J.J. Book 1 S0-ARH-473

BS RMC
l BB

LP   Peart, Jane
F   The pattern
PE

98-403

DATE DUE		
NOV. 1 3 2001		
Nov 27 2001		
JUN 0 7 2002		
AUG 1 4 2003		
SEP 1 6 2004		

THE PATTERN

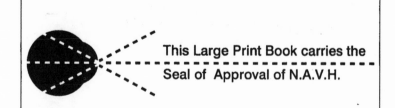

This Large Print Book carries the
Seal of Approval of N.A.V.H.

THE PATTERN

JANE PEART

Thorndike Press • Thorndike, Maine

Published in 1998 by arrangement with
Zondervan Publishing House.

Thorndike Large Print® Christian Fiction Series.

The tree indicium is a trademark of Thorndike Press.

The text of this Large Print edition is unabridged.
Other aspects of the book may vary from the original edition.

Set in 16 pt. Plantin by Al Chase.

Printed in the United States on permanent paper.

Library of Congress Cataloging in Publication Data

Peart, Jane.
    The pattern / Jane Peart.
      p. cm. — (American quilt series ; 1)
    ISBN: 0-7862-1304-3 (lg. print : hc : alk. paper)
    1. Quilting — Fiction. 2. North Carolina — Fiction.
3. Large type books. I. Title. II. Series: Peart, Jane.
American quilt series ; 1.
    [PS3566.E238P38 1998]
    813'.54—dc21   97-32569

Acknowledgments

The author would like to acknowledge the following authors for their books, which proved to be invaluable in the research and writing of this book.

Dennis Duke and Deborah Harding, *America's Glorious Quilts*

Wilma Dykeman, *The Tall Woman*

John Parris, *Roaming the Mountains*

Suzy Chalfant Payne and Susan Aylsworth Murwin, *Creative American Quilts Inspired by the Bible*

Lillian W. Watson, editor, *Light from Many Lamps*

Part One

Chapter One

Johanna Shelby, eighteen and recently having returned home from boarding school, stood looking out through the rain-smeared bedroom window. It had started raining early in the morning and had continued steadily all day. Now it was coming down in sheets.

Sighing impatiently, she turned back into the room. She gave a rueful glance at her new scarlet taffeta party dress hanging on the ledge of her armoire. She was looking forward eagerly to wearing it tonight at the first party of the holiday season, held at the home of her best friend, Liddy Chalmers. But if this kept up, it might be impossible to get there, country roads being what they were.

On her way across the room, she practiced a few dance steps, ending up by holding on to one of the bedposts, where she twirled around a couple of times before plopping down and bouncing onto the feather mattress. There she sighed again.

Although she had only been home a few

days, she already felt restless, at loose ends. Why? At school, she couldn't wait to get home for Christmas. And now it certainly was not that she missed school! For a free-spirited girl like Johanna, the rules, regulations, routine, the tedious hours in needlework class, and the memorizing endless verses to recite in the weekly elocution programs were boring and meaningless. In fact, Johanna was determined not to go back. That is, if she could convince her parents that she was quite "finished" enough. After two and a half years at Miss Pomoroy's Female Academy in Winston, she had had enough!

No, it certainly wasn't the lack of boarding school schedule that made her feel so fidgety. It was that she couldn't seem to settle down now that she was home. She felt so betwixt and between. She had changed more than she realized while being away. She'd gone off to school when she was sixteen and didn't seem to fit back into the family nest so neatly.

Johanna didn't really know what made her feel so uncomfortable back in the Shelby family circle. Maybe it was her prickly relationship with her sister Cicely, the next oldest. After her first greeting, Cissy had slipped back into her old adversary role with Johanna. Of course, Elly, the youngest, was adorable and as loving and lovable as ever. It was something else Johanna couldn't define. Even though she tried, she had the uneasy feeling she didn't really belong here anymore.

That is why after only a few days, Johanna found herself strangely at odds with everyone. It wasn't that she didn't love them all. It was just that she had the strangest feeling, as if she were on the brink of something, something unknown, something that was both exciting and a little daunting.

Johanna walked over to the window again. Putting her palms up against the steaming panes, she pressed her face against the glass. Just then the sky seemed to split open with a jagged streak of lightning that zigzagged down through dark, purple-edged clouds, sending the bare trees outside into stark silhouettes in a blinding flash. This was followed by a loud crackle of thunder that caused Johanna to jump back from the window in alarm.

In a panic reaction, Johanna turned and ran out of the room and down the stairs into the parlor, where the rest of the family was gathered, in time to hear her mother declare, "My good gracious, that was quite a jolt. It's a regular downpour. The roads will be rivers of mud by evening. I've a mind not to set out in this weather —"

"Not *go?*" a chorus of protest came from both the other girls. Cissy ran to stand beside her mother, peering out the window. Elly jumped up from the hassock, dropping her cat, which she'd been holding in her lap, to exclaim, "Not go to the *party?*"

"Oh Mama, surely you don't mean *that!*" cried Johanna, looking at her father for support and mainly concerned about having another evening confined at home and about losing the opportunity to wear her new dress.

"Well, I don't know. . . ." Mrs. Shelby's voice trailed into uncertainty. "Just getting from the carriage to the house, we'll get drenched for sure."

"Oh, it will be all right, Mama. We can bundle up and wear boots and carry our slippers 'til we get inside," Cissy assured her. At fifteen, she was the practical one.

"I suppose." Mrs. Shelby's voice still sounded tentative.

"Please, Mama, don't say we can't go!" wailed Elly, who at nearly eleven had been promised this treat, her first time to attend a really "grown-up" party.

"Oh, come now, Rebecca," boomed Tennant Shelby, the girls' father, who had caught Johanna's pleading look. He laid aside the book he had been reading to say chidingly to his wife, "Can't let a little rain deprive these pretty young ladies of the first party of the holiday season."

His wife gave him a cautionary look. Tennant was so indulgent of their three daughters, especially Johanna, that it was *she* who sometimes had to exert discipline or take the stern parental role. However, she was already inclined to put aside her own misgivings about the weather. The Chalmerses' party *was* the first of the holiday season. After all, she wasn't yet too old to remember what fun a dancing party could be. More to the point, with three daughters to eventually marry off, it was important that they get out socially. Particularly for Johanna, their oldest, home after her years out of circulation here in Hillsboro. Now eighteen, ready to be launched into society and ready for a serious courtship and marriage proposal. Not that it would be much of a problem. Johanna was pretty, vivacious, and bright. Any number of eligible young men would no doubt find her attractive. It was only a matter of choosing the right one.

Rebecca felt all three pairs of anxious eyes upon her. Waiting an appropriate length of time, she said slowly, "Well, I suppose it will be all right. If we leave early enough and you make sure Thomas drives carefully." This admonition was directed at her husband. Her decision was greeted by exclamations of relief and delight by her daughters.

By dark, the icy rain had turned to sleet, and once more Mrs. Shelby voiced her doubts about the wisdom of venturing out over rutted roads in the stormy night. Again she was the lone dissenter, and again she was coaxed, cajoled, persuaded. Finally, at half-past seven, swathed in hooded cloaks, shod in sturdy boots, their portmanteaus containing dainty slippers into which they could change upon their arrival, they were at last ready to leave. In high spirits, the three Shelby girls climbed into the family carriage. Inside the narrow interior, settling their crinolines, they seated themselves opposite their parents. As the carriage jolted along the country roads now running with streams of mud, the girls chattered merrily, giggling at whatever nonsensical things one or the other of them said. Elly, squeezed between her older sisters, was wildly excited to have been allowed to come along. She was ecstatic at the prospect of the evening ahead.

Upon reaching the Chalmerses' house,

Thomas, the Shelbys' coachman, pulled up as close to the covered side porch as possible. With Rebecca issuing warnings to be careful, the three girls, giggling with nervous excitement, descended from the carriage. Jumping over puddles, they ran through the pelting rain up the front steps of the house, through the door opened by the jovial Mr. Chalmers, and into the front hall.

The warm, candlelit house was already filled with the sound of fiddle music, lighthearted laughter, and happy voices. Someone took Johanna's cape, and as she stood there for a minute looking about, Liddy Chalmers, her closest friend from childhood, came rushing up to her. "Oh, Johanna! I'm so glad to see you! I was afraid you might not come! Isn't this weather dreadful?" She gave Johanna's arm an excited squeeze. "Come on. You can primp in my bedroom before we go in to dance." She lowered her voice significantly. "Burton Lassiter's been pacing up and down like a madman, waiting for you to arrive! I hid your dance card so he wouldn't fill up every slot."

Liddy propelled Johanna back through the narrow hall to her downstairs bedroom, chatting all the while. "I absolutely *love* your dress, Johanna! It's a perfect color for you."

Sitting on the mounting steps to the high,

four-poster bed, Johanna bent to pull off her boots and get her dancing shoes out of her bag. Liddy continued to talk as Johanna took out the red satin slippers with the tiny silk roses on the toes and slipped them on her feet.

"It's going to be such a fun party. I wish you could spend the night so we could stay up till all hours and talk." Suddenly Liddy clapped her hands. "Maybe the weather will worsen and you'll have to! Anyway, come along. Papa's about to call the first reel."

At the entrance to the parlor, now cleared of furniture for dancing, the eager Burton Lassiter was quick to find Johanna and claim her as his partner for the Virginia Reel, which was usually the dance to open a party.

When they finally came to a breathless halt after the lively dance, Johanna's gaze swept the room. It was then she became aware of the young man leaning against the pilaster in the archway.

He was very tall and his dark shaggy hair needed a good trim. He was not handsome, and his features were too irregular, with a strong nose and a determined mouth. However, the combination was oddly attractive. His gray eyes, regarding her so steadily, were intelligent yet held a hint of humor.

As the stranger glanced at her, Johanna

16

experienced the strangest sensation, as if somehow they knew each other, as if they'd met somewhere. Of course, that was impossible! Yet the strong feeling lingered.

She and Burton took their places with other couples lining up for the quadrille. The music struck up and she was swept into the promenade. Again Johanna caught sight of the stranger, and to her immediate confusion, found he was looking at her as well.

Who was he? she wondered curiously. In spite of her odd sense of recognition, she couldn't place him. In as small a town as Hillsboro, a stranger stood out. Surely Liddy would know. For some reason, Johanna felt an urgency to find out. Fanning herself briskly, she told Burton she was perishing from thirst and sent him off to fetch her a glass of punch. Then she quickly darted to Liddy's side. Taking her by the wrist, she led her aside and whispered, "Come with me. I have to talk to you!"

Puzzled but compliant, Liddy followed Johanna's lead down the hall to her bedroom. Some of the other girls were already there, restoring hairdos and primping in front of the mirror as they came in.

"What is it?" Liddy asked.

"Who is that tall fellow standing beside Dr. Murrison? Is he new in town? A relative? A nephew? Who?"

"That's Dr. Murrison's new assistant."

"What's his name?"

"His name is Ross Davison. He's been with Dr. Murrison for a few months now. He came after you left for school in September."

"Where's he from?"

"If you heard him talk, you wouldn't have to ask where he's from," a voice behind them said with a snicker. Unaware that they'd been overheard, both girls turned around. Emily Archer, a girl Johanna had never liked very well, was standing in front of the full-length mirror. Her face in the glass had a know-it-all smirk. But at the moment, she had the information Johanna wanted, so Johanna swallowed her dislike to ask, "What do you mean? Is he a foreigner?"

Emily giggled shrilly. "No, silly, he's from the *mountains!*"

"Mountains?"

"From Millscreek Gap, for pity's sake!" Emily fluffed her corkscrew curls and patted her skirt, turning this way and that as she surveyed herself in the mirror. "I suppose he *must* be educated — I mean, to be a doctor and all," she remarked indifferently. "But he still has that hill twang." Emily mimicked, *"You kin jest tell."*

Johanna frowned. She suddenly remembered why she had never liked Emily very much. Emily had a sharp tongue. She was always quick with a snide remark, a mean comment, or a sly innuendo. For some reason, it made Johanna cross to hear Emily make fun of that young man with his serious expression and deep-set, thoughtful eyes. But Johanna let it pass, not wanting to appear too interested in the newcomer. Emily had a razor-like tongue, liked nothing better than to tease. Johanna was not about to become her target by giving her anything to turn into a joke.

"Come on," she said to Liddy. "Burton's waiting for me with punch." She slipped her hand into Liddy's arm and they made their escape.

"What a cat that Emily is!" commented Liddy as they hurried out into the hall. "Actually, Dr. Davison is very well mannered and pleasant. Dr. Murrison sent him over when my little brother Billy had croup, and he couldn't have been nicer."

Back in the parlor, Burton was nowhere in sight, and Johanna allowed her gaze to seek that of the young doctor. As her eyes met his, he turned and spoke to Dr. Murrison. Then, to her surprise, they both crossed the room. "Well, Johanna, my dear, it's nice to see you home from Winston and looking so well," Dr. Murrison said. "I don't believe you've met my new assistant, Ross Davison."

Johanna's heart gave a little leap. "No, Dr. Murrison, I've not had the pleasure. Good evening, Dr. Davison," she managed to say, fluttering her fan to cool her suddenly flushed face.

"Good evening, Miss Shelby. I trust you are having a pleasant time?"

His voice was deep. There *was* a trace of the mountain twang to it, as Emily had said. However, Johanna did not find it at all unpleasant.

"Yes, indeed. And you?" As she looked up at him, Johanna felt a tingling in her wrists and fingertips.

It was uncanny, Johanna thought, this feeling of recognition. As though somehow they had been parted a long time and were, at this very moment, seeing each other again. The sensation was bewildering.

"If you have not already promised it, may I have the next dance?" His question brought her back to the present moment.

Even though she *had* promised the next three, Johanna simply put her hand in Ross's, felt his fingers close over it. He bowed from his great height, and she moved with him out onto the polished dance floor

20

as the first notes of the next set began. Out of the corner of her eye, she saw Burton, looking bewildered and a little indignant, glancing around in search of his missing partner. But she didn't care. She knew she was exactly where she wanted to be, dancing with this tall newcomer.

Ross was not the best of dancers. He was a little unsure and stiff, his height making him rather awkward. It did not matter to Johanna. She felt as if she were floating, her head spinning as fast as her feet. They circled, his hand firmly on her waist, her face upturned to his, and she could not remember ever feeling so happy. The piece ended and as they waited for the next one, they smiled at each other — as if they had danced together many times before.

The music started again, and again they seemed to move in perfect step. At length the melody ended. Yet, they remained facing each other. Mr. Chalmers's booming voice jovially announced, "Line up, ladies and gentlemen, for musical chairs."

Reluctantly Ross stepped back, bowed slightly, and relinquished Johanna. A row of chairs, numbering one less than the assembled guests, was placed down the middle of the long room.

The musicians started playing a lively

march, and the company began moving in a circle around the room, giggling, shuffling a little, attempting to anticipate when the music would stop and they would have to rush for a seat. As one by one a chair was eliminated and one or more persons had to drop out, the circle grew smaller and the fun and hilarity of the suspense grew louder. Every once in a while Johanna would catch Ross's glance. He was so tall and lanky that watching him scramble for a chair was comical. What pleased her the most was that he seemed to be thoroughly enjoying himself and had lost that slight awkwardness. Although his shyness touched her, she was elated that he could enjoy such fun.

Soon there were only a handful of marchers left, Ross and Johanna among them. The musicians, enjoying the sight as much as the onlookers clustered around the periphery of the room, changed the tempo from fast to slow to trick the hopeful remaining players. Johanna was almost weak with laughter, and once when the music stopped abruptly, she and Ross landed unceremoniously on the same chair. In a gentlemanly manner, he shifted and stood up, leaving her seated while a more boisterous young man slid into the only other chair left empty. Ross joined the spectators as Johanna stayed in the game.

With two chairs and three people left, the room became noisier than ever, people cheering on their favorites. When the music halted, Johanna made a dash for a seat, and as she did she lost her balance and went crashing, sending the chair sliding, herself collapsing in a heap with upturned crinolines and taffeta ruffles. One small dancing slipper, with its tiny heel, went skittering across the polished floor and out of sight.

Burton ran to help the laughing Johanna to her feet. Leaning on his arm, she hopped to the side of the room, where someone pushed a chair for her to collapse into. Johanna's laughter suddenly came to a swift halt when, from across the room, she saw her mother's disapproving expression. Johanna felt a sinking sensation, which was quickly replaced by one of rebellion. What had she done that was so horrible? Just played a silly game to the fullest. What on earth was wrong with *that?* She turned away from the admonishing face just as Ross came up to her, bearing her small satin shoe in his open palm.

He knelt to slip it back on her foot. As his hand held the arch, Johanna felt a tingle running up from her foot all through her. Involuntarily she shivered. He glanced up at her, and for a single moment their gazes met and held, as if seeking an answer to an unspoken question. Then people gathered around, and their voices crowded out the sound of Johanna's heart beating so loudly she was sure everyone could hear it.

Hours later Johanna was sitting in front of her dressing table, dreamily brushing her hair, when her mother entered her bedroom.

Johanna had been reliving the evening. At least the part after she had been introduced to Ross Davison. Following that, the rest of the party had simply faded into a backdrop. She hardly remembered the carriage ride home, the excited voices of her sisters discussing the evening. She had seemed to float up the stairs and into her own bedroom on some kind of cloud. Now her mother was talking to her in a tone of voice that was edged with severity, chiding her about something. Johanna blinked, looked at her mother, and tried to concentrate on what she was saying.

"I simply cannot believe it, Johanna! I thought your years at Miss Pomoroy's had taught you some reticence, some proper behavior. I am shocked to see that — given the opportunity — you are as much a hoyden as ever!"

Johanna, outwardly submissive, listened to her mother's lecture while continuing to brush her hair. *Eighty-two, eighty-three, eighty-four,* she counted silently, wondering if her mother's tirade would end at the prerequisite one hundred strokes.

"I expect you to set a good example for your younger sisters, Johanna. This was Elly's first grown-up party, and she worships you, you know, imitates everything you do: your mannerisms, your likes, dislikes — unfortunately, your bad traits as well as any good ones you might exhibit. I am thoroughly ashamed of your lack of decorum tonight, Johanna. And with that — that rough-hewn young man, whose parlor manners also need a great deal of improvement." All at once Rebecca realized Johanna was not really listening. Hadn't she heard a word? Maybe the child was tired. Perhaps this could wait until tomorrow.

"You *do* understand, don't you, Johanna? Anything you do reflects on the family. People are ever ready to gossip or spread untrue rumors. I would not want anyone to get the idea —" Again Johanna's expression looked faraway. Her sweetly curved mouth was — smiling. Rebecca's voice sharpened. "Johanna!"

"Yes, Mama. I do. I didn't mean to — I

was just having fun."

"I'm sure that was all there was to it, dear. But we can't give the wrong impression — you see?"

"Yes, Mama," Johanna replied demurely.

Rebecca leaned down and kissed the smooth brow, cupping her daughter's cheek for a moment with her hand. Her eyes swept over her daughter. Johanna was fulfilling her childhood promise of beauty. Her complexion was lovely, her eyes, with their sweeping lashes, truly beautiful, Rebecca thought fondly. *But we must be careful that her gaiety and vivaciousness aren't misunderstood.*

As soon as the door closed behind her mother, Johanna put down her hairbrush and studied her reflection in the mirror. Was it possible? Did she really look different? Something had happened tonight, and she seemed changed somehow.

In a way, that shouldn't have surprised her. She *felt* different. Ever since she'd come home less than a week ago, she had felt oddly displaced. The familiar seemed unfamiliar. Even getting used to being with her parents and two younger sisters again had presented problems. However, Johanna knew it was something more than that. Deep inside, there was a heart hunger she couldn't explain or even understand. A need for something to give her life meaning and purpose.

Johanna blew out her lamp, climbed into bed, and pulled the quilt up to her chin. She shut her eyes, squeezing them tight, and the image of Ross Davison came into her mind. He was different from most of the young men she knew, the ones she'd smiled at and teased at picnics, flirted with and danced with at parties.

He might be a bit awkward and unsure of himself socially, perhaps not good at small talk or such. He was already into a man's life, a doctor, healing the sick and injured, saving lives. It made the lives of most of the other young men she knew seem shallow by comparison.

Up until recently Johanna's life had been that of a schoolgirl — simple, uncomplicated, filled with friends, fun, light flirtations. Now Ross Davison had stepped into her life. His eyes seemed to look into her very soul. It had been almost as if he recognized that longing within her she had not ever spoken of to anyone.

Suddenly Johanna saw a possibility of something deeper and more important. She wasn't exactly sure just what happened tonight. She only knew that something had and nothing would ever be the same again. It both excited and frightened her.

Chapter Two

At breakfast the following day, Rebecca announced, "Johanna, I want you to take the fruitcakes around to the aunties. You may take the small buggy. If you don't dawdle or stay too long at each house, you should be back by noon. No later, because I shall need it myself this afternoon when I go to help decorate the church for Advent services."

Delivering fruitcakes to her cousins was Rebecca's holiday custom. Since she used a secret Shelby family recipe handed down to her by her mother-in-law, she knew that this was one thing none of them could duplicate. Fond as they all were of each other, nonetheless an unspoken but very real rivalry existed among the cousins.

"Yes, Mama, I'll be happy to." Johanna cheerfully accepted the errand, glad of the opportunity to get out of the house and thus escape some of the household chores Rebecca daily allotted to each daughter.

Immediately Cissy protested. "Why does Johanna get to do all the fun things?"

The difference in their ages always rankled Cissy. It was something she had not had to deal with while Johanna was away. After her first welcome to Johanna at her homecoming, Cissy had reverted to petty jealousy. Rebecca sent her a disapproving glance. "Because Johanna can drive the trap, for one reason. For another, the aunties haven't seen her since she came home." Then she added, "And stop frowning. Your expression is as unbecoming as your attitude." To Johanna she said, "I'll put the fruitcakes in a basket and then have Thomas bring the trap around."

Her mother's reprimand subdued whatever else Cissy might have argued. At least temporarily. However, when Rebecca left the table, Cissy stuck out her tongue at Johanna, who ignored her and went to get her hooded cape. She was pulling on her leather driving gloves as Rebecca emerged from the kitchen area carrying a willow basket packed with the gaily beribboned rounded molds of fruitcakes. Johanna drew a long breath, relishing the combined smells of brandied fruit, cinnamon, nutmeg. "Umm, smells delicious, Mama."

"Take care, and try to be back on time," her mother's voice followed her as Johanna took the basket and started out.

"Yes, Mama," Johanna promised as she opened the front door. She gave a cheery wave to her sisters, a pouting Cissy and a resigned Elly, both assigned to polishing silver.

Outside, Thomas, the Shelbys' "man of all work," waited beside the small, one-seated buggy at the front of the house, holding the mare's head. Thomas was husband to their cook, Jensie, brother to Bessie, the maid. All three had worked for her family as long as Johanna could remember.

"Morning, Thomas," Johanna greeted him, then paused to rub Juno's nose and pet her neck before climbing into the driver's seat.

"You be careful now, Miss Johanna. She's feelin' mahty frisky this mawnin'," Thomas cautioned, handing her the reins.

"Thank you. I will," she said. She gave the reins a flick and started down the winding drive out onto the county road.

The morning was bright, sunny, the air crisp and clear, and Johanna felt lighthearted and free. She was glad to be home, back in Hillsboro, after the long months away. At boarding school, her independent, happy-go-lucky spirit felt hopelessly suppressed by the strict rules. She had the secret intention that during this Christmas vacation, she would persuade her indulgent father to let her stay home rather than go back to the academy. She felt she'd had enough education and enough of the restrictive life at school. Cissy could go in her place!

As they moved along at a brisk pace in the winter sunshine, Johanna enjoyed traveling over the familiar roads, breathing deep of the pine-scented air. She was actually looking forward to having a visit with each auntie as she delivered her mother's special holiday gift.

Johanna's "aunties" were not *really* her aunts. They were her mother's first cousins. And they all had the same first name: Johanna. Their grandmother, Johanna Logan, had five daughters and one son. Each daughter named their first daughter Johanna in honor of her. The only one not named Johanna was Rebecca, the daughter of the son. *His* wife, the only daughter-in-law in the family, had refused to have *her* daughter christened Johanna. All the first cousins named Johanna were called by other names to distinguish them from each other. Thus there was Aunt Hannah, Auntie Bee, Aunt Jo McMillan, Aunt Honey, Aunt Johanna Cady.

Thinking of the aunties, Johanna often wondered if her mother ever resented the fact that *her* mother had broken with tradition and not named her Johanna. She never said and somehow Johanna had resisted asking. Her mother rarely talked about her childhood or her life before marrying. It was as if everything began for her when she became Mrs. Tennant Shelby. It seemed she had become part of his life and left her own completely, proud of her husband's prominence, their place in Hillsboro society.

Families were funny things, Johanna mused as she turned off the main road and took the rutted lane that led to the Breckenridges' home, the one closest to the Shelbys', her first stop. She and her sisters were the only girls in the family. The other relatives on both sides who had children had boys. Johanna had never given it much thought, but recently she had noticed that her mother quite bristled when the other aunties talked — or the better word was *bragged* — about their male offspring. Would her mother have rather had sons? Johanna wondered. However, she'd heard several of the aunties sigh and verbally declare they pined for a daughter, making such remarks as, "such comfort, so companionable, considerate in old age." So maybe it all evened out in the end, Johanna decided as she pulled up in front of her Auntie Bee's. She knew this would be a happy reunion. Auntie Bee, childless herself, doted on the Shelby girls, and secretly Johanna was her favorite "niece."

Winding the reins around the hitching post, Johanna ran up the porch steps. She raised the brass knocker and banged it a few times before Auntie Bee, who was somewhat hard of hearing, opened the door. "Why, Johanna, how lovely to see you! Come in, dear!" she said, beckoning her inside. "My, you get prettier every time I see you."

Johanna gave her a hug, relishing the familiar fragrance of violet eau de cologne she always associated with this aunt. "I've brought you Mama's Christmas fruitcake!"

Looking as surprised as if receiving it weren't an annual event, Auntie Bee declared, "How dear of her! And I know it's delicious. Let's slice a piece and have some tea. You can stay for a visit, can't you?"

"I probably shouldn't. Mama wants the trap back by noon."

"Not just for a wee bit?"

"Well, I guess — why not!"

"Why not, indeed! Come along inside. No mistake about its being December, is there? Lots of frost this morning when your Uncle Radford set out for his office." Auntie Bee took Johanna's cape and hung it up, saying,

"Now you go right on in the parlor, where I've a nice fire going. That'll take the chill off you after being out in the cold air. I'll get our tea and slice the cake."

"Can I help you, Auntie?"

"No, dearie, you just go on in and make yourself comfortable. I won't be but a minute." Auntie Bee bustled out to the kitchen.

Auntie Bee's quilting frame was set up in the cozy parlor, and Johanna went over to examine the one she was working on. When her aunt came back in carrying the tray with tea things, Johanna told her, "This is very pretty, Auntie, and I like the colors — what's the pattern called?"

"It's called the Tree of Life. In the Bible, a tree is the symbol of all the good things of life: plenty, goodness, and wisdom. All God's gifts to humankind we're to enjoy on this earth — our families, our home, what he provides — the abundant life the Scripture speaks about."

Johanna regarded her aunt's serene expression, the sincerity with which she spoke. Surely she never had a doubt or an uncertainty, unlike Johanna, who always questioned everything. "You really believe that, don't you, Auntie?"

"Of course, dearie. What's not to believe?"

Bee put one hand on the open Bible on its stand beside her quilting frame. "As it is written in Proverbs 3, 'Happy is the man that findeth wisdom. She is a *tree of life* to them that lay hold upon her.' "

After consuming a large piece of fruitcake and a cup of tea, Johanna turned down her aunt's urging for a second helping of each and departed for her next stop.

As she drove away, waving her hand to her plump aunt standing on the porch waving back, Johanna wondered: had her aunt never had a rebellious thought, a longing for something different than a placid existence? Was she always so at peace, as perfectly content as she appeared? Johanna sighed. She herself had so many unfulfilled dreams, so many romantic fantasies and desires. Perhaps her aunt's kind of serenity came eventually with age? She didn't really know. In her own heart a restlessness stirred, a deep yearning for an experience that did not even have a name. Was she to constantly search for something she might never find?

⁕ ⁕ ⁕

As she approached Aunt Hannah Mills's house, Johanna hoped she would not have to listen to a prolonged recital of her aunt's ailments. Aunt Hannah tended to complain at length of various aches. The consensus of family opinion was that most of them were imaginary. Today Johanna was in luck. At her knock, the door was opened impatiently, and Johanna got the immediate impression she had come at an inopportune time. The household was in the midst of holiday cleaning. Behind Aunt Hannah, through the door to the parlor, Johanna saw Suzy, the maid, kneeling at the hearth, polishing the brass fender, the fire tools, and the andirons. The frown on her aunt's face faded at once when she saw Johanna.

"Why, Johanna, child! What a surprise!" she spoke, trying not to sound irritated by the unexpected visit. This aunt was known in the family as a fuss-budget about her home — for her, cleanliness was truly next to godliness — and twice a year the entire house was scrubbed, cleaned, polished to a fare-thee-well. Christmas was one of those times. Yet since hospitality was a cardinal rule practiced by all the family, she welcomed Johanna inside.

"One of your mother's lovely fruitcakes!" she exclaimed with feigned surprise as Johanna handed it to her. "My, my, I don't see how your mother manages to do all she does. A houseful of girls to look after, a large household to run, all the entertaining she does, besides her charitable activities. Of course, *she* has been blessed with good health!" Aunt Hannah sighed lugubriously. "Not like some of us." She drew her small bottle of smelling salts from her apron pocket and inhaled. "I have felt quite unwell since . . . well, I believe I overdid it when —"

"I'm sorry to hear that, Aunt Hannah," Johanna said brightly, determined not to be an unwilling audience to a long list of Aunt Hannah's hypochondriac complaints. "I do hope you will take care so that you won't miss the holiday festivities. New Year's dinner is at our house this year."

Aunt Hannah looked aghast. "Miss our family dinner? Of course not! I wouldn't miss *that* even if —"

Before she could add the phrase "if I were on my deathbed," which Johanna anticipated might be next, Johanna said quickly, "I must be on my way, Aunt Hannah. I have the other fruitcakes to deliver, and Mother explicitly told me to be back home by noon. She is expected to be at the church to help decorate."

"Go along then, child. How I wish I had the strength to volunteer for such active things, too, but I just haven't felt up to it —"

Johanna moved to the door. One hand on the knob, she said, "Do give Uncle Roy my love. We shall see you on Christmas Day at Aunt Honey's." The door was open now.

"Yes. That is, if —"

Before her aunt could finish her sentence, Johanna stepped outside onto the porch, into the crisp, cold morning.

Aunt Hannah gasped, saying, "Oh, I must shut the door quickly, Johanna, or I'll catch my death —"

"Sorry, Auntie," apologized Johanna, then she ran down the porch steps and climbed back into the buggy. Glad to escape, she picked up the reins with a long sigh of relief. Next stop was Aunt Cady's. Johanna Cady was what Johanna called her "fashionable aunt." She was exceptionally attractive and youthful looking, with fine hazel eyes, silvery blond hair. She had a distinct style, impeccable taste, and a rather superior air. As Johanna arrived, she saw her aunt's carriage in front of the house, and when her aunt answered the knock at her door, she was dressed and ready to leave. Her peacock blue faille ensemble was elegant, and her bonnet sported curled plumes and velvet ribbon.

"Oh, dear me, Johanna, I'm just about to depart," Aunt Cady said. "With the holidays upon us, I moved up my visiting day so as to get all my calls in before I get caught up in the season. Munroe and Harvel will be home from college day after tomorrow, you know — and then there'll be no end to it!" She threw up her hands in mock dismay, but Johanna knew her aunt was looking forward with great pleasure to the arrival of her two handsome sons.

"It's all right, Aunt Cady. I just came to leave Mama's gift."

"Oh, how nice." Her aunt accepted it distractedly, placing it on the polished Pembroke table in the hall behind her. "When the boys come, we shall have to have some kind of party, invite all their friends — I don't know just when, but we shall of course let you know. They shall be so pleased to see you, Johanna." Her aunt's gaze traveled approvingly over her. "The boys will be amazed to see how pretty and grown up you are since last year!"

Johanna wasn't so sure. Her older boy cousins had always rather ignored her, being busy with their own social activities. Years ago it might have mattered to her to be noticed by her two attractive cousins, but somehow now at the mention of them, she mentally shrugged.

"Do tell them hello for me, and of course, tell Uncle Madison," she said as she went back out to the buggy.

"We'll see you at church on Christmas

Day and at dinner afterward. And be sure to thank Rebecca for me, won't you, dear?" Aunt Cady called after her.

Johanna had one more stop to make before heading home. She had purposely saved this one till last, because Aunt Johanna Hayes was her favorite. She was called Aunt Honey, because that was the name her husband Matt called her in his loud, jovial voice. He was a large man, measuring at least two feet taller than his petite wife. That name suited this aunt perfectly, Johanna thought as she approached the fieldstone and frame house surrounded by tall pines at the end of a lane. Honey had remained a great deal like the lighthearted girl she had been, frivolous, charming, fun-loving, the pampered pet of her husband and three strapping sons.

Up to her elbows in flour, Aunt Honey was making the decorated Christmas cookies of all sorts of shapes and sizes for which she was famous in the family.

"Darling girl, how happy I am to see you! But you've just missed Jo," Honey told Johanna. Her plump face showed dismay. "She'll be sorry to miss you. But she would go out riding! I told her I thought it was too cold, but you know how she is!"

Aunt Jo was spending Christmas with the Hayeses. Johanna knew Aunt Jo was an excellent horsewoman and no matter what the weather, she would go riding. "Yes, I know. I'll leave her fruitcake from Mama anyway and see her another time."

"Ah yes, there'll be plenty of family get-togethers during the holidays," Aunt Honey agreed. "Want to sample one of my cookies?"

"I can't stay, Aunt Honey, but I'll take one along to munch on."

"Of course. Come along into the kitchen with me. I have a batch almost ready to take out of the oven."

Suddenly a startled look crossed Aunt Honey's face, and she sniffed the air suspiciously. "Oh, my! I'd better get them out quick, or they'll be burned."

Johanna followed her into the deliciously fragrant kitchen. Aunt Honey scurried over to the stove and slipped out the tray of bell- and tree-shaped Christmas cookies. "Uh-oh, they're a bit brown at the edges!"

"They'll be fine, Aunt Honey," Johanna consoled. "Once you've covered them with colored sugar."

"What a clever girl, you are, Johanna," her aunt declared happily. "That's just the thing."

"I really must go, Auntie."

"Do tell your mama thank you for our

cake. Matt always looks forward to Rebecca's fruitcake," Aunt Honey said as she walked to the door with Johanna. "Your mother is so organized, no one can keep up with her! And here I am, not finished with my baking, not by half. I'm hopeless, it seems, no matter how early I start."

"You're just right, Aunt Honey." Johanna gave her a hug and went out the door. "And we'll see you on Christmas!"

Her errands done, Johanna decided to ride through town on her way home. With only a half-formed thought in her mind, she slowed her horse to a walk as she went by Dr. Murrison's house. Ever since the Chalmers' party, Johanna had spent a great deal of time thinking about the tall, young doctor with his slow smile and disturbingly penetrating eyes. However, as she passed the brown-shingled house, there was no one in sight. She felt disappointed, but then, what had she hoped for? A chance to talk to him again? There was just something about Ross Davison. . . .

In no hurry to get home, where household chores awaited her, Johanna decided to do a little shopping. She had a good half hour before her mother expected her back. Why not stop at the little notions shop that carried ribbons and lace and look around for a bit?

42

She had started making handkerchief cases in needlework class months ago as Christmas gifts for both her sisters. As usual with such things, she had lost interest in the project, and she had brought them home with her, unfinished. With Christmas only a few days away, maybe she could find some lace or trim to add a finishing touch.

She found a space in front of the shop and, hitching Juno to the post, went inside. It didn't take long to find what she wanted. Her purchases made, she was just leaving the store when she saw him crossing the street, coming straight toward her!

At the exact same time, Ross Davison saw *her*. Her scarlet cape, caught by a sudden wind, swirled up behind her like a bright fan, framing her dark, flying hair. He thought Johanna the loveliest thing he had ever seen.

"Miss Shelby," he greeted her. "What luck!"

"Luck?"

"Yes, quite a coincidence."

Or a hopeful wish come true, Johanna thought, amazed. Trying to conceal her pleasure, she teased, "Don't tell me you just happened to be thinking of me!"

"As a matter of fact, I *was*."

Johanna was taken aback. Most young

men of her acquaintance were not so frank expressing their feelings. In her social circle, an unwritten law was never to say what you meant — a game played equally by ladies and gentlemen. Johanna had always thought it ridiculous nonsense. Ross's frankness was as refreshing as it was startling.

"Yes," he said, "I *was* thinking about what a good time we had at the Chalmerses' party —"

"Musical chairs, you mean? Yes, it was fun." She laughed and Ross thought Johanna was prettier even than he had remembered, her face all glowing and rosy, her smiling mouth showing small white teeth.

"I hope we may enjoy other such times, or" — he frowned suddenly — "will you be returning to school after the holidays?"

Although she had not launched her planned campaign to persuade her parents to let her stay home instead of going back to the academy, she hesitated. "I may not be going back. I hope to be through with all that —"

"With boarding school? Or learning in general?" he grinned.

"Oh, there are lots of things I want to learn — *outside* the schoolroom." Her eyes sparkled with mischief.

"I see." Ross regarded her so seriously,

she began to feel uncomfortable. Recalling her mother's recent lecture on deportment, she hoped that her remark did not sound too flippant, too flirtatious. An awkward silence stretched between them. To break it, Johanna asked, "And why are you not going about doing good, curing illnesses, and that sort of thing, Dr. Davison?"

"At the moment, it seems most of Hillsboro's citizens are in good health or too busy with Christmas preparations to be sick."

For a minute, they simply stood smiling at each other. Since she could think of no plausible reason to delay longer, Johanna shifted and moved as if to go. "Well, I must be on my way, Dr. Davison."

"May I help you with your packages, Miss Shelby?"

There were so few, it seemed an almost ridiculous suggestion. But grasping at anything to prolong this chance meeting, Johanna just as ridiculously replied, "Why, thank you, Dr. Davison."

"Where's your buggy?"

It was right in front of them, a matter of a few steps. "Over there."

"I'll see you to it," Ross said quite solemnly. His hand slipped under her elbow, and they walked over to where Juno patiently waited. Ross helped her climb in, then said with obvious reluctance, "Well, I have patients to see —"

"Yes, and I'd better get home."

Before relinquishing her small parcels, he asked, "When may I hope to see you again?"

"Perhaps at church on Sunday," Johanna blurted out impulsively, then blushingly amended, "— that is, *if* you attend?"

"Not always, but" — he looked amused — "*this* Sunday I will."

She picked up the reins. Their gaze still held. Johanna was amazed that so much had been said, and yet so much remained unspoken but somehow understood. At last she said, "Good-bye, then. Until Sunday."

"Yes, 'til Sunday. Good-bye."

Feeling unreasonably happy, Johanna started for home.

⬥⬥⬥

The following Sunday, Johanna was already up when her mother came into her bedroom to awaken her with a cup of hot chocolate. In fact, Johanna was standing in front of the mirror trying on her new bonnet while still in her nightie. Surprised, Mrs. Shelby raised her eyebrows but said nothing. Johanna was usually the hardest of the three girls to get up and moving in the morning.

What had prompted this early rising? Surely it wasn't sudden religious fervor? Rebecca regarded her oldest daughter curiously.

Rebecca was inordinately proud of her three pretty daughters, and this morning as they made their way to church, she noted that Johanna looked especially attractive. Her new bonnet of russet velvet, with a cluster of silk bittersweet berries nestled on green velvet leaves on the band, and wide brown satin ribbons tied under her chin, was most becoming. She was also being extremely amiable and sweet-tempered, moving over at Cissy's demand for more room in the carriage, looking demure with folded hands over her prayer book. Something was stirring, Rebecca felt sure, but she could not pinpoint what it might be.

As for Johanna, when they reached the churchyard, her heart was pumping as fast as if she were on her way to a ball. When they all got out of the carriage, she saw Dr. Murrison and his tall assistant mounting the church steps. She dared not look to the right or left to try to locate where they were seated as she followed her parents down the aisle to their family pew, indicated by the small brass identifying marker engraved SHELBY.

Before she sat down, she glanced around as casually as possible and saw that the two were seated toward the back of the church. Then she remembered it was well known that Dr. Murrison always sat in the rear near the door in case a medical emergency called him away from divine service. She ducked her head, studying the hymn book. After reading the same line over at least three times, none of it making sense, she realized she was much too aware of the young man three pews behind her. It became suddenly hard to breathe, much less sing.

Somehow Johanna got through *this* Sunday's seemingly endless service. When her mother stopped to chat with friends on the way out of church, she had to curb her irritation. *Oh, please don't let him leave,* she prayed. Stepping outside onto the church steps, to her delight she saw her father engaged in conversation with Dr. Murrison, and Ross stood quietly beside him. She heard her father saying, "But of course, you both must join us. Am I right, my dear?" He turned to Rebecca as she and Johanna approached them. "Wouldn't we be pleased to have Dr. Murrison and his assistant join us for dinner on New Year's?"

Dr. Murrison, a ruddy-cheeked, gray-whiskered man with a gruff manner that his small, twinkly blue eyes belied, demanded, "But wouldn't we be intruding?

A family occasion, surely?"

"Not at all, my good fellow," Mr. Shelby denied heartily. "Holidays are no time to be alone. Now, we'll say no more about it. But expect you both."

Rebecca murmured something appropriate. Johanna shyly smiled at Ross. His eyes seemed to light up, replacing his serious expression with one of pleasure. A few more pleasantries were exchanged, then good-byes were said.

Once in the family carriage, her father announced, as if in explanation of his impromptu invitation, "Couldn't let Alec spend the most festive day of the holidays alone, could we? He used to spend the holidays with his sister over in Clayton County. But she passed away last summer — and that young fellow, Davison, he'd never get to his home in the mountains in this weather. Snow's made the road up to Millscreek impassable."

Johanna did not listen to the rest of her parents' discussion. She was too happy planning what she would wear when Ross Davison came to the house for dinner. Ten days seemed a long time to wait.

Chapter Three

"I don't want to go!" pouted Elly at the breakfast table. "I don't want to have my music lesson. Why do I have to do it during the holidays? I didn't think I'd have to go to lessons at all, with Johanna just come home."

"That will do, Elly," Mrs. Shelby said sternly. "You will take your music lessons as usual. Miss Minton is paid for each pupil's lesson. If you don't go, she doesn't get paid. She is the sole support of her invalid mother, and it is only right and proper that you go. Besides, I heard you practicing yesterday, and you certainly *need* the instruction. You fumbled quite badly on your piece. Now, that's all I have to say. Go and get ready."

Elly's lower lip trembled and tears filled her eyes.

"I'll take Elly over to Miss Minton's, Mama," offered Johanna. "And maybe we can go have a little treat afterward. You'd like that, wouldn't you, Elly?"

Her little sister's face brightened. "Oh,

yes!" She jumped up from her chair.

"That's very generous of you, Johanna." Mrs. Shelby looked approvingly at her but added, "Still, I believe, Elly must learn responsibility without the promise of reward. *This* time, however, it will be all right."

Within twenty minutes Johanna and Elly were on their way. Elly took Johanna's hand, swinging it happily.

"I've missed you, Johanna. It's really lonely at home without you."

"I missed you, too, punkin." Johanna smiled down at the rosy, upturned face.

"I hate taking piano lessons. But Mama insists. She says every young lady should play a musical instrument and must have accomplishments." Elly had some trouble with the word. "When I ask *why,* Cissy says, 'So that suitable gentlemen will want to marry you.' As if I cared about *that,*" she sniffed disdainfully. "But Cissy *does.* She plays the flute and *she* likes it. She can't wait 'til she's old enough to have beaux." Elly looked sideways at Johanna. "Do you have beaux, Johanna? I mean, someone special you want to marry?"

"Not really, Elly," Johanna laughingly replied, but a small, secret smile played around her mouth as she thought of Ross Davison. Although she couldn't as yet consider him

51

a beau — or even a would-be suitor, there was something tucked deep inside her heart that whispered "possibility."

Caught up in thoughts of the mysterious, unknown future, Johanna was surprised when they reached Miss Minton's house in what seemed to her like no time at all. Elly yanked the leather thong, setting the pewter doorbell clanging and bringing a flustered-looking Miss Minton.

When she saw Johanna, she gave her head a little jerk. Johanna had not been one of her best students nor a favorite. Too restless, too uninterested, and one who had not progressed much, in spite of all Miss Minton's efforts. In her opinion, *she* had not been at fault — it was simply that Johanna had not applied herself.

"Well, Johanna, I see you're back from school. Were *they* able to give you some appreciation of the value of a musical education?"

Trying to keep a straight face, Johanna replied, "I *was* in choir, Miss Minton, but that's about all."

"Humph. Let's hope they were more successful than I at teaching you to sing on key," was Miss Minton's rejoinder. "Come along, Elinor. I hope you're prepared today. Go in the front room. I have another student in the parlor." From inside the house, the scratchy sound of a squeaky violin could be heard. Johanna suppressed a wince. She certainly didn't intend to remain here listening to Elly's stumbling fingers on the piano, accompanied by the agonizingly dreadful rendition of the violin student. Helping Elly off with her coat and bonnet, she whispered, "I'll go do some errands and be back for you in an hour. Then we'll go have our treat."

Elly threw Johanna a hopeless look. No prisoner on the way to the gallows could have looked more desperate. Before Elly reluctantly followed Miss Minton's rigid back down the narrow hall, Johanna gave her a little wave and a sympathetic smile.

Outside in the crisp winter morning, Johanna walked briskly toward the center of town. She had no particular place in mind to wile away the hour Elly was enduring her music lesson. Johanna window-shopped at the milliner's and manteau maker's, then went to the stationer's. Browsing the displays of handsome desk sets, she wished she could buy one for her father as a Christmas gift. Of course, they were all much too expensive, some elaborate silver ones consisting of inkwells, sealing stamps, quill holders. She sighed. She would probably have to finish embroidering the spectacle case she had started and never completed, for his birthday, and give it to him for his Christmas present.

Outside again, she walked slowly down the street, in the direction of Dr. Murrison's residence. A wooden sign with his name and the words "Physician and Surgeon" underneath swung on the gate. In smaller letters, another name — Dr. Ross Davison — had been painted by a different hand. She put out a tentative hand and traced the name over a couple of times with her gloved finger.

"Miss Shelby!" a deep male voice called and she whirled around. Ross Davison was running out from the side entrance of the house, without his coat, his hair tousled by the wind. Johanna felt her face flood with color.

When he reached her, Johanna saw obvious happiness in his face. He leaned forward on the gateposts. His eyes shone, his smile wide.

"Miss Shelby, what brings you out this chilly morning?"

"Yes, it is chilly." She raised her eyebrows, noting he was in his shirtsleeves, as if he had come flying out when he saw her, in too much of a hurry to put on his jacket.

To her amazement he stated, "I saw you

from the window and was afraid you might pass by without my having a chance to speak to you."

What honesty! What lack of pretense or guile! Johanna thought of all the silly chit-chat most young gentlemen dealt out in conversing with young ladies. Ross Davison was certainly different.

"As to what I'm doing out," she replied, "I'm on my way to fetch my youngest sister from her music lesson." Johanna laughed. "Actually, I should say *rescue* her. She was very reluctant to go, and only the promise of a treat afterward would persuade her."

Ross was spellbound. Just looking at her, her lovely eyes sparkling with merriment and her cheeks as glowing as twin roses, listening to her voice, her laughter, made his heart happy. As a doctor, he was aware of his own physical reaction at the sight of her. His heart rate had quickened alarmingly, and probably his blood pressure rose as well. Diagnosis: decidedly unmedical. He knew he was in fine health, so there must be another explanation.

A little uneasy under his steady gaze, Johanna said, "I must be on my way. It should be nearly time for the prisoner's release."

"Can you wait until I get my coat?" he asked. "I'd like to accompany you, if I may?

Maybe buy both of you a treat?"

"Why, thank you, Dr. Davison. That would be very nice." Johanna was too delighted to dissemble.

"Good. Then, I'll be right back," Ross promised and, turning, ran back to the house. A minute later he emerged, still thrusting his arms into his coat sleeves. He twisted a long knitted scarf around his neck and fell into step alongside her, breathless.

"My goodness, Dr. Davison, you could win a marathon!"

"I'm what town folks call a 'ridge runner,' " he laughed heartily, turning the word used often as a derogatory name for mountain folk into a matter of pride.

On the short walk over to Miss Minton's, they talked and laughed easily, as if they had known each other a long time. Being with Ross was so natural, Johanna felt relaxed and happy. Elly, her snub nose pressed against the window next to the front door, was already anxiously awaiting Johanna's arrival. Her coat was buttoned crookedly, her bonnet jammed on her head, its strings tied carelessly into a crooked bow.

Miss Minton stood behind her, arms folded. Seeing that Johanna had not returned alone but accompanied by a young man, her eyes sharpened disapprovingly behind her spectacles.

Johanna made quick work of the introductions, then took Elly's hand, and the three of them hurried down the path and out the gate. "Dr. Davison has kindly offered to stand for our treat, Elly," Johanna explained.

"What would you say to a candied apple on a stick, Miss Elly?" Ross asked. "When I was in the bakeshop earlier, they were making them. And the smell of brown sugar, cinnamon, and apples was almost too much."

"Sounds wonderful, doesn't it?" Johanna squeezed Elly's hand.

Elly's eyes lit up and she smiled shyly, nodding her head.

The trio were blissfully ignorant that behind a stiff, lace curtain, the watchful gaze of Miss Minton was following them.

Miss Minton's mouth pressed in a straight line. What a bold baggage Johanna was! And that young assistant of Dr. Murrison. Shouldn't he be tending sick folks instead of gallivanting around with that Shelby girl? Miss Minton intended to pass on her opinion to the next mother who showed up today with one of her pupils.

Outside, the subjects of Miss Minton's negative consideration were having a merry time. They stopped to get their candy apples, then walked down to the duck pond while they ate, the sweet, sticky coating blending deliciously with the tart taste of the juicy apples. The three of them carried on a jolly conversation. Both Johanna and Ross included Elly, giving her attention as an equal.

Finally Ross said he had to go back to his office. "But I've had a wonderful morning, thanks to you two. You don't know how much it means to a doctor to be with healthy, happy folks for a change."

Elly looked wistfully at the tall departing figure and sighed. "Isn't he nice? I'd like him for a beau, wouldn't you, Johanna?"

Out of the mouths of babes! But Johanna didn't dare admit her wholehearted agreement with Elly's opinion. The little girl might just pop out with something at the wrong moment. For now, Johanna wanted to keep her still uncertain feelings about Ross Davison to herself. So not answering, she just gave her a quick hug and said, "Come on, Elly, I'm cold. I'll race you home." Then picking up her skirt, she started to run, forgetting altogether that she was now a young lady and this was unseemly behavior for someone who was eighteen.

For the next few days, Johanna's thoughts

swirled, circled, and whirled around Ross Davison. It was a delicious secret that she hugged close, too precious to share with anyone. Was it real, had it truly happened? Her inner happiness softened and sweetened her, touching everything she said and did with a remarkable gentleness.

Rebecca thoughtfully noted this "weather change" in her oldest daughter. Perhaps some of Miss Pomoroy's influence had taken its hoped-for effect on Johanna. Usually when Johanna was home, she created all sorts of small tempests. Frequent spats between her and Cissy, careless neglect of household duties, a general disregard for anything but her own pleasurable activities. Maybe all the trouble and expense she and Tennant had lavished on Johanna was at last reaping some benefits. Johanna certainly seemed to be maturing. Of course, she had always been generous, cheerful, maybe too fun-loving but certainly a joy to be around. Now if she could just become more interested in the womanly skills that would be necessary assets when she married. Of course, there was still time for that. Johanna had another year to complete at the academy. . . .

Unaware of her mother's concern, Johanna was fully enjoying her vacation, free from ringing bells, boring lessons, required stitchery classes. Every day, she received fistfuls of invitations to holiday parties. Each one a potential chance of seeing Ross Davison, now a part of the social circle of Hillsboro's young people. Whatever people like the snobbish Archers might say, an eligible bachelor was always welcome, and as the respected Dr. Murrison's assistant, Ross had an assured acceptance.

As she wrote her replies to these invitations, Johanna could never have guessed that her next meeting with Ross would be pure "happenstance" or that it would have such unexpected repercussions.

Two days before Christmas it snowed. Snow in Hillsboro was unusual. Snow of this depth and of such lasting quality was really rare. The temperature dropped and the foot or more of snow that blanketed the town formed an icy crust, perfect for sledding. Elly was beside herself with glee, and Johanna was still young enough to love the snow and see its possibilities for enjoyment.

Excitedly they got out the seldom-used wooden sled and waxed the runners. Bundled up with scarves and mittens, Johanna and Elly went to join some other adventurous ones who had made a sliding track on the hillside.

The air was as keen and stimulating as chilled wine, stinging the eyes and turning noses and cheeks red as ripe cherries. Up and down the winding hill the girls went, swooping down the slopes and shouting at the top of their voices as they sped to the bottom.

It was when they reached the bottom for about the fourth time and were starting the slow climb back up to have another spinning ride that Johanna spotted Ross coming along the street. Holding on to the brim of his tall hat with one hand and his doctor's bag with the other, his head bent against the wind, he plowed along the path through high drifts on either side.

Unable to resist the impulse, Johanna bent over, quickly scooped a handful of snow, formed it into a ball, and sent it winging through the air. It hit its target exactly, knocking Ross's hat clear off. Startled, he halted and spun around, looking for the culprit. Then he saw Johanna and Elly holding on to each other as they convulsed with laughter. His first puzzled expression instantly broke into a wide grin. "You rascals!" he shouted. Dropping his bag, he swiftly rounded a ball of snow with both hands and threw it. It landed on Johanna's shoulder as she turned to avoid being his target. There followed a fierce snowball fight, two against one. Elly and Johanna alternately fashioned snowballs and pelted Ross while he struggled valiantly to return as good as he was getting. Finally it ended in a laughing truce, with Ross pulling out a large white handkerchief and waving it. He retrieved his hat, dusted the snow off its brim, and picked up his medical bag. Smiling broadly, he approached the two girls, who were still laughing merrily.

"Enough! I surrender. I have sick people who are down with the croup, chills, and fever!" Ross pleaded submissively. "How can you two justify delaying me on my rounds of mercy, waylaying me and attacking me so viciously?"

For an answer, Johanna reached down and molded another snowball and tossed it with all her might, only to be hit by one herself as she turned her back and started running out of range. Her laughter was ringing out in the air when unexpectedly she heard her name spoken admonishingly. She whirled around to see Emily and Mrs. Archer approaching along the side of the street. Emily's mother had a shocked look on her face. Johanna blushed scarlet, feeling like a child caught with a hand in the forbidden cookie jar. Not only was she positive Mrs.

Archer would relay *this* escapade she had observed to everyone, including Johanna's mother and aunties, but Johanna knew Emily was delighted to have a spicy tidbit to pass along to her chosen friends. Johanna Shelby and the young doctor carrying on in broad daylight on the street! Emily's eyes were wide with curiosity as she and her mother came to a stop within a few feet of both Johanna and Ross.

Johanna attempted a semblance of poise and started to make introductions but did not have a chance. With lifted eyebrows Mrs. Archer said coolly, "Oh, we've met Dr. Davison, Johanna. I wasn't aware *you* two were acquainted."

Emily interjected too sweetly, "Don't you remember, Mama? Johanna and Dr. Murrison were the last left playing musical chairs at the Chalmerses' party." She glanced over at Johanna with the look of a tabby cat licking a bowl of cream.

Johanna flushed, gritting her teeth. That Emily! What a spiteful person she was. However, Ross, unaware or undisturbed by the fact that Emily was trying to embarrass them, bowed slightly, acknowledging Mrs. Archer. Then he laughingly declared, "That was the most fun I've had since I was a tadpole."

Mrs. Archer gave him a cold look that might have chilled a lesser individual. "*Really?* How odd, Dr. Davison." Then, turning to her daughter, she said, "Come along, Emily. We must get on with our errands." She added pointedly, "Johanna, do give your dear mother my kind regards." With that parting jab they walked off. Johanna bit her lip in frustration, knowing for certain she would hear about this later.

Ross seemed hardly to notice their departure. His mind was too taken up with Johanna. Did she have any idea how pretty she was? Her dark curls escaping from the red knitted cap tumbled onto her shoulders. The rosy laughing mouth. The blue, blue eyes shining with fun.

After exchanging a few more silly jests, Ross set his hat straight and gave them a small salute. "Good day, Miss Shelby, Miss Elly. Regrettably, I have work to do while *others* may play!" He made an exaggerated bow. "And may I take this opportunity to wish you both a very happy Christmas."

"I like him," Elly declared as she and Johanna started back up the hill.

"I do, too," said Johanna, knowing it was much more than that.

"He doesn't seem at all like a stuffy old doctor, does he?"

"No," replied Johanna. They went back to sledding, the playful incident with Ross part of a happy day. A day when Johanna had seen yet another side of Ross Davison. A side that appealed to her own fun-loving self.

***

This year Christmas dinner was at Aunt Bee and Uncle Radford's home. Since it was also their twentieth wedding anniversary, the whole family was in an especially festive mood for the double celebration. As they gathered around the table for dinner, Aunt Hannah's husband, Uncle Roy, who was an elder in church, was asked to say the blessing. All heads bowed as it was ponderously intoned, and afterward the light buzz of conversation resumed as plates and platters were passed.

Then something happened that startled Johanna. During one of those lulls that sometimes occur even in the most congenial company when everyone is simply enjoying the good food, Aunt Hannah remarked, "By the way, Johanna, Emily Archer's mother said the strangest thing to me when I saw her the other day." Aunt Hannah pierced her with a sharp look. "She mentioned that she had seen you and Dr. Murrison's assistant in quite a rowdy display, throwing snowballs at each other in broad daylight on the street! I told her she must be mistaken, that I thought it unlikely that a girl with your background and breeding and so recently come from Miss Pomoroy's establishment would be making a spectacle of herself in public!"

The silence that followed was so absolute that one could have heard the proverbial pin drop. Johanna felt her cheeks flame as everyone either looked at her or avoided doing so. Worst of all, she felt her mother's gaze rest upon her. What could she say in her own defense? Besides, it was true. It had happened, there was no use denying it. Johanna opened her mouth to explain, but as it turned out, it was Elly who did.

"Oh yes, Aunt Hannah. It is true! Johanna and I both did. It was ever so fun! Dr. Davison is so kind and jolly. Johanna and I had such a good time."

Aunt Hannah looked a trifle sheepish at the little girl's enthusiastic explanation, but she still had the last word. Giving a little clucking sound of disapproval, she said, "One would hardly expect a *physician* to engage in such sport."

"And why not?" boomed Uncle Matt. "He's a young fella, even though a man of medicine! I admit to feeling like frolicin' myself sometimes in the snow!" he chuckled heartily.

There was a murmur of amusement at this around the table, then a general, noncontroversial conversation continued.

Johanna cast her uncle a grateful look, then glanced at Aunt Hannah. Known in the family for a talent of turning a joyous occasion into something else, she had certainly been true to form today. Thankfully, Uncle Matt, was jolly enough to make up for it.

Johanna avoided her mother's questioning eye, knowing she would have some explaining to do later. Inwardly she fumed. The Archers had wasted no time carrying their tidbit of gossip to willing ears. However, evidently Aunt Hannah's *informant,* Mrs. Archer, had failed to tell her that her younger sister was there, too.

Although the meal proceeded without further ado, Aunt Hannah's acid remark about Ross had spoiled the family holiday dinner for Johanna. Auntie Bee's lemon meringue pie could have been cardboard for all Johanna could tell.

At least her little sister had saved the day. And Uncle Matt's comment had dashed some cold water on Aunt Hannah's criticism. But only temporarily. Back at home, as Johanna had known she would, Rebecca came into Johanna's bedroom. "Why didn't you mention seeing Dr. Davison and having a snowball fight the day you took your sister sledding?"

"I didn't think it was important." Johanna shrugged. "It was just a silly game —"

"It seemed important enough to Mrs. Archer for her to speak of it to Hannah. You know how it upsets me to have my daughters the subject of criticism or comment."

"Oh Mama, you know Emily's mother is a terrible gossip. She was just trying to find something to talk about. Why is she so interested in what other people do? I say she's much too inquisitive. She should mind her own affairs."

"Don't be disrespectful of your elders, Johanna," her mother corrected sharply, then added with a raised eyebrow, "Besides, the only people who mind others being inquisitive are those who have something to hide." She paused. "Do you have anything you'd like to tell me, Johanna?"

"No, Mama, I don't." Johanna pressed her lips together stubbornly.

Rebecca sighed and went to the door. Her hand touched the knob and was about to turn it, when she glanced again at Johanna.

"Remember, Johanna, anything you girls

do or say reflects on us — your parents, your home, your upbringing."

Without looking at her, Johanna replied, "Yes, Mama, I know."

New Year's Day 1840

Chapter Four

Coming as it did at the end of the festive holiday season, New Year's Day had always been rather a letdown for Johanna. After the round of parties and festivities, it used to mean her reluctant return to the strict regime of Miss Pomoroy's. This year was different. After much pleading, she had received parental permission to remain at home.

Johanna, jubilant with that victory, had other reasons to be happy. This year it was the Shelbys' turn to host the traditional family gathering, and the fact that Dr. Murrison and his assistant had been invited to share it with them made it special.

Since this was Rebecca's first time in six years to have everyone at Holly Grove for the holiday dinner, everything had to be perfect. Right after Christmas, preparations began to ready the Shelby house for the occasion. Ordinarily Johanna dreaded the uproar of housecleaning. However, this year she pitched in with energy and enthusiasm that surprised Rebecca. The fact that Ross would be a guest was, of course, the spur.

Rebecca directed the work, allotting certain tasks and jobs to everyone. Their cook, Jensie, asked her sister, Aster, to come over and help Bessie with the heavier work of cleaning. Every nook and cranny had to be thoroughly dusted, every piece of furniture polished, the pine floors waxed. The Shelby girls were all put to work as well. All the silver had to be shined, brass candlesticks polished, the Christmas greenery refreshed, and the red bayberry candles replaced on the mantel sconces and windowsill lamps.

Cissy frequently complained of fatigue, of being overworked, and begged to rest. Elly sighed and dawdled over every task assigned. However, Johanna's mood was merry as she hummed at any job she was asked to do. Her cheerful attitude made her sisters alternately resentful or suspicious and mystified her mother. Even so, Rebecca appreciated her willingness to help with everything. For the time being, Rebecca's mind was concentrated on the result of her efforts: perfection. The annual New Year's Day dinner was an unadmitted competition among the ladies, each one trying to outdo the others when it was her turn. Secretly Johanna thought the beginning of a new decade was terribly exciting. *1840!* What would the next year hold?

The next *ten?* She had been a mere child at the beginning of the last — now she was a young woman with everything to look forward to. The possibilities seemed endless. Johanna's imagination went soaring. Heavens, she would be twenty-eight at the end of another decade. All sorts of things would have happened to her by then.

At last all was in readiness. The house sparkled and shone. The smell of lemon wax, almond paste, the fragrance of balsalm potpourri from bowls set about the rooms, the spicy aroma of cinnamon, ginger, and nutmeg from baking pies, mingled with the scent of cedar boughs and evergreen pine wreaths still hanging at the windows.

New Year's Day dawned with overcast skies. Gray clouds hovered with the promise of more snow. Before leaving for the special New Year's Day services at noon, Rebecca made a last-minute survey of her domain, satisfying herself that all was in perfect order. She anticipated that her cousins would give the Shelby household a polite yet precise appraisal. At length, everything met her approval, and the family went off to church.

Johanna hoped she would see Ross there. Although the shape of her bonnet kept her eyes reverently toward the pulpit, precluding any possible sidelong glances, under her jade velvet pelisse trimmed with beaver, her heart raced. He might be there observing *her!* But there was no sign of him, either in the back pews as they left or in the churchyard. An emergency of some sort? A sick child? A dying patient? A doctor's life was full of such unexpected happenings. What might have prevented his attendance at church could also cause him not to come to dinner. Such a possibility dismayed her.

Johanna had no time to dwell on such a catastrophe, because no sooner had the Shelbys reached home than the aunties and their husbands began to arrive.

Each lady brought her very best culinary effort to add to the veritable feast Rebecca and Jensie had prepared. Each cousin prided herself on being a fine cook, so each dish presented was to be profusely praised. By the time everyone gathered in the parlor for a holiday libation, all were in a good mood, ready to see the old year out and welcome in the new.

Although she circulated among her relatives, chatting with each in turn as her mother would have her do, Johanna kept stealing surreptitious glances at the grandfather clock in the hall. Each time she passed a window, she glanced out hopefully, longing to see Ross coming through the gate. Even while trying to respond to some of the parlor conversation, she strained her ears for the sound of the knocker on the front door.

She knew dinner was planned for five o'clock. *Please don't be late,* she prayed. Delaying dinner would upset her mother, and she wanted Ross's first visit to come off well. Even a medical emergency would not be an excuse if her mother's sweet potato soufflé collapsed.

In an uncharacteristic state of mind, Ross Davison walked through the gathering winter dusk on his way out to Holly Grove. This would be the first time he would see Johanna in her own home, one he knew was far different from his own. During his time in Hillsboro, he had been in enough homes of people like the Shelbys to realize just how different their backgrounds were.

Ever since he'd met Johanna, his feelings both daunted and excited him. Every time he saw her, his pulse rate was erratic, his heartbeat accelerated. He had to ask himself a dozen times a day what kind of madness this was. His hopes were probably impossible. All week he had debated whether or not to find some way to get out of the invitation Dr. Murrison had accepted for them both.

He had argued both sides, vacillating. It would be wiser not to go, something told him. However, the thought of missing a chance to see her, be with her again, proved too much. Now here he was, on his way.

Holly trees lined the curving driveway up to the impressive house of pink brick with white columns and black shutters. Standing at the gate, Ross looked up at the Shelby home. In the twilight, all the windows, adorned with scarlet-bowed wreaths, were lit with candles.

He swallowed hard, then opened the gate and went forward, up the porch steps. At the paneled door, there was another moment of hesitation. Then resolutely he raised his hand to the gleaming brass knocker in the shape of a pineapple, the traditional symbol of southern hospitality.

When Johanna opened the door for him herself, Ross was caught off guard. In a red and green plaid dress that rustled crisply, she looked so enchanting that it quite took his breath away. "Oh Ross, I'm so glad!" she said impulsively, then attempted to regain a proper manner. "Good evening. Do come in." She stepped back so he could enter.

Feeling tongue-tied, Ross struggled for words. He fumbled to take off his hat, held it awkwardly until he realized she was holding out her hand to take it so she could place it on the rack by the door. "Where's Dr. Murrison?" she asked.

"He'll be along soon," Ross assured her. "Just as we were leaving, an old patient stopped by to bring him a Christmas present, and nothing would do but that he come in for some cheer. You know how it is at holiday time."

A burst of laughter and the sound of voices floated out from the parlor. Ross glanced in that direction, an unmistakable look of alarm on his face. Johanna caught it and realized how shy he was. Immediately she sought to put him at ease. "Don't look so startled. It's only family. Of course, there *are* quite a lot of them," she laughed gaily. "But they're all quite harmless." She lowered her voice conspiratorially. "Just try not to sit down by Aunt Hannah, or she'll regale you with all her symptoms. I'll seat you by Auntie Bee. She's a dear and will want to know all about you." Smiling encouragingly, she took his arm and led him into the parlor.

To Ross the elegantly furnished room seemed filled with dozens of pairs of eyes, all turned to him. Johanna began to introduce him. The names went in one ear and out the other, the faces all became blurred.

76

Ross was grateful to sit down at last. A jovial, gray-whiskered gentleman handed him a cup of eggnog. Later he unobtrusively placed it on the small pie crust table at his elbow. He was sure it contained spirits, and he was not a drinking man.

Seated across the room, between Uncles Matt and Radford, Johanna looked at Ross fondly. Even his awkwardness touched her. However, Johanna tried to see him through the appraising eyes of her mother, her aunties. Johanna knew they would probably not consider him handsome in the slightest. However, to her there was such strength in his rugged features, sensitivity in his expression, depth of intelligence in his eyes, that she thought him one of the finest-looking men she had ever seen.

Within twenty minutes the front door knocker sounded and Dr. Murrison arrived. He and Tennant Shelby were old friends and he knew the others, so he was completely at ease. At once he was drawn into the general conversation of the group. The Shelbys, Millses, Hayeses, Cadys, McMillans, and Breckenridges never lacked for topics to discuss, debate, or argue about. The fact that the young doctor was sitting quietly, observing Johanna, went quite unnoticed — *except* by her mother.

Rebecca had excused herself to give her beautifully set table a last critical look before inviting the company to come into the dining room. Pleased that her best china, with its sculptured edge of flowers, gleamed in the glow of candles in two six-branched silver holders, she gave a final touch to the centerpiece, an artistic arrangement of fruit and pinecones. Then Rebecca returned to the parlor. She stood at the threshold, waiting for the appropriate moment to invite everyone to come in and be seated. It was then, with a sudden sharpening of her senses, that she saw Ross unabashedly staring at Johanna.

It struck her with that alertness one recognizes as impending threat or danger. Immediately she glanced at her daughter. Her face illuminated by firelight, Johanna was indeed lovely. Her dark hair, parted in the middle, with bunches of curls on either side of her face, was tied with crimson ribbons. A fluting of ruffles framed her face and slender neck. However, it was her expression that caused Rebecca's intake of breath. Johanna was gazing across the room at the young doctor, with the same raptness in her eyes as *his!*

Johanna's eyes held nothing back. Their glance was softly melting. Rebecca knew her daughter so well. *Why, the girl's in love!* Rebecca felt heat rising into her face. *How in the world did that happen?* There was only time for those fleeting thoughts. No time for her awareness to do more than register. Just then, Tennant caught her attention lifting eyebrows in a silent question. At her nod, he got to his feet, announcing, "Well, ladies and gentlemen, I believe my dear wife has come to fetch us in to dinner."

Seated across the table from him, Johanna watched Ross from under the fringe of her lashes. She felt a tenderness she had never known for anyone, along with the realization that he was feeling uncomfortable. He moved the lined-up silverware at his place nervously as he tried to pay close attention to what Uncle Madison Cady was expounding. Ross seemed so stiff, so different from the joking, laughing young man she had danced with, pummeled with snowballs, and talked with so freely at other times. Of course, it was meeting all her relatives. That must be hard on a stranger. Her sympathy came to the surface as she watched how he remained mostly silent after answering a few questions politely put to him. But to Johanna, everything about him seemed somehow so endearing and sweet. For example, how he had bent his head considerately to speak to Auntie Bee so that her deafness would not demand his repeating.

Rebecca's practiced glance passed over the table, her hostess's eye making sure everyone was enjoying the meal. Her gaze rested upon Johanna and, alerted, moved quickly across to young Dr. Davison, then back to her daughter. Neither of them were eating! Johanna had hardly touched her food! Where was her normal hearty appetite, an appetite that Rebecca had often claimed was *too* hearty, unladylike? She was only nibbling, pushing her carrots around her plate with her fork.

Something was going on between those two. Rebecca remembered she had felt that same little dart of alarm watching them together at the Chalmerses' party earlier in the month. But she thought her word of caution to Johanna about her frivolous behavior had settled it. Even as that thought passed through her mind, she saw an exchange of glances between Johanna and the young doctor. Rebecca knew that look, recognized it for what it was. Surely not *love* but certainly romantic *infatuation*. A twinge of possible problems pinched Rebecca. No question about it, she must speak to Johanna *again*.

Dinner finally came to an end, with everyone declaring they had eaten too much and enjoyed it immensely. They all returned to the parlor and settled back into chairs, on sofas, and a kind of desultory conversation ensued. For a few minutes Rebecca lost track of the topic everyone seemed to be discussing. She was distracted by the sight of Johanna and the young doctor sitting together at the other end of the room, conversing. Johanna's attitude was that of someone intently listening to Dr. Davison's every word. The scene had the look of intimacy Rebecca felt inappropriate. If she could have overheard their conversation, she would have been even more upset.

Ross was saying, "There are some things I've been wanting to talk to you about — some things I'd like you to know about me. Maybe I'm speaking out of place — I don't know. I don't have all the social graces I know you're accustomed to — I know your family, your background, is a great deal different from mine." He hesitated. "But Miss Shelby, I come from good folks, honest, hardworking, God-fearing folks with a lot of pride. I am the oldest in my family. My father died — was killed logging, actually. I didn't get much schooling after that. That is, until a friend of Dr. Murrison's, a teacher, saw something in me — a hunger to learn, maybe — and talked my mother into letting

81

me come with him into town, live with his family, go to school. I always wanted to be a doctor — I don't know why — always wanted to help things that were hurt, animals, children, anyone who was sick." Ross halted. "I wanted most of all to learn doctoring so I could go back to the mountains and minister to my people. I've seen children die that didn't need to, men die from blood poisoning, women — well, all kinds of sicknesses and disease nobody knew how to treat or cure. And since I got *my* chance, I want to give something back. Can you understand that?"

"Oh, yes!" Johanna said breathlessly, completely entranced by his earnestness. No young man had ever spoken to her like this, about serious things, important things, things that counted. She was amazed and touched and thrilled that Ross Davison wanted to share these things — evidently so dear to his heart — with her.

"You may wonder why I'm telling you all this. I don't usually talk so much, not about myself anyway. But I needed to tell you. I felt you'd understand, Miss Shelby —"

"Oh, please, call me Johanna!"

Ross looked doubtful. "I've never known anyone like you before. I haven't had much time for socializing. When I was at college,

I had to work, and then there were my studies. I'm not much at dancin' " — his eyes twinkled — "as you found out!"

"You did quite well," Johanna smiled, "experienced or not!"

Ross paused for a moment. "I was looking forward very much to coming to your home tonight. Your mother was very kind to include me. She didn't have to just because Dr. Murrison is an old family friend."

"But you couldn't be alone on New Year's Day!" exclaimed Johanna. "It's such a special occasion."

"Yes, I suppose it is. We never made much of holidays at home —" He then stopped. "Anyway, it was very gracious —"

"It was lovely to have you."

Rebecca decided it was time to interrupt. The two were completely absorbed in each other. Someone was bound to notice, then there'd be questions. She would ask Johanna to go to the kitchen, bring back fresh coffee to replenish everyone's cup. Before she could put idea to action, Dr. Murrison rose, declaring he must take his leave. Immediately his assistant also got to his feet. Reluctantly, Rebecca was sure, from the way his gaze lingered on Johanna.

After bidding everyone good-bye and thanking Rebecca for her hospitality, the two physicians went toward the hall. Mr. Shelby accompanied them, and before Rebecca could invent some excuse to stop her, Johanna quickly followed.

While Dr. Murrison and her father finished up their conversation, Ross asked her shyly, "I wondered if you'll be going to the taffy pull at the Chalmerses' next Wednesday?"

"Yes! Will you?"

"Miss Liddy was kind enough to invite me."

"Then we shall see each other there," Johanna said brightly.

"Yes," Ross replied solemnly. "I shall look forward to it."

When the door closed behind them and her father returned to the parlor, Johanna spun around a couple of times in an impromptu dance. She felt her spirits soaring outrageously. Spinning to a stop, she suddenly *knew*. Why, *this* was falling in love!

The night of the Chalmerses' party, Johanna had felt something happen between them. She hadn't quite known what. Startled, her lips formed the words: I love him! To her own astonishment, she knew it was true.

Chapter Five

The evening of the taffy pull, Johanna was invited to stay overnight with her friend Liddy.

Winter taffy pull parties were one of the most popular kinds of social get-togethers for young people. Although it was not openly admitted, the romantic potential of such an evening was widely accepted. At least, the young people themselves regarded it as romantic. If their parents did not, it was only because their memories were short. Often such a casual, spontaneous evening of two-by-two candy making developed into a more serious courtship. Under the laughter and gaiety and visible adult supervision, it afforded a means for couples to pair off without raised eyebrows. Within the guise of making candy, there was the chance for a quick hug and kiss in an alcove or corner. In fact, it was one of those well-circulated sayings, part joke and part truth, that a winter night of pulling taffy often resulted in a June wedding.

For that reason alone, knowing Ross had been included in the guest list, Johanna was particularly looking forward to the evening. Without being closely observed by chaperones, there was a real possibility of having another private conversation with Ross.

She was thrilled he'd confided in her about his family, his life, his hopes, his ideas of being a doctor. None of the other young men she knew had ever talked to her that way; as if she were an equal, as if she had intelligence to understand serious things.

As Johanna was about to leave on the afternoon of the party, Rebecca had a moment's uneasiness. Johanna had been to dozens of taffy pulls, and Liddy had been her friend since childhood. Why was she acting so excited, so eager to be on her way?

Although, ever since gaining permission not to return to Miss Pomoroy's, Johanna had been a shining example of obedience, cheerfulness, and helpfulness. She did her chores without complaining, was tolerant of Cissy and kind to Elly. Then, why did Rebecca feel troubled? It was the dreamy look she sometimes saw in Johanna's eyes, how she went about smiling as if she were listening to music. Instead of the volumes of history her father had assigned for her to study in order to continue her education in lieu of going back to school, Rebecca had found an open book of poetry on Johanna's bedside table! Poetry, indeed! Still, she did not see any tangible evidence that there was anything to chastise Johanna about.

Of course, Rebecca had no idea of how many "happenstance" meetings there had been with the young doctor on the days Johanna had eagerly volunteered to do errands for her mother.

So Johanna kissed her mother's cheek and went gaily off in the buggy that had been sent for her, neither of them dreaming that this evening would be a turning point in both their lives.

A big iron pot filled with sorghum was already boiling and bubbling on the stove in the Chalmerses' kitchen when Johanna arrived. She knew almost everyone there, and there was much chatter, everyone exchanging news and telling each other about their Christmases. They gathered around the stove, waiting for when the sugary mixture reached the proper consistency, while Liddy's father, red-faced, perspiring, shirtsleeves rolled up to his elbows, kept stirring. Suddenly he bellowed, "Get your plates buttered, folks!"

Mrs. Chalmers and the other mothers in attendance stood by the kitchen table, handing out solid white ironstone plates on which butter had been slathered. One by one, people filed up to the stove, and Mr. Chalmers ladled out dipperfuls of the syrupy liquid onto the greased plates, where it had to cool. When it was cool enough to be lifted off with the hands, the fun of pulling began.

With much laughter and conversation, everyone rubbed their hands with lard. Then the boys selected a partner and the pulling started. At first the molasses was stiff and hard to handle, but once it got started, it was easier to work, and it would be stretched into a kind of rope. The boy would grab the rope in the middle and pass the end on to his girl partner. Of course, sooner or later a few of the girls managed to get all mixed up in the rope of taffy. When this happened, the boy had to get his arms around the girl, standing behind her to free her hands from a wad of taffy. The point of the pulling was *supposed* to be to make the taffy more brittle and tasty. The longer it was pulled, the whiter it got. This was done with a great deal of giggling, squealing, and laughter, the hilarious "shenanigans" all taking place under tolerant chaperonal surveillance.

When Mrs. Chalmers felt the "tomfoolery" had gone as far as it should, she called for the taffy to be coiled onto the buttered plates. There was provided a second round of fun as people twirled and swirled the candy, making designs of hearts and links, and fashioning a fancy final assortment of the hardening taffy. When the taffy was ready for breaking up, couples took their pieces and, pairing off, went to find a place to chat, eat, and enjoy.

As it turned out, Johanna didn't have the worry of wondering how Ross would get into all the playing around. For the first part of the evening, she kept watching for him. Her distraction annoyed her partner, Burton Lassiter. "Pay attention, Johanna! Pull! Stretch it before it hardens," he told her in vain.

Johanna was finally rewarded when Ross arrived. She saw him before he saw her. He stood in the doorway with Liddy, appearing to listen to whatever she was saying while his gaze searched the room. When he saw Johanna, he distractedly excused himself from their hostess and came straight across the room to her. Suddenly everyone else in the crowded room simply disappeared for her. He was standing right in front of her, his thick hair and his shoulders glistened with raindrops. Had he come out in this storm without a coat, forgotten his hat? Johanna wondered.

"Good evening, Johanna. I'm sorry to be late and I cannot stay, but I must speak to you." Ross held out his hand and she put hers into it. He looked around and, seeing an unoccupied corner in the crowded room, led her over to it.

They sat down. Still holding her hand, he said, "I have to leave soon. The Barlow children are pretty sick. I saw them earlier today, but I'm uneasy about them. I want to check on them again."

"I understand," Johanna said, nodding her head.

Neither of them cared if curious eyes were upon them as Ross covered both her hands with his and leaned toward her, saying earnestly, "But even if it were only for a few minutes, I didn't want to miss the chance of seeing you. You see, Johanna, there is something I must say to you. Something important. In fact, I can't think of anything else." He paused. "I know this isn't the proper time or place — could you possibly meet me tomorrow? Say about two in the afternoon? I should be finished with office hours by then —"

"Yes. Where? You didn't say."

Ross's heavy brows drew together. "Someplace where we can talk without — what about the bandstand in the park near the skating pond past the stone bridge? You know where I mean?" His hands tightened on hers. "And if anything should delay me, will you wait?"

"Of course I'll wait," she said. "No matter how long." She was already planning what excuse she'd use to get out of the house that time of day. She felt wildly happy. Secret meetings, the stuff of romance novels. Johanna reveled in the excitement of it.

For a full minute they simply gazed into each other's eyes. What she saw in his told her what she had longed to know. Johanna was suddenly breathless.

Reluctantly Ross said, "I have to go. It may seem impolite to Liddy, but I don't want to disturb the Barlows by coming by too late."

"I'll walk out with you," Johanna offered, rising. She waited while he made his apologies to Liddy, then, ignoring Liddy's puzzled glance and Mrs. Chalmers's soaring eyebrows, she followed Ross out the front door.

They came out onto the porch. It had stopped raining but the night was cold and damp. Johanna shivered. Immediately Ross was concerned. "You shouldn't be out here. You'll get chilled."

"I wanted to come."

They moved closer to each other. She half turned toward him, and the moment was vibrant with all that was between them yet undeclared. Then, in a low voice, Ross spoke.

"I love you, Johanna."

That was what she had hoped, wished for in her heart, but now that it had been said, it startled her. She drew in her breath, then with something like relief whispered, "I love you, too, Ross."

"Oh, Johanna." He held out his arms and she went into them. He drew her close, held her tight. Her cheek rubbed against the scratchy texture of his rough wool coat. Her ear was pressed hard against his chest so that she could hear his pounding heart. "Oh Johanna, I love you so much —" Then, almost in a groan, he said, "But it's impossible."

She pulled back, looked up at him. "*Impossible?* What do you mean, impossible?"

"How can I make you happy?"

"You already have."

"I mean — what have I to offer someone like you?"

"Yourself. That's all I'll ever want," she replied softly.

Ross put his hands on either side of her face, raising it so he could look deeply into her eyes. Then he gently lifted her chin, leaned down, and kissed her mouth. His lips were warm in the cold air and the kiss was sweet. There was a kind of desperation in his voice when he asked, "What are we going to do, Johanna?"

When Ross left, Johanna went back into the party. For the rest of the evening, Johanna moved as if in a daze. She spoke to others, laughed, pulled taffy, and chatted merrily with everyone. She felt as if she were in a puppet show, mouthing lines spoken by someone else, with somebody pulling the strings. She didn't remember what she said once the words were out of her mouth. Liddy kept glancing at her curiously, Burton sulked, and Mrs. Chalmers gave her several disapproving looks. It didn't matter. Johanna knew now that what was between her and Ross was no mere flirtation. It wasn't only her own dreams and fantasies about him. Ross Davison was in love with her.

Ross had asked, "What are we going to do, Johanna?"

Do? What did he mean, *do?*

In the Chalmerses' guest room, Johanna propped the lavender-scented pillows behind her and sat up in bed. She was not the least sleepy, even though, with an exaggerated yawn, she had discouraged Liddy from coming in to gossip and chitchat as they usually did after a party. Liddy had gone away miffed, and although Johanna was sorry about that, she needed to be alone. Something important had happened between her and Ross tonight, and she wanted to think about it, sort out her feelings.

Everything she felt was so new. Yet there was a sweet familiarity about Ross. The odd feeling that they had known each other for a long time lingered. It was as if she had been waiting for him all her life.

She heard the steady patter of rain on the windowpanes. Where was Ross? Was he home yet? Or driving back to town along some country road? Or was he still with those sick children? Her heart felt tender as she thought of what a good doctor he must be. Was he thinking of her, as she was of him?

How conscientious Ross was. Her heart softened further as she contemplated his innate nobility. Yes, nobility. That best described him.

It made her feel humble that such a man *loved her!* She still couldn't quite believe it. She must change, become *worthy* of his love.

She needed to mold herself into something better, stronger. Johanna closed her eyes in remembered delight of his kiss. She hugged her knees and smiled. Being in love was so wonderful!

Again Ross's question came into her mind.

"What are we going to do, Johanna?"

Do? Although she wanted to keep this happy secret to herself for a little while, of course in time they would tell everyone, share their happiness. That's all they would *do*. She couldn't imagine what else Ross meant.

Johanna slid down into the pillows, shutting her eyes at last and, with a happy sigh, went to sleep.

Chapter Six

Hurrying through the blustery January afternoon, Johanna hugged her happiness close. Oh, how wonderful it was to at last be free to say "I love you" and mean it! Ross was everything she had ever dreamed of in a lover — more, even! How had she been so lucky? She had never been so happy in her life. She had gone to meet him today from Liddy's house, where she had stayed overnight after the taffy pull party. She had invented an errand so that she could go alone. Liddy had seemed suspicious. Johanna could not share her secret — at least, not yet. Promising she would return so that she would be there when Mr. Chalmers arrived from town to drive her back to Holly Grove, she had rushed out without further explanation.

Ross was waiting for her at the appointed place. Johanna rushed toward him, but instead of looking happy, Ross looked worried. He hadn't slept, he told her. He had been wrong to speak of love to her as he had last night, he began. But she would not let him finish.

"No, no, it wasn't! I love you, too, Ross. And I know it's right."

"But what can we do, Johanna?" The words seemed wrung from the depths of his heart.

His question puzzled her. What would they do? What did any two people in love do? They got married.

He acted as if there were insurmountable problems. She wouldn't listen to any he tried to tell her about. He had house calls to make, and nothing was really settled as he hurried away.

She was so happy, she felt her heart might burst. She couldn't wait to tell her parents. Of course, they did not know Ross very well, but they knew Dr. Murrison. He was an old family friend. They certainly knew and respected Dr. Murrison and must realize he would not have chosen Ross from among all the medical students he could have brought in as his assistant, if he had not been convinced of his character and ability.

And of course, her parents would probably be surprised, call theirs a whirlwind romance, but what was wrong with that? After their first surprise, they would be happy for her. She was sure.

Johanna could not have been more wrong.

The minute the words were out of her mouth, Johanna knew she had made a mistake. She saw the stricken expression on her mother's face. Immediately Johanna was contrite. She was furious with herself for having upset her mother so much. But even though she realized she had not picked the right moment, she hadn't expected this intense opposition.

"It's out of the question. You're much too young and I won't hear of it."

Her mother's reaction chilled Johanna with its cold vehemence. Perhaps it was mostly because she would be the first one to leave the nest. At first Johanna did not realize that the real problem regarded her choice.

Though her father was surprised, his objections were milder. "Well, Johanna, I thought it was young Burton Lassiter you were interested in. He certainly has hung about here looking at you with calves' eyes long enough. What's wrong with Burton? Good family, nice fellow."

"Oh, Burton!" Johanna scoffed. "I don't love Burton. I never could. You can't make me love someone I don't. You certainly can't make me marry someone I don't love."

"Who was talking marrying?" Tennant protested. "Anyway, I agree with your mother. You're far too young to be thinking about marrying anyone."

"Mama was seventeen when she married *you*, Papa. And I'm eighteen and will soon be nineteen."

"That's quite enough, Johanna," her mother interrupted sharply. "We'll speak no more about it. And we will certainly make our wishes plainly known to Dr. Murrison that we do not appreciate Dr. Davison's attentions to our daughter without our permission."

Johanna turned pale. "Oh Mama, you wouldn't! That would humiliate Ross, and he is so sensitive."

Rebecca looked at her coldly. "He should have had the good manners to address your father before he spoke to you of love, Johanna — assuredly before he spoke of marriage. It is just more evidence that he has neither the breeding nor background that we would accept in a prospective husband for our daughter — any of our daughters. And as I have told you many times, as the oldest it is up to you to set the example for your younger sisters. Now, that is all. I suggest you go to your room and give some thought to your rash, reckless behavior and the upset you have caused your parents."

Mute with misery, speechless with frustration and resentment, Johanna turned and went out of the room, ran upstairs and into her bedroom, letting the door slam behind her. She flung herself down and, in a torrent of tears, wept into her pillow for some time.

She knew she had done everything wrong, had approached her parents in the worst way. She'd ruined everything! She had foolishly hoped they would be happy for her. She had not thought of all the objections her mother had listed. It seemed so petty, so cruel, to judge Ross on such shallow measurements. What could she now do to put things right? To make Ross acceptable to her parents?

She woke the next morning with a blotched complexion, eyelids puffy from her frequent bursts of tears during the sleepless night. When her mother sent Cissy to call her down for breakfast, she pleaded a headache and said that she was going to stay in bed. When her mother peeked in the door later in the day, Johanna pretended to be asleep. She had lain there through the hours trying to come up with a new way to present

Ross to her parents, to ask them to try to get to know him, to discover his fine qualities. If they did, she knew they could not help but be impressed with the same things she saw and loved in him.

The winter afternoon darkened, and Johanna knew her father would soon be home. When she heard the front door open and her father call out "Rebecca!" as he always did when he entered the house, she tiptoed out of her bedroom, leaned over the banister, and heard the murmur of her parents' voices. She felt sure they were discussing her. She crept downstairs, in her nightie and barefooted, and huddled on the steps, straining to hear what her father and mother were talking about.

She heard her mother say, "She's buried herself in her room all the day, won't eat a bite, determined to be stubborn. She has upset the whole household over this foolish thing. She won't listen to me. She won't listen to anybody!"

"It's her fondness for melodrama, that's all. It will all be over in a few weeks, I'm sure."

At her father's rejoinder, Johanna stiffened indignantly. If there was anything that infuriated her, it was indulgent amusement, that her earnest pleading could be dismissed as a whim not worth considering.

Her father was always inclined to be amused at whatever Johanna did. All her life, when she had popped up with something she had just discovered or thought, he had looked at her indulgently. She could remember numerous times when he had done exactly the same as he had last night when she broke her news about Ross. He had smiled at her, stood up, and patted her on the head as if she were a recalcitrant child who needed to be pacified and reassured that somehow, in time, she would get over her silly notion.

Well, *this* time he was wrong. He'd see. They'd both see. She was serious. She loved Ross Davison, and in spite of anything they said, she was going to keep on loving him and someday they would marry.

Then she heard her mother say firmly, "You must speak to Alec Murrison, Tennant. That's all there is to it. I am sure he would not countenance his assistant pursuing a courtship that was unwelcome. Even if it is only a matter of our friendship, I am sure he will see that our wishes are respected."

Johanna's hands balled into fists and she pressed them against her mouth. Oh, no! That would hurt Ross so dreadfully. He revered and admired Dr. Murrison so much. To have him rebuke him for — what? For loving her! It was too awful. Johanna crept back upstairs and into her room, choking back new sobs.

Across town in the house of the town's physician, another conversation was taking place. Remembering that this was the man who had taken him in, treated him like a son, rendered the hospitality of his home, given him the benefit of his own knowledge and skill, been his mentor and his instructor, Ross hesitated. Perhaps it was too much to ask for Dr. Murrison to champion his cause. Perhaps Dr. Murrison would be risking his friendship with the Shelbys if he gave his blessing to Ross's asking for Johanna's hand in marriage. But how else could this ever come about? At least he could ask Dr. Murrison if he should try.

"I want to marry Johanna Shelby. Do you think there is any hope? I don't want to take advantage of you, sir, but I do need your opinion."

Dr. Murrison pursed his mouth as if giving the statement considerable thought. He knocked his pipe ashes on the stone edge of the fireplace, took his time refilling it and lighting it again before answering Ross's question.

"Have you addressed the young lady herself as yet?"

"Not formally asked her to marry me. However, truthfully, I have told her I love her." He paused in anguished embarrassment. "I couldn't help myself. But I didn't speak of marriage. I wanted to talk to you first, and if you think it would be all right, I would then, of course, approach her father and ask his permission."

"Well, that certainly is the usual way of things," Dr. Murrison agreed, but there was a degree of hesitancy in his words that sent a cold chill through Ross. Something more was coming, and instinctively he braced himself for it.

Then Ross suddenly decided that whatever it was — and he suspected what it *might* be — he didn't want to hear it. Abruptly he got to his feet and said, "I shouldn't have taken advantage of our relationship. I was wrong to place you in an awkward position. Forgive me." Without waiting for Dr. Murrison's reply, Ross left the room.

He went quickly upstairs to his room. He sank into the one chair in the sparsely furnished space and stared at the flickering light shining through the door of his small stove.

Why had he been so stupid? Why hadn't he seen what should have been obvious to him from the first? The Shelbys, one of the most prominent families in Hillsboro, accepting a poor, backwoods doctor with no future for the husband of their daughter? He gave a short, harsh laugh. For that's what it was — laughable! Ridiculous. Impossible. How could he have been foolish enough to entertain such a thought — to dream?

⁂

At church the following Sunday, Johanna was sitting in the family pew, beside her mother. Rebecca's head was bowed in private prayer before the service. Johanna bowed her head also. She wasn't praying, exactly — she was pleading in anguish and fear. Fear that what she wanted most in the world would not be allowed her. *Please, please, God.*

While her mother stopped after the service to compliment the minister on his sermon, Johanna stepped outside, looking for Ross or Dr. Murrison in any of the groups of men gathered in the churchyard, talking. But the tall figure she hoped to see was nowhere in sight.

It was bitterly cold and frosty, and when Johanna's mother joined her on the church steps, she took her arm, urging sharply, "Come along, Johanna. Get into the carriage. It's too cold to stand around in this wind."

Chapter Seven

Rebecca, her back very straight, sat at her quilting frame in the parlor. Seven stitches to the inch, in her hand the needle, poised daintily, moved expertly in and out. She had placed a lot of hope in Johanna. Much careful thought and consideration had been given to her rearing. Expense too, sending her to a fine female academy for the kind of education necessary for a girl who would assume the role of a wife in a prestigious marriage. Johanna had shown little interest in housewifely skills. She had acquired exquisite manners and social graces, could set a beautiful table, and was a graceful dancer and a gracious conversationalist. Of course, if she married someone from a wealthy family, such as Burton Lassiter, she would have plenty of servants. However, a woman still needed to master all sorts of tasks to enable her to teach her servants, show them how the work was to be done.

Rebecca gave a small shudder. Although her face was expressionless, she was concerned about her oldest daughter. Through the years, Rebecca had learned to conceal her emotions — disappointment, hurt, anxiety. Pride might be her besetting sin, but it was also her shield.

One deep wound she had suffered and tried to conceal was that she was the *only* one of all Grandmother Logan's granddaughters not to bear her name — Johanna. As if that weren't humiliation enough, then there was her own failure to produce a son for her husband. After two miscarriages and one stillborn, with much difficulty she had delivered Johanna. Three years later Cissy, and five years after that, Elly. But no male to carry on the family name.

Thinking of her own mother, Rebecca had to suppress her resentment. Why had she refused to follow the tradition of the family she married into? Rebecca had hardly known the rebellious young woman who had been her mother. She had died when Rebecca was only four. But of course, the story of her own christening had been told to Rebecca by anxious "do-gooders" and busybodies. It was a family scandal that could not be hushed up, because it had been witnessed by so many. A whole churchful, as a matter of fact. Possibly the whole congregation. The time had come for the minister to ask the question,

"And by what name shall this child be known?" and instead of replying as expected, "Her name shall be Johanna," her mother, dark eyes flashing, had responded in a clear voice, audible to the very rafters of the small stone church, "Rebecca." There had been, Rebecca was told, a collective gasp of shock.

The story had been repeated many times to Rebecca over the years, and she grew to dislike hearing it. She'd had to live with the legacy she had been left. It had, in a way, made her the outcast. She had tried to make up for it by excelling in many ways, always competing for attention among her cousins, for her grandmother's affection. But in the end, no one really seemed to care. Bee and Honey and Jo McMillan and Johanna Cady and even Hannah never mentioned it.

Was blood thicker than water? Had somehow Johanna, her carefully taught daughter, inherited the wildness of her maternal grandmother? The rebellious spirit? Flaunting what was expected, falling foolishly in love with an unsuitable man? Ross Davison might be a fine young man — certainly Alec Murrison thought the world of him. Still, he was not the right husband for *her* daughter. Johanna Shelby had been reared to marry a man of wealth, society, good family, refined background.

Well, it would not be. She would not allow it. Not let all her dreams, hopes, plans, go amiss because of a foolish girl's fancy.

Rebecca bent her head again over her work. This quilt, on which she was spending hours of meticulous care, tiny stitches outlining the lovely pattern, was for Johanna. Her wedding quilt. Rebecca had carefully traced the pattern from the ancient design, adding some of her own creative interpretations. It was called the Whig Rose by most, although the more romantic name was Rose of Sharon, which was taken from the beautiful Scripture in Song of Songs, the love song of Solomon to his bride, a part of the Bible that was now taught to describe Christ's love for the church.

As the Rose of Sharon, the pattern was a dazzling declaration of human love, the joy and passion between man and woman, honoring the sacredness of marriage. Secretly that is how Rebecca thought of it as she appliquéd the delicate scrolls, the buds, stems, and leaves, white thread on white. To her it represented all those hidden expectations she had brought to her own wedding, the special dreams of happiness she had hoped would be fulfilled. Now, years later, she was a mature woman who had survived the cares and concerns, the sorrows and losses, the disenchantments of life. As she sewed, Rebecca reflected on her own memories. If all those hopes and dreams had never been fully realized, still she had experienced a satisfying life, once she had faced realities, put away fanciful dreams. As she stitched into this quilt for her daughter renewed promises that yet might be for her happiness, Rebecca's mouth tightened. Rebecca rapped her thimbled finger on the edge of her quilting frame resolutely. *I won't let her make some stupid mistake, throw her life away.*

The following afternoon was the cousins' weekly quilting session. Alternating homes, the ladies of the family gathered to work on each other's quilts. Each cousin had her own special quilt in progress on which the others sewed. Of course, this was more than simply a sewing session. It was a time to exchange events and town gossip, discuss relatives and friends and upcoming plans, or contribute a bit of interesting news. Dessert and coffee and tea were served, perhaps a new recipe to be tasted, commented upon, and enjoyed. It was always a congenial time, and Rebecca always looked forward to it with pleasure. However, in her present state of mind, she was tempted to promote her slightly scratchy throat into a full-fledged cold to avoid going.

These get-togethers had started before they all had married, at the time all were working on quilts for their hope chests. Now it had become a weekly ritual in their lives. Nothing but a serious illness or a life-and-death crisis was an acceptable excuse for not attending. To not go was bound to cause concern of one kind or another.

Only the most unobservant person could have missed the effect of Hannah's remark at Christmas about Johanna's snow frolic with Dr. Davison. Since not one of her cousins could be qualified as that, Rebecca was also sure her canny relatives had noticed Johanna's obvious gaiety brought on by the arrival of the young doctor on New Year's Day. Surely one of them had guessed her high spirits were prompted by something other than a family gathering.

Nothing in the family was ever a private matter. Although kept within the family enclave, everything that happened or was about to happen or needed to be decided was always discussed at length among the cousins. Rebecca was sure someone, some way or other, would mention Johanna's escapade, her interest in Dr. Murrison's assistant.

Although Rebecca felt ill-prepared to answer any probing questions, at length she decided she had to go. There was no possible way out. However, she was determined to maintain a discreet silence on the subject, no matter what the provocation. She anticipated that if there were any, it would most probably come from Hannah. With no children of her own to make excuses for or explanations about, Hannah had an insatiable curiosity about others' offspring.

Resignedly Rebecca hooked the braided fastenings of her mauve pelisse, settled her bonnet on her head, tying its brown satin ribbons firmly under her chin, and set out. Today's meeting was at Johanna Cady's house, only a short distance from the Shelbys'. The brisk walk would clear her head for whatever lay ahead.

As she stepped inside her cousin's door, she was greeted by the usual buzz of conversation from the already assembled ladies, which only halted briefly as she was welcomed. The hostess for the day, Johanna Cady — called Josie by her cousins — rose to take Rebecca's cape, compliment her bonnet, and relieve her of her muff.

"You're late, Rebecca. I thought something might have happened."

"I'm sorry. A little delay, that's all."

"Well, you're here now, and that's all that matters." Josie lowered her voice. "You missed all the discussion about the new pattern we're starting. Of course, Hannah had to have her say, which took a while. So we got started later than usual."

Rebecca took her place at the quilting frame, between Honey and Hannah, and threaded her needle. The pattern stretched out was called Caesar's Crown. It was an array of geometric shapes forming an intricate design, on which Hannah was unfavorably commenting, "Why ever did you pick such a complicated one, Josie?"

"Because it's beautiful. Why else?" Josie retorted, adding tartly, "When it's done properly."

Honey, always the conciliator, spoke up. "I've seen one or two of these finished, and they're outstanding."

"Did Munroe or Harvel use drafting tools to cut your material from?" Hannah persisted.

"No. As a matter of fact, I did it all myself. I used bowls and teacups and folded paper," Josie said with a little toss of her head. "It just takes a little imagination."

"Well, I prefer the Double Wedding Ring pattern to this — it's every bit as handsome and much simpler," sniffed Hannah, anxious to have the last word. Then, in order to keep Josie from another sharp rejoinder, Hannah turned her attention to Rebecca, asking, "Has Johanna finished her twelve quilt tops yet, Rebecca?"

Traditionally, a young woman completed twelve quilt tops for her hope chest. A quilt was supposedly finished by the time she was ready to be engaged. Before Rebecca could think of a noncommittal answer, Bee appeared with the tray of cakes and the tea service. "Let's take a break, ladies," she suggested, and the ladies left their sewing for a welcome time of refreshment. Hannah's question was left dangling.

Rebecca had always been provoked by Johanna's lack of interest in quilting and needlework of any kind. Cissy was much more amenable in every way toward the womanly arts so necessary in a genteel woman's preparation for marriage. If only Johanna were more diligent and less imaginative and adventurous. If she *were*, there would certainly not be this need to worry over her.

Josie used Hannah's comment to introduce a subject she wanted to bring up. "Speaking of the Double Wedding Ring pattern, I think we should start working on one soon," she smiled smugly and sat back, waiting for her cousins' eager curiosity.

"What do you mean, Josie?" asked Bee.

"Well, it isn't official," she began tantalizingly, "but I think Harvel is about to propose to Marilee Barrington. He's just spoken to her father over in Cartersville, and —"

She was immediately the target of enthusiastic inquiries, demands for a description of the young lady, the possible date of the nuptials, and other pertinent questions. Of course, it was Hannah who had to put a chill into the happy conversation. She pierced Rebecca with a long look and pursed mouth, remarking morosely, "What a shame we couldn't be planning a lovely quilt for Johanna!"

Every eye, albeit tactful ones, turned expectantly toward Rebecca. She could easily have said something scathing to silence her cousin, but that would only have revealed her own inner upset. Instead, keeping her voice even, a tolerant smile in place, she replied, "No news from that corner, I'm afraid." Inside she was indignant at her cousin's bluntness. Somehow Hannah always managed to strike a sour note.

For the rest of the afternoon, Rebecca sewed quietly, not adding much to the hum of conversation that flowed around her. Her mind was busily plotting a sure way to remove Johanna from the dangerous ground on which she was treading because of her foolish infatuation with the young doctor. Johanna was always drawn to the different, the out of the ordinary, the unusual. And Ross Davison certainly fit all those criteria.

If only Tennant hadn't given into Johanna's pleas not to be sent back to Miss Pomoroy's. Rebecca had been against it and yet had allowed herself to be persuaded. Privately she had decided Johanna was as "finished" as she need be. They could apply the saved fee to Cissy's turn to go next year. Rebecca had to admit that the thought of enjoying Johanna's company at home had influenced her decision. Now she regretted her quick capitulation.

How cleverly Johanna had managed to manipulate her parents for her own purpose. Rebecca could but wonder how she herself had been taken in by Johanna's persuasiveness. All Johanna had ever wanted was to stay in Hillsboro, near the young doctor. It's my own fault, Rebecca chided herself. I saw it on New Year's Day! They only had eyes for each other. Johanna attempted to hide it, but *he* was too honest to try. Rebecca sighed. Even then it was probably too late. It had gone too far by then.

But of course, this courtship was impossible. And now it was up to *her* to do something, Rebecca decided.

Quite unexpectedly she was handed the opportunity she had been searching for. She was brought back from her own troubling thoughts into the present when she heard Honey announce, "I'm planning to go to Winston with Jo when she returns home."

Winston! Of course! Rebecca thought immediately. Winston, where the McMillans lived, was a lovely place with two colleges and a seminary, a cultured atmosphere. It was a hospitable and friendly town. What a perfect solution! Get Johanna out of town. Her cousin had a wide circle of friends, most of whom had children Johanna's age who could introduce her into their lively social life. Johanna could accompany Honey on her trip. Honey adored Johanna, and if Johanna could be persuaded —

No, not persuaded — *told* she must go. Rebecca was through with indulging her. They would have to be firm. Johanna must be kept from a mistake that might ruin her life.

Rebecca decided to have a private word with Honey. As soon as Honey got up to leave, Rebecca quickly followed. Once outside walking together, she tucked her arm through her cousin's and outlined her plan, confiding the reasons she had not wanted to share with the others.

Honey was delighted with the idea. Encouraged by this response, Rebecca felt led to open up more about her concerns, about how unsuitable she felt Johanna's interest in Ross Davison was and how anxious she was to remove Johanna even temporarily from an impulsive attachment.

Honey looked doubtful. "Well, of course, I'm sure Jo will be happy to introduce Johanna and perhaps even give a party or two for her while we're there, but I've never seen parental interference do more than intensify a romance, sometimes even making it the reason to flourish."

"Be that as it may, Honey, it's a risk I shall have to take. You know how impulsive Johanna is, and I just cannot take the chance of her rushing headlong into something as disastrous as this match could be."

Johanna had heard her mother leave and knew she would be gone several hours for the weekly quilting session. She could not remember at which auntie's house it was being held this week. It didn't matter. She knew that sooner or later her situation would be circulated on the family grapevine. Johanna expected this, anticipated it, both dreading and looking forward to the opinions they would express. All would be different, she was sure. She wasn't counting on allies because, despite their contrasting views, the cousins usually stood together on such things. All she could hope for was some understanding.

The house was empty. Now that the holidays were over, her sisters had started back to the dame school they attended in town, and she was alone.

It had been a horrible week. She had stubbornly refused to join the family for meals since the terrible scene with her parents two nights before. Johanna was not proud of the chaos she had brought into the usual harmonious atmosphere of the Shelby home. But they were being so unreasonable. They were refusing to even allow Ross to come and talk to them, ignoring all his fine qualities in an unyielding assertion that he was "unsuitable."

Her parents were giving her a studied silent treatment, maintaining a rare period of unity about the issue. That her father was as adamant as her mother was a bitter pill to swallow. Always before, he had been willing to let Johanna present her case, whatever it was. It especially hurt that this time he stuck with her mother, and her mother was entirely inflexible.

They had forced her to be deceitful, she justified, slipping out of the house on the chance that she would meet Ross as he went about making house calls in town. By some sort of unspoken agreement, they had found that the curved stone bridge near the churchyard was an easy place for their paths to cross by "happenstance." That's where she hurried on her way today. She felt a little uneasiness, a kind of nervous apprehension. She had not yet told him of her parents' reaction to telling them they were in love. She knew how deeply wounding it would be to his pride to learn they did not approve of him as a prospective husband for their daughter.

At the little bridge, Johanna looked anxiously for the familiar figure she hoped to see. She had only a few minutes to wait. Soon she saw Ross, his head bent against the wind, striding toward her.

As soon as she saw his expression, she knew something was very wrong. There were circles under his deep-set eyes, as if he had not slept. He looked drawn and there was a vulnerability about him she had never noticed before. Something had happened. Had someone in her family gone to him, told him they considered his courtship unacceptable? Her father? No, not him. Her mother? One of her uncles?

Perhaps they had even gone to Dr. Murrison? She had been foolish to think they could keep their love secret — not in *this* family, she thought with some bitterness. Not when everyone lived in everyone else's pockets. Her heart felt heavy and she felt almost sick. Ross's step slowed as he approached her, almost as if he were reluctant to see her, to tell her what she felt in her heart of hearts he had come to say.

Shivering with cold and nervousness, Johanna wasted no time. She had already broken so many rules of so-called ladylike deportment as related to him, it would be better to know at once what was the matter. It was too important. She had to know.

"What is it, Ross? You look so troubled."

"Johanna, we cannot go on meeting like this. Your parents would be angry if they knew. We must not see each other again."

"Not see each other? What do you mean? Not ever?" How did he know about her mother and father's disapproval? "Ross, why? Is this your idea? But you said —" She hesitated. Then she had no pride left and finished, "you said that you loved me."

"I shouldn't have, Johanna. It was wrong of me."

"*Wrong?* How is it wrong? You did say

you loved me, didn't you? Or did I imagine it? Dream up the whole thing?" Her voice trembled, tears glistening in her eyes.

"No, of course not. I do love you, Johanna. Maybe I should never have told you, because it was wrong —"

"I don't understand." She shook her head.

"The fact is, Dr. Murrison himself has discouraged me from pursuing my courtship. He says I should never have spoken to you about love — or anything — without first speaking to your parents. Dr. Murrison pointed out that this was probably the first thing they hold against me. That I don't know the proper thing to do, that I don't have the manners or the right background for —"

"Oh, for pity's sake, Ross, has he threatened you? Would he dismiss you?"

"No, of course not. He just pointed out the simple truth. You come from a home, a family, a life, so different from mine or what I have to offer —"

"Does love mean nothing? That we love each other — did you tell him *that?*"

Looking abject, Ross slowly shook his head. "No, I didn't. Because in my heart, I know they're right."

"No, they're not. They're very, very wrong. I love you. I won't hear any more of

123

this." Johanna placed her fingers on his lips to keep him from saying more.

Ross pulled them gently away from his mouth and went on speaking.

"We must be sensible, Johanna. What *do* I have to offer you? A doctor without a practice of my own. I'm going back this summer when my apprenticeship with Dr. Murrison is over. Back to the mountains — you don't know what living there would be like. There'll be hardly any money, because most of the folks I'll be caring for don't have any. They'll pay in potatoes or corn or fire-wood, most likely. Johanna, how can a man ask his wife — a girl like you, who's been used to so much more —"

"I don't care about that!" she protested.

"But *I* do. And if I were your father, I would. Dr. Murrison's right. He told me he worked years before he could get married. I have nothing to offer you —"

"That's not true, Ross. You have every-thing to offer me. Your life, your love, your whole heart — that's all I want, all I'll ever want."

She put her gloved hand on his arm. His head was turned from her, and she longed to see his face, to try to read what he was thinking in his eyes. "Look at me, Ross." Her voice was low, urgent, sweet to his ears.

He turned, took both her hands in his, brought them to his chest, looked down into her upturned face.

"Oh, Johanna. I love you, but I want to do the right thing."

"This is the right thing," she whispered. "Let me talk to my parents. Surely they want me to be happy."

"I believe they want your happiness, but I also believe they don't think I would be part of the happiness they want for you."

"I think it was a surprise — even a shock — but when I tell them how I feel, how I really feel about you, I think they'll understand."

Ross did not look so sure. "I don't want you to be alienated from your parents, Johanna —" His voice deepened with determination. "I won't go against your parents' wishes. I respect them too much for that."

A shaft of wind blew Johanna's bonnet back, her hair about her face, and she pushed it back impatiently, tucking the strands behind her ears, then straightened her bonnet.

"I've always been able to convince my parents when I really and truly wanted something. *This* time it's the most important thing in my life." Johanna tried to sound convincing. However, Ross's expression, the uncertainty in his eyes, shook her confidence.

When they parted, she felt cold and a little afraid. It was beginning to get dark as she walked home. The damp, gusty wind blew wet leaves, scattering them, plastering them on gates and fences along the way. The glow of being with Ross, the warmth of his kiss on her lips, began to fade. She shivered. She had never before felt like this. The loving closeness of her family had always protected her, sheltered her. No one could understand how miserable she was, how desolate, how totally alone she felt. There was no one to comfort her, support her. She was in this by herself. It would take all her courage to see it through, to stand fast. Even Ross doubted the wisdom of what they were doing. He was even willing to give her up — for what? For people to whom wealth, privilege, and standing in society meant more than love?

Her mother was already home when Johanna returned red-eyed from her walk, hoping she could blame it on the cold wind. She halted briefly at the door of the parlor, made some comment about the weather to her mother, then went upstairs.

Johanna seemed oddly subdued, Rebecca thought. The suspicion that she might be hiding something confirmed her own decision. She had made the wise choice, done the right thing. The sooner Johanna was out of harm's way, the better.

In her room, Johanna paced agitatedly. She must get this over, get everything out into the open. The sooner, the better. She would wait until after supper, after both her younger sisters were in bed. Then when both parents were together, she would go to them. The only way she could hope to make her parents understand that she was serious was to tell them in clear, brave, simple language, "I love Ross Davison and intend to marry him." Over and over she rehearsed just what she would say. But she never got to say those fiercely independent words.

Johanna worked herself up to such hope that she never imagined she could fail to convince them. She did not take into account that her parents were just as determined not to let their daughter "throw herself away" on a penniless doctor from the hills.

Chapter Eight

The following evening during dinner, the atmosphere was strained. Even the two younger girls seemed affected by the hovering storm. Finally everyone finished and as Johanna rose, preparing to do her assigned job of clearing the table, Rebecca spoke, "Leave that, Johanna. Cissy and Elly can do it tonight. Your father and I want to speak to you in the parlor."

Johanna followed, half glad that although this was unexpected, it might be the chance she was waiting for. She drew a long breath and followed her parents across the hall.

Her mother stood at the door and closed it after Johanna entered. Rebecca moved to stand at her husband's side, and they both turned to face her. Johanna felt a premonition — of what, she wasn't quite sure. Then her mother spoke.

"We have been shocked and saddened by your rebellious spirit, your unfilial behavior, your unwillingness to obey us as your parents, who are wiser and far more competent to judge what is best for you. This unsuitable attachment must be ended at once. Since you do not see fit to obey us out of love and submission, we are sending you away from the occasion of your willful disregard of parental guidance until you come to your senses. Tomorrow you are leaving with Aunt Honey for an extended stay at Aunt Jo's in Winston. We hope this will give you the opportunity to examine your recent behavior, come to your senses, and once more trust that we know what is best for you."

Stunned, Johanna gasped. "You can't mean that! You wouldn't! How could you, Mama?" Her voice broke into a sob. "To send me away like this — like I've done something wicked! I don't deserve to be treated like a child!"

"You *are* little more than a child, Johanna — a foolish, stubborn one, we have to concede. However, you are still under our supervision, and we are responsible for your actions, certainly for your future. You will do as you are told."

"Papa, do you agree?" Johanna turned in desperation to her usual advocate. But Tennant's face was averted. He stared into the fire and did not turn to look at Johanna. But her mother spoke, drawing Johanna's attention back to the one who was the real originator of the idea to exile her.

"Your clothes and other things are packed, and you will leave first thing in the morning."

Unable to speak, blinded by tears, Johanna whirled around and ran out of the room, tripping on the hem of her dress as she stumbled up the stairs to her room. She let the door slam behind her, then stood there for a moment looking wildly around as if for some escape. Then her gaze found her small, humpbacked trunk at the foot of the poster bed. The lid was raised but it was neatly packed, just awaiting a few last minute belongings to be placed in the top layer.

A sob rose and caught in Johanna's throat. So it was true. They were sending her away. Well, if they thought that would make her forget Ross or change her mind about him — they were wrong. Johanna's jaw clenched.

* * *

Later, coming upstairs, Rebecca paused on the landing. From behind Johanna's closed bedroom door, she heard muffled sounds. One hand gripped the banister. Her sobs were pathetic, heartrending to hear. Consciously Rebecca stiffened, stifling her maternal urge to go in, to comfort. Then her sensible nature took over. No, Johanna needed to learn that life wasn't simply a matter of choices. There was a reason. She could not allow her daughter to throw away her life, all she'd been groomed and trained for, on a nobody — a man from who knows what kind of family? Slowly Rebecca mounted the rest of the stairs and passed her daughter's door without stopping.

⬥

The next morning when Aunt Honey's coach was sent around for her, Johanna came downstairs to find her father had already left the house for his law office. Puzzled, she asked, "Didn't Papa even wait to tell me good-bye?"

"You have hurt your father deeply," Rebecca replied tightly.

Her words stung Johanna as much as if she had been slapped in the face. She stepped away from her mother, feeling both guilty to have caused her beloved father unhappiness and wounded by this rebuke. She knew she had behaved impulsively, spoken disrespectfully. Much she wished she could retract. She was remorseful and if he had been there, she might have begged her father's forgiveness. But to let her leave like this seemed too cruel a punishment.

"It's time to go, Johanna. Matthew and Honey want to get an early start, and you still have to pick up Aunt Jo."

Her mother turned a cool cheek for Johanna to kiss, and dutifully Johanna bid her good-bye. She prayed that someday all this hurt between them would be healed. She dearly wanted this, but not if it meant giving up Ross.

The night before, she had committed one last rebellious act. She had written to Ross, planning to post it somehow on the way. In her letter, she told him of her departure, adding,

Ross, I am doing what my parents wish by going to my aunt's without complaint, if only to prove that this imposed separation will not change my feelings toward you. In fact, I believe the old adage "Absence makes the heart grow fonder." I trust that you feel the same as I do. I trust that when you said you loved me, you meant it and are willing to wait and hope that this forced parting will have been worth it when my parents give their consent.

After writing those lines, Johanna had put her pen aside for a moment. She knew she had laid her heart bare and it may have been reckless to do so. But Johanna knew Ross was a man to trust — his word was his bond.

He had told her he loved her, and that was enough for her. Both of them knew that the feeling between them was too strong to be denied. It wasn't as simple a matter as her parents thought. What was between her and Ross was deeper than that.

A future together seemed threatened, but Johanna felt that whatever the future held, she wanted to share it with Ross. No matter what price she had to pay. Otherwise, she foresaw for herself a life of bitter regret, a loss that nothing else would ever fill.

Now as she looked through the oval window in the back of Uncle Matthew's carriage and saw the house she had left grow smaller and smaller as they went down the lane, Johanna's heart was wrenched. Home, with all it implied, meant a great deal to Johanna. She had often been homesick when away at school, had longed to be back in the warm, harmonious atmosphere with her parents and sisters. But now it was almost a relief to be going. The strain between her and her parents had become unbearable. On the other hand, leaving Hillsboro meant that even a chance encounter with Ross was impossible.

Well, she would have to make the best of it. Ross would know she had not given up, and however long her exile would be, her parents would see it had not achieved its goal. When it was over and she came back, surely they could work things out.

Aunt Jo and Aunt Honey were companionable fellow travelers, and the daylong trip was not too arduous at all. Even though Johanna was sure her aunties had been advised of the reason she was accompanying them, they did not mention a word, and the day passed pleasantly. Uncle Matthew fell asleep almost as soon as they had passed the town limits, and he slept most of the way.

The McMillan's house was a rambling fieldstone-and-clapboard structure a little distance from town. Aunt Jo's husband, Mac, as everyone called him, came out on the porch to greet them heartily as the carriage came to a stop in front. His warm welcome was the key to the rest of Johanna's visit.

There was an assortment of relatives from odd branches of all the families that were merged with the Logan clans, and all of them outdid themselves to entertain the visiting cousins. Everyone contrived to make Johanna's visit pleasant. There were parties of all kinds, dancing, skating, suppers, and teas. Aunt Jo had many friends with sons and daughters Johanna's age. Most of the young men attended the local college and always came with two or three classmates to any sort of gathering to which they were invited. Johanna never lacked for dance partners at any of the events, even though she felt less like dancing and partying than she ever had. She missed Ross terribly. In the midst of any party, her thoughts would stray to the one person who wasn't there, and her vivaciousness would visibly fade, her attention span falter, her conversation become distracted.

The days passed, one after the other, until Johanna had been in Winston almost two weeks. One morning she woke up close to despair. She felt so helpless. If only she could do something instead of sit it out and drearily wait for her parents to alter their decision. She had no idea what her mother had arranged with Aunt Honey about how long she was to stay at Aunt Jo's. She was getting very weary of the seemingly endless round of Winston social life — it struck her as inconsequential and meaningless.

Her forced "exile," as Johanna privately termed her visit, did provide a chance for some rare introspection, something she had little time for at home. In Rebecca's well-run household, every chore was assigned, checked upon, every moment of the day accounted for. But here Johanna often lay awake at night after the rest of the house was quiet, its occupants asleep. Then most often her thoughts flew to Ross. She wondered what he was doing, tried to imagine him meeting with patients or perhaps sitting at his study table at night, his dark head bent over his huge medical books.

In the long nights before sleep overtook her, Johanna examined her reasons for her strong attraction for this man, who had come as a stranger into the town where *she* had grown up. Yet there had been an immediate bonding. It was as if heart spoke to heart, soul to soul, as if they had looked deeply into each other's eyes and found life's meaning there.

It must be unusual, it must not happen often. She readily understood why her parents found it bewildering. She did, too. Even though she didn't fully understand it herself, she knew it was real.

Johanna decided to confide in Aunt Honey. She had always been easy to talk to, quick to sympathize, ready to understand. There was a disarming innocence about her, maybe due in part to Uncle Matt's take-charge attitude toward her. He treated her with such caring affection, almost as if she were a child. But Honey was far from childish. She was a keen observer of and had a tolerance for human behavior, its foibles and failings. She never seemed critical nor surprised by anyone's failures.

One afternoon Johanna came into the parlor when Aunt Jo had gone riding, and she found Aunt Honey was alone. Her aunt raised her eyes from her knitting. "Well, dearie, are you enjoying your visit?"

Johanna walked over to the window, fiddled with the drapery tassel, staring disconsolately out the window for a few minutes. Then spinning around, she faced her aunt. "It's not working, you know," she said bluntly.

Honey surveyed her niece warily. "What do you mean, dearie?"

"Oh, I know you had to join in the conspiracy," Johanna blurted out. "And I don't blame *you*, Aunt Honey. I know my parents think they're doing the right thing, separating me from Ross. They think I'm going to change. But I'm not."

Aunt Honey lowered her knitting and looked at Johanna. "You think not, eh?"

"I know not!" replied Johanna firmly. "I love him and he loves me. And they should just accept that."

"Can't you try to see this from your parent's viewpoint?" Aunt Honey suggested mildly.

"I can't. How can I?"

"I suppose you're right, dear. How could anyone expect you to?"

"You do understand, don't you, Aunt Honey?" Johanna sighed. "It's so unfair. They won't even let him come to the house, let themselves get to know him." She paused, then turned to her aunt eagerly. "When we get back to Hillsboro, would you let Ross visit me at your house?"

Startled, Honey looked at Johanna, then slowly shook her head. "Johanna, dear, I couldn't possibly go against your parents' wishes. It would be wrong —"

"But it's wrong of *them* to keep us apart. All I want to do is be happy! Why don't they want me to be happy?"

"Don't be so harsh on your parents, Johanna. They *are* thinking of your happiness. They just don't think what you want to do will make you happy."

"Ross *will* make me happy."

Aunt Honey looked pensive. Her eyes rested thoughtfully on her niece.

"No other person can guarantee you happiness, Johanna. Much as you think they can. Life isn't a fairy tale with everyone's story having a happy ending."

But she saw that Johanna wasn't really listening. There was a bemused expression on her face, a faraway look in her eyes. She was gazing somewhere into the future, a future with Ross. Honey realized she might have been talking to a stone for all the good her warning was doing. A fairy-tale romance was what Johanna was living, what she wanted. All true love, glorious sunsets, moonlit nights, music, eternal bliss. Honey sighed, perhaps she'd better write a letter to her cousin Rebecca.

However, Honey procrastinated. Maybe it would just take more time. After all, Johanna seemed to be trying to enter into the social activities Jo arranged for her.

At least for another week or so. Then came a day when Johanna did not come down to breakfast. She complained of a headache. When her aunt took her up a tray of tea and toast, she found Johanna's eyes swollen from crying. The next day she remained in bed. She refused to eat, no matter what dainties or delicacies the McMillan's cook fixed for her. She grew pale and wan. The aunties became concerned, then worried.

"This won't do," Aunt Jo said severely to her cousin. "It won't do at all." So Honey sat down and wrote the letter she had put off writing to Rebecca and Tennant.

My Dear Cousins,
    I hesitate to write this letter, but both Jo and I feel it is necessary to apprise you of the rather alarming decline in Johanna's

physical condition, which causes a great deal of concern. We know the reason you felt a change of scene from Hillsboro would be beneficial (her interest in Ross Davison, whom you consider an unacceptable suitor). However, we must inform you that her interest in him has not diminished, nor has her determination wavered. Her symptoms would seem grave if we all did not know their source to be emotional. To put it quite plainly, Johanna is "heartsick" and fading fast like a flower deprived of sunlight. She is without energy, enthusiasm, takes little food or liquids — in other words, she is gravely depressed. We are really concerned that she may be moving into melancholia. She no longer takes any interest in the social life here in Winston, although she has been both welcomed and sought after by the young people of Jo's acquaintance. We therefore have come to the conclusion that it would be best if she came home, where she can have parental care.

Your devoted cousin,
Honey

Within a week word came back that Johanna was to return to Hillsboro on the next stagecoach.

Chapter Nine

Johanna arrived back home looking considerably thinner and quite pale. Her first look at her daughter gave Rebecca a start. Gone were the rosy cheeks, the sparkle in her eyes, the lilt in her voice. Even if Johanna were dramatizing herself, the result was effective. Determined not to soften her attitude to her recalcitrant daughter, Rebecca simply saw to it that she ate every bite of the nourishing food placed before her, got plenty of rest and a daily walk in fresh air.

For her part, Johanna was glad to be home, glad that her parents seemed reasonably happy to see her. Things settled back to the normal routine of life Johanna knew before she had disrupted it with her rebellion. Elly, of course, was delighted to have her adored older sister home, while Cissy seemed aloof. During Johanna's absence, she had strenuously played the dutiful daughter, in contrast to Johanna. It amused Johanna somewhat to see her sister take advantage of the situation. It also saddened her, because although no one spoke of it, she could tell her own place in the family was not quite what it had been.

Secretly Johanna was biding her time, trying to find some way to contact Ross or prevail on her parents to change their minds about allowing them to see each other.

Liddy Chalmers, her first visitor, seemed shocked at her appearance. "My goodness, Johanna! What's wrong? You look so thin and pale! Have you been ill? What has happened?"

Tears welled up in Johanna's eyes at the sympathy in Liddy's voice. "*Everything's* happened!" she wailed. "Everything in the world. My heart is breaking. I'm in love with Ross Davison, and I don't know what I'm going to do about it."

Liddy's eyes widened. "Ross Davison? *Really?* I mean, I noticed you only had eyes for each other at the taffy pull, but then you went away, and —"

Johanna poured out her heart. Liddy was titillated by the details of Johanna's description of her secret meetings with Ross, which to Liddy's imagination had all the elements of one of the romantic novels she devoured about star-crossed lovers. But sympathetic as she proved to be, Liddy still was shocked that Johanna had defied her parents. It just wasn't done. Not in their ordered world. Johanna soon sensed that her friend was not as supportive as she had hoped she might be and that it would be wiser to keep her own council rather than confide in her.

During the days after her homecoming, Johanna spent a great deal of time in her room. Ostensibly, she was working on her album quilt or otherwise putting her time to good use. Actually, she was doing much soul searching.

Johanna knew that her parents' purpose in sending her away to forget Ross had been a failure. It had confirmed her feelings for him, deepened her conviction that their two lives were meant to be joined.

Johanna felt that with Ross her life would take on new depth. None of the young men her parents deemed eligible had stirred her heart, her imagination, her spirit, as Ross Davison had done. Observing the lives of the women in her family, Johanna found them a tedious round of shallow pleasures and rigid duties, restricted by limiting social rules. Johanna desperately wanted something else. She wanted her life to have meaning, to have it matter that she even existed.

She believed strongly that by sharing Ross's life, she would find the meaning she was searching for in her own. Johanna was convinced this was her chance. She even dared to think it was God's purpose for her life, if she just had the courage to grasp it.

On the brink of despair, deep in her heart she believed that if they were *not* allowed to marry, the rest of her life would be lonely, dissatisfied, unfulfilled.

At length she came to the important decision to take matters into her own hands. She would send a note to Ross asking him to meet her at the bridge near the churchyard. That would be easily enough arranged, since her mother insisted on her daily "constitutional." Whether he answered or met her or not, Johanna would accept it as God's will. She was willing to risk leaving the result to God.

She wrote only a few lines.

My Dear Ross,
  I am home again and must see you so we can talk. Please meet me at the bridge near the churchyard.
                    Ever your Johanna

A little before the hour she was to meet Ross, Johanna hurried past the steepled church and, winding through the graveyard,

144

to the arched stone bridge. The day was gray and overcast, and the willows bending over the river were bare. Johanna arrived breathless with anticipation and anxiety. What if Ross did not come? Not showing up could be his way of telling her he was not going to defy her parents' disapproval. As she came in sight of the bridge, to her relief she saw Ross already there. She saw his tall figure, the shoulders hunched slightly, folded arms on the ledge, staring down into the rushing water below.

She ran the last few steps toward him. At the click of her boots on the bridge, he turned, and as he did, Johanna remembered how at their first meeting she'd had the strange sensation that they were being reunited again after a very long separation. What she had felt before was some kind of mysterious precognition. Only this time it was true. This time it was *really* happening.

Johanna halted and there were a few seconds of hesitation before either of them moved. Then simultaneously they both rushed forward. He caught her hands tightly in his. His gaze embraced her hungrily.

"Oh Ross, I missed you so!" Johanna cried.

Ross did not reply. His eyes said so much more. He simply drew her to him, holding her so close that she could feel the thud of his heart next to her own. Then, his arm around her waist, they walked down closer to the water.

"Johanna, was this wise? I feel so guilty deceiving your father and mother by meeting you. And Dr. Murrison too. But when I got your note, I couldn't *not* come. I never meant to cause such . . . trouble."

"It's not your fault, Ross. I had to see you. I had to be sure. . . ." Johanna paused and looked at him anxiously.

Ross shook his head sadly. "It's wrong to meet like this when your parents have made it clear that —"

"Ross, don't say that. Just listen. *Listen!*" she begged. "I love you. Nothing else matters if you love me, too. You *do* love me, don't you?"

"You know I do, Johanna, but I had no right to speak without first —"

"If you love me, Ross, I have no intention of forgetting you or giving you up. I shall go to my parents, tell them. And if they still —"

"No, Johanna." Ross's tone was firm, decisive. "That's not your place. It is mine. I have given this a great deal of thought. In fact, I have thought of scarce else since you went away. I will go to your father like any honorable man would do, ask him to give me, to my face, the reasons they consider me unworthy to . . . court you." The corners of his mouth lifted slightly at the use of the old-fashioned word. "I love you, Johanna, and I intend to fight for you."

During the next few days, the March weather was as unpredictable as Johanna's emotional seesaw. One day she would awaken to gusty winds, rain dashing against the windows — the next morning sunshine would be drenching her bedroom. Johanna's mood vacillated from hope to despair. Had Ross acted as he had told her he intended to? Had he gone to see her father? Written him? Life in the Shelby household seemed to go on its usual smooth way, neither parent giving Johanna any indication that Ross had taken the step he had promised.

Then one late afternoon Johanna's father came home earlier than usual. He came to the door of the room where Rebecca sat at her quilting frame, beckoned her to follow him into his study, then closed the door.

Johanna had been in the room with Rebecca, dusting her mother's collection of porcelain figures. Evidently her father had not seen her. As her parents disappeared, Johanna put the Dresden shepherdess back on the mantelpiece and tiptoed across the hall. She paused briefly at the closed study door, straining to hear some of their conversation. But all she could hear was the steady flow of her father's deep voice, interrupted occasionally by her mother's. However, she could not tell anything from the tones of their voices.

Johanna's heart beat a staccato. She felt sure she and Ross were under discussion. Had there been a meeting? Had Ross been dismissed, his suit rejected? Had he been humiliated? No, her father was first and foremost a gentleman. He was also a compassionate, understanding man, a gentle father.

In an agony of uncertainty, Johanna crept past the closed room, up the stairway, and into her bedroom. There she flung herself on her knees and prayed. She tried to pray as she had been taught, a submissive, surrendered kind of prayer, the kind she had been told was most pleasing to God. However, such learned prayers were in conflict with the desperate ones of her heart. Even as she murmured, "If it be your will . . . ," deep down it was *her* will she wanted done. Her stubborn, rash, reckless will to have Ross no matter what the cost.

Johanna was not sure how long she had prayed when there was a brisk knock at her bedroom door. Quickly she scrambled to her feet, just as Cissy poked her prim little face in, saying importantly, "Johanna, Mama and Papa want to see you right away." She delivered this message with the unspoken implication, *You're in trouble!*

⁂

Johanna entered the room with a sinking feeling. Her mother was seated at her quilting frame and did not look up. Her father stood, his back to the door, staring into the fire blazing on the hearth. At her entrance he turned. His expression was unreadable.

"You wanted to see me, Papa?" Johanna asked in a voice that trembled slightly.

"Yes. Your mother and I want to talk with you, Johanna. Come in, please, and take a seat."

Johanna wasn't prepared for the gentleness in her father's voice. In fact, she had been half afraid they had discovered her secret meetings with Ross and she was about to receive a stern lecture on deceitfulness and disobedience. She came in and closed the door behind her and walked across the room to the chair he'd indicated.

Her knees were shaking, so she was glad to sit down. However, she perched on the edge of the chair, clasping her hands tightly together on her lap. Holding her breath, she looked from one to the other of her parents.

Her mother continued stitching and did not meet her daughter's gaze. Johanna then looked toward her father expectantly. There was a tenseness in his posture unlike his usual relaxed attitude when at home.

"First, I want you to know, Johanna," he began in a rather lawyerly manner, "that we respect you, admire you even, for your courage to withstand our persuasion — yes, our attempts to influence you from making what we deem an unwise decision. It shows character —"

Her mother stirred as if in disagreement, and Mr. Shelby glanced over at her. He paused a few seconds before he continued, amending his statement. "At least a determination that, while perhaps misguided, is nevertheless commendable."

Johanna braced herself for whatever was forthcoming.

"As your parents, we feel it our responsibility to guide you in matters that your youth, inexperience, may not give you the wisdom to decide for yourself. When someone is young and in love, clarity is often blurred." He paused again. "Your mother and I have spent many hours in prayerful discussion of this situation." He spoke slowly and very deliberately. "We feel that as your parents, we should point out to you that with such a man as Ross Davison, his lifework, which he intends to pursue in a remote, very poor mountain community, will always come first. The needs of the people he serves will always be his priority. Much like that of a dedicated minister of the gospel. A wife and family will always have to take second place, even though that might not be his conscious choice. Do you understand what I mean? "

"Yes, sir, I think I do."

"You and this young man, Ross Davison, have very different backgrounds, as you must know. You have been reared in a comfortable home, provided with all the necessities — and what's more, some of the luxuries. You have been sheltered, privileged. From what I understand, he was raised in poverty, hardship, but through his own efforts and those of some who believed in him, he has managed to get an education and is now a skilled physician."

Mr. Shelby turned, picked up one of the fire tools from beside the hearth, poked at the logs. The sizzling hiss of a breaking log filled the temporarily silent room. It was a full minute before he began to speak again.

Johanna pressed her palms together in suspense. Where was all this leading?

Slowly her father turned back, and in a

voice thick with emotion, he said, "We have met with our trusted friend Dr. Murrison, who told us that Dr. Davison is a man of unquestioned integrity and honor as well as being a fine doctor. The young man you have chosen and wish to marry is one of remarkable intelligence, character. Still, I feel I must tell you, Johanna, that if you marry this man, you will be going into a kind of life for which you have no preparation. It will be a hard life, a life of work, privation —" He halted, as though he felt it difficult to go on.

"Yes, Papa?" Johanna prodded breathlessly.

He looked at her and she saw on his face infinite resignation, sadness. Then he said, "We have agreed nothing is worth the stress and discord that have been constant in this household of late." He cleared his throat. "So we want you to know that if you truly believe that a marriage to Ross Davison will bring you fulfillment and happiness — then we consent to it."

Stunned, Johanna glanced at her mother, then back to her father.

"Oh, Papa, do you really mean it?"

"Yes, my dear. I would not say so if I did not. We give our consent." He shook his head. "That is not to say that we approve of it or have reconsidered the obstacles we see in such a marriage. What we are saying is that we give our permission for you and Dr. Davison to see one another and" — Mr. Shelby shrugged — "the rest is up to you."

Johanna jumped up and rushed over to him. "Oh Papa, thank you, thank you!" She spun around toward her mother. Rebecca held up a hand as if to ward off a hug.

"No, Johanna, don't thank *me!* You have had your way in this matter. Over my disapproval, my objections. I hope it won't bring you unhappiness."

Johanna was too relieved to let even her mother's coldness dampen her joy. "I'm sorry if I've hurt you, Mama, but I know it's the right thing." She paused. "May I have permission to let Ross know your decision?"

She glanced at her mother, whose mouth tightened as a flush of anger rose into her face. Johanna turned to her father for the answer.

"Dr. Davison has already been told. Through Dr. Murrison. It was Alec Murrison who came to see me at my office to plead the young man's cause. His arguments were valid, convincing. I told him he should have become a defense lawyer instead of a doctor." Mr. Shelby smiled but it was a tight, rather grim smile. "I'm sure Dr. Davison now knows he can pursue his . . . courtship."

Johanna moved to the parlor door. Tears of happiness sprang into her eyes. Her hand on the knob, she turned back into the room. "Thank you," she said again, then went out and started up the stairs. She saw her two sisters leaning over the balcony at the top of the stairway. She recognized by their guilty faces that they had been doing their best to eavesdrop on the conversation in the parlor. But too happy to be cross, she laughed. Running the rest of the way to the top, she grabbed each girl by one hand and spun them around, pulled them with her down the upstairs hall in a merry, exultant dance.

The next morning, in the cold light of day, her euphoria wore off.

She had dashed off a note to Ross informing him of her parents' decision, hoping he would call upon her that evening. That done, Johanna's soaring spirits had suddenly departed. The impact of what had taken place began to filter through her elation of the night before. Reality flooded Johanna.

The full impact of what her parents had done hit her. They were not forbidding her to see Ross. They were giving her the freedom to make up her own mind. It was to be her choice, her decision. It was overwhelming and a little frightening.

It was rather like, she remembered, how she had struggled with the doctrine of free will when she had attended confirmation classes. "But why did God give us free will when he knows we will sin and might lose heaven? I'd much rather God made us be good and be *sure* I was going," she had argued with the baffled young assistant minister who had taught the young applicants.

She had rushed headlong into this exciting experience of falling in love. Perhaps she had not thought long or far enough ahead. All she had been aware of was that she loved Ross, wanted to be with him, was thrilled he loved her.

Her parents had given her permission to exercise her free will and marry him. Now she could make her own choice. As she fully realized this, she felt some trepidation at being told she was responsible for her own life.

She had won her fight to have her own way. But what had she lost? Somehow Johanna had always known that she was her father's favorite, his chosen companion for walks in the woods, where he had pointed out to her the flora and fauna. Botany was one of his many interests. And he had a love of words, of Shakespeare's plays and poetry, which he shared with Johanna. However, in the past few months their old easy camaraderie had disappeared.

Johanna desperately wanted it back, wanted to be reconciled with her father. Yet truthfully she felt it was too late to regain what was lost. Ever since Ross had become an issue, Johanna's father had kept his distance from her. Certainly he'd been influenced by her mother's disapproval. But the look on his face the night before, even as he gave Johanna her "heart's desire," had been a mixture of sorrow, regret.

She hadn't meant to hurt anyone. Especially not her beloved father. Was there always a shadow side to happiness?

❦

Within the week, Ross arrived at Holly Grove in the evening to begin what was to be his formal courtship of Johanna.

Johanna waited upstairs in her bedroom, its door half open, listening for the brass knocker on the front door to announce Ross's arrival. When it came, her heart echoed its clanging. Next she heard footsteps on the polished floor of the downstairs hall, the murmur of male voices, and knew Ross was being greeted by her father. Breathlessly she prayed, *Oh, dear Lord, let it go well.*

Then, at the rustle of taffeta skirts on the stairway, Johanna shut her bedroom door quietly, holding her breath until there came a tap and her mother appeared in the doorway. Her expression was bland. Whatever she was feeling, she concealed it well.

"Johanna, Dr. Davison is speaking with your father now. In ten minutes you may go down and join them."

Johanna nodded, smiling at her mother, a smile that was not returned. Rebecca left and Johanna stood, hands clasped against her breast, feeling the pounding of her heart. She went out into the hall and remained at the top of the steps, counting silently to herself until the clock struck ten minutes past the hour. Then she slowly walked down the stairway.

Her father held open the door to the parlor for her. Beyond him she saw Ross standing, his back to the fireplace.

"I'll leave you two now — I am sure you have much to say to each other," her father murmured and went across the hall to his study, leaving the door slightly ajar, as was only proper.

Johanna started toward Ross just as he took a few steps forward, holding out both his hands to her. "Johanna, Johanna —"

Tears of joy sprang into her eyes. Her

tongue tried to form his name, but her throat was too tight to speak. They stood inches apart, simply looking at each other. Then Ross took one of her hands and kissed her fingertips. "At last, Johanna, at last," he whispered. "Your father has given us his permission." He did not say "his blessing," and Johanna wondered if Ross realized the difference. However, at the moment she was too consumed with happiness to pursue the thought. She had won — *they* had won — and that was all that was important for *now*.

She moved closer and lifted her face.

"I love you, Johanna," he said, almost in a sigh, then leaned down and kissed her softly.

With a small indrawn breath she returned his kiss. A sensation of pure joy swept over her. This was it, the answer to all her prayers, hopes, and dreams.

***

Each evening thereafter, unless some medical emergency prevented him, Ross appeared at the Shelby home to spend some time with Johanna. Johanna lived for those moments alone with him, albeit the parlor door was always discreetly left ajar.

One evening, Ross was delayed and Johanna waited impatiently for him to come.

A family had come down with some kind of fever and he'd had to attend them, he explained when she rushed to welcome him. In the parlor, his arm around her waist, Ross led her over to the sofa. "I have something to show you, Johanna. Something I've had for a long time. Something I had made while you were in Winston, with only my faith that this time would come, that this would happen."

Ross held out his hand, and in its palm lay something round, shiny, a circlet of gold, her wedding ring!

"Look inside," he urged her. Johanna held the small band up to the light shining out from the glowing fire.

"Love, Fidelity, Forever. JS–RD," she read aloud.

She looked up at Ross with eyes glistening with tears. For a minute emotion made her unable to speak. She remembered Ross once saying, "What do I have to offer you, Johanna?"

Here lay the answer in the palm of her hand. A circle of love, embracing, enveloping, protecting love, that's what he was offering her now and forever, as long as they both should live and on afterward into eternity.

Chapter Ten

Once the aunties and other family members were told and her engagement was formally announced, Johanna — her heart's desire granted — became the daughter Rebecca had always dreamed of. She could not have been more docile, more open to suggestions, directives, plans. Johanna was ready to compromise on any detail. Rebecca found this new side of her oldest daughter remarkable. Though easier to deal with than the one that had balked at so much Rebecca had wanted in the past, it was a little difficult to get used to and somewhat unnerving.

The plans for Johanna's marriage to Ross went forward smoothly, at least on the surface. Rebecca was still given to moments of deep doubt. She would think that if she and Tennant had simply held out longer, not given in to Alec Murrison's championship for his young assistant nor to Johanna's alarming melancholy, perhaps — *perhaps* — it all might have eventually resolved itself. But Rebecca was too pragmatic to spend much time in vain self-reproach. There were too many details to be attended to, too much to be accomplished and completed to waste any time in useless regret.

The wedding was to be a quiet one, not in church but in the Shelby's parlor, with only the immediate family attending, which in their case made up quite a crowd. To Rebecca's secret relief, Ross informed her — without seeming embarrassment — that none of his family would be able to come. His mother never traveled, he told her, and his sisters were too young. Spring planting would keep his younger brother Merriman and his family from coming as well. Although Rebecca accepted his explanation and assured him she understood, privately she had not been sure if the Davisons would be comfortable among the Hillsboro people. Of course, they would have been welcomed graciously. Still, it was one less problem to worry about, she told herself complacently.

Johanna could hardly wait to tell her best friend, and a few days following the Shelbys' acceptance of the inevitable, Liddy was invited over so that Johanna could share her news.

"Oh Johanna, are you *sure?*" Liddy's eyes

were wide, marvels of ambiguity. She was both excited and sad. A romantic, she was thrilled at the happy ending of this star-crossed love story, and yet she felt uneasy about her friend's future.

"I've never been more sure of anything in my life!" declared Johanna. The two girls were sitting on Johanna's quilt-covered bed a few days after the Shelbys had given their consent to Ross's marriage request. "Ross is everything I ever dreamed of, Liddy, and so much more. I am beside myself with happiness." Johanna's smile and eyes radiated joy. Her whole expression glowed.

"But to go live up in the mountains, Johanna, miles away from everyone you know, from everything you're used to." Liddy's voice held doubt.

"I've been away from Hillsboro before, for goodness' sake, Liddy! Almost three years at Miss Pomoroy's. And if *that* wasn't different from what I'm used to, nothing is! I love Ross and we're going to have a wonderful life together. And it will all work out. Don't worry about me." Johanna reached over and squeezed Liddy's arm.

"I don't know, Johanna. I heard Mama talking to one of your aunts, and —"

"I hope you didn't pay any attention to any of that? Who was it, Aunt Hannah? She always takes the gloomy side of everything."

"Well, Mama agreed with it, Johanna. She said when love is blind, there's a rude awakening."

"Oh, fiddle! That's one of those typical old wives' tales ladies say to each other when they don't agree about something. I just hope *I* never get old and narrow and view anything that is different as bad. Of course, Ross is different from most of the insipid men we know here, Liddy."

"Not all of them. Take Burton, for instance —"

"*You* take him, Liddy!" Johanna said indignantly, then giggled.

"I *would* if I could!" Liddy retorted snappishly. "The problem is, he's brokenhearted over *you*, miss!"

"I'm sorry, Liddy. I was teasing. Burton is a dear, lovable fellow. I just don't love him. Not all his persuading would ever change that. You can't just decide to love someone. It just happens. Like it did with Ross and me. Neither of us was expecting it or even looking for it. But we *knew* when it *did* happen, and that's what makes me so sure."

"Johanna, be serious for a minute, please. I just have to talk to you!" Liddy suddenly burst out. She began to sniff and her eyes filled. "It's all wrong. You must give it some more thought before you go and do something you'll regret for the rest of your life! I just hope you won't be sorry. As Mama agreed with your auntie, 'Marry in haste, repent in leisure.' "

Johanna looked at her, startled.

"Oh Johanna, he's just not right for you!"

"What do you mean, *not right?*" Johanna echoed, bewildered.

"I mean — well, it's not that he isn't fine, honorable, and a good doctor, but to *marry* him, Johanna, and go so far away to live, on the edge of nowhere, in the hills, with people you don't even know, will have nothing in common with. . . . Oh Johanna, you just *can't!*" Liddy's eyes filled with tears that began to stream down her face.

"I don't see what you mean, Liddy."

"That's because you're not willing to look, Johanna."

"Pish tush!" Johanna said scornfully. "You're a regular old lady, Liddy. Where's your sense of romance?" She teasingly tossed a small embroidered pillow at her friend.

Liddy tossed it back, pretending to pout. "Well, don't say you weren't warned."

"Not warned? No, I'd never say *that*. If you only knew how many times I've had to listen to the same sort of thing you've been saying. I think every one of the aunties, one way or another, have delivered such warnings." Johanna smiled. "And I'm going to prove them all wrong! So there!" She stuck out a small, pink tongue.

Her friend ignored Johanna's attempt at comedy. "Mama says Millscreek Gap is real backwoods, Johanna. You're not just going to move everything from your home up there like it was a paper cutout and fit it in there and everything will be the same. Don't you understand how *primitive* mountain people's lives are? You've never even met his folks, never been to his home, seen how they live — my goodness, some of those mountain people that come down to town to sell their baskets and chairs . . . why, they're just not like *us*, Johanna. I mean, some of them don't even know how to read or write, Johanna, do you realize that?"

Indignantly Johanna stared at her. "I can't believe you're saying this, Liddy. You sound like Emily Archer! Place Ross beside any other man in all of Hillsboro, and he'd stand head and shoulders above them all. Ross is a *doctor*, an educated man. You should hear him discuss things — all sorts of things. Not just about medicine and all. Even Papa had to admit that he is very intelligent."

"Maybe. But that's a man's world, Johanna. You're going to miss things you

165

don't even realize now."

"Like what?" Johanna demanded.

"Well, like things you take for granted. Things we all take for granted, everyday things as well as special things. Up in the hills, there are no shops or stores or theater or —"

"None of that matters." Johanna's eyes grew dreamy. "Don't you understand that, Liddy? Not when you're in love the way Ross and I are. The question isn't, Is he good enough for *me?* but, Am I good enough for *him?*"

"Johanna, will you just listen?" begged Liddy.

"No, I don't think I will," retorted Johanna, getting up from the bed on which the two had been seated. "I thought you were different, Liddy. I thought you would understand, be glad for me. Not come here talking to me as though I'm some half-wit that doesn't know what she's doing. Telling me that I'm making a mistake. What kind of a friend are you?" Johanna was getting choked up as the words rushed up on her. "I'm so lucky that Ross loves me. I have to pinch myself at times to make sure I'm not dreaming." Johanna turned her back on Liddy and went over and stood at the window, her shoulders stiff with anger.

At length the sound of sobbing caused her to turn back into the room. Liddy was bent over, her head in her hands, crying broken-heartedly. Johanna's soft heart melted. She went over to her weeping friend, put her arms around her.

"It's all right, Liddy. Don't cry anymore. I know you just said what you thought you should. But believe me, I'm going to be so happy."

"Oh Johanna, I'm sorry," Liddy sobbed, her arms tightening around Johanna. "I'm just going to miss you so terribly."

"And I will miss *you!* We've been friends *so* long! But you will be one of my brides-maids, won't you? I'd ask you to be the maid of honor, but Mama says I must have Cissy — it's only proper for the sister of the bride and all that. But I do want you specially, so will you?"

"Of course!" Liddy said and the two girls hugged.

During the rest of the visit, the two girls discussed colors, material, and design of the bridesmaids dresses. By the time Liddy left, things had smoothed out between them. At least on the surface. But Liddy's criticism had wounded Johanna, and she knew that somehow their friendship would never be quite the same.

One afternoon just a few days later Johanna had another visitor, an unexpected one. Bessie stuck her head in Johanna's bedroom door and announced, "Miss Johanna, dere's a young gemun to see you."

"Dr. Davison?" Johanna asked excitedly, jumping up from her desk and dropping the quill pen with which she was addressing wedding invitations.

"No'm, it's Mr. Lassiter."

"Oh, dear!" Johanna's exclamation was dismayed. She had not seen Burt since her engagement had become common knowledge in Hillsboro. She wasn't looking forward to this, she thought as she gave a quick peek in her mirror, smoothed her hair, and straightened her lace collar. But there was no help for it. She had to see him, even if it turned out to be unpleasant. Burton had never made a secret of his feelings toward her, at least as much as she would allow him to. Johanna had consistently tried to avoid his getting serious. She knew it was only her efforts that had delayed his proposing. She knew Burton had planned to talk to her father as soon as he completed his year of reading law with his uncle. Well, it was all neither here nor there now, she sighed and went downstairs.

As she entered the parlor, Burton turned from where he stood staring moodily out the window. Johanna had no trouble reading his expression. His face was a mixture of disappointment and indignation.

"Johanna, how could you have done this? You hardly know the fellow. No one does!" were the first words out of his mouth.

This declaration immediately infuriated Johanna, and she lost no time indicating that to Burton.

"*I* know him. *Dr. Murrison* certainly knows him. And who are you to make such a statement?" She drew herself up, attempting to look both angry and dignified, a hard combination to achieve.

"But *I* love you, Johanna. I always have. I always intended to ask you to marry *me!* You must have known that."

"I'm sorry, Burton. I knew you were fond of me. Why, we've been friends since — since we were children almost. At least from the time we went to Mrs. Clemens's dancing classes. And we shall always be friends. But I never led you to believe there would be anything else between us. I certainly never *meant* to, if you somehow got that impression."

"That's beside the point, Johanna. We have everything to make a really good marriage. We have the same background, we grew up at the same time, we go to the same church, we know all the same people. I am my parents' only son, and I will get all the family silver, seventeen acres of land on which to build you a beautiful house, provide you with a home, a life that you're used to — there's no reason at all why you wouldn't accept my proposal."

"The most important reason of all, Burt," Johanna said softly. "I don't love you — not the way a woman should love the man she marries. I'm sorry, but that's the truth. Hard as that may be for you to accept."

Burton shook his head vigorously and went over to her.

"Johanna, you've got to listen to sense. This is a foolhardy thing you're doing. Marrying a man who's practically a stranger, going off into the mountains, to who knows what kind of a life? It's ludicrous. Everyone agrees."

Anger rushed up in Johanna. The idea that Burton's family and, as he indicated, *everyone* in Hillsboro, were talking about her, discussing her decision, infuriated her.

"Burton, I'm sorry if you're hurt. I'm sorry if you think I'm making some kind of terrible mistake, but there it is. And despite what you or anybody else — *anybody* at all — has to say about it, I'm going to marry Ross Davison, and I'm more proud and happy about that than anything I've ever done in my entire life."

Burton looked crestfallen. He threw out his hands in a gesture of helplessness.

"I always knew you were stubborn, Johanna, but mark my words, what you're doing is beyond reason." His mouth tightened into a straight line. Then quite suddenly his expression changed into one of inconsolable regret. "I *know we* could have been happy, Johanna. If you'd just given me a chance. . . ."

Johanna's sympathetic heart softened at the sheer dismay in his face, the sadness in his voice.

"Oh Burt, if it were as easy as that. Someday you'll understand. I mean, I genuinely hope that someday you'll find someone and feel the way I feel about Ross. You'll recognize it *then*. You'll understand what I'm saying and know you can't settle for anything less."

Burton shook his head again. "How can you be sure that isn't the way I already feel about *you*, Johanna?"

Johanna took a step back, moved toward

the parlor door leading into the hallway. "I'm sorry, Burt, I truly am. I never meant to make you unhappy." She knew there was really nothing else to say. She wanted him to leave, to have this painful confrontation over.

Head down, Burton crossed the room and, without looking back, walked past Johanna into the front hall. There he picked up his hat and cloak, opened the door, and went out.

Johanna sighed. It had been a difficult half hour. But what else could she have said or done? Truthfully she did hope Burton would find someone to love. Someone he could love as much as he thought he did Johanna. As much as she loved Ross.

However, much as she tried to dismiss it, Burton's words hung like a shadow over her own happiness. He had said a great many things that she didn't want to agree with but knew were true. Of course, the conventional wisdom was that you married someone from a similar background, someone with whom you had much in common.

She and Ross *did* come from different worlds, but a strong love could bridge those differences. And the one thing of which Johanna was sure was that their love was strong enough.

Burton's emotional plea for her to reconsider her decision to marry Ross was not the only such experience Johanna had after her engagement was announced. A visit from her paternal grandmother proved even more difficult. The old lady had arrived one morning, earlier than she usually went out anywhere. Johanna was called down to the parlor to find her father's formidable mother seated by the fireplace, one hand clutching the top of her gold-headed cane. Her small, bright eyes pierced Johanna as she entered the room.

Hardly before Johanna had kissed her withered cheek and greeted her, Melissa Shelby demanded, "What's this I hear about you, young lady? I couldn't believe my ears when your father came to inform me that you were to be married to someone I never heard of!"

Johanna had tried to explain that Ross was Dr. Murrison's assistant and a doctor, but her grandmother waved her ringed hand in a dismissing gesture.

"Tut, tut. Alec Murrison, what does *he* know? I've known *him* since he was a lad, and never did think him too bright!" she had said sharply. "Being a doctor don't give him insight or the ability to make a good match." She shook her head, making the silver corkscrew curls under the black lace widow's cap bob. "*His* say-so don't make it the right thing for *you*." She glanced over at Rebecca. "Neither does your mother and father's *reluctant* approval of this engagement. In *my* day, daughters married whomever their parents picked out for them. Not just any Johnny-come-lately that happened along."

Patiently Johanna attempted to placate the indignant old lady. "Grandmother, I truly believe that if you met Ross, you'd change your mind."

The old lady's chin had risen disdainfully. "Well, young lady, I'd planned that you would have my Georgian silver tea set when you married, but I thought you would chose someone from one of the Hillsboro families I know. What's wrong with some young man from among your parents' friends?" She turned to Johanna's mother accusingly. "I just don't understand young people these days — *or* their parents, for that matter. My papa ruled with an iron hand, and we all snapped to, I'll tell you." She tapped her cane sharply on the floor.

"We certainly intended to bring Johanna's young man to call on you, Mama-in-law," Rebecca had replied. "It did all come up rather unexpectedly. We thought —" She never got to finish what she might have said, because Melissa interrupted.

"*Intended?* What good does that do *now?* As I told my son, everyone knows what is paved with good *intentions.*"

"I'm sorry," Rebecca had murmured, then sent Johanna an angry glance that said, Now, see what you've done?

Impulsively Johanna had gone over to her grandmother, knelt down in front of her, and looked up into the frowning face.

"You want me to be happy, don't you, Grandmother? I'm sure if you allowed yourself to know Ross, you'd see how very kind and good he is and you'd see that I was making a good choice, the *right* choice for *me.* Please, may I bring him over?"

Rebecca had looked at her daughter, mentally shaking her head. There she goes, turning on the charm. And she'll have her way. She always does! In front of her eyes, she saw her daughter wield the magic she had seen her use so often on her father.

In the end, Johanna had received a grudging invitation from Grandmother Shelby to bring Ross for tea the following Sunday afternoon.

That evening while waiting for Ross's

usual, often brief visit, Johanna wondered if all the opposition they were getting had made her more stubborn or strengthened her love. It was a tossup. The more people told her she was making a mistake, the more she dug her heels in, declaring they were wrong. Ross often seemed distracted, and she worried that he might have the same kind of doubts. They had stepped onto this path together, and there was no turning back now. The question was, Was it true love or pride? Johanna quickly dismissed these troublesome thoughts. Of course she loved Ross. Of course she wanted to marry him. When they were together, nothing like that entered her mind. She basked in the love she saw shining in his eyes. The clasp of his hand on hers, his kiss on her lips, thrilled her, and then she knew she wanted nothing more than to spend the rest of her life with him.

During the next few weeks, the Shelby household was as busy as the proverbial beehive. The local seamstress had all but moved in to work on Johanna's gown and the bridesmaids' dresses.

Concentrating on filling a suitable hope chest for Johanna, Rebecca often asked herself in frustration, What in the world would the girl need for a log cabin in the mountains? If Johanna were marrying a young man from Hillsboro and doing things properly, there would have been at least a six-month engagement and they would have spent a year embroidering and monogramming linens. Rebecca sighed. So much for that. What was expected of a bride in town had nothing to do with what her housekeeping requirements in Millscreek Gap might be.

Johanna did not appear at all troubled by whatever doubts others had with her marriage plans. As she basked in her love, her days passed in a kind of euphoric daze. She would soon have her heart's desire. However, she *was* sensitive enough to realize that Cissy was jealous of all the attention she was getting. For weeks the wedding had been the center of activity at Holly Grove, and Cissy's attitude had become increasingly noticeable. Johanna did not want her sister to be unhappy, even if only because her pouting face sometimes intruded on Johanna's own happiness. She decided to do something. One night at bedtime she crossed the hall, tapped gently at the door of the bedroom Cissy shared with Elly, and entered.

Elly was already asleep. Cissy was perched on the bed, brushing her hair their mother's required one hundred strokes. She looked up in surprise at Johanna's entrance. Cissy neither smiled nor gave Johanna an opening.

Probably brooding over some imagined slight or something that had happened that made her feel neglected, Johanna thought. However, she continued with her intended mission. She held out her hand, in which she held a folded, lace-trimmed hankie.

"Cissy, I'll soon be gone and you'll be the oldest one," she began. Cissy gave her head a little "So what?" toss. Undaunted, Johanna continued, "And I want you to have something special to remember me. Here."

Cissy's eyes widened in surprise. "What is it?"

"Take it and see."

Looking cautious, Cissy took it into her own hands and slowly unfolded the dainty linen handkerchief. Lying within the folds was a pair of earrings, small garnet drops surrounded by tiny pearls.

"Oh, Johanna!" Cissy exclaimed. "Thank you. I've always loved these."

"I'm glad."

"Are you sure? I mean, do you really want *me* to have them?"

"Yes. And you're to wear them on my wedding day. They'll look perfect with your dress." Cissy's gown was to have pink draped puffs over rose taffeta.

Impulsively Cissy hugged her. "Thank you, Johanna!"

Suddenly Johanna felt sorry for all the spats, all the spiteful words they'd carelessly flung at each other in the midst of small tiffs and little arguments. She wished she and Cissy had been closer all these years. She wished she could have loved this sister as easily as she had Elly.

For now, anyway, their particular bridge of built-up resentment and disharmony had been crossed. Johanna was satisfied she'd responded to her inner nudging to make amends with her sister. She was going on to a new, wonderful life with Ross, and she didn't want to have any regrets about unmended fences left behind.

* * *

The aunties had combined their talents and many hours to make their niece a beautiful quilt in record time, to give as a wedding present. Although Rebecca knew what they were doing and why they were meeting more frequently, she used the explanation that her demanding duties as mother of the bride-to-be prevented her from coming to the regular weekly sessions. This left her cousins free to discuss the situation regarding what was commonly agreed to be an "unsuitable" match.

"Johanna's marriage is a terrible blow to

both Rebecca and Tennant," Hannah declared.

"If that's so, Rebecca is holding up very well under the circumstances," remarked Jo McMillan.

"Of course. Rebecca's got too much pride to admit it," snapped Hannah, bristling that her opinion would be contradicted.

"But I think Dr. Davison is a fine young man," Honey ventured mildly.

"If he's Johanna's choice, what difference should it make to anyone else?" demanded Jo McMillan.

"That's fine for *you* to say, Jo — *you* don't have a daughter. I'm sure Rebecca hoped Johanna would do her proud and make a prestigious marriage. That Lassiter boy, for example. Or Judd Sellers," persisted Hannah.

" 'Love laughs at locksmiths in spite of parents' plans,' to misquote Shakespeare. Didn't Rebecca and Tennant try locking Johanna up, so to speak?" demanded Jo. "Wasn't that what the trip to visit us after Christmas was all about?"

Hannah pursed her lips. "Well, even if they gave in, it has still all happened too fast. A proper engagement should last at least one year." Hannah gave a definitive nod. "And as long as we're quoting or misquoting,

'Marry in haste, repent in leisure.' That's all I have to say."

Honey and Jo exchanged an amused look, sharing their doubt that it was all Hannah had to say.

"It's really not for us to judge. If Johanna is happy, what else matters? She's the one who will suffer if it's a mistake," commented Bee.

"I agree, and when you come right down to it, I've never seen anyone look happier. Why, Johanna's become quite beautiful in the last few weeks, haven't you noticed?" Josie asked.

"The two of them absolutely adore each other. He can't keep his eyes off her. The way he looks at her . . ." Bee's voice trailed off, and a dreamy expression passed over her plump, pink face. "Humph —" *was* all Hannah seemed to be able to say after that.

The wedding was set for a Tuesday, the first week in June. It was a far cry from the wedding Rebecca had wished for her oldest daughter. It had always been her hope to put on an elaborate wedding reception appropriate for the Shelbys' standing in the community. But if Johanna noticed the lack of what would have been extravagant preparations had there been another type of celebration, another bridegroom, she was too blissful to care.

The ritual service would be read by Reverend Moresby, and the couple would respond standing in front of the fireplace, which was to be decorated with simple arrangements of flowers and candles. Afterward, cake and wine would be served to the company.

The morning promised as pretty a day as anyone could have wished for a June wedding. The first thing Johanna saw upon awakening was her gown, which was hanging on the pine armoire opposite her bed. It was of oyster white faille and, touched by the sunlight flooding in from the window, seemed to sparkle with iridescent light.

Elly was her first visitor. She came into Johanna's bedroom proudly bearing a tray with hot chocolate and biscuits. "Mama said I could bring you your breakfast this morning, Johanna," she announced. "See, I picked this myself for you." She pointed with one chubby finger to a single white rose, drops of dew still sparkling like diamonds on its velvety petals faintly blushed with pink.

They were soon interrupted by a quick tap on the door, and Cissy came in, her hair still wrapped in paper curlers, to sit beside Elly on the foot of the bed while Johanna sipped her cocoa.

Cissy had dropped the superior air she had maintained while Johanna was in their parents' disfavor. After Johanna's gift, she had changed and had entered into the wedding preparations helpfully and happily. She gloried in the position of being the maid of honor as well as in knowing that once Johanna had departed, *she* would be the oldest daughter in the home. Privately she intended to learn by her sister's folly and only have beaux her parents approved. In the meantime, there was no harm in being close to her sister again. In fact, down deep Cissy knew she would miss Johanna. Terribly. Throughout their childhood, Johanna had always been the lively center of fun games and merriment and mischief. Cissy realized that something sparkling and delightful would disappear out of all their lives with Johanna's departure from their home.

Elly too was caught up in the general prewedding excitement and anticipation, but Johanna had always been especially sweet to her little sister Elly, her pet. There was enough difference in their ages that there had never been any competitive rivalry between them as had existed between Cissy

183

and Johanna, Cissy and Elly. When she realized that Johanna would actually be leaving them, going off to live with Ross far away, Elly felt very sad. And she was quite fond of the tall, gentle man who, Johanna had explained, was going to be her "brother." Having them both leave together would be hard for Elly to take.

The entrance of Rebecca soon sent the two younger girls scuttling to get dressed. "Hurry now. I'll be in later to tie your sashes," she told them. "And do your hair, Cissy." Cissy was the only one of the three who did not have natural curls.

When they had left, Rebecca turned to Johanna. "Come, Johanna, it's time," she said briskly. Her daughter's glowing eyes and radiant face brought sudden, unexpected tears stinging into Rebecca's eyes. To hide them, she quickly turned her back, went over to the armoire, making a pretense of smoothing the shimmering folds of the wedding dress.

When Johanna was bathed, her hair brushed, braided, and wound into a coronet, with four ringlets on either side, bunched and tied with white ribbon, Johanna stood in front of the mirror while her mother buttoned the twenty tiny buttons down the back of her bodice.

Where was Ross? Johanna wondered. Was he getting himself into a white shirt, uncomfortably submitting to the requisite fastening of a high, stiffly starched collar, a silk cravat, getting some last-minute advice from Dr. Murrison, who was to stand up with him at today's ceremony? Dear Ross, she thought with a tender sympathy — it will only be for a few hours. One can withstand anything for a few hours. And then — a lifetime of happiness together.

Johanna was so preoccupied by her own happy thoughts that she missed the expression on her mother's face reflected in the mirror as she stood behind her. Rebecca looked at her with a mingling of sadness and hopelessness. *If only . . . If only . . .* were the errant thoughts flowing restlessly through her mind.

But Johanna was unaware of such maternal regrets. Her heart was singing. At last! At last, all her dreams were coming true.

"Now the skirt, Johanna," her mother said, and the silk overskirt slid over her taffeta petticoat with a delightful whispering swish.

Throughout the morning, the aunties had arrived one by one, peeking their bonneted heads in the bedroom door, whispering, "Could I be of any help?" Only Aunt

Honey's offer was accepted, as she had brought the bridal bouquet Johanna was to carry, lilies of the valley, picked fresh that very morning from Aunt Honey's garden, then encircled in a paper lace ruffle and tied with satin ribbons.

Cissy came in next, looking very grown-up in her maid of honor gown, gazing at herself in the mirror as she moved her head back and forth to make her new garnet earrings swing. Next Liddy and Elly were admitted, looking like two spring flower fairies in their pastel dresses, wreaths of fresh flowers on their heads. Finally Johanna was ready, just as there came a discreet knock on the door, and her father stood on the threshold.

When Johanna turned to greet him, she was caught off guard by what she saw in her father's eyes as he gazed upon her in her bridal gown. For perhaps the first time in her life, she grasped the intensity of his love. Mingled there also was something she could not quite discern. It was a moment filled with a depth of emotion she had never plumbed. Her instinct was to lighten it. Affecting a coyness she had often mimed on other occasions to amuse him, Johanna put her forefinger under her chin and curtsied, asking, "How do I look?"

Tennant cleared his throat, said huskily,

"Beautiful, my dear." They had survived the emotional moment, and Johanna moved swiftly across the room and placed her hand on his arm. He patted her hand and asked, "Ready?" She nodded and together they went into the hall to the top of the stairway, then slowly descended the steps. At the bottom, they turned to enter the parlor, where the preacher and Johanna's bridegroom waited.

The familiar parlor had been transformed into a bower of fragrant loveliness. All the aunties had contributed the choicest flowers from their individual gardens, and arranged them in milk glass vases on the mantelpiece and in baskets fanning out from the fireplace.

For Johanna, who was seeing it all with starry eyes, the room shimmered with light from hundreds of candles, although actually there were only two four-branched candelabra behind Reverend Moresby, creating an angelic haloed aura around his head. Then her gaze met Ross's, and her breath was taken away by the impact. All nervousness left her. Never before in her life had she felt so calm, so confident, so sure, as she did going forward to take his outstretched hand.

All past tragedies were forgotten in that one triumphant moment. Having one's dream come true was a very satisfactory state of affairs.

As her father took her hand and placed it in Ross's extended one, Johanna felt the symbolism of the act, which signified a transfer of responsibility, protection, and caring between the two men. Up to this moment Tennant had been her "cover." From this day forward it would be Ross's duty to love, honor, and cherish her.

Johanna was fully aware that in the exchange of vows, she was not only giving herself into Ross's care but promising to hold him in esteem, give him reverence and obedience, "as long as you both shall live." It was the most solemn, sacred pledge she had ever taken, and she intended to carry it out with all her mind, soul, spirit.

She held her breath as the minister intoned the closing admonition of the marriage ritual. "The sacrifices you will be called upon to make, only love can make easy — perfect love can make them joy." *Sacrifices?* she thought, glancing up at Ross's serious profile. All she could think of was the *joy*.

A smile played at the corners of her mouth. Of course she promised to "love, honor, and obey." She pushed back the lace mitt on her third finger, left hand, so that Ross could slip on her wedding band. Then she heard the thrilling words before the benediction. "I now pronounce you man and wife."

A long moment of quiet followed that pronouncement, then suddenly it was broken by a rush of voices. Hugs, kisses, and congratulations followed as the assembled family crowded around the couple.

Soon after the ceremony, other guests began arriving for the reception. The Shelby parlor had been too small to accommodate all their acquaintances and friends for the actual ceremony. In a daze of pure happiness, Johanna took her place beside Ross and her parents to greet them.

As the guests came through the receiving line, Johanna read in their glances — although they were all too polite to say anything — a startling message. It was the same look that had puzzled her when she saw it in her father's eyes earlier. Now she understood it clearly. *Pity!* She could almost hear the whispers of some of the wedding guests, the comments. "Imagine! A pretty, popular, accomplished young woman throwing herself away to marry a penniless doctor and go live in a remote mountain community."

Even as it made her furious, she felt a slight chill slide through her veins.

If she had not been so completely in love

with Ross Davison, it might have caused her deep anger. Or worse still, fear. But just then she felt his hand clasp hers in a reassuring squeeze. Looking up at him, she saw in *his* eyes all that mattered — unabashed, unconditional, unswerving love.

Auntie Bee, young in heart and a romantic, had offered her home for the newlyweds to stay in for the three days before they left for their home in the mountains. She and her husband, Radford, were leaving right after Johanna's wedding for a long-planned visit to her husband's ninety-four-year-old mother in Pennfield. Therefore their house would be empty and thus provide the young couple privacy for a short "honeymoon."

In a flurry of rice and rose petals, Johanna and Ross, hand in hand, left the reception in the buggy lent by Dr. Murrison, drove the short distance to the Breckenridge house. Auntie Bee's housekeeper of many years, Tulie, met them at the door.

"Evenin', Miss Johanna. Evenin', Doctor," she greeted them, her wrinkled brown face creased in a wide, toothless smile.

Tulie had known Johanna since she was a little girl, so the curtsey was in deference to Johanna's husband the doctor and her new status as a "married lady."

"Miss Bee and me got the guest room all ready," she told them. "And Miss Bee thought you-all would like to eat your supper on de balcony oberlookin' de garden."

"That sounds lovely, Tulie." Johanna smiled and, still holding Ross's hand, followed the old woman up the winding stairway to the second floor.

At the top, Tulie turned as if to be sure they were behind her, then waddled down the corridor to the end and opened a door, gesturing them to enter. They stepped inside the spacious, high-ceilinged room scented with lilac and rose potpourri, and the door clicked shut behind them, signaling Tulie's quiet departure.

Johanna had been in and out of her aunt's house dozens of times, she realized, but she had never been in the guest room. She looked around with pleasure. Everything — colors, fabrics, and furnishings — was in exquisite taste. In the white-paneled fireplace, a fire had been laid, ready for the touch of a match should the evening turn cool. A golden maple tester bed was covered by Auntie Bee's prize Double Wedding Ring quilt.

Johanna walked over and opened the French windows to the balcony, where a round table covered with white linen cloth and set with sparkling crystal goblets and fine china awaited them. To one side was a wheeled cart on which were placed several silver-domed serving dishes and a coffee urn.

"Come look, Ross," she called.

He followed her out and stood behind her.

"Isn't it perfect?" she said.

He slipped his arms around her waist, leaned down and kissed her cheek. "Yes, perfect," he whispered.

Johanna turned in his arms. Ross's hands smoothed over her ringleted curls, causing Johanna's ornamented hair combs to drop with a plink to the polished floor, loosening masses of lustrous hair to tumble onto her shoulders. She lifted her face for his kiss. This was the kiss they had waited for, the kiss that expressed a love they both knew would be forever.

***

At Holly Grove, in the master bedroom, Rebecca stood at her window looking out into the moon-drenched night. A tumult of emotions had kept her awake. This was her daughter's wedding night. Oh, Johanna! Dear child, foolish child. Rebecca closed her eyes, twisted her hands together, and leaned her forehead against the glass.

Her heart was full of pain, yet hope mingled with anxiety, resignation with prayer. Could she have done anything more to prevent this marriage? That thought still anguished Rebecca's mind. Was the premonition she felt just imagination gone wild? Didn't Paul exhort his followers to bring vain imagination into captivity? She must not borrow trouble but hope the best for a marriage that, in her opinion, was doomed to bring unhappiness to her beloved daughter.

She heard a stirring in the bed behind her, then Tennant's concerned voice. "My dear, is anything wrong?"

She half turned toward him, shook her head. "No, nothing. Just couldn't sleep."

How could she tell him how her thoughts of the past had rushed over her, overwhelming her with echoes of another love — someone whom she had weighed and found wanting, contrasted to *him?* In Tennant Shelby she had seen what she wanted in life. Tennant had never known that Rebecca had made so difficult a choice. She had already met Tennant when this other young man entered her life, and love — spontaneous, impulsive, unexpected — had flamed up between them. But she had let him go. His last words, flung at her in anger, still haunted. . . .

Rebecca shuddered, drew her shawl closer about her shoulders. There are two tragedies in life, the old Arabic proverb says. One is not getting what you wish for — the other is getting it.

Tennant's voice came again. "Come to bed, love. You must be exhausted. It's been quite a day. . . ."

Part Two

Chapter Eleven

A second-day reception was held at Holly Grove for friends of the family who had not been invited the day of the ceremony. A glowing Johanna, in a dress of red-and-white dotted swiss, its eyelet-ruffled neckline edged with narrow red velvet ribbons, stood beside her new husband and her parents to receive guests. Her pride was apparent as she introduced Ross to those who had not yet met him. She was all smiles, sweetness, and gaiety.

Rebecca observing her, thought with mild irony, *Of course, now that you've got what you wanted, my girl, butter would melt in your mouth. Let's hope that it doesn't turn to sour cream.*

The aunties were in full force, darting here and there, seeing that the refreshment table and punch bowl were kept replenished, buzzing like happy bees, murmuring among themselves, nodding and smiling as they gazed fondly at the newlyweds.

Ross, never all that at ease at social occasions, was glad when it was over. While Johanna, her sisters, and relatives gathered to ooh and aah over the many wedding gifts, Ross sought the respite of the side porch.

It was approaching evening and the breeze was cool, refreshing on his hot cheeks. He had been acutely aware of the curiously speculative looks of the Shelbys' friends who were meeting him for the first time. He could guess some of the comments being made, such as "What can a girl like Johanna see in *him?*" or "What can the Shelbys be thinking of to let their daughter marry him?" Perhaps he was oversensitive. However, even as strongly as he loved Johanna, he'd had moments of deep uncertainty himself. He had been brought up to respect his elders, to listen to their advice, heed their warnings, which had often been right. He hoped, for Johanna's sake, he had not allowed good judgment to be swayed by his emotion. He hoped he could make her happy — even though he wasn't sure just how.

<hr/>

Early the morning of the third day after the wedding, Ross and Johanna started out from Hillsboro for the mountains. The fare-wells to her parents and sisters were blessedly brief. Happy and excited as she was to begin her new life with the husband she adored, Johanna did not trust herself to say good-bye without tears. Leaving her childhood home was hard enough. Leaving her parents, knowing that the hurt and disappointment she had caused them had not completely healed, was even harder.

Saying good-bye to Cissy, who had already assumed her coveted role as the oldest Shelby daughter at home, amused Johanna more than it saddened her. However, when it came to Elly, the dam of tears broke. The little girl hugged Johanna tight around her waist, wailing, "Don't go, Johanna, or take me with you!"

Kissing the child's wet cheeks, Johanna cuddled her, saying in a choked whisper, "You can come visit me, honey, if Mama will let you! But I have to go with Ross now." Finally she had to almost pry the little girl's fingers away from her clinging hold. Rebecca stepped forward and took Elly by the shoulders.

"That will do, Elly. Shame for being such a crybaby. Johanna is married now and must go with her husband." Almost the same words Johanna had used, but they sounded so different in her mother's voice. Startled at the hard edge to Rebecca's usually melodious voice, for a moment Johanna looked at her mother. But her expression was composed, controlled. Johanna started to say something. Something foolish, like "Mama, do you love me?" But the words caught in her throat. She felt Ross's hand on her arm.

"Come, Johanna," he said gently. "We must get started if we want to get there before dark."

With another kiss and hug for Elly, Johanna put her hand through Ross's arm and turned to go.

To her surprise, at the last minute Cissy came running down the porch steps after them. "Wait, Johanna, wait!" she called. Johanna turned and Cissy flung herself into her arms. "Oh Johanna, we're going to miss you." Johanna could feel Cissy's tears against her cheek. Surprised at this show of emotion from the sister who usually kept her distance, Johanna hugged her hard and whispered back, "Take care of Elly. Be sweet to her, won't you?"

Cissy nodded. Then they heard their mother's voice. "Come, Cissy. Don't delay them. They must be on their way."

They would be riding on the two horses that were the McMillan's wedding gift to them. Some of Johanna's belongings had already been sent ahead to the cabin where they were to live in Millscreek Gap. Later

Johanna's trunk and other belongings would follow in a wagon.

"Come, Johanna," Ross said again.

The sisters' embrace loosened. For one long minute they looked into each other's eyes. Johanna wished she had taken time to become closer to Cissy, tried to understand her better. But now it was too late. Her real parting with family had come.

"Good-bye," she said over the hard lump in her throat.

Ross handed her up into her sidesaddle and tightened the straps of her small traveling bag behind her, then mounted his own horse. With one last look and wave to the group standing on the veranda, Johanna turned her horse's head and followed Ross down the drive. They rode side by side but were silent as they passed through town. Johanna was dealing with a myriad of emotions that had suddenly rushed up inside her. Ross was sensitive enough to understand that she was saying good-bye to what she was leaving behind.

At the town limits, they took the narrow, rutted road that led through the dense woods and upward into the mountains. It was nearly a day's journey to reach Ross's homeland. Johanna had never seen the sky so blue. A rising mist shimmered with the golden sunlight. The farther they got up into the hills, the sweeter the air, which was fragrant with the mingled scents of wild honeysuckle, sunbaked pine needles on the trail, ferns, spicy spruce. All along the paths and deep into the forest that flanked them on both sides, were masses of mauve and purple rhododendron, orangey azalea, and delicate pink mountain laurel, more beautiful in their random profusion than the arranged bouquets in church.

The deeper they went, the more the silence surrounded them, yet it was alive with all sorts of sounds. They heard the rustle of meadowlarks rising out of the brush, startled by the noise of their horses' hooves, muffled as they were by the carpeted trail. There were butterflies hovering over the blue-purple violets, half hidden by the shiny-leafed galax on the forest floor. Graceful sprays of white flowers hung from the sourwood, with clusters resembling the more cultivated wisteria on her Grandmother Shelby's porch. High in the treetops, there came the song of birds and the humming of bees. The singing of the creek could be heard far below them as they climbed higher. It was June in the high country in all its glory. Ross turned in his saddle and smiled at her. Johanna felt her heart melt with happiness. After all this time, all this waiting, hoping, and praying, she and her husband were on their way to their own home high in the mountains — could anything be more wonderful?

Soon Johanna noticed a wooden board nailed to a tree, on which was crudely painted the words MILLSCREEK GAP with an arrow pointing north. A little farther along, they passed through what could only be described as a wide place in the trail. There on one side was a slightly listing wooden building with a sign over the door that read GENERAL STORE AND POST OFFICE.

Was this it? Johanna wondered. Was this all there was to the town of Millscreek? Had Liddy been right? Johanna remembered that her friend had called it something like the far side of nowhere.

Ross turned again and smilingly pointed to the sagging, weathered structure but didn't even bother to stop. Is that where she would come to buy supplies and get her mail? A small frisson of anxiety stirred in the pit of her stomach, but she quickly quelled it. Everything was going to be all right, everything was going to be fine. Just different, Johanna reassured herself.

The trail began to climb now, and every so often they would pass a weather-beaten, gray house perched on the side of a hill.

Sometimes they would see a sunbonneted woman with a couple of children out in a garden. As they passed she would lean on her hoe for a few minutes, watching them go by. Ross would always shout, "Howdy!" and Johanna would wave tentatively. Rarely were these greetings acknowledged or returned, except by the children, who would run forward at the sight of the two on horseback, then stand staring, their fingers in their mouths. Perhaps they were shy of strangers. *Not that we will be strangers for long,* Johanna thought optimistically. *Once Ross takes his place here as the only, much-needed doctor, these people will lose their shyness and become my friends, too. I'll visit and they'll visit. . . .*

This was her first chance since the wedding to give serious thought to what her new life with him might be like. Of course, Ross had spoken about his family at length, told her about his stalwart father, killed felling a tree when Ross was only fourteen. His mother, Eliza, was left a widow with four children and forced to scratch a living on the small plot of land to provide food, clothing, for her family. Johanna could tell Ross was proud of how Eliza Davison had kept the small farm going, reared the four children by herself, with only young Ross to help.

His brother, Merriman, had been just twelve when Ross had gone to live with the schoolteacher in town and get his education. His mother had been fiercely insistent on this. "I was torn," Ross had confided to Johanna, "thinkin' I oughta stay and be the man of the family, but she wouldn't hear of it. She told me, 'Son, the Good Lord give you a brain, hands to heal, and it would be like throwing away a gift if you didn't take this chance Teacher Gibbs is offerin' you.' I was determined then and there to come back. I'd do what she expected me to do, then give Merriman his chance."

"And did he take it?" Johanna had asked.

A kind of sadness had come into Ross's expression at her question. "No, he's married now and got two young'uns. I reckon he knew what he wanted. Sis Jenny is a sweet girl, and they have a home and a farm just up the hill from Ma. Merriman still helps her as much as he can. I guess folks do what they think will make them happy. You can't give something to someone if they don't want to take it."

Johanna had sensed Ross's regret that his younger brother had passed up on the opportunity Ross had been prepared to give him. It had also probably left Ross feeling sort of lonely as the only member of the family who'd furthered himself, she thought. That left his two little sisters, Sue and Katie, now eight and ten, still at home.

Johanna was both looking forward to and dreading meeting them all. What kind of a mental picture did they have of *her?* she wondered.

They climbed steadily upward, twisting back and forth along the winding trail. The forest was silent, beautiful, but Johanna found it rather foreboding with its impenetrable shadows even on this sunny morning. Just then Ross turned and called back, "We're almost there, honey. Up over this next rise and Ma's cabin is right on the ridge."

At the prospect of meeting Ross's mother for the first time, Johanna felt slightly apprehensive. She knew Eliza Davison must be a woman of strength and courage to have reared such a man as Ross. How proud she must be that he'd become a doctor! Johanna wanted desperately for Ross's mother to accept her, to think she was worthy of her fine son. And Johanna wanted to be a loving daughter to *her*. Ross had tried to tell her not to expect too much show of emotion at this first meeting. "You know, mountain folk are different. Not that they aren't as hospitable as, say, people in Hillsboro are. Ma is as kindhearted and generous as you'd find anywhere. She's just not talkative." In spite of his reassurance that his mother was looking forward to her coming and would welcome her, Johanna felt a little ripple of nervousness as they approached the rambling, weathered log house.

Ross turned his horse under the shade of a drooping pine tree, tethered him to the rustic fence, then came over to lift Johanna down from her saddle. His hands spanned her waist and he held her for a minute, smiling down at her.

"Don't look so scared," he teased. "Nobody's gonna bite you."

"Don't tell *me* that! You said you were shaking in your boots when you went to see *my* parents for the first time. Anyway, who said I was nervous?" Johanna demanded with mock severity. "Do I look all right?" She adjusted the brim of her tricorne.

"You look just right," Ross grinned.

"Really?" Johanna tugged at her jacket and fluffed out the lacy jabot of her blouse. She hoped her blue, braid-trimmed riding habit didn't look too fancy.

Before Ross had a chance to reassure her again, a tall woman stepped out from the house and came to the edge of the porch and said, "Well, howdy!"

"Ma!" Ross waved one hand. "This is Johanna, Ma." Turning to Johanna, he held out his hand. "Come on, honey." They walked toward the porch. "This is my mother, Eliza."

"How do you do, Mrs. Davison. I'm so happy to be here."

Holding Ross's hand tightly, Johanna went with him up the steps. At the top, Johanna debated whether she should kiss her new mother-in-law or not.

Eliza Davison was thin as a reed, with dark hair heavily peppered with gray. Her calico dress was crisp, covered by a spotless cotton apron. Immediately Johanna saw Ross in his mother's strong features — the firm mouth and chin, the deep-set, slate gray eyes under dark, straight brows. Under their searching gaze, Johanna felt exposed, disconcerted. The woman seemed to be staring right into her, taking her measure. In spite of the sun on her back, Johanna felt chilled. Face to face with Ross's mother, she wondered how Eliza Davison, born and raised in these mountains, *really* felt about her oldest son marrying a girl from town.

However, Eliza's greeting was warm and friendly enough. "Well, Johanna, I'm right pleased to meet you. My son has shure spoke highly of you. Now, do come inside and out of the day's heat."

Ross held the door so that Johanna could follow his mother into the house. The interior was dim and cool, smelled of wood shavings, soap, and some delicious cooking aromas emanating from the kitchen area at the far end of the room.

"These are Ross's sisters, Sue and our baby, Katie." Eliza gestured to two skinny little girls standing in the shadows. Both were dressed in starched calico dresses, the hems of which they were twisting. Their hair was plaited in tight braids, but Johanna could hardly see their faces, because they'd ducked their heads at her entrance.

"Sue, Katie. Come on over and meet your brother's wife," their mother beckoned them. Heads still down, they took a few steps forward, then stopped a few feet from Johanna, bare toes wiggling.

"Hello!" Johanna bent toward them, smiling. "I have two younger sisters, too," she said. "I hope we'll be great friends."

The two smiled shyly but didn't speak. Ross stepped over and swung one up in each arm, and they burst into giggles. Johanna could see at once that they adored their older brother. It made her feel a little more at ease to see how quickly he acted completely at home and didn't appear anxious or uneasy.

It was as though he were trying to show her that this was a place where one could act naturally, not have to put on airs of any kind or be especially mannerly.

"You must be hungry, comin' sech a long way, startin' out 'fore dawn. Sit ye down." Eliza indicated the long, rectangular, scrubbed pine table, with half-sawn log benches on either side, their surface worn smooth. "I asked Merriman and Jenny to come for dinner, but he was gettin' his garden in and not shure he'd be done by supper. But I reckon they'll both be here 'fore too long. And bring their young'uns. They've two boys, Johanna. Three and five, and they're a handful." She shook her head and a slight smile touched her thin lips. She looked at Ross. "Puts me in mind of Ross and Merriman at their ages." Then she motioned to the two girls. "Come on, you two, help me put things on the table." Over her shoulder, she said to Ross, "Do you want to show Johanna where she can wash up?"

Johanna was glad to be taken to the side of the porch, where a basin of fresh water, a clean towel, and a cake of soap were set on a wooden table under a small mirror. She took off her hat and unwound the veil, smoothing back her hair, tightening the ribbon that held it. She rinsed her face and hands. Then, as it was getting very warm, she took off her snug jacket.

Ross was waiting by the front door. "Merriman and Jenny just came," he told her and led her back inside.

Merriman was a head shorter than Ross but had the same lean good looks. He was very tan, however, and the bronzed skin made his eyes seem very blue. His wife, Johanna decided, would have been exceptionally pretty if she weren't painfully thin and pale-skinned. Her light brown hair was drawn severely back from her face into a plain knot at the back of her head. She seemed very shy and kept her remarkably lovely eyes downcast. She mumbled her hello, then immediately scooted over to help Eliza in the kitchen area.

"All right now, gather round, folks. Everything's ready," Eliza said as she brought two large platters to the table, one of fried chicken, one of roasted ribs. Jenny and Sue followed with bowls of sweet potatoes, hominy, greens, and an apple pie. Jenny and Merriman's two small, towheaded boys scrambled up on the benches on either side of the long table just as their grandmother set a black iron skillet of cornbread from right off the stove onto the table.

Once everyone was seated, a silence fell.

It lengthened. Johanna felt her stomach tense. No one moved or spoke. Was this a kind of silent grace? Like the Quakers', maybe? She had never thought to ask Ross. At home, the Shelbys held hands around the table while Papa said the blessing. Under lowered lashes, she looked around warily. To her surprise, both of Ross's little sisters were watching her gravely. Eliza's head was bowed. The silence seemed to stretch. Johanna stirred uncomfortably. She felt Ross's hand squeeze hers gently, and she raised her head cautiously. Eliza was looking at her and said quietly, "If you'll do the honors, Johanna." Suddenly she realized that as the guest at the table, *she* was supposed to say the blessing. She glanced at Ross for confirmation. He nodded, smiling slightly. Quickly she bowed her head, trying frantically to remember the one so often said at home. In a low voice that sounded more like a mumble, she recited it. A moment later plates were being passed, and she let out a breath of relief.

It took her a few moments to regain herself. She ventured two or three attempts to engage Jenny in conversation but failed. She did notice, however, that once or twice Merriman's wife glanced at her furtively. Actually, Jenny was looking at her blouse! Given the plain gray calico Jenny was wearing, Johanna understood. It was only natural. Jenny couldn't be more than nineteen. Like any young girl, she loved pretty things. Probably she had nothing of her own like Johanna's Cluny lace-trimmed blouse.

Johanna tried hard to think of some comment to make, but all she could think of was to compliment Eliza on the food. It seemed insane. She had never before felt so tongue-tied. She wanted to please Ross by being friendly to his family, but everything she said seemed to fall flat. She ended up being quiet while Ross and Merriman talked about mutual friends, the crops planted, the weather. Maybe the Davisons didn't talk much at meals, unlike her own family, who always entered into a lively discussion at mealtimes. She should stop trying so hard, she decided. It wasn't that Ross's family disliked her, she assured herself. *It's just that I'm a stranger, an outsider, that I don't belong here yet. It will take time for them to get to know me, for me to know them.*

Johanna had heard somewhere that to find out what kind of a husband a man would be, watch how he treats his mother. She was touched by the gentle way Ross spoke to Eliza, the respect he showed her.

Johanna was relieved when Ross got to his

feet, saying they must go if they were to reach their own home before dark. Johanna thanked Eliza, said good-bye to Merriman and Jenny, urging her new sister-in-law and brother-in-law to come see them as soon as they were settled. She gave the little girls a special invitation to come up and visit. Ross kissed his mother's cheek, hugged his sisters, then brought the horses around and helped Johanna mount, and they started back up the hillside.

In spite of the fact that she had wanted it so much, that first meeting, brief as it was, put Johanna off slightly, put her on her guard. Although she had not known exactly what to expect, it had not been the welcoming she had hoped for.

Ahead of them the mountains loomed, clouds, wreathing the summits, or opened to reveal peaks crowned with a glorious golden light. The path zigzagged upward. In the clear evening light, the mountain was bathed in sunlit isolation. "There it is, honey." Ross pointed and Johanna saw the peaked roof of a log cabin with a wide stone chimney just ahead. "That's *our* place."

Johanna's heart lifted. "Our place," Ross had said. The place where they would live as husband and wife. After all these months of longing and waiting, here at last they would begin their life together.

When she stepped inside the cabin, it seemed dark after coming in from the brilliant sunset. She looked around. One large room with a stone fireplace at one end. Ross was behind her, waiting for her reaction. He had spent the previous week getting it ready for her. Then she saw the rocking chair. She walked over to it, admiring its smooth finish.

"It's a wedding present from Uncle Tanner," Ross said. He gave it a gentle push and stood there smiling as it moved back and forth without a sound, without a creak. His hand smoothed the gleaming arms caressingly.

"Who is Uncle Tanner?" Johanna asked.

Ross smiled. "You'll find out soon enough. I reckon they'll be by to visit 'fore too long. He and Aunt Bertie —"

"Your aunt and uncle?" Johanna was curious because she'd never heard Ross mention them.

"Not really, but we've always called them 'Aunt and Uncle.' I think actually they're Ma's cousins."

"Oh, I see, like my 'aunties' are *my* mother's first cousins."

"That's right," Ross agreed, then said, "Now I'll show you the spring." He took her hand and led her outside. He guided her up a little rise to a clump of poplar trees, over to a ledge, and pointed, "There it is." Johanna looked to see a natural bowl of water standing clear as glass, surrounded on three sides with a ledge of rock and a tangled web of roots. Around the spring and beside the stream that flowed from it were beds of moss, and galax, and vines of other plants that bloom in summer. On the far side, overhanging the spring, were a dozen wild blackberry stalks. As they drew nearer, Ross said, "This is the lifeblood of our place, Johanna. The purest, sweetest water you'll ever taste." He reached down and picked up a dipper lying on the stone, filled it, and handed it to her to drink. It was just as he said, icy, delicious. She closed her eyes as she swallowed, and then she felt his lips warm on hers.

He took the dipper from her, laid it back on the stone, put his arm around her waist, and together they walked back down the path.

On the porch, Ross turned and pointed. "Look there, Johanna." A summer moon was rising slowly over them. Arms around each other, waiting, they watched until it hung, a great silver dollar, above the trees. It was so exquisitely beautiful, Johanna drew in her breath.

Then Ross swung her up into his arms and carried her into the house, saying softly, "Welcome home, Johanna."

Chapter Twelve

Johanna stirred slowly out of sleep. Not fully awake, without quite opening her eyes, she was aware of brightness under her closed lids. She felt warmth. Sunlight. *It's morning,* she thought drowsily. She felt a floating sensation, almost like flying. *This is happiness! What I'm feeling is real, true, and it's me and I'm happy!*

She stretched and reached out to the pillow next to hers. She opened her eyes, blinking. The bed beside her was empty. Raising herself on her elbows, she looked around.

From the alcoved bed, she could see across the center room into the kitchen. She smelled the unmistakable aroma of freshly made coffee. Ross, she smiled. He must have got up early and made it. Just then the cabin door opened and he walked in.

He looked over at the bed and, seeing her, asked, "Sleep well?"

"Perfect!"

He came over and stood at the foot of the bed. "I love you, Mrs. Davison."

She held out her arms to him. "Say that again."

"Which? I love you? Or Mrs. Davison?"

"Both!"

He laughed, came over to the side of the bed, and took her into his arms. He buried his face in her tangled curls, and for a moment they just held on to each other. Then Johanna leaned back and smiled up at him.

"What shall we do today?"

"We could go pay Aunt Bertie a visit," Ross suggested as Johanna threw back the covers and got out of bed. "I saw Uncle Tanner yesterday when I went down to Ma's, and he asked me if the 'honey was still on the moon.' " He grinned. "Folks figure a new couple need a few weeks alone to get used to each other or find out they've made a mistake."

"Mistake?" Johanna pretended indignation. "Well, at least not *me*." She tossed her head. "I don't know whether your kin think *you're* the one that might have made one."

She slid her bare feet into the small velvet slippers, reached for her dressing gown. Ross held it for her to put on, then wrapped his arms around her.

"No, ma'am, no mistake. Best thing that ever happened to me." He leaned down, kissed her cheek, her neck, until she wiggled around laughing and turned, hugged him.

"Oh Ross, I'm so happy!" she sighed.

"Well, so am I."

Aunt Bertie and Uncle Tanner's cabin was nestled among shaggy rhododendron bushes as big as trees, and shadowed by balsams. Aunt Bertie was a treat. Just as Ross had told her, Johanna liked her right away. Who could not?

She was spare, straight backed, her movement as brisk as a much younger woman. Daily use of hoe, shears, washboard, and skillet had made her hands strong. Her wrinkled face had a rosy tan, and her snapping dark eyes held a twinkle. There was a youthful lilt in her voice. Cocking her head to one side like an inquisitive bird, she asked Johanna, "How old do you take me for?"

Afraid to offend if she guessed wrong, Johanna hesitated, and Aunt Bertie laughed, "Goin' onto seventy-nine next January. I 'spect to go on jest as I've been doin' 'til the Good Lord takes me home. I been working a garden and spinning wheel since I was eight years old. My mama had a passel of young'uns, and I was the oldest girl, so I took over a lot of the chores. I've been workin' all my life, and I don't want to end my days in a rockin' chair, although Tanner makes the best ones." She pointed to the two on the porch and urged Johanna, "Sit over there and try it."

"Uncle Tanner made one for us, Aunt Bertie," Ross said. "It was sitting in our cabin when we came. Figured it was a wedding present."

"Of course it were! I plum forgot. When he heard you were gittin' married, Ross, he started on it." She fixed Johanna with bright eyes. "Don't it rock nice and smooth?"

"Yes, ma'am. It's beautiful."

"Now, you-all sit down and we'll have a nice visit. Ross, Tanner's out there gittin' his cider press cleaned up, ready for when our apples are ripe." She glanced at Johanna. "Wait 'til you taste Tanner's sweet cider. But first you gotta try my pie," she chuckled. She bustled into the cabin.

Ross gave Johanna a "Didn't I tell you?" look just as a tall man came from around the house.

"Reckon I heard voices," the man said.

Ross went down the steps and greeted him. "Uncle Tanner, we just wanted to pay you and Aunt Bertie a call, thank you for the chair. Come meet my bride."

"Don't mind if I do," Uncle Tanner said, a grin cracking his weathered, tan face. He was thin as a whip, rather stooped in the shoulders, but moved with a lively gait. If

Aunt Bertie was almost eighty, Johanna thought, Uncle Tanner must be that old or maybe older.

Uncle Tanner took the steps spryly. "Mahty pleased to meet you. Looks like Ross got not only what he needed and wanted but somethin' fine and purty, too," he chuckled and held out his hand to Johanna.

Johanna extended her own, and the old man grasped it and gave it a good, strong shake. Under his steady gaze, she felt herself weighed, measured, and not found wanting.

Johanna was pleased to feel she'd passed muster of someone she knew her new husband held in high regard.

Aunt Bertie appeared at the door. "Y'all come on in now." After the three of them were seated at the scrubbed pine table, Aunt Bertie came in from the kitchen, carrying a pie plate in one hand and a jar of honey in the other. She put the pie on the table and the jug of honey beside it, then started cutting generous wedges, lifting them one by one onto the plain, cream-colored pottery plates beside the tin.

"Now, if you want something tasty, spread some of this here honey over the top," she said as she handed around the plates. The pie was hot and its flaky crust a golden brown. The honey looked like clear liquid sunshine. Hesitantly but afraid she might offend Aunt Bertie if she didn't follow her suggestion, Johanna tentatively drizzled the honey over the top of her piece of pie.

A smile twitched Aunt Bertie's lips. "Never tried that before, I reckon?" Watching Johanna take a bite, Aunt Bertie said, "See? Good, ain't it?" With satisfaction, she turned to Ross. "How about you, Ross? You ever tried it?"

"No, ma'am, not that I can remember."

Aunt Bertie looked shocked. "You're funnin' me, ain't you? Can't believe you've lived this long and never had apple pie with honey."

When Johanna and Ross left, nothing would do but that they carry away with them a willow basket loaded with goodies from Aunt Bertie's larder — jars of strawberry jam, peach preserves, apple butter. "My apple butter's known in these parts," she told Johanna. "Come fall when the apple crop is in, I'll teach you how to make it with my recipe," she promised.

<hr/>

"So what do you think of Aunt Bertie and Uncle Tanner?" Ross asked.

"I think they're wonderful!" Johanna answered.

"Good." Ross seemed satisfied. "I could tell *they* liked *you*."

What Johanna didn't say, afraid she might be misunderstood, was what she had found so surprising and so refreshing — their lack of artifice of any kind. They spoke, acted, responded, in such a natural, unaffected way. Johanna found it utterly charming. She was used to society's polite shallowness, especially in a first meeting with someone, when people tended to be somewhat formal. Aunt Bertie and Uncle Tanner had just taken her in, showing her the same warmth they bestowed upon Ross, whom they'd known all his life. Of course, she was sure they would have welcomed her just because she was Ross's wife. Still, Johanna hoped to win her own place within his family circle before too long.

Chapter Thirteen

Johanna woke up and even before she opened her eyes, she knew she was alone. The cabin was quiet. Ross must have already left. She sat up feeling somehow bereft, deserted, even though she'd known this day was coming. She recalled their conversation of the night before, while Ross had been packing his medicine bag.

"Well, darlin' mine, I have to be about my doctoring. I've got people who've been waiting for me, and I had a whole passel of messages passed on to me — the Henson's baby has colic, Molly Renner needs a tonic, Tobias's leg is actin' up again, all kinds of ailments to see to up and down the mountainside."

Johanna had sighed, "I guess so. That's what we came up here for, wasn't it? For you to be a doctor and for me to be your wife! But what shall *I* do without you all day?"

"I don't know." Ross had looked puzzled. "Ma always found something that needed doing."

Johanna had felt somehow rebuked and said no more. As they kissed good night, Ross told her, "I'll be up and off at the crack of dawn, most probably. Got a lot of mountain to cover tomorrow."

Still, Johanna wished he had wakened her so that she could have fixed him breakfast, seen him off like a proper wife. She got up and looked around the small cabin. Here there were not the kind of household tasks she had been assigned at home — polishing silver, arranging flowers, or practicing her music. Or the social calls or visits from friends for tea in the afternoon, such as there had been in Hillsboro.

The long day stretched ahead of her emptily. Oh, there were chores enough to do, but Johanna did not feel like tackling any of them. She longed for — what?

She did not even want to admit that what she missed was the very thing she had run away from. Used to the activity of her busy home, Johanna was not accustomed to spending a great deal of time alone. Even at Miss Pomoroy's, there had been her classmates and the set pattern of the day.

There wasn't even anything really to do. Housekeeping, with no mahogany furniture to dust or polish, no brass candlesticks to shine, was simple.

When they arrived here, Johanna had found their shelves stocked with home-canned fruits and vegetables, deer jerky, and there had been a cured ham, a side of bacon, fresh eggs, butter, and milk in the spring-house. At the foot of the bed, a cedar box had been supplied with coarse sheets, home-spun blankets.

Johanna's own belongings, her trunk of clothes, boxes of wedding presents, and her hope chest had not yet come. Perhaps when they did, she would have more to do, placing them, arranging things, putting her own touch on their home.

She poured herself a cup of the coffee Ross had made and left on the stove, then went over to stand at the open front door, looking out. An unwanted thought came into her mind. What would she do with the rest of her life, here on this isolated hillside with no family, no friends? Surely the novelty of marriage or coming here had not worn off so quickly.

Their cabin was surrounded by the tall pines, and suddenly she had a feeling of being closed in. Frightened, she turned back into the room. Maybe she should go down and visit Ross's mother. That would probably be a good thing to do, get better acquainted. Getting out in the open in the fresh air and sunshine would ease that strange feeling of being up here by herself, cut off from the world.

Johanna put on a fresh dress and did up her hair. She felt a little shy about just showing up at Eliza's with no invitation. But wasn't that foolish? She was sure that mountain folk didn't stand on any sort of ceremony, especially not among family members. As Ross's wife, Eliza's daughter-in-law, *she* was family now, wasn't she? She tied on a wide-brimmed straw hat and set out. She thought she remembered the way, although the last two times they had been there, they were on horseback. She had only to follow the path, and she would soon be at Eliza's house. However, the path had several forks winding in different directions, some quite overgrown with brush, laurel bushes, sweeping pine branches. Soon Johanna became confused and wondered if somehow she had taken a wrong turn.

At a little clearing she stopped, trying to orient herself. Suddenly she heard the sound of childish voices. Within a few minutes two little girls came into sight. Sue and Katie, Ross's sisters! Recognizing them, Johanna was filled with relief. They would show her the way, of course, even take her there themselves. "Good morning! I'm so glad to see you," she began, waving her hand to them. But their reaction stunned her. Immediately their smiles disappeared. The smaller of the two slipped behind the older, her finger in her mouth, while the other girl looked startled.

Knowing they were shy, Johanna smiled and took a few steps toward them, saying, "I'm on my way down to see your mother. Am I on the right path? I felt lost."

They stared back at her, eyes wide, but said nothing.

Johanna tried again. "Is this the right way?"

They nodded in unison and then spun around and ran, stumbling over their bare feet in their hurry to get away, running back the way they had come. Left so unceremoniously, Johanna felt bewildered and hurt. Was it just shyness or didn't they like her? She had always been good with children. Elly adored her and so did all her little friends. Johanna sighed. She probably had a lot to learn about mountain people, children as well as grownups.

All desire to visit with her mother-in-law vanished. She was unsure of her welcome in the middle of the day, when Eliza might be busy with many chores and wonder why *she* wasn't similarly occupied. It might be an interruption or, worse still, an intrusion. Not willing to risk another rejection, Johanna turned around and retraced her steps back up to their own cabin.

That evening when she told Ross about her encounter with his sisters, he brushed it off casually. "They're just shy. Not used to talking to strangers."

"*Strangers?* I'm their sister-in-law," she protested.

Seeing Johanna's expression, Ross quickly said, "You won't always be a stranger, honey. But right now they don't know you, and to them you *are* a stranger. It'll work out in time. You'll see."

In spite of his reassurance, Johanna still felt uncertain. Day after day, she kept putting off going down to see Eliza. That is, until Ross brought up the subject himself, saying, "I stopped by Ma's on my way home today, Johanna, and she was wonderin' if you were poorly? I said, 'No, she's fit as a fiddle.' I think that was her way of asking why you hadn't been down to see her. Better go tomorrow, honey. Else she might feel slighted."

The next day, Johanna went down to see Ross's mother, and it was a pleasant enough visit, although she still found Eliza rather standoffish. That too could be shyness — or was it wariness of *strangers?* However, it made Johanna determined to win her over. She wanted desperately for Ross's mother to love her.

The weeks of summer went by. Still Johanna had to fight the feeling of being an outsider. She did not know how to break through the wall they had put up. She was longing to be friends. She couldn't summon the courage to bring up the subject again to Ross. At length she decided that all she could do was be herself, whatever the mixture was that made her who she was. Whether his family liked it or not, liked *her* or not, Ross had found that mixture exciting, desirable. Certainly enough to stand up to her father and, against all odds, ask for her hand in marriage.

Sometimes Johanna would stand on the porch of their cabin after Ross had left for the day and look down into the valley. She saw plumes of thin blue smoke rising over the treetops and knew they came from the piled stone chimneys in the dozens of log cabins scattered all along the way, up and down the hillside. Each of those cabins had people, families, women who would possibly be her friends. All she had to do was reach out. It was a new experience. Johanna had always been open to people, had always had friends. Why not now? Was she *really* that different that they didn't want to know her? As the weeks passed, she became even more reluctant to try.

One day, she saw Ross's little sisters come by on the trail below the cabin, carrying buckets. Johanna ran out onto the porch and invited them to come in. However, they shyly shook their heads. Sue, the older of the two, said, "No'm, we cain't. It's black-berry-pickin' time. Ma's goin' to make jelly, and we best get on with pickin'." She held up her bucket. "Ma don't like us gone too long."

Johanna was tempted to offer them some cookies and lemonade, cool from the spring-house, but then decided she wouldn't. Watching them go on down the path with their buckets, Johanna realized she missed her own sisters. More than she expected to, more than she had when she was away at school. The fact was that there were more and more times during the day when Johanna's thoughts flew home to Hillsboro.

The tiny twinge of homesickness Johanna had consciously tried to push away surfaced when her trunks finally arrived. They were brought up the hill by mule, delivered by the taciturn Jake Robbins, the postmaster in charge of the small post office in back of the general store. As soon as he deposited them with the few words Johanna could wrest from him, she eagerly started to unpack them.

The first trunk contained the wedding presents that, before the ceremony, Johanna had been too excited to really appreciate. She put those beside the gifts of linen and china to wait so that she and Ross could look at them and enjoy them together. It was unpacking the second trunk that caused her first excitement and delight to vanish. An unexpected depression swept over her when she saw the contents. Her mother had seemingly emptied her bedroom of all traces of *her*. As if she had never lived there at all! Her books, vases, throw pillows, knick-knacks. Her mother had sent Johanna her childhood, her girlhood, her life at home! As though she were never coming back! The emotional blow was stunning. It cut a deep wound. Johanna sank to the floor, her knees having suddenly gone weak.

Holding a small pair of blue Delft candlesticks that had once graced the little fireplace in her room, Johanna felt as though she had been cut adrift from everything dear and familiar. She glanced around the cabin.

Where would these go? Where would any of these things fit into her new environment, these surroundings? For the first time since she had come with Ross to the mountains, Johanna felt a sense of loss, a void that nothing came quickly to fill. Had she cut herself off from home, family, as completely as it seemed?

Chapter Fourteen

By the end of the summer, Johanna had organized herself to accomplish certain everyday chores, although there were still ones she hadn't got the hang of yet. Johanna realized she had a lot to learn about housekeeping.

She had no one to teach her the considerable skills necessary for her to learn if she was to keep house properly here, make a home for Ross. She wanted it to be a haven of warmth, comfort, and peace after a long day on horseback visiting the sick.

She was hesitant to ask Eliza, fearing that her mother-in-law would be scornful of her inadequacy. She didn't want to impose on Aunt Bertie, who had already been more than friendly and who was always busy and never seemed to know an idle minute. Why, Aunt Bertie would think Johanna plum daft not to be able to find enough to do to fill her days.

What Johanna did not understand was that far from being unfriendly, the mountain people were hesitant to intrude on someone they considered smarter, more accomplished than themselves. They would never offer help or advice that wasn't requested.

Ironically, Johanna discovered that among the books her mother had packed in her trunk was the well-thumbed dictionary her father had given her when she was ten. There was a needlepoint marker in the P's, the last section in which she had looked up a word, memorized the definition. She smiled, a trifle nostalgically. Her father's admonition was still a good one. She would continue to learn a new word every day, even if there was no one to test her on it.

"Perseverance," "persistence," "patience," were all good goals to pursue in this new life she had taken on. She needed them all as she tried to "perfect" her wifely skills. All had been badly employed as she groaned over lumpy rice, burned biscuits, scorched cornbread.

But Johanna was determined she would learn. And slowly, gradually, painfully, she did.

<hr />

Johanna's inner doubts were transitory, usually lasting only the length of a long day spent alone when Ross was late coming home from "doctoring." She *was* happy, Johanna told herself over and over. She loved Ross and she tried to keep her moments of melancholy well hidden from him.

One night Ross was out very late. He'd been called to tend the children of the storekeeper, who all had bad earaches. The Millscreek Gap store also housed the post office, and while there, Ross had been given a letter addressed to Johanna.

When he got home, he found Johanna asleep in the rocker by the fire. Ross placed the letter on the mantelpiece, then gently wakened Johanna and carried her to bed. She sleepily acknowledged his presence but went right back to sleep. It wasn't until morning that he told her about the letter.

For some reason, she waited until Ross left to open it. She recognized her mother's fine penmanship and opened the letter at once. As she read it, she felt a rush of unexpected emotion. Pictures of Holly Grove flooded into her mind. She could almost smell the scent of potpourri, flowers from her mother's garden, the mingled smells of polished wood, baking apples, and beeswax candles. Turning page after page, other familiar images came. Things she hadn't realized she cared much about or missed, now became cherished memories. Johanna had left all of this happily for "love and the world well lost." A dear, familiar world, as it turned out.

Johanna read on.

Cissy is growing into a very pretty young woman and is agreeable in every way. We had a length of silk, striped in pale blue and cerise, made into a lovely gown for her to wear to the Pettigrew's party, at which she was quite the belle of the ball.

Impatiently Johanna put the letter down for a minute. She could just imagine how Cissy was "toeing the mark" to her mother's satisfaction. She could read between the lines her mother had written, could almost hear all the same things her parents had tried to tell her. If she had listened . . .

Johanna got up and walked restlessly around the room. Why should news of the social life in Hillsboro bother her now? She didn't really miss it, *did* she?

When she had first come to the mountains, the possibility of unhappiness had seemed *impossible,* but now . . .

Suddenly the cabin door opened and Ross stood there. Startled, Johanna winked back her tears and got to her feet.

"Why, Ross! What are you doing back?"

He remained standing there for a full

minute, then said, "I'm not sure, Johanna. I just thought maybe you might need me."

Johanna's heart lurched. She dropped the letter as she ran to him.

"Oh, Ross!" She flung herself into his outstretched arms. As they closed around her, she rejoiced in their strength, in the safety and security she felt in his embrace. Why should she ever regret anything? She could not stop the tears, but now they were not tears of self-pity but of thankfulness. How lucky she was to have this love. How ungrateful to ever question it or doubt that it was meant to be.

It frightened her that even for a little while, she had allowed herself to waver as to whether she had made the right decision. Ross was real, not the romantic myth they had tried to describe him as. He was the reason she had resisted all attempts to persuade her to give him up.

That night, the mountains echoed with the first summer storm. It began slowly, with big raindrops pattering on the roof then quickly becoming a deafening thudding. Thunder boomed, echoing through the ridges and valleys of the mountains that surrounded the cabin. Great jagged forks of lightning crackled in the darkened sky. Awakened, Johanna moved closer to Ross, who slept on, as if used to this kind of nature's noise. He was of these mountains, Johanna thought, born and raised here. Nothing about them disturbed or frightened him. Without waking, he drew her close. His nearness thrust away the uncertainties and doubts she'd had that day. Fear brought on by the storm disappeared as she moved closer to Ross, felt his lean, warm body. A warmth, a sense of security, took its place. This wonderful man who loved her, who understood her, to whom she was important, was her protection against foolish regrets. Here in his arms was safety, tenderness. She must value them, know how richly she was blessed.

Ross was her life now. She would prove her parents wrong.

<hr />

Johanna knew she needed something to help her cope with her new life. She didn't know what. She had not thought beyond marrying Ross, getting her heart's desire. She had not anticipated the standoffishness she had encountered in Millscreek. Other than Aunt Bertie, none of the women she had met had invited her to visit nor taken her up on her invitations. Not even Merriman's wife, Jenny. Every time they were all at Eliza's house, Johanna had asked her. Jenny seemed even shyer than the little girls.

Johanna's feelings about Ross's mother troubled her most of all. She did not feel Eliza really accepted her. No matter how hard she tried, Ross's mother maintained an aloofness that Johanna could not seem to bridge.

Help for her anxious heart came from two unexpected sources. The first was from Uncle Tanner, who happened to drop in at the worst possible time. Johanna was crying tears of frustration over a batch of burned biscuits when his knock at the door and his friendly "Howdy, anybody home?" came.

Johanna hastily wiped her eyes, banged down the tin, and hurried out onto the porch to greet him. She invited him in but he said, "I reckon just some water will do me, as Bertie's expecting me home right quick." Johanna walked with him up the stone path to the spring. While Uncle Tanner helped himself to two dipperfuls, Johanna's expression must have told him something, because he said gently, "I gotta 'spicion you're feelin' some sorriness. Anythin' I kin do might help?"

"Oh, it probably sounds silly, Uncle Tanner. I just burned a whole batch of biscuits." Tears filled her eyes again. "Sometimes it seems I can't do anything right, and" — before she knew it, she was unloading to him — "and nobody seems to like me here!"

"Now, girly, let me give you a piece of advice. Go slow. Mountain folk don't make up to strangers easy, but once they take you in, nobody in the world could have kinder kin. You mark my words. Eliza will come 'round. My Bertie'll show the way, but you'll see. You're one of the family now —"

Uncle Tanner's soft-spoken voice fell like soothing balm. She had longed for just such comfort. His words were as much a gift of love as the beautifully crafted rocker. His genuine warmth, his smile, and his gentle way touched her deeply. As she waved him off, she felt much better. She went back inside, tossed out the "burned offering," and started mixing up another batch of biscuits.

One morning not long after Uncle Tanner's visit, Johanna was out weeding in the small vegetable garden Ross had started for her, when she heard the sound of horse's hooves plodding up the hill. She sat back on her heels, one hand shading her eyes, and looked to see who her visitor might be.

A stocky man in a shabby swallow-tailed coat, battered hat, and dusty boots dismounted and nodded toward Johanna. He had a scruffy red beard, prominent nose, but twinkly, bright blue eyes. He took off his hat, showing a balding head, then grinned and greeted her. "Howdy, ma'am. A good day to you and praise the Lord! Nathan Tomlin here. I'm the circuit preacher. Come to pay you a call."

Johanna got to her feet, aware of the skirt she had tucked up, the sunbonnet that had fallen back from her perspiring face. Self-consciously she wiped her dirty hands on her apron.

"Good morning." She tried to sound welcoming. Meanwhile she was hoping she had left the kitchen tidy before coming outside, and wondering what-on-earth refreshment she could offer him.

"Mighty pleased to meet you, ma'am. I knowed Ross from the time he were knee-high to a grasshopper. Growed up to be a doctor!" Preacher Tomlin shook his head as if in amazement. "Eliza told me he had his-self a peart wife, now. So I come up to see if it were true," he chuckled, "and to make your acquaintance."

"Please, won't you come inside?" Johanna asked, feeling flustered. She should be better prepared for company, she told herself, even if she rarely had any. Her mother was always prepared, serving without seeming fuss a dainty tea tray, whether it was a neighbor or their minister making a pastoral call.

"Thanky kindly, ma'am." He took out a red bandanna and made a swipe at his perspiring forehead. "Mighty hot morning, and something to wet my whistle would go down mighty fine."

Johanna untied her sunbonnet, stuffed it into the deep pocket of her apron, patted her hair, then ushered the preacher into the house. Inside, a quick look around assured her it didn't look bad. The floor was swept, the place neat. She was happy she had picked a bunch of wildflowers earlier and set them into a glazed pottery jug on the table.

Johanna picked up the kettle to heat water for tea, but Reverend Tomlin held up his hand. "Don't trouble yourself, ma'am. I got a passel of visits to make this day, so I can't stay long. Just a dipper of your spring water is all I need."

"You're sure?" she asked.

"Yes ma'am, thanky kindly," he nodded.

As she took out a tumbler and started to fill it, she saw his gaze sweep the room as if looking for something. After he took the glass of water she handed him, drained it, and returned it to her, he commented, "No Bible, young lady?" His eyes were kind, if curious. "In most mountain homes, it's in a place of honor, like yonder on the mantelpiece, or at the table so's it can be read mornin' and night."

At the mild reproach in his tone, Johanna blushed. Quickly she pointed to her small leather New Testament she'd had since school days, beside her prayer book on the hutch.

Preacher Tomlin shook his head and said gently, "That ain't enuf. Not by a long shot. Gotta have the *whole* Word, read it every day! The Prophets, the Psalms, and Proverbs. Next time I ride by, I'll bring you one," he promised, then he moved toward the door. "Now I'll bid you good day. Got places to go, people to see," he laughed. "Didn't mean to admonish you, but remember, 'Who the Lord loveth, he chastiseth.' The woman is the heart of the home, you know. Ross needs to hear the Scriptures every day to give him the strength he needs in his chosen work. You need to provide that for him."

Johanna stood on the porch and watched Preacher Tomlin mount his horse, turn around, and start down the mountainside. She felt strangely sobered by his visit.

As much a surprise to *her* as it might have been to Nathan Tomlin, a verse came into her mind just then — "Be not forgetful to entertain strangers, for thereby some have entertained angels unaware." Johanna almost had to smile in astonishment. Surely *that* was from Scripture! But from whatever unknown memory source it had come, Johanna knew it was important. However, she had no idea at the time how it would affect her life.

***

Johanna had never been what people call "religious" — she was certainly not "pious," as Aunt Hannah was — but there was a deep core of spiritual longing that she had never been quite so aware of as she was now. Although she had attended church with her family regularly every Sunday, whatever the subject of the sermon was, it was quickly forgotten. Johanna had never thought deeply about spiritual things. Lately, however, surrounded by the natural beauty of God's creation wherever she looked, Johanna was filled with awe and reverence. There had been no channel for it, no way she'd found to express it. Ross said a perfunctory blessing over their evening meal, but he was usually so tired when he finally got home that it was short. Often he hardly got through supper before his eyelids would droop, and not long after the meal ended he would kiss her good night and go to bed, exhausted by the rigors of his day. Many nights, Johanna sat by the fire long afterward, gazing into the flickering flames until they burned into glowing embers. It was at times like this when she most felt the emptiness within.

After Preacher Tomlin's call, Johanna felt chastened. She did not know exactly what to do about it. However, a few days later, true to his promise, he stopped by and brought her a Bible.

"You're goin' to find God's very close up here in the mountains, little lady," he told her before he rode off. Johanna soon discovered that as untaught as the disheveled-looking preacher seemed, as much as he altered the King's English, there was a goodness of heart, a genuineness, that she had never encountered before.

In the Bible he gave her, there were dog-eared pages, notations in the margins, verses underlined. She began to read it daily. First, the marked chapters, out of curiosity as to what Preacher Tomlin might feel was important. Then more and more she found her own favorites. On warm afternoons, she would sit on the small porch of the cabin, in the sunshine, the Bible on her lap. Gradually some of the verses became familiar, and she began to say them softly to herself, memorize them. Quickly Psalm 121 became a favorite. "I will lift mine eyes unto the hills — From whence cometh my help? My help comes from the Lord, the maker of heaven and earth." Johanna felt she needed help badly — to adjust to the loneliness of her new life, to become a good wife to Ross, the helpmate he needed. She loved him more than ever, and she never wanted him to be sorry he had married someone not up to the challenge of being the wife of a mountain doctor. She often recalled Aunt Hannah saying, "You can't live on love, my girl." Well, *without* love it would have been impossible.

⁂

Church was only held if Preacher Tomlin was in the neighborhood over a Sunday. The announcement that he was going to conduct a meeting would be circulated by word of mouth up and down the mountain. Ross usually brought home the news, but if there was sickness or a baby to be delivered, he could not accompany Johanna that Sunday.

The service was informal. No set ritual seemed to be observed, and it did not have a certain time that it was over. People brought their children, went up for healing prayers, commented with "amens" during Reverend Tomlin's sermons, which were apt to ramble and get diverted when his eye found someone in the congregation he wanted to address. Often he would break off in the middle of a sentence to say, "Good to see you, Sister Anna. How's your rheumatiz? Do say? Well, come up for prayer." Although this rather startled her the first time she attended, Johanna began to regard it as a real, down-to-earth way of reaching people — perhaps even the way Jesus might have done it when folks gathered around him and he talked, touched, and taught them. The hymns were sung without benefit of an organ. Someone would start and others would join in. The same verse might be sung over and over, and finally just fade away. "On Jordan's stormy banks I stand / And cast a wishful eye / To Canaan's fair and happy land / Where my possessions lie" or "O brother, it's how will you stand / And it's how you will stand on that day?" or "Sowing on the mountain / Reaping in the valley / You're going to reap just what you sow."

Johanna could not help but compare the services here with the formal services of the Hillsboro church she had always attended. There an air of solemnity reigned — the measured tones of the organ, the ritual that never deviated for that particular day of the church calendar designated by the prayer book. Here the small, frame church rang with hands clapping, feet tapping, spontaneous "hallelujahs," and joyously sung hymns. When Johanna looked around at the smiling faces, even the little children swaying to the rhythms, she thought that as different as the forms of worship were, maybe both were equally pleasing to God.

One Sunday when she and Ross had gone to church together, outside afterward Aunt Bertie had urged, "You-all come along home with us." Johanna always enjoyed being with the old lady, who she found was a fount of wisdom, humor, and good advice.

Ross went outside with Uncle Tanner to his apple press. It was soon going to be time to make cider and for Aunt Bertie to make her apple butter. The smell of biscuits baking and sausage frying crisply filled the cabin with delicious odor. "Can I do anything to help?" Johanna asked.

"No, thanky kindly, not this mawnin', but come time for me to make my apple butter, I might need some help a-stirrin'. You see, it's a daylong job. Them apples gotta be stirred every single minute. If a body don't stand right over the iron pot and keep that paddle moving, the apples'd burn and the apple butter would be plum ruined. A heap of folks ruin their apple butter by not doing so. There's nothin worst than scorched apple butter."

Aunt Bertie went to the door and called out to Uncle Tanner and Ross to come in and eat. Coming back to the table, she said to Johanna, "Apple butter makin's not for a lazy-body or a weakly person. That's what I meant by mebbe you could come help me the day I do mine. Take turns a-stirrin."

Johanna said, "I'd be glad to, Aunt Bertie," having no idea what she had let herself in for.

Chapter Fifteen

One evening when Johanna stepped out on the porch to hang up the dishpan, she called to Ross, "Come out here and see this!" She pointed to a new moon, a pale, thin crescent in the dark cobalt sky. "Have you ever seen anything so beautiful?" Standing behind her, he put his arms around her waist, bent his cheek against hers.

"Yes ma'am, many a time," he said softly. "Mountain moons are the prettiest, and I'm glad you're beginning to appreciate them."

"Oh, but I do! Did you think I wouldn't?"

"I guess I thought that come fall, you might miss all those parties, dancing, and taffy pulls." There was a hint of laughter in his tone.

"Not when I have *you* and the moon," she smiled in the darkness, snuggling against him. "It's very romantic."

He laughed. Then, stifling a yawn, he murmured, "I'm off to bed, darlin'. Must've rode a hundred miles up and down the mountain today." He kissed her cheek and went back inside. For the tiniest moment Johanna felt deserted. But she realized his days were long, arduous. He would be up before dawn, upon his horse, and on to making his calls. He needed his sleep. Still, it was so lovely out here, not a bit cold, and the moon was so beautiful. She didn't want to go back inside. But such beauty ought to be shared. It was the kind of night to be with someone you loved, maybe quoting poetry to each other. . . .

Johanna sighed. Suddenly she felt a little lonely. Her thoughts wandered. What were they doing at home tonight? Was Cissy getting ready to go to a party? Or were they all playing a parlor game together — snap-rattle or charades? Irrationally she wished she were there — and then, almost immediately, she knew she didn't want to be. That part of her life was over. She had what she wanted. It was just that there was a void that nothing here had quite filled for her yet. Not that Ross wasn't enough. He was everything to her. It was just that a girl needed a friend. Someone her own age. Another girl to laugh with, someone to share secrets with, someone to talk to. . . .

Ross was completely at home here. He moved confidently where she felt so strange. She remembered how only a short time ago *he* had sometimes seemed awkward where she was so at ease. It was that very awkwardness that somehow had seemed so endearing to her, made her want to reach out to him, make him comfortable. His shyness and inarticulateness around her parents only made her love him more, made her feel protective. Her thoughts grew tender as she thought of her husband. His gentleness undergirded his strength and skill. He'd gone away to learn "doctoring," but he still belonged — he'd come home to heal and help them. She had seen the looks of awed affection that followed him, the respect in the eyes of people as they greeted him with "Howdy, Doc."

Now it was *she* who was in a different environment. What was that Scripture verse? Hadn't the captive Israelites complained that they couldn't sing in a strange land? That's how she felt sometimes, "a stranger in a strange land." She wanted so much to be liked, to be understood. Would it ever happen?

One sunny morning early in September, Johanna had taken her mug of coffee out onto the porch steps to drink in the sunshine. Ross had left before daybreak and had not wakened her. Since he usually returned at night exhausted from the long, work-filled days, mornings before he set out were the only real time they had together. Johanna cherished that time, and today they had missed that. A long day alone stretched out before her.

Suddenly a piercing scream caused her to jump up, spilling her coffee. She looked around to see where it was coming from. Then, stumbling out of the brush, Ross's sister Sue came running. "Oh ma'am, ma'am, Miss Johanna, ma'am!" she called when she saw Johanna.

Johanna set down the mug and hurried to meet the little girl rushing breathlessly toward her. "Oh ma'am, it's Katie. She's —" Sue stopped a few feet from Johanna, panting. "She's — she's — oh, please come help her!"

"Of course! Where is she? What's happened?"

Sue was sobbing. Her small, freckled face was flushed, tear-stained. She gulped and tugged at Johanna's apron. "Please, ma'am, come. Up yonder!" She pointed to the craggy hillside above their cabin. "We wuz out pickin' berries and started to crost the creek, over a log that had fell, and I got to the other side, but Katie, she — she got skeered, I reckon. Anyhow, she couldn't move no more. She jest sit down and started a-yellin'. I tried to git her to come. But she jest kept lookin' down at the water rushin' over the rocks, and —" She halted, gulping. "She cain't move!"

All the time Sue was talking, she was pulling Johanna by the hand up the hill. It was steep and rocky, and Johanna's own breath was coming fast and hard. From what Sue told her, she had a mental picture of what had happened. But she had no idea how bad the situation was until they reached the top. There she saw how high above the rushing mountain stream was the log where the little girl was stranded.

She had stopped screaming and was clinging to the rough bark of the log with both thin little hands. Johanna saw that the child's eyes were glazed and staring, a look of stark terror on her face.

"Why in the world did you try to cross there?" she asked Sue in a hushed voice. The child shook her head. "Dint know it was so high, I reckon. 'Til I got on it — then I knew I had to go on, but Katie got skeered and couldn't."

Sue, older by two years and having long, skinny legs, had probably made it across on sheer pluck. The younger, smaller Katie probably made the mistake of looking down, got dizzy, and panicked.

However it had come about, the situation

was dangerous. Johanna tried to figure out how deep the water was, how she could get to the child to rescue her. First she had to calm her so she wouldn't get more frightened, lose her grip on the log, and fall off. The current was fast, the stream full of huge rocks. If Katie fell, she could hit her head on one of the jutting stones or be swept away in the swift waters. Johanna knew she had to act quickly.

"Don't worry, Katie," she called. "Don't be afraid. I'm coming to get you!"

She sat down on a large rock on the bank and untied her boots. She'd have to wade out to the middle, reach up, grab the child, and pull her into her arms, then carry her to shore. She had to do it fast, before Katie got dizzy, lost consciousness, tumbled into the water. From things Ross had told her, Johanna knew most accidents happened because people panicked.

Johanna's heart thundered. Her hands trembled as she loosened her laces, pulled off her boots and stockings. Standing up, she lifted her skirt, unbuttoned the waistband of her petticoat. Letting it drop, she stepped out of it and tossed it aside. Then, gathering up her skirt, she tucked it into her belt. The less she had on, the less chance that the water would soak it, weigh her down, drag her into the current.

Behind her she heard Sue sobbing, but she had no time to stop and comfort her. She had to save her little sister.

The first shock of the icy water on her bare feet made Johanna gasp. She would have to move quickly so that its freezing temperature would not hamper her progress. Hard rocks under the tender soles of her feet made her steps torturous. The cold water rose to her ankles and calves as she plunged forward. It was deeper than she thought and the current stronger. What if the water was even deeper in the middle, at the point on the log where Katie sat motionless, dazed with fear? Now she felt the water rushing around her knees, the edge of her turned-up skirt. Clenching her teeth against the onslaught of icy water, she pushed on. Nearing the fallen log, she almost lost her footing in a sudden drop of the riverbed.

"I'm coming, Katie. Hold on, honey," she called through her chattering teeth.

The water had reached her thighs, and she could feel the wet cloth of her soaked pantaloons chillingly against her skin. The rush of the swirling water made it hard to get a foothold. She stretched out one hand. The scaly bark scraped her palms. Gripping it desperately, she inched her way closer to

Katie. *Please, God, help!* she prayed. At last she was just below Katie. In a voice that shook, she said, "Now, Katie, I want you to let go of the log, lean down, and put your arms around my neck. I'll hold you — just come slow and easy." Johanna put up one arm toward the child, holding on to the side of the log with her other hand to steady herself against the current.

"I cain't, I'm skeered!" wailed the little girl weakly.

"Yes, you can, Katie. Come on, honey. I'm here and I'll catch hold of you. Just let go."

Every minute the child hesitated was agony. Johanna knew she had to get through to the child, who was now numb with cold and fear. Time was of importance, the situation desperate. Johanna was losing the feeling in her legs from the freezing water, and she still had to make it back to the bank safely with Katie.

"Katie, come on!" she cried.

All of a sudden she felt the child throw herself forward onto her. The thin little arms went around her neck in a choking hold. Katie's trembling little body pressing against her nearly unbalanced Johanna. *Dear God, help us!* Words of Scripture Johanna didn't even know she'd memorized came pouring into her mind.

I have called thee by name, thou art mine. When thou passeth through the waters, I will be with thee and through the rivers, they shall not overflow thee.

Struggling with the added weight of Katie, Johanna turned, the strong current pressing against her, and made her way painfully back across the sharp stones, through the cold, rushing water, toward the bank. Finally, gasping for breath, her feet cut and bruised, she stumbled onto the grassy bank and fell on her knees, still holding the shivering Katie.

Sue hunkered down beside them, alternately sobbing and sniffling, "Oh, thanky, ma'am. Thanky." Then Katie began to sob. Johanna felt salty tears roll down her own cheeks. Then she started laughing. Both girls looked at her, startled, then gradually they too began to laugh. Johanna knew it was mostly hysterical. But it didn't matter. She'd rescued Katie. That was the important thing.

At last, breathless from laughter, she wiped her tears away, scrambled up. Her bare feet were beginning to have some feeling again. In fact, they felt hot and tingling. She picked up her stockings and boots, slung them over one shoulder by the laces, and threw her discarded petticoat over one arm. "Come on," she said, reaching out a hand to each of the girls. "Let's go back to my place and get dry and have a treat."

Johanna thought of the tin of powdered chocolate her mother had sent in her last box from Hillsboro. She guessed maybe Sue and Katie had never tasted it. She'd make some hot cocoa and wrap Katie up in a quilt, and they'd all feel better.

Without even realizing it at the moment, Johanna had crossed over whatever line Ross's family had placed between them. By coming to Katie's aid that day, she had definitely won over Sue and Katie. The very next day, Eliza came up the mountain to thank her personally, after hearing the children's story of Johanna's rescue. She brought a rhubarb-and-berry pie and shyly told Johanna that if she wanted the recipe, it was one of Ross's favorites. On a deeper level, something even more significant happened to Johanna after the day she rescued Katie. She realized that the Bible reading she had been doing lately had taken hold. She was not even sure from which chapter, what verse, she had drawn that passage she'd remembered. In the midst of panic but still with faith that she would be heard, Johanna had cried out for help. "I called on the Lord in distress, the Lord answered me and set me in a broad place." As Preacher Tomlin told her, "He does what he promises to do."

Chapter Sixteen

The whisper of autumn fell like a soft melody on the mountains. The air had a crispness in the mornings, a tart sweetness like a ripe apple in the afternoons. The hills were russet touched with gold, asters blue-gray swayed in the wind, goldenrod nodded on the banks of the winding road up to their cabin. In the October mornings, mist veiled blue hills, frost sparkled on the sumac in roadside thickets, hickory log smoke curled up from stone chimneys within the log cabins that hopscotched down into the valley, as breakfast fires burned on hearths inside.

Aunt Bertie sent word that she was going to start her apple butter. "You're to be there at dawn," Ross told her, his mouth twitching slightly, his eyes mischievous. Johanna's eyes widened. "Uncle Tanner gets the fire going before the sun peeks over the ridge. She's spent the last two days peeling and paring the choicest apples, and she'll be ready to start by sunup."

By the time Johanna ate a hasty breakfast

and made her way down the hillside to their cottage, Aunt Bertie stood with a wooden paddle, stirring the boiling apples in a big black iron pot over the hickory fire. Uncle Tanner was sitting on a bench nearby, whittling. They both greeted Johanna cheerily.

"You come in good time, girly. My arm gets wore out a lot sooner than it used to, so I'd take it kindly if you'd spell me once in a while."

"Of course, Aunt Bertie. Now?"

"Not yet. Look at this and I'll show you what's next." Aunt Bertie motioned her closer with her free hand. Johanna bent and looked into the pot, where the apples were boiling, bobbing and making little popping sounds. "I've poured in a jug of Tanner's fresh cider, and now it's 'bout time to put in sugar and spices," Aunt Bertie said. "You can take over, Johanna, whilst I add it in."

Johanna had never imagined it would be such hard work. After Aunt Bertie had poured in the sugar and spices, Johanna took the paddle and slowly began stirring. The sun climbed into the sky, time passed, and still the apples kept boiling, puffing and popping like soap bubbles. Wood smoke got in her eyes, and she shifted arms for stirring, wiping her forehead with the back of her arm and pushing back her perspiration-dampened hair. Still, it seemed, the apples weren't ready.

Uncle Tanner kept feeding the fire, and he insisted on taking a turn stirring, because as the liquid got redder and stickier, the stirring got harder and harder. When Aunt Bertie protested, he gently but firmly told her, "Now, Bertie, don't fuss. I do my share of eatin' your apple butter — 'tis only fair I pitch in on the makin'."

Johanna knew it was his way of giving Aunt Bertie a needed rest. She herself found the stirring very tiring and wondered when this famous apple butter would ever be called "done and ready."

She soon offered to do her spell of stirring, and it was hard going. The wind rose and a cool breeze blew on Johanna's red, hot face. It seemed an age before Aunt Bertie came to her side, peered into the pot, took the paddle from Johanna, then said to Uncle Tanner, "It's done. Lookahere, it's so nice and thick, you could cut it with a knife. Come on, you can move the pot offen the fire."

Aunt Bertie gave a couple of extra stirs, then lifted the paddle, tapped it on the side of the iron kettle. Holding it in one hand, she swiped some of the apple butter onto her finger and stuck her finger in her mouth. Her eyes brightened as she tasted it, then smacked her lips. "Umhmmm!"

"How is it?" Johanna asked eagerly, feeling she'd had some small part in making it.

"It'll do," was all Aunt Bertie said. "Right tasty. Not a bit burned. Try some?"

When Johanna got a sample, she knew that Aunt Bertie's comment was a vast understatement. It was absolutely the most delicious apple butter she had ever tasted.

***

A week later Uncle Tanner stopped one day to bring Johanna several jars of the product. Johanna felt a particular pride to have helped make it. "Won't you come in?" she invited.

"No, thanky kindly, but can't stay. Too much to do. Firewood to cut and store. Winter's a-comin', rhododendron leaves is rolled up tight as a tobacco leaf. Soon it'll be November, and the frost in the mornin's means cold weather ahead," he predicted. Then he went on his way.

Johanna stood on the porch for a moment, her arms holding a basket filled with Aunt Bertie's bounty, and watched gray squirrels rattle in the leaves under the hickory trees, stopping every once in a while, shoe button black eyes darting back and forth, bushy tails quivering, then scrambling up the oak tree.

Shivering, Johanna went back into the house. Uncle Tanner was probably right, she thought. October was fast slipping away, and now in the mornings, the wind rustled the tree branches and whistled down the chimneys.

Very early the next morning, she was awakened to the delicate patter of rain. She raised herself on her elbow and sleepily looked out the window. She saw silver needles of rain falling steadily. She cuddled back down into the quilts and went back to sleep. By the time she woke up for the second time, it was raining hard. Afterward, she wondered if she had experienced some kind of premonition. For some reason, she felt reluctant to get up and start her day. It was as if somehow it held something to dread. However, it was a fleeting feeling, and she soon was out in the kitchen, where Ross had a blazing fire going and had made coffee. As he poured her a cup, he said, "I'm riding down to Hayfork to the store to see if the medicine I ordered has come in yet."

"On such a bad morning?" Johanna asked with a worried frown.

"Ain't goin' git no better," he told her, grinning. Sometimes when he was teasing her, Ross deliberately lapsed into "mountain speech."

After he left, Johanna got busy with her chores. But to her surprise, only a short time later she heard the sound of his horse outside. She hadn't expected him home before late afternoon. Puzzled, she turned from the stove just as he came in the door. He was dripping rain from the brim of his wide hat, the shoulders of his slicker. There was something about his face that should have warned her. But it didn't. At least, not until he brought a letter out from under his coat, held it out to her. "It's from your mother — addressed to both of us. So I opened it, and —"

Somehow Johanna knew even before he spoke the words.

"I'm sorry, darlin' —" Ross's voice wavered slightly. "Your father is dead."

Unable to speak, Johanna moved stiffly toward him, then went into his arms, closing her eyes against the awfulness of those words, leaning against him.

"No," she murmured. "No. *No!*"

They stood holding each other wordlessly for a long time.

Then Johanna looked up at him, asking numbly. "How? What happened?"

His expression was one of infinite tenderness, pity. "He was only ill a few days. They didn't think it was serious, or they would have sent for you — he went very quickly."

Before he could say anything more, Johanna burst into tears. She gasped, "It's my fault. I caused it. If I hadn't disobeyed . . . If I hadn't left home . . ."

"Oh Johanna, you mustn't say that. Don't. Don't blame yourself." His voice broke and he just held her tighter, unable to find anything to stop the pain she was inflicting upon herself. It was a pain she had not known nor understood nor even knew existed, one she did not think she could endure.

Throughout that long, cold night, Ross held her. Outside, the wind howled around the house, moaned through the tall pine trees, sighing like the keening sound of mourners. Johanna shivered and he drew her closer. She felt the deeply buried aching, the longing, rise within her. *I want to go home. I must go home.* She lay awake through most of the night, unable to stop thinking. When the gray light of dawn crept through the windows, she eased herself out of bed, crouched in front of the hearth, where the one remaining log left burning when they had gone to bed glowed red, making a whispering sound. She felt cold clear through. Her hands were icy, and she held them out to the fire to try to warm them. Johanna's eyes burned watching it and filled up with tears again.

She heard movement behind her, and Ross was beside her, holding her in his arms, rocking her like a baby while she sobbed on his shoulder. After a while he carried her back to bed.

When she awoke, Ross's place beside her was empty. She heard him moving around in the kitchen. A fire already blazed in the hearth, and she heard the clink of pottery, smelled the scent of boiling chicory. After a while he came to the foot of the bed. "I let you sleep. You needed the rest. But I'm taking you to your mother's today. You must see your father buried."

The rain had stopped and there was the smell of wood smoke in the air, which had a touch of frost. They rode down to his mother's house to tell them they would be gone to Hillsboro for the funeral, to spend some time with Johanna's grieving family.

While Ross explained, Johanna sat huddled on a bench and stared into the fire, her mind pain-paralyzed. She was unable to speak. Eliza's voice was gentle as she said, "Of course you must go. Your ma needs you."

Johanna did not answer. She started to say something, tell the truth. Her mother did not need her. Her mother had never *needed* her. The truth was, *she* needed her mother.

Or at least everything her mother symbolized — comfort, safety, childhood.

She felt Ross's tender gaze upon her, saw him exchange a glance with his mother, a bid for understanding. Johanna made an effort to speak very politely. She longed for sympathy but could not seem to respond to it. Eliza poured a mug of tea and placed it in Johanna's numb hands. "Drink this afore you go. It'll help," she said softly.

During the long, jogging journey along the trail that zigzagged down the mountain, Johanna was racked by grief and burdened by guilt. Was her stubborn, rebellious behavior in some way the cause of her father's death? Her mother had often mentioned in her letters,

Your father is often downcast and without his old cheerfulness. He misses you, Johanna, always having relied on your special companionship.

Could such a thing have brought on a depression leading to illness? It didn't seem possible — her father had always been hearty and vigorous.

I deserve everything I'm feeling, Johanna

thought bleakly. But even in her misery, she was reminded of Preacher Tomlin's exhortation — "Condemnation is not from God. In Christ Jesus there is no condemnation." She wanted to believe that. Why then did she *feel* so guilty? But could God forgive her if she couldn't forgive herself?

At last they came into Hillsboro. It was raining here as well. The roads were wet. On walkways, sodden clumps of leaves were piled under the dripping branches of the bare trees. As they rode through the familiar streets, past the familiar houses, out the familiar road that led to Holly Grove, Johanna felt as if she had been gone forever, much longer than five months.

On their way down the mountain, several times Ross had drawn his horse up beside Johanna's, asked anxiously if she wanted to stop, take a short rest. She had shaken her head. Her only thought was to get home.

At last they saw the road, fenced with split rails, that led up to Holly Grove. In the curving driveway were several buggies and one carriage drawn up in front of the house. At first that startled Johanna, until she realized that of course the aunties would all have gathered to do all the things caring relatives did in times of sorrow. She could just imagine them flocking there in proper mourning

271

attire, like so many blackbirds.

Drenched in spite of her wool cape, and saddle weary, Johanna put her hands on Ross's shoulders and let him lift her down.

"I'll see to the horses later. I want to get you inside," he told her. His arm supported her as they went up the steps of the porch. Before they reached the top, the front door flew open, and Elly flung herself into Johanna's arms.

"Oh Johanna, you've come! I *knew* you would! I've been waiting and waiting. Oh Johanna, poor Papa —" And she burst into heartbroken sobs.

Johanna leaned over her, smoothing back the silken curls from the small, tear-streaked face, murmuring comfortingly, "Hush, sweetie. I know, I know."

"Do come in. You're chilling the whole house," spoke another voice with a trace of irritation. Johanna looked up and over Elly's head and saw her other sister standing there, holding the door open.

Cissy looked different, more grown-up even than a few months ago. She was dressed in black taffeta, her hair held back by a wide black velvet band. However, it was her expression that puzzled Johanna. She had a fleeting impression that her sister was not all happy to see her. Quickly Johanna dismissed that thought. She was probably wrong. Her cool attitude must be Cissy's way of handling her grief, Johanna thought, and she went forward to embrace her.

"Where's Mama?" Johanna asked. The words were no sooner spoken than Aunt Honey and Aunt Cady appeared from the parlor, followed by Aunt Hannah. Immediately Johanna was smothered with hugs and sympathy. Ross was taken in hand and led to the dining room, where, as Johanna knew it would be, food was spread out in abundance.

"I must go see Mama." Johanna extricated herself from the lilac-scented embrace of Aunt Cady, who was handsome in an elegant mourning ensemble.

"Of course you must, my dear. I'll bring up some tea for both of you," Aunt Honey promised, and Johanna shed her hooded cloak and went swiftly up the stairway.

Johanna opened her parents' bedroom door quietly. Her mother, dressed in a wide-skirted black dress, was sitting in the wing chair by the window, her chin resting on one graceful hand. At the sound of the door opening, she turned her head. In that brief moment, Johanna thought again how beau-

273

tiful her mother was. Her dark hair rose from a distinct widow's peak. When she saw who was standing there, Rebecca gave a little cry, "Oh, my dear!" and held out her arms, and Johanna went into them.

For a long moment, mother and daughter clung to each other. Rebecca was the first to let go. Drawing back, she regarded Johanna thoughtfully.

"He loved you so, Johanna . . . so very much." In those few softly spoken words, Johanna sensed something else. A reprimand, an accusation, a judgment? Without actually saying so, her mother had deepened Johanna's own feelings of guilt. It was almost as if she had said, "If you hadn't gone away, this would not have happened."

There was no time to think that through, because Rebecca gestured for her to sit on the tufted hassock beside her chair.

Rebecca was unusually pale yet composed and as exquisitely groomed as always, onyx pendant earrings set in silver filigree swung from her ears, and an onyx cameo was pinned at the throat.

"Oh Mama, I'm so —" Johanna's voice broke. Her sense of loss and sadness was too deep for her to express. Her mother patted her hand. "I know, dear, I know."

"How did it happen? Was he sick long?

Was it a heart attack, what?"

Still holding her daughter's hand, Rebecca began, "He came home one evening, chilled. There had been a cold drizzle all day that turned to a freezing rain. He was thoroughly soaked, not having taken an umbrella with him. He refused my suggestion to change and get to bed immediately to ward off any possible effect. He wouldn't hear of it — just took off his boots and had dinner with us as usual. But the next morning —" Rebecca shook her head, her eyes moistened. "He awoke with a rasping cough, pains in his chest. I sent for Dr. Murrison, but he was out delivering a baby in the countryside and did not come calling until that evening —"

Johanna clasped her mother's hand. "Oh Mama, how dreadful — did he suffer much?"

"You know your father, Johanna, how he always makes — *made*," she corrected herself, "light of any physical problem he might have —" She paused. "I don't think any of us realized how serious it was. He did agree to stay in bed that day, however. He asked me to bring his writing tray, some papers from his desk. Although I protested he should rest, he insisted. He worked for some time, then said he felt tired and would sleep for a while. But by the time Alec — Dr.

Murrison — came by, he was already far gone — the congestion had gone into his lungs, and he had a high fever. Dr. Murrison thought he might be able to fight it." Rebecca sighed. "But he never really rallied. Spoke only a few mostly incoherent words, then — slipped into unconsciousness."

"Oh, Mama." Johanna felt as if her heart were breaking. Tears rolled unchecked down her face. She put her head on her mother's lap, felt Rebecca's hand laid lightly upon it.

After a few minutes, Rebecca said, "I must go downstairs now, Johanna. People will be calling. People have been kindness itself, and I must receive them. That's what your father would want me to do." With a rustle of taffeta, she rose to her feet, then said to Johanna, "You don't have to come, not just yet, anyway. Tomorrow after the funeral, there will be those who will want to see you." Rebecca moved over to her bureau, peered briefly into the mirror to check her appearance. She lifted one of the two boxes on top, took out an envelope, then turned and held it out to Johanna. "He wrote you a letter."

Johanna got up and walked over to where her mother stood, and took it. Her mother was watching her with appraising eyes, the ones Johanna had always felt could see and

276

judge beneath the outer shell of a person. Rebecca seemed to hesitate, as if to wait for Johanna to open it and read it while she was there. But Johanna simply stared down at the familiar handwriting, the classic swirls and loops of her father's Spenserian script. Her finger traced the wax seal imprinted with the familiar crest of her father's signet ring. Torn by wanting to read it and somehow dreading what her father might have written to her, Johanna hesitated. Rebecca waited only a few seconds before going out the door, saying over her shoulder, "We've put you and Ross in Elly's room, Johanna. Cissy took yours when you left, and Elly can sleep with her while you're here."

Those words sent a chill through Johanna that her mother surely could not have guessed or intended. Although Johanna had relinquished her privileged place as the oldest daughter at home to Cissy before she left, the fact that Cissy had taken over the room *she'd* had since she was born made Johanna realize that things had truly changed in this regard.

That explained the enigmatic look on her sister's face upon their arrival. It was the unspoken fear that by Johanna's coming, she might be displaced. The old instinctive rivalry. Johanna smiled ruefully. It was *she* who felt displaced.

Leaving her mother's room, she walked down the hall and opened the door to Elly's room, went in, and closed the door. She went over to the window, then with hands that shook broke the seal on her father's letter and drew out two folded pages and began to read.

My Dearest Daughter . . .

In the months that were to come, Johanna would read that letter again and again. Its pages became stained from the tears that fell as she read what her father had written. In these lines, Johanna discovered the parent's heart she had never known. His love, his dreams for her, his hopes, his disappointment, his loneliness for her. In spite of what had happened to cause their estrangement, her willful insistence on making her own marriage choice, his love for her had never changed. Now that it was too late, she understood it was that very love that had seemed so strangely cruel to her. This letter, written when he was so ill, perhaps when he knew it was a mortal illness, was undertaken to release her from any remorse or guilt. It was his last will and testament to a beloved child.

On the day of Tennant Shelby's funeral, the sky was overcast. In the church, Johanna sat in the family pew, beside Rebecca on one side, her sisters on the other. Behind them were all the aunties, their husbands. Johanna's eyes, swollen from all her weeping, were hidden behind the veil that one of the aunties had hastily sewn onto her bonnet the night before because Johanna had been too shocked to come prepared with the mourning attire expected to be worn by members of the family. Tears blurred the print as Johanna tried to read the words of the service in her prayer book.

The church was filled. Tennant Shelby had been an outstanding man of the community, revered for his integrity. However, none had known him as Johanna remembered — a kind, gentle, loving father. Why had she not appreciated him more? She had taken his sheltering care, his indulgence, his concern, for granted. She had stubbornly resisted his counsel, his advice. Johanna thought of the times she had turned away as he had tried to embrace her during those awful months when he had opposed her marriage.

If only she could go back — do it over.

Not that she would have loved or wanted Ross less, but she could have been less selfish, tried to see her parents' side more.

Winter sunlight shone weakly through the arched window behind the altar but soon faded, leaving the interior of the church gray, full of shadows. Johanna shuddered. Elly, sitting beside her, glanced at her worriedly and slipped a small hand, wearing a black kid glove, into hers. Johanna gave it a reassuring squeeze. She must be strong and brave for Elly's sake, for Cissy's too. At least *she* had Ross, while her sisters were left without a wise father, a protector.

The service ended and Johanna, with the rest of the family, followed the pallbearers carrying the casket out of the church to the adjoining cemetery.

The aunties were all appropriately draped in crepe veiling, which flowed from their bonnets in the November wind. With their caped shoulders and black-gloved, folded hands, they looked like a flock of black-winged sparrows hovering around their cousin, the widow.

Johanna tried to concentrate on the minister's words.

The minister began reading the final words over the casket before it was lowered into the newly dug grave. "In the midst of life, we are in death. . . ."

Standing among the granite crosses, the engraved headstones, the flowers and wreaths, Johanna knew a sense of intolerable loss, of terrible aloneness. Frightened, she glanced around and still felt apart.

She looked over at Ross for reassurance. But his head was bowed. She felt separated from him too. *I am a stranger here. Among my own people.* Involuntarily she shivered. She must pay attention. She clenched her hands. She felt as if she might faint and stiffened her body, willing herself not to.

The minister's words came again, intoning the words of commitment, consigning her father to his heavenly rest. "Most merciful Father, who has been pleased to take unto thyself the soul of this thy servant, grant unto us who are still in our pilgrimage and who walk as yet by faith . . ."

Something in Johanna's heart refused to be comforted. Inside she was wrenched with a terrible need for her father. She didn't want to let him go. *Not yet. I don't want you to go. I have so much I want to say to you, so much to explain. . . .*

It began to sprinkle, large drops falling slowly. Umbrellas opened up. The mourners huddled closer together, and the minister's voice picked up speed.

"Thou knowest, Lord, the secrets of our hearts. Shut not thy ears to our prayers but spare us, Lord by thy gracious mercy. . . ." He hurried to the last part of the service. "The Lord be with thy spirit. And so we say together, Our Father, who art in heaven, hallowed be . . . ."

The assembled mourners joined in the Lord's Prayer as the rain began to come harder, the wind stronger. Johanna's throat thickened and she could not get past the hard, painful lump lodged there, to repeat the familiar words. "Forgive us our debts . . . ."

Back at the house, the aunties bustled about, setting out the dishes, the cakes, pies, and other things they'd baked and brought for the funereal feast. *Feast!* What a name, Johanna thought bleakly. She sipped the tea Auntie Bee urged upon her, wrapping her icy hands around the cup, trying to warm them. She accepted condolences from family friends, nodding, murmuring thanks. All she could think of was her father out in the graveyard in the rain.

The afternoon lengthened painfully. Toward dusk, the last of the guests began to straggle to the door with last-minute expressions of sympathy, platitudes of solace, offering to provide whatever the grief-stricken family needed. Soon the aunties began gathering up their assorted dishes and containers, promising to replenish or refill them before they too departed.

Ross came to Johanna and led her into the small alcove off the dining room.

"I'm going over to Dr. Murrison's tonight, Johanna. I've already spoken to him. As a matter of fact, he came over to me at the funeral, asked me to come. I'll have to leave early in the morning to go back, anyway. As you know, I've got a lot of sick folks in Millscreek that need me. If I'm over there with him, my leaving won't disturb your family." His eyes showed concern. "You look exhausted, Johanna. You *all* need your rest. It's been a long, sorrowful day. But I think you'll be a real comfort to your mother if you stay here a few days. Whenever you feel you can leave her, just send me word and I'll come for you."

Johanna was a little taken aback by Ross's decision. Truthfully, she had made no plans. She had not even thought as far as the next day. However, she could see that his was the wisest course. Perhaps he was right — maybe her mother did need her, more than she had thought.

He held her for a long time, kissing her gently before he left. When she realized he was actually going, she felt suddenly bereft. Perhaps, in a part of her mind, she had thought how comforting it would be to be in his arms tonight — where he would kiss away the tears that all day had been near the surface.

But he was already putting on his coat, slinging a knitted scarf around his neck, reaching for his hat. It was too late to ask him to stay.

However, that evening her mother, accompanied by Cissy, retired earlier than usual, and Johanna found herself alone. Elly, worn out, had gone to bed before the company had all departed. In Elly's borrowed bedroom, Johanna found she was restless, too upset to sleep. She wished she had not agreed to Ross's leaving. She missed the feel of his arms enfolding her, comforting her.

The events of the day, and her father's letter, had been emotionally wrenching. Before long, Johanna began weeping uncontrollably, trying to smother the sound in her pillows.

The squeaking of the bedroom door startled her. She sat up in time to see a small, white-gowned figure, like a little ghost, slip into the room and with a rush of bare feet run to the bedside and jump up.

"Oh Johanna, I woke up and thought

about Papa. I couldn't go back to sleep. Can I come in with you?" Elly whispered urgently.

"Of course!" Johanna said and threw back the covers. The two sisters clasped each other and, close in each other's arms, wept together for all they had loved and lost.

<hr/>

One day followed the next. Soon Johanna realized she had been at Holly Grove for over a week and had not sent word to Ross. The flow of visitors continued, because Tennant Shelby, a man of wide acquaintance, had been well liked, respected, held in affectionate regard by a number of people. Johanna took it upon herself to act as hostess in her mother's place, greeting guests. This became sometimes tedious and stressful, given her own emotions, yet Johanna considered it a labor of love, deeply appreciating the esteem in which her father had been held. In spite of their shared grief, Cissy's attitude toward her remained guarded. Employing newly gained sensitivity and tact, Johanna tried to ease the tension between them, to show her in small ways that her coming home did not threaten her sister's place. Gradually Cissy softened. The two older daughters were able to divide the many varied tasks in the wake of Tennant Shelby's death.

There was much to be done. There were thank-you notes to write for all the gifts of flowers, food, and visits from neighbors, friends, and acquaintances. Their father's office had to be closed with all the moving of books, papers, files. There were meetings with his law partners, arrangements to be made, and matters to be decided concerning disposition of property.

With all this to deal with, two more weeks passed before Johanna realized that she had moved back into the rhythm of life at Holly Grove. Her life with Ross in the mountains seemed to have faded into the background.

It wasn't until she had been there four weeks that the full truth of this came to her. Dr. Murrison was called to the house because of Elly's earache. Johanna had been taking care of her sister and was in the bedroom with her when Dr. Murrison arrived. He looked surprised to see her. "You *still* here, Johanna?"

After he finished examining Elly, he left a small bottle of oil on the bedside table with instructions on how to administer it. "Heat it slightly and put two or three drops in each ear every few hours." Then he turned to Johanna and gave her a sharp look. "So when will Ross be down to fetch you back *home?*"

The blunt question and almost accusatory tone startled Johanna. Her cheeks got hot under his appraising glance. Busying herself smoothing Elly's coverlet, she replied defensively, "Soon, I suppose. Right now I'm needed here."

"Oh? Is that right?" was the doctor's only comment as he repacked his medical bag, patted Elly's hand, saying, "You'll soon be up and around, young lady. Won't need any more of your sister's fussin' and coddlin', I expect." With another glance at Johanna, he departed, leaving her indignant and confused.

Johanna spent another few minutes plumping Elly's pillow, then went to refill her water jug. Why had she let Dr. Murrison's remarks upset her? Wasn't she doing what she *should* be doing? Didn't her mother *need* her during this terrible time? After all, her mother had lost the husband on whom she had depended for over twenty years. Didn't Dr. Murrison realize she needed support, comforting? Maybe he was just not sensitive to such things.

Later, still bothered by what the crusty old physician had implied, Johanna knocked at her mother's door. At her answering call, she went in.

"Can I do anything for you, Mama?"

Rebecca was seated at her escritoire, writing replies to the many condolence notes she had received. She looked up at her daughter's entrance. For a moment, she studied the slim figure standing in the doorway. Johanna seemed fragile, vulnerable somehow — Rebecca had not missed her roughened hands. And she was thin, too thin. What had she been doing all these months to bring about these physical changes?

Rebecca bit her lower lip. Was her new life as the wife of a hill doctor in that primitive backwoods community too hard for her? Johanna was still lovely looking, the prettiest of all her daughters. But youth and beauty were fleeting, and a life of deprivation and hard physical work could age a woman too soon. Rebecca curbed her inclination to say something — something she might regret, something that might bring pain or, worse, remorse. Besides, there were other things she had noticed, all to the good — a patience, a gentleness, a genuine sweetness in Johanna that had not been there before.

Life teaches hard lessons. Evidently, Johanna was learning this. Rebecca sighed, then answered Johanna's question. "Nothing, thank you, dear." She went back to the note she was writing.

Johanna remained standing there. "You're sure?"

Rebecca signed her name to one of the black-edged note cards she was writing. "Quite sure."

Johanna still hesitated.

Rebecca looked up again. There was something in Johanna's expression that Rebecca had never seen there before. An uncertainty — a pleading in her eyes. Ever since she had returned to Holly Grove, there had been something about Johanna that puzzled Rebecca. It was utterly unlike Johanna. She had been at Rebecca's beck and call, interpreting a gesture, a glance, a word, anticipating her slightest wish, volunteering to fetch a shawl, a footstool, seeking to please, anxious to help.

"Wouldn't you like a cup of tea?"

All at once Rebecca understood. Johanna was "doing penance" for what she perceived was her guilt. Somehow she blamed herself for her father's death. As if her being here would have changed anything!

Rebecca knew in her soul that she had often been jealous of Tennant's closeness to Johanna. She had sometimes been stricter, perhaps, to counteract his indulgence.

Things had always come so easily to Johanna — love, popularity, happiness. Rebecca had told herself she didn't want her to be spoiled. But was it more than that? Had she wanted the intimacy Johanna shared with her father for herself?

With sudden clarity, she saw that it was possible for her to have what she had always longed for from her oldest daughter — closeness, companionship, dependency even. In this moment, Rebecca knew it was in her power to bind Johanna to her more closely than she had ever been with her father. It would be easy, because Johanna wanted it, too. She could keep Johanna here, keep her from returning to where she had never wanted her to go in the first place. It would be so easy — *too* easy.

Then came an image of the tall, young, awkward man who loved her daughter. In her mind, Rebecca saw his compassionate expression, his thoughtful eyes, the way he looked at Johanna with unselfish love.

Pain slashed Rebecca's heart. That kind of love was no longer *hers*, but it was Johanna's. And she could not rob her of it. Johanna was a married woman, with duties that took precedence over any need her mother might have. Johanna must be made to see that. Johanna must go home to a husband who loved her, missed her, longed for her, wanted her *home*. The home he had made for her, the home that was theirs to live in together! It would be dreadfully wrong of Rebecca to delay Johanna any longer here at Holly Grove.

"Mama?" Johanna ventured hopefully. "Isn't there *anything* I can do for you?"

"No, dear, nothing," Rebecca said firmly and turned away from the eagerness in Johanna's eyes, back to her correspondence.

"Don't you need help with your notes?" Johanna persisted.

"I'm almost finished." Rebecca tapped the pile of black-rimmed envelopes with one finger. "Besides, Cissy can help me if there are any more."

Her mother's tone was definite. Of course Cissy was here to help her with anything that might come up, Johanna thought. Why hadn't she realized that? Johanna went out of the room, closing the door quietly behind her.

* * *

At the click of the door being shut, Rebecca's hand clenched compulsively and a blob of ink dropped from the point of her quill pen onto the neatly written note. With a stifled exclamation of annoyance, she crumpled it up and tossed it into the wastebasket by the desk.

Rebecca knew she had hurt Johanna. However, she had deliberately sent her away. She also knew that when she was gone, she would miss her daughter dreadfully. Even with Cissy and Elly still at home, Rebecca knew she would be alone in a way she had never been before. Rebecca winced, placing her fists against her eyes.

Johanna was the child of her heart, the way the others were not. However, she had done the right thing — she had "freed" Johanna. A mother's sacrifices never end.

* * *

Outside her mother's closed door, Johanna stood for a few minutes. Slowly the myth of her mother's need for her dissolved. The truth of her mother's self-sufficiency was obvious. Rebecca Shelby had not been prostrated, become unable to function, or fallen into a melancholic depression with her husband's death. She did not need Johanna here any longer. The household at Holly Grove hummed along as it always did, even without Tennant Shelby. Especially, it did not need Johanna to see that things ran properly.

The truth was, she had stayed longer than necessary, deceiving herself into believing that she was needed. The truth was that *she* had been the needy one. She had welcomed sliding back into the ease and comfort of her old home. Meals appeared on the table without her lifting a finger, hot water was brought upstairs for her morning bath by Bessie, fresh sheets appeared on her bed, and clean towels were there like magic when she needed them.

Why had she not seen what was happening? It had taken bluff old Dr. Murrison's words to turn the key. He had unlocked this truth in her mind by asking her when Ross was coming to take her *home.*

Hillsboro and Holly Grove were no longer her home. Home was with Ross, in the mountains, his beloved mountains — *her* beloved mountains. In her heart, understanding burst like a bud opening into a beautiful blossom.

That very day she wrote a letter to be sent in the next day's post. That night she packed her things.

When at the end of the week Ross came, no word was spoken. None was needed. They rushed into each others arms as if it were the first or the last time they ever embraced.

When Johanna caught sight of the cabin,

her heart gave a lurch. It stood there as if waiting for her return. *What an imaginative ninny I am*, she said laughingly to herself. Then she turned to smile at Ross, who was looking at her as if anxious to see her reaction.

"I'll take the horses down to the barn, rub them down, and feed them, then I'll be in directly," Ross said as he helped her out of her saddle.

When Johanna walked up the porch steps, she saw firewood neatly stacked at the far end. Often people paid Ross back with such things — suddenly there would be split logs piled beside the barn, with no clue as to who had left it there in payment. Or jugs of cider would be left outside the door. It was the mountain folks' way. No money but too proud to accept charity. These evidences of how much Ross was appreciated touched Johanna. She wished her relatives in Hillsboro who still thought she'd married beneath her could know this.

Opening the door, she walked inside the cabin. Immediately she breathed in mingled delicious smells — pumpkin pie, apple, cinnamon. Over the stove hung strings of red peppers, dried onions, pods of okra, striped gourds, rainbow-colored Indian corn.

"Aunt Bertie's doings, I expect," she said

to Ross when he came inside.

"And Ma's too," Ross said quietly.

Johanna felt stricken that she hadn't thought of Eliza first. Ross's mother had not been nearly as forthcoming and friendly to her as Aunt Bertie.

"When she heard I was going down to bring you home," Ross added, "she said she'd bring up supper so you wouldn't have to cook when we got back. She knew you'd be tired. I think there's beans and ham and bread. Probably other things as well."

"How kind," Johanna murmured, making a mental resolution to make a real effort to get to know her mother-in-law better.

Chapter Seventeen

That winter seemed long and cold and lonely to Johanna. Although Ross had suggested she might want to spend Christmas with her family in Hillsboro, Johanna felt a strange reluctance. Without her father's jovial presence, there would be a terrible void.

As it turned out, there were heavy snows, and with the mountain trails impassable, traveling was out of the question. It was hard enough for Ross to trek to the isolated homes in Millscreek Gap to make necessary sick calls. There was a great deal of illness that year — children with whooping cough, the older people with severe rheumatism and colds. Ross came home late most evenings, exhausted, too tired and chilled to do more than eat and fall into bed.

The snow kept away even her rare visits from Aunt Bertie and Uncle Tanner, as well as Sue and Katie, who had become frequent visitors since the rescue. Left much alone, Johanna experienced some melancholy about her father, thinking about what she might have said or done differently. She thought of the letter she had procrastinated about writing to him after her marriage, a letter expressing her love, her sorrow at having hurt him, her assurances that her choice had been the right one. She wished she had told her father that Ross was a good and loving husband. However, she had put it off time and again, not sure of exactly what to say. Now it was too late.

Little by little, Johanna gained peace of mind. With her newfound faith, she believed her father *did* know.

With the coming of spring, the mountains burst into glorious beauty. The air was filled with lovely smells — damp moss, sweet clover. There were warm, lovely days, longer afternoons, lavender evenings.

It was in these first weeks of April 1841 that Johanna knew she was going to have a baby.

After her first excitement at the prospect, Johanna had most of the same nagging little worries of any about-to-be mother. Tears came and went like April rain. *I'm as bad as we used to tease Elly about,* she admonished herself, *crying at the drop of a hat!* She knew it was the early stages of her condition. She had heard that expecting a baby sometimes made a woman fanciful and silly. After those first few weeks, a marvelous calm overcame Johanna, and with it a lovely glow.

Ross was deeply happy and proud and couldn't wait to tell everyone. Johanna wanted to wait to first share the news with his mother. Johanna felt somewhat shy about confiding some of her qualms about her approaching motherhood. Eliza was so strong and capable, she probably wouldn't be very understanding. After all, she had birthed four of her own with no seeming problem. However, Johanna instinctively felt it was the right thing to do to tell her mother-in-law first, before Ross, in his own happy pride, blurted out the information to someone else.

The path down to her mother-in-law's house was steep, winding its way precariously between the dark woods on one side, the rocky cliff on the other, with a sheer drop down to the glistening river snaking through the cove below.

Eliza's thin, lined face broke into a wide smile at the news Johanna shyly confided.

"I'm right pleased for you, Johanna. Havin' a baby, becomin' a mama — why, I reckon it's one of the happiest times in a woman's life. I 'spect Ross is beside hisself, ain't he?" Eliza nodded. "He'll make a fine daddy. He was always so good with the younger ones. Patient, kind to 'em. Even

Merriman, who could be ornery," she chuckled. "He's got all that from *his* pa, and that's what makes him such a good doctor, I reckon."

In that afternoon she spent with Eliza was the first time Johanna began to feel close to her mother-in-law. Telling her about the coming baby seemed to have narrowed the gap between them.

"Now, of course, you're going to have to have quilts for the young'un. And it'll pass your waitin' time to be makin' some."

"I'm ashamed that I don't really know how to put one together," Johanna confessed. "I guess I was too impatient, too restless, always wanting to be doing something else."

"Well, you'll be sittin' plenty in the next few months and the further along you git. It's a nice, peaceful thing to do, sittin', dreamin' 'bout the baby to come. It was fer me. I musta made a half dozen each time I was expectin'."

Eliza went over to the blanket box and opened the lid. The smell of cedar rose as she did so. Inside were neatly folded quilts. She brought one out, smoothed it with her gnarled, work-worn hands, then unfolded it to show it to Johanna. "This here is one like I'd made for Jenny's last little 'un. I had some pieces left over, and I dunno why, I jest made up another one. It was even 'fore you and Ross got married. Mebbe even 'fore I knew about you."

"Oh, it's beautiful — *Ma*," Johanna said softly, using the name for the first time, then reaching out a hand tentatively to touch the quilt.

"You gotta be right careful about what pattern you use for a baby cradle," Eliza went on, warming to her subject. "It's just not the color or a pretty design you're lookin' for. There are some old tales about quilt patterns. Not to say I believe all of 'em. . . ." She shrugged. "I've always called this here one Turkey Tracks, that's the way it was taught to me. But some of the old women say it used to be called Wandering Foot, and nobody would use it for a child's bed."

"Why ever not?" Johanna was curious.

Eliza shook her head. "Oh, there's lots of old stories about it — things like iffen a child sleeps under it, it'll grow up discontent or with a roaming mind. You hear lots of things like that. Not that I pay a lot of mind to them. But there's lots of other pretty patterns to pick from."

"My mother quilts and so do all my aunties."

Eliza looked somewhat taken aback.

"Then mebbe when they know about the baby, they'll all be sending you one they'll make up special. You won't need this 'un." She started folding the quilt up, as though to put it back in the cedar box.

"Oh, please no, Ma. I *want* this one," Johanna protested, then added shyly, "I think for our baby's first quilt — it should come from his daddy's ma."

For a minute Eliza almost seemed startled. Her eyes glistened and she turned her head quickly. "Well now, iffen that's what you want —"

"Yes, it is," Johanna assured her, then hesitantly asked, "Ma, would you teach *me* how to quilt?"

"You really don't know how?"

"Not really. I was never much interested, I'm afraid. I've made a few patches but never put together a whole quilt."

"Well, now." Eliza sat back on her heels, her expression thoughtful. "I've got a pattern — ," she said slowly. "Made up a few patches but haven't got 'round to finishing it. Mebbe you could start on it. It's simple enough for a beginner." She leaned over the cedar chest again and brought up a brown paper package and slowly unwrapped it. Inside were layers of folded cloth, some cutout patterns, and other pieces of material. On

301

top were two or three finished blocks on cream-colored cotton, each banded with deep pink. In the center of each block was appliquéd three stylized, pink-petaled flowers accented with green stems and leaves.

Johanna smoothed her hand over the delicately sewn pieces. She imagined Eliza bent over her quilting frame, taking the tiny stitches painstakingly by firelight after all her chores were done. It was a thing of simple beauty, crafted out of the creativity within her that needed expression.

"Oh Ma, it's truly beautiful," Johanna said softly. "What do you call this pattern?"

"Hit don't have any right name. I jest always admired the mountain lilies that bloom along in July. I didn't have a pattern — I just drew it off on paper from looking at it, then used that to cut out my material."

"Mountain lilies, of course," Johanna smiled. "Carolina Mountain Lily. That's what we'll call it."

She slipped her hand over Eliza's worn, rough one, awed that it could make something so exquisite as well as chop wood, churn butter, hoe corn.

On her way back up the mountain, the package containing the quilt pattern and materials strapped behind her saddle, Johanna felt excited, as if she were launching into a whole new phase of her life. It was funny, actually. Back at Holly Grove she'd had to practically be dragged to the quilting frame, constantly be made to pull out her indifferent stitches and do her part over. Now she was looking forward to learning how to make a quilt of her own. For the first time, Johanna felt a real bonding to Ross's mother and to the mountain community that was now her home.

The news spread fast among the extended Davison family up and down the mountain. Aunt Bertie and Uncle Tanner were the first to come visit and congratulate them, bringing a cradle made by Tanner's own skilled hands. As Ross and Johanna stood around it admiringly, Bertie told them, "Tanner's cradles are the best. Made out of buckeye log. He worked on it like he was makin' something fit for a king. He likes buckeye 'cause it's light and hollows out so easy and it's a pretty wood. He pegged it with oak pins to two hickory rockers, curved just so. His rockers never creep. It's somethin' I never saw in no other cradle." She gave the cradle a gentle press of her foot. "See there, it jest rocks so nice and easy. I always called Tanner's cradles a lullaby of buckeye."

Trying to look indifferent, Uncle Tanner beamed at his wife's praise.

Later the men went up to check the few apple trees on the hillside, and Johanna brought sassafras tea for Auntie Bertie and herself to drink out on the sunny front porch.

"When your time comes, honey, Tassie Rector's the one," Aunt Bertie said. "She's been bringin' babies for nigh on forty years, I reckon. Never lost a baby nor a mother in all that time. Iffen I wuz you, I'd go make her acquaintance, let her know you'll be needin' her," Aunt Bertie advised.

"But Ross is a doctor, Aunt Bertie. He knows all about babies. He's already delivered dozens since we came back up here," Johanna said.

"Doctor or not, he's a man, ain't he? I think you'd be glad if you go see Tassie and talk to *her*. A woman needs another woman at a time like that."

"I'm sure Ross's mother, Eliza, will come," Johanna said tentatively, wondering if maybe there was more to having a baby than she realized. She had a sudden longing for her own mother or Aunt Honey.

"You jest take my advice, Johanna, and go see Tassie," was Aunt Bertie's last word to her before she and Uncle Tanner took off.

One Sunday after service, outside church Ross got into a conversation with Merriman, and Johanna was left standing with Jenny. She had always felt a little awkward with her sister-in-law. Jenny was one of the few people her own age — at least, one of the few girls — whom Johanna had not been able to win as a friend. She didn't know what made her feel so awkward around Jenny. She never seemed to be able to bring up a subject Jenny would respond to. Although Johanna told herself the girl was probably just shy, she had begun to feel that somehow Jenny disliked or resented her. This made it almost impossible whenever they were in each other's company. Most of the time, that was when they were all together at Eliza's. Then there was always so much to do, helping set food on the table or doing the clearing away or washing up. But sometimes, like now, Johanna found herself with a blank mind and a silent tongue.

Jenny seemed just as ill at ease as Johanna. Shaded by the broad-brimmed sunbonnet, her eyes were cast down, and her thin mouth worked nervously. At home, her father used to tease Johanna that she "couldn't stand a moment's silence," and this proved true at this awkward instant. Johanna surprised herself by impulsively bursting out, "Jenny, I'm really pretty scared about having this baby. You've had two — I wish you'd come up to visit me one day and talk to me about it. It would really help to talk to someone else — I mean, someone my own age."

Jenny's face flushed and she looked startled. She opened her mouth and started to say something, then swallowed and seemed too taken aback to go on.

"Please, Jenny, I mean it. I'd really like you to come. Will you?"

"Yes, yes. Shure I will," Jenny finally murmured.

Just then the two brothers sauntered up to where their wives were standing. Ross smiled at them both. "What're you two ladies gossiping about?" he asked teasingly.

"Babies!" Johanna laughed and glanced over at Jenny merrily. To her surprise, Jenny had blushed beet red. Belatedly Johanna realized that maybe mountain women didn't talk openly about such things, even in front of their husbands, even when one of them was a doctor. She was sorry if she embarrassed Jenny, and she leaned toward her and gave her a reassuring touch on her arm, saying, "Now don't forget, Jenny — I'm looking forward to your visit."

Two days later Jenny did come, still shy, still pretty untalkative. She did, however, bring a gift of a beautiful little knitted baby shawl. She also endorsed Aunt Bertie's recommendation that Johanna go see Tassie.

"She helped brung both my boys," Jenny told her. "None better in all the mountainside."

Some weeks later Johanna decided to follow both Jenny's and Aunt Bertie's suggestion. On a beautiful early fall morning, she saddled her horse and went down the mountain. The air was clear, with a definite sharpness to it. There was the smell of ripening apples, burning leaves, and she noticed the sharp-tanged fragrance of chokeberries.

"Tassie's home is easy to find," Aunt Bertie had told her. "If you get lost, ask anyone you see. Everyone knows her, will tell you how to get there." She was right, and soon Johanna came in sight of a weathered frame house on the side of the hill. As she got off her horse, leading him by his reins up the rest of the steep path, Johanna saw a woman sitting on the porch on a rush-seat rocking chair.

"Howdy," the woman called.

Johanna gave an answering wave. "I'm Jo-

307

hanna Davison," she said as she walked up to the porch. When she came closer, she saw the woman's strong, sensitive face, wreathed in wrinkles and a welcoming smile, and her deep-set, kind eyes.

"Well, I'm right happy to meet you. Doc's wife, ain't ye? Come and sit a spell."

For the next hour or so, Johanna felt as though she had been warmly hugged and comforted by this dear lady.

At once offered refreshment and the other rocker, Johanna was soon hearing the story of Tassie's life. "Was born right here, only a stone's throw from where we're sittin'. Married at twenty and had ten young'uns, all healthy, alive to this day. Now have thirty grandchildren and eight great-grands and brought 'em all into the world." She rocked and smiled with satisfaction. "I began midwifin' while my own was still little. It jest seem to be my callin' in life." She nodded. "We all come into this world with a mission. The Lord saw fit to give me this one, and so he was present with me all the time, at every birthin'. God give me the talent to bring babies safely, and that's what I've tried to do. I take no credit myself, you understand? I've had no real trainin' but what God give me. I jest always put my trust in him, and as Scripture says, "My grace is sufficient.""

When the sun was getting low, Johanna stood up, ready to leave. Tassie said, "I know your man is a doctor, and from what I heard, a fine one. But if you want me, jest send word and I'll be on my way."

"That's very kind of you," Johanna said as she tied her sunbonnet strings. She didn't think she'd really need Tassie, not with Ross there, but she didn't want to hurt the old lady's feelings.

On her way back up the mountain, Johanna wished she'd paid more attention when she still lived in Hillsboro, wished she'd listened when the aunties were discussing some friend's confinement or a birth in their circle of acquaintances. Then marriage and motherhood had seemed something in the distant future. Now that it was soon to be her own experience, she realized she knew next to nothing about it. Of course, Ross would be with her and certainly knew what to do when the time came. He was well trained and capable. And Eliza would also be on hand. She wouldn't have to rely on a backwoods midwife, thank goodness.

Eliza helped Johanna begin her quilt. Uncle Tanner willingly made her a frame to set up. Once she got started, Johanna discovered she actually enjoyed doing it. She liked arranging the pieces of bright calico material and pinning them into the design more than the actual stitching. However, gradually and with Eliza's patient instruction, her stitches got smaller, neater, and after Ross moved the frame up to their own cabin, she found she could work while daydreaming about how life would be once their baby arrived. Being pregnant made her less active, and often Johanna found herself getting sleepy after only a half hour or more at her quilting frame, so it went slowly. She would often have to lie down and take a nap on the long afternoons as fall turned into winter and the wind blew around the cabin corners, sending the cedar boughs sighing against the windows, making the sound almost of a lullaby.

Chapter Eighteen

Johanna felt her shoulder shaken gently and heard Ross whisper, "I've got a nice fire going, honey, but you stay in bed until the house gets good and warm. I've got a few visits to make, but I should be home early afternoon."

Johanna murmured something drowsily, felt Ross kiss her cheek, his hand smooth her hair, then she snuggled deeper into the quilts and went back to sleep.

She wasn't sure how much later she woke up. A fire was burning brightly but low in the big stone fireplace. Slowly she roused herself, pulled on her voluminous flowered flannel robe, got awkwardly out of the high bed. Six more weeks and she wouldn't be able to sleep in late like this, she thought with a smile. Neither would she have all this extra weight to carry around with her. She slipped her feet into slippers and went to the window. Outside the sky was a chalky gray. Snow? The edges around the glass pane were frosted slightly.

The kettle Ross had left hanging on the crane over the fire was sizzling. Johanna put a few spoonfuls of herb tea into a mug, poured in water, and stirred it into a fragrant brew. As she leaned over to replace the kettle, she felt a strange sensation in her back. Straightening up, one hand went to the curve of her spine. Had she imagined it? Probably pulled a muscle slightly when she reached for the kettle, she thought. Her body wasn't familiar to her anymore. She had all sorts of queer aches and pains now, in places she could never have imagined before. Sitting down at the table, she cupped her hands around the steaming mug, inhaling the spicy aroma of the tea. The room was pleasantly warm, the tea delicious. Johanna glanced around, thinking how happy and content she had felt in recent weeks.

Everything about the little cabin pleased her — the polished gourds on the mantel, the blue and white dishes on the pine hutch, the rocking chair, which she had enjoyed more and more these last months. Then her gaze rested on the cradle and the quilt folded over its side. Soon their precious baby would be nested within that. *Their* child, hers and Ross's. She didn't care whether it was a boy or girl, either way she would love it.

She looked out the window again. To her

surprise, she saw a few snowflakes floating lazily down. If it snowed, it would be the first of the season. Autumn — or Indian summer, as they called it here — had lingered longer than usual in the mountains this year. It wasn't until way into November that the mornings had become really frosty and the evenings chilly.

Johanna got up from the table to go over to the window, when a quick, darting pain traveled down the back of both her legs. She gasped, clutched onto the edge of the table. What in the world? Had she slept in a cramped position so that her muscles were stiff? A fleeting worry passed through her mind. It couldn't be anything to do with the baby. Or could it? She took a deep breath. She put her weight back on her feet and straightened up. Nothing happened. It was all right. Just a twinge of some kind. Nothing more.

She walked over to the window, leaned on the sill, and watched the snow fall slowy, as if it were not in any hurry. Still, it was sticking, she saw, watching the steadily falling snow cover the ground with a light powder.

It looked beautiful. The sweeping branches of the pines and hemlocks that rimmed their property were dark green under the fluffy fringe of white, the rail fence like dark rickrack against the drifting snow.

Johanna moved back over to the stove, where the oatmeal she had set on the back burner the night before was now thickened, ready to eat. She started to dish herself out a bowl, when she again felt another strange little clutch in the middle of her back. This one lasted longer than the first one. She frowned. She waited a full minute. Nothing happened. She filled her bowl, poured milk and honey over her oatmeal, and went to sit by the fire and eat.

She hoped Ross would get home before the snow got any deeper. It was hard enough traveling the narrow ridges on the mountain to out-of-the-way cabins in good weather.

Finishing her breakfast, Johanna decided to work some on the quilt she was making for the baby. Then she wouldn't worry about Ross. Eliza had been right — making the quilt was a pleasant, "mind easin'" experience. Johanna enjoyed it more than she ever imagined. Wouldn't her mother and aunties be amazed? It used to seem a pointless occupation back when she would rather have been doing something else. Now, anticipating a baby, Johanna found it enjoyable. Working on the quilt, she dreamed of all sorts of happy things. With the baby, she felt that the life she and Ross shared would become even happier, more complete.

Johanna shifted her position. She seemed to become uncomfortable sooner than usual as she sat in the straight-backed chair at the quilting frame. She started to get up to get a pillow to wedge behind her back, when a sudden pain struck her. It was longer and stronger than either of the others. This time it traveled swiftly from the middle of her back down the length of her legs, causing her knees to cramp. She sat down quickly, holding on to the chair arms.

For a long while she remained absolutely still. What was going on? It *couldn't* be the baby. *Could* it? The last time Tassie stopped by, she had looked Johanna over with a practiced eye, declaring she had a good six weeks yet to go. Over a month.

Alarm coursed through Johanna. Was something wrong, then? Oh, if only Ross were there. She waited tensely but nothing else happened. Reassured, she got up and walked over to the window again. It was now near noon. The snow was coming down with a driving force. The ground was covered and the wind was blowing the snow in drifts along the fence and against the windowsills. Johanna put her hand on the pane and felt the cold.

Where was Ross? He'd better get home

before it snowed any harder. She watched with increasing anxiety as the snow continued falling steadily.

Restless and unable to go back to her quilting, she felt suddenly chilly. She went over to the wood box, got a few smaller logs out, and threw them on the fire, sending up a spiral of sparks. She got down her shawl and wrapped it around her shoulders. Drawing the rocker closer, she sat down near the fireplace.

Suddenly a grinding sort of pain gripped her. She gave a startled cry. Was that the kind of pain that signaled the start of labor? Oh, no! Surely it was too soon. It couldn't be happening. Not now! When she was there alone! It couldn't be starting, could it? Please, God, no. A deep shudder went all through Johanna. She knew that once it started, there was no stopping it. What was it Tassie had said? "When a baby's ready to come, it comes!" Could this be how it begins? Slowly, so that you're not sure, then more often, harder, with sensations unlike anything else you've ever felt?

Holding the shawl close about her, she made her halting way back over to the window. The day was darkening quickly, clouds heavy with still more snow hovered, the boughs of the pines and hemlocks surrounding the cabin were now burdened with clumps of snow, and the wind-blown snow was now banked along the rustic fence along the horse trail down the mountainside.

Ross had better get home soon, or the way would be impassable. Fear stirred in the pit of her stomach, tightening her throat. If this *was* the baby coming, she couldn't go through it all by herself. She *couldn't* — dear God, she just couldn't! She felt her eyes fill with tears of fear and frustration. It just couldn't happen like this. Her body seemed almost apart from her mind, which became surprisingly clear. If this *was* the baby — and she was getting to the point where she *knew* it was — she should do something, get ready somehow to handle this alone, if she had to.

Before she could move or turn around, another slow pain clutched her, making her bend over and cling to the window sill, causing an involuntary groan. There was no mistaking it. This was it!

She closed her eyes for a minute, prayed frantically. *Please, God, make me brave, show me what to do. But please send someone! Bring Ross home!*

Boil water! That somehow tugged at her memory as something to do. She wasn't sure quite why, but she filled the kettle anyway and hung it over the fire. The fire was roaring, crackling, and the smell of apple wood was pungent as it burned. Still, Johanna could not get warm. She shivered and braced herself for another pain.

It came and she held her breath until it passed. Fifteen minutes later another one began. Between pains, Johanna heard the ticktock of the clock. She counted the time, clenching her hands on the arms of the rocker, waiting for the pain she knew would soon overtake her. Between those times, she prayed, *Please, someone come.* Outside the steady, silent snow continued.

The wind howled around the cabin, sounding like a hundred screeching owls. Johanna gritted her teeth, set her jaw, shuddered. How could this have happened to her? To the pampered daughter of well-to-do town folk? To be up here all alone in an isolated log cabin in a snowstorm that was gradually shutting her off from any help? At a time like this, she should be surrounded by loving, comforting, caring people — people who, for heaven's sake, knew what to do!

Panic set her heart to pounding. She hugged herself and moved closer to the fireplace, shivering in spite of its warmth.

She thought of the day Liddy Chalmers had come to see her before she got married, begged her to reconsider marrying Ross. "You *can't,* Johanna, you just can't!" Liddy had cried. Johanna thought of that scene in detail now. "To go so far away, to live on the edge of nowhere," Liddy had said.

Well, that's exactly what she *had* done. If she'd gone to Hillsboro months ago to have the baby there, as her mother had written to suggest, she wouldn't be in this awful situation. But Johanna had refused. *This* was her home now, she'd insisted in her letter back to her mother. Was she now paying for her stubbornness, her self-will, her pride?

Johanna imagined how it would have been for her now if she'd accepted her mother's invitation. A picture came to her of her own bedroom, with its slanted ceiling, the dormer windows looking out onto the garden, the four-poster bed, her little desk and white-paneled fireplace, her bedside table with her favorite books. She remembered how when she had some slight childhood illness, trays were brought up to her with cinnamon toast or lemon pudding, and if she had a fever, her mother's cool hand would be on her forehead. Ruefully she knew she'd never appreciated it enough.

Just then another wave of pain swept over her. Johanna clamped her teeth together, accidentally biting her tongue. Tears rushed into her eyes. Finally the pain passed and again Johanna made her way haltingly over to the window, peering out. Snow piled up on the window ledge and around the small panes shut off any view. Johanna saw that the trail was almost obliterated by the drifts. And it was still snowing. There was little hope that Ross would come now. He might be caught somewhere up the mountain. Perhaps he'd stayed too long at some remote cabin with a patient. Ironically, maybe even to deliver a baby!

First babies often took a long time, Tassie had told her. On the other hand, she'd said, some babies were in a hurry. What this baby would do, Johanna had no idea. She bit her lower lip as a strong spasm gripped her again.

She tried not to think of some of the horror stories she'd heard whispered among the girls at boarding school. Of course, none of them *really* knew anything about it. All they circulated were old wives' tales passed from one ignorant girl to the next. However, she *did* know that sometimes women died having babies. What if she died here all by herself? What if they came and found her dead, and the baby too?

If she died, how sad everyone would be. Even Cissy. The idea struck her that when people died, they always left a will. To distract herself from the next pain, which she knew would be coming soon, Johanna thought of what she would bequeath to her sisters in her nonexistent will. She really should have made a will, she thought. Facing what she was now, there was always the possibility of dying. If she *were* to make a will, she'd leave Cissy the cameo pin Grandmother Shelby had given *her* on her sixteenth birthday. Cissy had been really put out about that. She had always admired the delicate Grecian profile carved in ivory on a pale lavender background, framed in gold, circled with seed pearls. And Elly. What could she leave to her youngest sister. What would Elly want of hers?

That was as far as Johanna got in her melancholy thoughts. She perked up suddenly. Didn't she hear something? Above the wind, beyond the pattering of the icy snow against the windows — was that the sound of voices? Oh, dear God, was someone actually coming? She got up from her crouched position, staggered to the door. It *was!* She heard shouts! It wasn't her imagination. Someone was actually coming. Thank God.

Pressing her face to the window, wiping away the frost that veiled her view, she looked out. Stumbling through the blowing snow, the piled-up drifts, were two bundled figures, hanging on to each other, making their way toward the cabin.

With all her strength, Johanna slid back the wooden bars on the door. The wind pushed against it, and she was hard pressed to hold the door open enough for the two people to come inside.

Woolen mufflers around their heads hid their faces, and Johanna could only see their eyes, which were fringed by snow-crusted lashes. The tips of their noses were red with cold. Heavy shawls stiff with frozen snow were wrapped around them, disguising their shapes. Then as they began unwinding the long knitted scarves, she saw who they were. The first face revealed was Tassie's, the second that of Ross's mother, Eliza.

"Oh Ma, I'm so glad you came," Johanna gasped, clutching Eliza's arm. "I think the baby's on its way! But how did you know to come?"

"Tassie come by, told me she'd seen Ross up on the ridge near the Coltons' cabin early in the day. She heard tell that Milt had broke his leg felling a tree, and thought Ross might have trouble gettin' down the mountain agin iffen it kept snowin' so heavy. We both decided you shouldn't be up here alone in case — well, just in case. So we come."

"Thank God you did!" Johanna said fervently. "But what about Sue and Katie?"

"They'll be fine. Took them over to Jenny and Merriman's 'fore I set out," Eliza told her. "Now, don't you worry 'bout nuthin' but bringin' this here baby into the world."

Even as her mother-in-law spoke, Johanna felt another pain coming. She nodded and braced herself. Her fingers clutched Eliza's arm. Immediately she felt the swift support of both women holding her firmly. When the pain had passed, Johanna let Eliza help her over to bed. There quilts were tucked around her, pillows piled beneath her head, shoulders, back. She could hear Tassie moving around in the cabin. Soon she brought Johanna a mug of steaming herbal tea, a mixture of red raspberry and chamomile. "Here, you sip on this, honey. It'll ease you and make you feel better."

After that, things became blurred. There was the rhythm of pain, each one closer and harder. Always in the background were the comforting voices of the two women, who held her hand, rubbed her back, soothed her with quiet, calm instructions.

Outside the day darkened. Between pains, Johanna asked, "Ross? Is Ross here?"

"Not yet, honey. Now, you jest quiet yourself. Everything's goin' fine. Your baby'll be here 'fore long."

Johanna couldn't remember just when she lost track of time — possibly hours passed. Everything centered on the cycle of ever-increasing pressure, Tassie's encouraging voice. Then she heard the slam of the cabin door as it was thrust open and banged against the wall. The next thing she knew, her hand was covered by two large ones, her name whispered. "Johanna, darling, I'm here."

She opened her eyes. Ross's face bent over her, his keen eyes worried. His cold cheek pressed against hers, and he said huskily, "It won't be long now, honey."

Relieved, reassured, Johanna clung tightly to his hand and gave herself up to the business of giving birth, feeling safe, secure, and completely comforted by his presence.

It seemed endless. Then, as if from a long distance off, Johanna heard the strong, unmistakable sound of a baby's cry! It was over. She'd had her baby. She fell back against the pillows, filled with a tremendous joy, a sense of accomplishment.

Johanna awakened to the sweet aroma of spice wood tea boiling, then the stirring of the little bundle tucked into the bed beside her. Her baby! she realized in dreamy surprise.

She looked down into the pink, crumpled little face. The baby's eyes were closed. Gently she touched the downy crest of hair on the small, round head, let her finger trace the cheek. How sweet, how dear. She was in awe of this perfection. This is what she had waited for all these months, their child. Johanna felt an emotion new and deep move within her. "Thank you, God," she whispered.

Slowly she became aware of other movement in the room, and then she saw Eliza come to the side of her bed, holding a cup from which a spiral of fragrant steam arose.

"You're awake, Johanna. Let's see if we can sit you up some so's you can sip this tea. It'll give you strength, then mebbe later you can eat somethin'." She paused, then asked hesitantly, "Kin I hold the baby for you?"

Johanna smiled up at Eliza, turning back the edge of the blanket so she could see the little face better. "Isn't she beautiful?"

Eliza beamed. "Yes, she shure is a right peart little'un," she replied, nodding her head. "Ross sez you're namin' her Johanna — that's the custom in your family for a first girl."

"Yes ma'am, but we're going to call her JoBeth — Johanna *Elizabeth*."

Johanna watched as her mother-in-law's face underwent a change of expression, from a startled look to a softness she had never seen there before.

" 'Lizabeth?" Eliza repeated softly.

"Yes ma'am, after *you*." Johanna said.

Eliza struggled not to show her emotion, but her eyes brightened suspiciously and her lips worked as if trying to say something. At length, not being able to express what she was feeling, she simply lifted Johanna's fingers and pressed them to her cheek. "I — well — thanky," she managed to say at last.

Chapter Nineteen

Johanna's third September in the mountains seemed particularly beautiful to her. Coming out onto the porch one afternoon, she lingered. High in the tall trees surrounding their cabin, the wind sang. Listening to its music, Johanna realized it was a melody she had learned to hear and love. She felt a part of all this now — these hills, the scent of wildflowers, wood smoke, the special light in summer evenings, the sweet scent of honeysuckle, the clean smell of freshly cut pine. She felt the satisfaction of belonging. A feeling that had been long coming.

Sometimes, Hillsboro and her own girlhood seemed a hundred years away. Her life now was centered here in the mountains, on the baby, and on Ross.

After her father's death, Ross had been her strength, her comfort. She had never before realized the depth of his love, the generosity of his soul, the strength of his devotion, the selflessness of his being. Johanna felt sure her father would be glad to know how beloved she was, how cherished, protected.

The baby was napping and Johanna was tempted to stay, enjoying the sunshine, but there were still chores to be done. She sighed and reluctantly went inside.

Her glance fell on the quilting frame Uncle Tanner had made for her before the baby was born. There was an unfinished quilt stretched upon it. She hadn't worked on it for weeks. Somehow there was always something else that needed doing. Besides, this one wasn't coming out as she had planned. Maybe she was too impatient, or maybe she didn't have the skill — it didn't seem to have a theme. Johanna went over to it, stood looking down at it. Shouldn't a quilt have some sort of theme, a message — shouldn't it represent something? Something was missing. Something was wrong. The colors? The pattern? The pieces she had selected? It was a daily reminder of something lacking in her — the will to continue, to complete. Whatever the problem, somehow it didn't please her. Something seemed to be missing, but she didn't know just what.

Johanna had finished two smaller ones for the baby. Eliza had sewed the tops to the matting and flannel backing, and JoBeth slept sweetly and soundly, wrapped up in their warmth. This quilt was supposed to be Johanna's showpiece, to exhibit the skills she had learned through much struggle, much ripping out and redoing, a masterful work to be displayed proudly. And yet it wasn't right. Why? Not feeling inclined to work on it, she went on to do other chores.

She still had trouble juggling everything there was to do. The baby took up most of her time. Johanna found her a source of endless delight. She knew she neglected other things to spend time with her baby.

JoBeth was a daily miracle to her. Everything about her seemed extraordinary to Johanna. She could hardly put her down or stop watching her. She loved caring for her, cuddling, feeding, rocking, admiring the rosebud mouth, the startlingly blue eyes, the way her silky dark hair was beginning to curl around her forehead and shell-like ears.

Hearing the sound of stirring from the cradle, Johanna hurried over and, greeting JoBeth with soft, cooing sounds, she lifted the baby. It was just too pretty to stay inside, Johanna decided. Then, taking one of the quilts Eliza had given her, she carried her outside. Spreading the quilt on the grass in the mellow gold of the autumn sunshine, she placed JoBeth on it. The baby was just about ready to crawl. She would get up on her fat little hands and knees and rock back and forth, as if she hadn't quite figured out just how yet.

Johanna never tired of watching her. She felt that time with her baby was precious, and she didn't want to miss a minute.

The afternoon lengthened. JoBeth had now been placed on her back, kicking her little legs, waving her arms. Her round, blue eyes watched a cluster of birds flying back and forth between the oak tree overhead and the fence nearby.

Above them, purple-shadowed mountains arched against the sky. Johanna realized how much she had come to love them. They no longer seemed threatening or ready to close her in, isolate her, but instead seemed to protect and surround her with love.

The light began to change, the wind began to stir the pine boughs. Ross should be coming home soon. Johanna picked the baby up and walked to the fence overlooking the trail, peered down to see if Ross might be making his way up. At a long distance on the mountainside, she saw him coming. Her heart lifted with a little thrill she astonishingly recognized as being much the same as the very first time she had seen him at the Chalmerses' Christmas party.

He sat somewhat slouched forward in his

saddle, his shoulders bent as though he'd had a tiring day, his hands easy on the reins. Johanna felt a rush of tenderness.

Coming near, he saw her and waved one hand.

" 'Evenin', honey," he called, then smiled at the baby. "Evenin', Miss Johanna Elizabeth."

At the top of the hill he dismounted. Taking off the horse's bridle, then the saddle, he placed them on the top of the fence, opened the gate, and turned the animal into the pasture.

Ross walked toward Johanna and held out his arms for the baby and placed her against his shoulder. Then he put his other arm around Johanna, and together the three of them went into the house. Inside, Ross leaned down, gave Johanna a long, slow kiss, then sighed, "It's good to be home."

Joy surfaced in Johanna. It *was* good to be home. *Their* home. She remembered hearing it said, "Home is where the heart is, where your treasure is." *Her* treasure was Ross and the baby. She felt a deep thankfulness for all that was there and for all the years ahead of them.

Johanna glanced at the quilt on the frame. She went over, stared down at it critically. Suddenly she began to see its design. She saw the pieces all coming together in a harmonious pattern. What she wanted it to represent was her life here with Ross and the baby. All the things home meant to her — love, laughter, devotion, belonging.

All at once Johanna knew what she wanted her quilt to say. There was still much of their life that was yet to come, just like the quilt. There was more to work on, more to bring forth. But the pattern was there underneath. Nothing was missing — not from her quilt nor from her life.

How to Make Johanna's Quilt

Appliqué allows you to create your own design by stitching bits of fabric on a foundation material. The Carolina Lily quilt is easy to make if you follow the step-by-step instructions. Allow your creativity to blossom by selecting your favorite colors for your own lilies. No two lilies are the same on the Carolina Lily design, but our instructions will allow you to make the flowers look symmetrical to each other.

First, sew two diamonds. Stitch from the bottom of the diamond to the top seam. Second, sew two pairs of diamonds together making one Carolina Lily blossom. Be careful to sew from the bottom of the diamonds to the top—do not sew through it. Now, sew the long side of a triangle to the base of the blossom. You may need to trim the ends of the petals within 1/8 of the sewing line, while gradually tapering the points. Next, make the stems by folding green strips along each long edge. Put the center stem on top of the side stems. You may need to trim the side stems where they meet the center stem to avoid bulk. Hand-baste or pin the Lilies onto the foundation. Trim the stems, allowing 1/4" under the flower. Finally, using small slip stitches, appliqué the stems and the Carolina Lilies. If you prefer to work with felt, wool, or non-woven materials use the buttonhole embroidery stitch instead.

Now to assemble the quilt top, trim the sides of the appliquéd block so they are all equal in length. Make three vertical rows of four blocks, joined with long sashing strips. Press each seam toward the sashing strips. Each of these rows should have the same measurements too.

Now you are ready to layer and quilt. The

backing fabric should be divided into two equal lengths.

Sew the two sides together. Outline-quilt around all the flowers and stems. Lastly, quilt the marked designs.

Finally, to complete the quilt sew the strips together in a continual diagonal seam. Stitch through all the layers around the quilt. When you reach the starting point overlap the ends.

Your Carolina Lily quilt will forever bloom the fruit of your needle art.

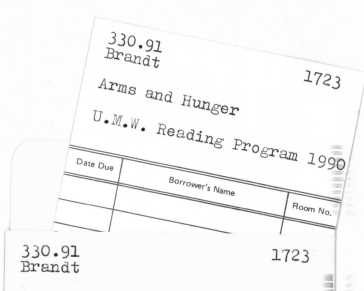

330.91
Brandt

1723

Arms and Hunger

U.M.W. Reading Program 1990

Date Due	Borrower's Name	Room No.

330.91   1723
Brandt

Arms and Hunger

U.M.W. Reading Program 1990
Christian Global Concerns

ARMS AND HUNGER

ARMS AND HUNGER

Willy Brandt

Translated by Anthea Bell

The MIT Press
Cambridge, Massachusetts

First MIT Press paperback edition, 1987

Published by arrangement with Pantheon Books, a Division of Random House, Inc.

Library of Congress Cataloging-in-Publication Data

Brandt, Willy, 1913–
  Arms and hunger.

  Translation of: Der organisierte Wahnsinn.
  1. Developing countries—Economic conditions.
  2. International economic relations. 3. World
politics—1985–1995. I. Title.
[HC59.7.B67713 1987]   330.9172′4   87-4057
ISBN 0-262-52127-X (pbk.)

CONTENTS

1723

FOREWORD

Why this book? I have often been asked what became of the recommendations of the Independent Commission on International Development Issues which I chaired. I have tried to give an honest answer; I cannot give a very positive one.

Over the last few years some progress has been made in some developing countries, but much further deterioration has also occurred, as is shown by both the famine disaster in Africa and the debt crisis in Latin America. This survey, however, which is not written for experts, does not suggest we resign ourselves. Instead, it calls for productive concern.

It is against our own interests to leave the developing countries to deal with their economic and social problems alone, instead of recognizing them as our partners. World peace is at risk if the East–West conflict and the arms race spread ever further into the Third World – and if funds are not at long last released from the build-up of armaments and made available for the struggle against underdevelopment.

I would therefore draw attention to the connections between East–West and North–South relations, between the arms race and world hunger.

I should like to thank Gerhard Thiebach for his work on the material, Fritz Fischer for helpful comments, and my wife for going through the manuscript.

Unkel, Spring 1985   W.B.

INTRODUCTION TO THE AMERICAN EDITION

Just before I started writing this introductory note I had been watching TV evening news. And I had marvelled at the almost unbelievable pictures of Uranus and its colourful rings, which Voyager II transmitted after travelling in space for more than eight years. Earlier that evening German TV had shown the first episode of Herman Wouk's *Winds of War*. Thus, within the span of two hours I had a glimpse of the future and a painful look back at the past, an idea of the human potential for good and for evil. And I wondered in which direction the world is heading.

In this book I present my views on what I consider the more important issues for the coming decade. My thinking naturally reflects a European perspective. But my own life and experience have been influenced and informed by many contacts with the world outside Europe and with people from all parts of the globe. To them, Europeans in general, and certainly I myself, owe a great deal. Sharing my views with them is but a small attempt at repaying some of that debt.

I am confident that what I have to say will be seen as the well-intentioned effort of a friend — even if it is rather critical in one respect or another. Above all I hope I have dealt with some of the issues and fears that worry people in all parts of the world but especially in Europe. That serious questions are being asked with great intensity and that people are deeply concerned is evident. I have become aware of that concern not only through my personal contacts but through many letters from individuals I have never met.

One instance I remember exceptionally well. (It helped me to write this book.) Some time ago a student of finance and economics at Berkeley, California, wrote me a letter expressing concern about the state of affairs in the world, especially as it affected relations between the United States and Europe. He believed the greatest danger to the stability of the world was Western economic competition rapidly deteriorating into open and violent hostility.

From his studies and observations he had concluded that the international economy was entering into a new cycle leading to worldwide depression around 1988–89. This would occur at least partly because of large US government deficits, but primarily it would be triggered by the lack of comprehensive American economic planning and policy and by the drying up of many sources of capital.

The world debt situation, in his view, would not permit repeated rescheduling of debts, and without a massive reordering of troubled financial markets, major debtor nations would opt for default.

Trade hostilities might well degenerate from mutual complaints to destructive rivalry, he felt. Without coordinated planning in the US, and in the absence of an integrated Western economic policy, 'these repeated blows of economic collapse must eventually lead to conflict'.

The conflict might readily have military expression. He observed that the US was urging Japan 'to defend itself by 1990', while many US politicians also wanted Europe to shoulder greater responsibility for NATO. Correspondingly, he suggested, the movement in my own country across party limits was steering the Federal Republic towards a European strategy for the reunification of Germany. If the isolationist trend in the US continued, it would result in the US pulling its forces out of Europe and Japan. The consequence, as talks with his European and Japanese fellow students seemed to have confirmed, would be policies 'independent of Washington's will'.

American foreign policy seemed to be obsessed with Soviet threats. Therefore the US saw political divisions within the West as aggravating obstacles to a unified response to the Soviet threat, not as the beginnings of an entirely new chapter in history. The US tended to overlook the underlying animosity among commercial competitors, where conflict arises among friendly neighbours whose self-interests collide. It was clear to him that the world economy could finally promise only two things: 'severely diminishing prosperity and, ultimately, nuclear war'.

The US, he continued, was an intensely fragmented society with strong economic, social, and racial polarizations. These had been successfully papered over by a trillion-dollar economy that continues to grow. But there was a grave prospect of a scenario in the near future in which the US, having mired itself and the rest of the West in perpetual domestic problems, would have to be saved by external forces.

He proceeded with what he called a worst-case projection:

- Economic cycle of recession, followed by partial recovery, followed by further recession, creating a long-term downward trend.
- Economic policies reacting too slowly to the crises or being misapplied. Emphasis on political diversion: propaganda about external threats, creating isolationist-military attitude.
- Prolonged wars further draining US strength (Middle East, Central America, Africa).
- Large-scale domestic disorders.
- Fierce international trade competition leading to embargos, boycotts, severe quotas, and retaliation.
- Rapid destabilization of the world. If the US falls, it will pull down the whole West.
- Europe and Japan reacting: rapid remilitarization, because the US would not provide economic leadership or defence.
- US domestic turmoil leading to need for allies to intervene.

Under these circumstances, he concluded, Europe would certainly regain its status as a great power, in order to fill the vacuum created by the decline of the US, whether slow or sudden. This process was already under way. Europe and Japan he saw as losing trust in America's stability. Therefore, 'They must either accommodate challengers or move to defend themselves.' The letter ended with an expression of hope for continued peace and for cooperation between the Federal Republic of Germany and the United States.

3

As the reader will learn from this book, I have been concerned with many of these issues for years, in various ways. Perhaps it takes more than one book – and maybe more than one lifetime – to deal with these problems adequately. Nevertheless, this in a way is my response to that letter and to many others.

It should also be evident that I have not given up hope. But the current world situation is very serious indeed, not the least because of the lack of clear vision and coherent policies – on all sides. However, I am hopeful that changing relations between the United States and the Soviet Union may reduce the threat to world peace.

Other developments affect and possibly threaten international stability and world peace. Let me just mention one example: In 1980 there appeared a book called *The Fate of the Dollar*. Barely five years later the questions on the cover of the book seemed almost funny: 'Why is the dollar worth less than it was ten years ago?' 'Where will the inflationary spiral end?' 'Will the dollar ever become sound again?' Meanwhile we have reached a different point in the cycle, with the dollar strong and inflation under control. But there is reason to fear that those same questions may become even more pertinent in the near future.

Less amusing and more telling is a story in that book, about a conversation between Otmar Emminger, then president of the Deutsche Bundesbank, and Anthony Solomon, then Undersecretary of the US Treasury. In 1979 Emminger is reported to have said, 'Solomon told me when he had been in office only a few months, "I don't like the idea of the value of the dollar abroad being at the mercy of the central banks." I said, "Good. Then finance the deficit yourself."'

The US deficit has grown ever since. And the US has not financed it itself.

Economists rarely disagree any more over how all the debts and deficits have grown. Whether conservative or liberal, they consider the strains on US farmers, the jobs lost in manufacturing, and rising delinquencies on home mortgage payments to be unsustainable. So *Let's Rebuild America* is more than just the title of a recent important analysis of what might remedy these circumstances; the phrase also reflects a very real and urgent need.

4

As to the international consequences of US policy, the recent change in attitude towards dealing with the international debt crisis allows us to feel some hope – unless the change came too late or the new measures turn out to provide too little support for the debtor nations.

Great damage has been done nevertheless. For it took three years of muddling-through crises, near panics in the financial markets, a million or so jobs lost in manufacturing, and social unrest in the developing world for the Reagan administration to recognize the debt crisis for what it really is: a long-term economic and political barrier to development that is slowly strangling world economic growth, as one analyst recently put it.

To deal with the deficit problem, Congress recently passed the Gramm-Rudman Act, a device designed to bring financial discipline at very high cost. If the Act is not ruled unconstitutional, it will deny both Congress and President discretion over a range of future spending. It has been called 'one of the most desperate acts ever to have come out of Washington'. It has been compared to a girl who knows she can't say no, so she buys a chastity belt and throws away the key. However, it appears that some politicians think Gramm-Rudman looks like a solution to the contradictions implicit in the economic policies they have followed since 1981. Tax cuts have indeed brought economic growth, but given the enormous outlays for 'defence' and the lack of substantial reductions in other expenditures, the growth in the economy has been matched by a growing budget deficit – not the promised revolution at all, but old-style recipes, one might add. As a result, the national debt, which was below $1,000 billion in 1981, is passing the $2,000 billion mark now. And the US has become the world's largest debtor – having been the world's largest net creditor nation as recently as 1982.

Enormous amounts of money are of course spent every year on what is called 'defence' or 'security'. Without these mind-boggling expenditures there would be no additional warheads, no new missiles, no launchers or silos, nor many of the other things allegedly needed for ever more 'reliable' defence. To many people the science of the physicists and the reasoning of the military experts has long since turned into fiction when it comes

5

to all those gadgets. The vast majority, however, long ago capitulated to the experts. But world peace cannot be left to the experts alone. And money is something most everybody understands.

As those things need to be paid for, it is worthwhile asking how such gigantic outlays are funded, where money comes from and how, who decides about its use, and whether there is any control at all. Only fools can still believe that today the financing of war – or 'security' or 'defence' – has much to do with defence budgets voted by Congress, or by parliaments elsewhere. One cannot claim that hundreds of millions of people around the world knowingly and actively support the huge arms build-up of the United States. But they do it nevertheless, through transfers of funds and savings to the US, funds that come from rich and poor alike, from industrialized and from developing countries, and even from the East.

Put another way, the present world monetary system serves to finance the ongoing arms build-up. Without their knowledge or intention, the citizens of many lands – but least of all those of the US itself – through their modest savings contribute to the financing of this obscene madness called the arms race. This is not to say that the United States is solely responsible. Nor are people forced to act that way. Indeed, they do it voluntarily.

All this happens for a simple reason. Our international monetary system is based on the US dollar as the main reserve currency. This establishes special privileges for the US that no other nation enjoys. Since the dollar is the yardstick for all other currencies, the US can pay for its trade deficits with dollars it does not first have to earn – as long as the rest of the world goes along and maintains confidence in the dollar. And as long as the rest of the world transfers its savings to the richest economy on earth, providing a kind of private development assistance to the US, there is little pressure on the US to change its policies.

However, the situation is not going to last forever. There are two likely alternatives. Either the privilege of the dollar will be abolished through an uprising of the debtors – all those suffering under the present system – or it will be abolished by the US itself – which is bound to happen once the advantage is exhausted –

when US debt service starts to exceed the inflow of new capital. At that point the US will devalue and inflate its currency, or even withdraw it from international circulation.

All this of course is nothing new. But memory is short, and the general optimism in the United States, the new feeling that America is Number One again – remember the Olympics? – tends to blur people's perceptions.

The Vietnam war and the Great Society had also generated large deficits, which for a while were financed from abroad. The dollar was overvalued, there was a trade deficit, and inflationary pressure was exported. But it could not go on forever. Devaluation of the dollar became necessary (1971 and 1973), leading to high US inflation, to recession all over the world, promoting the oil shocks and the debt crisis. From all this, the world has not yet recovered.

The present situation is much worse. And failure to act will bring incalculable damage to all of us. It is said that the United States and the Soviet Union could easily work together if there were a threat from Mars. I believe the threats confronting us here on earth are real enough and may even turn out to be deadly. This calls for rethinking, for cooperation worldwide – and between the two superpowers in particular.

What happened to the British pound in 1931 is bound to happen to the dollar sooner or later. And we should recall the dire consequences of earlier breakdowns of international economic peace. In the 1930s, the breakdown of the world economy led to the rise of Nazism in Germany, of fascism in other parts, eventually to Hitler's expansionism and to World War II – just remember *The Winds of War* . . .

This time we face only one alternative at best: either we leave the system to itself, let it break down, and make a fresh start thereafter; or we try to prevent this sequence of events before it is too late. I am not sure if the first option actually exists. After another catastrophe there just may be no one left who can start all over. And even for the second option, chances appear rather dim: if successful, the operation would be the first of its kind in recorded history. Nevertheless, we must try our best.

The only safe solution to our present international monetary problem is quite obvious. In fact, the groundwork has already

7

been done. We need an international reserve currency that does not give any special privilege to any country or to any international banking community. Basically, this currency exists in the form of the IMF's Special Drawing Rights (SDRs).

World peace does not depend on money alone. But a functioning international monetary system that is fair and that allows equal participation for all is a necessary precondition for peace. If we fail to understand the urgent need for change in the present system, the traditional cycle of boom, crisis, and bust will repeat itself with all its costs, suffering, and misery – unless the crisis explodes into World War III and a nuclear holocaust.

The international financial system has reached another historic crossroads. In the nineteenth century the world's great creditor nation was Britain. It encouraged global prosperity by exporting capital and permitting other nations free access to its markets, so they could service their debts. In the 1920s and 1930s, the international economy broke down as the creditor nations tried to solve their unemployment problems through protectionism. This, in turn, made it impossible for the debtor nations to service their loans. The German reparations crisis of that time must have seemed remote and unimportant to the average US citizen. As events transpired, however, it proved to have a direct bearing on millions of people's lives and fortunes. The present debt crisis may be similar.

All too often Americans – like Europeans – tend to forget some basic facts about today's world. Americans also may feel that being between two oceans makes them safe. But what about their southern border and a rising wave of immigrants? What about world population trends and population shift within the US? There are over 4 billion people in the world now, of which 2 billion live in Asia, and one out of eight people on earth is an African. Soon there will be 6 billion people, and most of the increase will occur in the Third World.

One earth but two worlds, a kind of feudalistic split into a rich world and a poor world, as a colleague on our Commission said, is not a viable prospect for the future. The way a society responds to the needs of the poor through its public policies is the test of its sense of justice or injustice. Aid and charitable gifts are necessary, but they are not enough. Organized social

8

efforts to secure justice and human rights are indispensable, at home and internationally.

US debt-crisis policy – which other major industrial countries pretty much accept without complaint – is being formulated as if bankers alone had a major stake in the outcome. Although it is widely recognized that US banks face the prospect of collapse if debtors do not pay, it is less well understood that US workers and businesses will lose jobs and markets if the debtors, especially the Latin American debtors, *try* to pay.

At present, the United States is experiencing its most dramatic transformation in its international financial position since World War II. America has become a debtor nation on recorded transactions for the first time since 1914.

Still, with more than a quarter of the world's annual income, the United States continues to play a pre-eminent role in an increasingly interdependent world economy. But the common crisis goes far beyond the monetary realm. Numerous reports in the United States and elsewhere have pointed to its various aspects. They warn that the world faces disaster on various fronts unless it changes course. They all point out that nations separated by geography, culture, and ideology are now linked in a single and complex technological network confronted with common challenges. The global ecology, which is under increasing stress, is only one very visible area with ever-growing problems.

But these same links also create hope, according to those who work on these questions and who possibly know more about them. There is hope for a new form of just global community. These interconnections call for much greater attention to the stark inequities in living conditions and in the control of resources within and between countries.

For what some see as growing interdependence is regarded by many as a pattern of domination and dependence. And the extreme inequalities are undeniable. Literally half the world's population lives in degrading misery and abject poverty, and hundreds of millions of people are suffering and dying every day because our global economy is not as just as it could be.

Under these circumstances there is no justification for the fantastic misuse of human creativity and material resources in producing weapons of war on a gigantic scale, aggravating our

9

economic difficulties and channelling resources away from the task of creating a more just and productive world economy.

In science, as in other spheres, our world is divided between the rich and the poor. In the North, in the industrialized countries of East and West with an income of $5,000 billion, we spend 2 per cent of this on nonmilitary science and development research – more than $100 billion a year. The poorer South, with one-fifth of the income – about $1,000 billion – spends no more that $2 billion on science and technology. This is the price tag for just one nuclear submarine – and there are more than a hundred of them in the oceans of the world. For the price of a single nuclear submarine, five hundred centres like the International Centre for Theoretical Physics in Trieste, Italy, could be funded for one year, as we are told by Professor Abdus Salam, who is not only the director of that institute and a genius in his field but above all a concerned scientist.

The growth of population and the limits of our resources are issues of equally deep concern, though we are concerned about the quality of life as well as its quantities. Poverty and hunger are not simply the result of large families. Family size depends on economic development, education, respect for woman and their role, availability of health care, and cultural traditions.

The gap between rich and poor – people both individually and as nations – is widening. Developing countries share the responsibility for their own failures and destinies. Yet the pervasive power and economic strength of the industrialized countries implies a greater responsibility to serve the causes of human dignity and human rights.

Although the United States cannot save the developing world alone, its strength gives it the opportunity to launch a worldwide effort for justice and economic rights. This effort would be in the best American tradition. Individual rights and community responsibilities are linked, not opposed, as the churches tell us. The common good, according to the *Second Draft of the US Bishop's Pastoral Letter on Catholic Social Teaching and the US Economy*, is the sum of those conditions of social life which allow social groups and their members access to their own fulfillment. These include the rights to basic necessities, fundamental freedoms, and the protection of relationships. The full range of human rights is outlined in John XXIII's *Peace on Earth*, which echoes and supports the United Nations Universal Declaration of Human Rights. They include the rights to life, food, clothing, shelter, rest, medical care, employment, healthful working conditions, a family income sufficient for dignified living, the possibility of property ownership, and security in the event of sickness, unemployment, and old age.

Economic rights are as essential as civil freedoms. They should be granted an analogous status. Securing these human rights will require hard work. There is need for dialogue and room for diversity of opinion on how to do it. But there can be no question of *whether* to do it. The various issues are interconnected. Their resolution requires difficult trade-offs. Many suggested reforms would be expensive, but not as expensive as the failure to act.

There was a time, not so many years ago, that US citizens prided themselves on their foreign-aid programs. During the late 1940s and again in the 1960s, economic-assistance programs were looked upon as vital expressions of American idealism. And I can testify what that generosity has meant for my country and for Europe, what it still means today as we continue to benefit from it with the local-currency counterpart funds of the Marshall Plan gifts and loans being recycled into new credits. Yet I know that among younger people, not all have even heard of the Marshall Plan, much less have any idea of its importance. A minority consider it to be a part of an imperial policy of the era, which they detest.

I can assure you that the magnificent idea of the Marshall Plan, its system of gifts and loans to shattered postwar Europe, made our recovery possible. It assured our survival and allowed democracy to flourish. The present generation owes its health to it. The Plan restored the fabric of European life. And I believe that there could be no better memorial for those who had that splendid idea than a major cooperative international effort to fight hunger and misery in the Third World, a major enterprise for peace and development. And the dimension of this enterprise should be commensurate with American generosity and largesse in the immediate postwar years.

The United States, which in the past had been a leader in

international cooperation and economic assistance, has substantially reduced its international-development efforts. Today, Americans spend proportionately far less on aid than people in a number of European countries. I understand many of the reasons for the dwindling commitment, but I cannot accept them. And I sincerely hope that this attitude will change again as understanding of the most critical world situation grows. I never believed that the American people could be indifferent to poverty and starvation anywhere in the world. The recent wave of support for the victims of famine in Africa was evidence of their compassion. I am convinced that government policies will once again come to reflect the deep-rooted ideals of the people.

When the nations of the world join in an enterprise to improve the chances of common survival, to overcome our common crisis, and to work for common security through the promotion of peace and development, the most powerful and richest nation cannot stand aside – and no one else would want it to.

It is my sincere hope that my views and arguments presented in this book will help convince the readers and, if necessary, convert them into believers in the moral state of man and the international ideal. For, as John Donne, the great mystic of the seventeenth century, put it:

> No man is an island, entire of itself;
> every man is a piece of the continent,
> a part of the main;
> if a clod be washed away by the sea,
> Europe is the less,
> as well as if a promontory were,
> as well as if a manor of thy friends
> or of thine own were;
> any man's death diminishes me,
> because I am involved in mankind;
> and therefore never send to know
> for whom the bell tolls;
> it tolls for thee.

Bonn, January 1986   *W.B.*

INTRODUCTION TO THE BRITISH EDITION

We live in times full of drama and confusion. What we are experiencing is not a process of measurable change, but a series of wide-ranging upheavals in science and technology, in economic affairs and in international relations.

Numerous crises in many parts of the world provide ample evidence of this radical change. But it would be quite wrong to allow ourselves to be hypnotized by that suggestive term 'crisis'. There is no hope of things simply returning to normal. We will continue to face radical change and we must find adequate solutions. Not to do so could be fatal.

To my way of thinking, worldwide change is necessary today for three main reasons. First, there is the need for a profound restructuring of the world economy to increase world productivity and to provide jobs. Secondly, there is the persistent East–West rivalry and arms build-up. And last, but not least, are the completely unsatisfactory North–South relations between the industrialized states on the one hand and the developing countries on the other.

First, the profound change in the pattern of the world's economy: The period of persistent economic growth on the scale which we experienced in the Fifties and Sixties would seem to be over for the foreseeable future. This holds true for the whole world. In western industrialized countries, in the eastern industrial societies and in the developing countries as a group – wherever we look there is now much slower economic progress. In some parts we even see output declining.

We do not need to look far for the social and political consequences. For many years, it was possible to offset social tensions in western democratic societies because there was enough economic growth to go around for all, or almost all. As a result, even the broad masses of our nations derived benefit from a steadily rising level of affluence. Whenever divergent interests met head-on, a material compromise was at hand.

Today, this sort of compromise is available only on a rather limited scale. In many countries, the pace of social strife has quickened, even if everyone may not yet be aware of it.

It will require a considerable amount of imagination and sensitivity to balance the various interests in our modern industrial societies within the limits to further growth which are now visible, and at the same time to maintain a smoothly functioning political process. Our democracies will not remain what they have been if our elected leaders leave the field uncontested to rival groups or simply stand aside.

If a new balance among the various factions and interests is not achieved, there will be an acceleration of a trend already noticeable in certain places: a loss of confidence in those in political office along with a dwindling faith in the viability of modern democracy. I see the possibility of an ever more widespread alienation – alienation of the sort expressed by quite a number of the younger people – an escapism inspired by a blend of political weariness and anxiety about modern civilization. Misgivings about the whole purpose of technical progress might combine with a dangerous nostalgia for the apparent peacefulness and tranquillity of former times – a peacefulness and tranquillity which never really existed.

Secondly: The arms race has not only continued apace, it has assumed dimensions which can no longer be grasped by the human mind. Every day the world spends millions and millions of dollars for military purposes; we stockpile more explosives than food, and we are more concerned with what is called military security than with hunger and malnutrition, which in the end may pose an even greater threat. Every warning seems to have fallen on deaf ears. All efforts to achieve concrete arms limitation seemed to be frustrated by the feeling of a growing threat from the other side. Sometimes, warnings miscarry because the overall situation becomes unstable. And regional conflicts expand. It is small wonder that many people were beginning to ask whether the policy of détente ever really existed, and if it did whether or not it had failed definitely, and if it had what alternative there might be.

It is still my feeling that the ideas underlying the efforts to reduce tension at the end of the Sixties and the beginning of the Seventies have not been futile. In my view, these ideas did not flow from illusions, but from the pragmatic desire to supplement defence with a political dimension for safeguarding peace, producing attempts to help evolve a common interest in arms limitation. That remains indispensable. And it has, as we know, led to reopening of talks between the two superpowers.

The further commitment of valuable resources to even more gigantic arms projects would render it impossible to devote one's attention to the great problems which exist side by side with the arms race, with equally frightening possibilities. And we may well fool ourselves when we see security as purely a military problem, as if population explosion and hunger, the limited resource base of our earth and the abuse of the environment were risks of a lesser category.

Still, we must not become discouraged. However painful setbacks may be, they don't give us an excuse for simply turning our backs. The important thing is to learn from mankind's mistakes and to stay on course for peace and cooperation: without illusions, but with steadfastness.

Thirdly: Reshaping relations between industrialized and developing countries – 'North and South', as it is often called in international discussions. In point of fact, this much used term 'North–South' inadequately conveys the complexity of highly different levels of development and gravely imbalanced relations between rich and poor peoples, richer and poorer nations. But it is certainly no exaggeration when I say that I regard this as *the* social challenge of our times – a challenge to all people with a sense of responsibility.

Today, one-fifth of humanity suffers from hunger and malnutrition in developing countries. The majority of these men, women and children live in South and South-East Asia and the sub-Saharan regions of Africa. During the last decade, many countries in these regions have been able to make but little progress. If no fundamental changes take place, then this decade cannot be expected to bring any improvements either. It might well mean more *under*development.

Therefore, it is perfectly understandable that the developing nations have been calling for fundamental reforms in the world economy for something like two decades. However, as in the case of domestic reforms in most of our own countries, the scope for international reforms has narrowed considerably.

The picture I have just drawn is not a very happy one, but it does reflect the real situation. Under these circumstances, we must try to implement adequate policies. It seems clear to me that employment policy and structural policy accompanying it cannot be left solely to the oft-invoked 'self-healing forces' of the market economy. Anyone who has held a position of responsibility in a country like mine in recent years will never be tempted to underestimate the thrust of the market-economy system. Nevertheless, experience at home and abroad, especially in less developed countries, lèads me to believe that an important role must be played by public responsibility in a number of sectors.

At the same time, everyone with a knowledge of the current situation in the public sector, and in large private enterprise as well, will realize the importance of avoiding bureaucratic excesses. In any case, gross materialism cannot be the sole *raison d'état* in a democracy. I am not pleading the virtues of high-minded renunciation; I am pleading the case of justice, solidarity and fair treatment, both within states and between states. In a period of rapid and deep-rooted change, we shall only survive if individual interests are embedded within an overall framework of social solidarity. From this flows the perception that government decisions must be taken with the closest possible involvement of the people concerned and affected by such measures.

The holders of political office must remain receptive to fresh ideas, whether they themselves are able to develop them or not. Those who believe that many things cannot continue as they have in the past must be taken seriously. Should we not be mounting a more active search for solutions which correspond to the economic and ecological requirements of our time in order to establish, wherever possible, a stable equilibrium?

So what is the plan of action? First and most important, the leaders of the two superpowers must discharge their specific responsibilities towards other nations. They must do what has to be done in order to create that minimum of confidence without which predictability is impossible. Otherwise, there will be no end to the arms race, and without an end to the arms race, détente cannot survive; and without détente there can be only a fragile security.

Europe has long ceased to be the hub of the world. Nevertheless, it remains of great importance for the whole of mankind that we in Europe prove capable of maintaining peace and thereby furnish an example of how differing interests can be reconciled without explosive conflicts. It is my firm belief that we need détente in order to safeguard peace and to find the strength for balancing the interests of North and South.

My conclusion derives from lifelong experience – a life marked by ups and downs, disappointments and encouragements. What humanity needs is not less détente, but more negotiations and cooperation. In addition to humanitarian and idealistic challenges, there is a good deal of legitimate self-interest involved. Peace is not only good for others. More exchange will be to our advantage as well as to that of others. The jobs of many of our young people, and even more so, of their children, will depend upon speeding up the process of development and exchange.

It will be difficult for anyone to escape the conclusion, after reading this book, that interdependence is the dominant fact of life in our era – that we are responsible for each other's wellbeing, and that we must learn to live together or face the prospect of perishing together.

I am not without hope. Indeed, realistic confidence in our capacity to build a better world for all has been the foundation of my thinking and the motivation of my work.

All of us are responsible for helping to create our common future.

W.B.

I

A QUESTION OF COMMON SURVIVAL

1. *Appalling Discrepancies*

Most of us have no idea of the alarming record 1986 will leave behind: very probably in that one year over 1,000 billion dollars will have been spent, worldwide, on military purposes of various kinds.

Look at this vast expenditure of funds in another way: every minute of every day of the week – work days and holidays alike – the nations of the world are spending around two million dollars on armaments and other military expenditure.

And every minute, some 30 children aged under five or six are dying because they do not have enough to eat, or there is no clean water for them, and because they are denied any kind of medical care.

In 1974, an admirable pronouncement was made: within a decade no child should go to bed hungry. This was directly after the Sahel zone and Bangladesh famine disasters of that time. In 1984 UNICEF, the United Nations Children's Fund, calculated that 40,000 children in the age group mentioned were dying every day.

The shocking television pictures of the latest East African disasters have roused many from apathy, although the pictures convey only a part of the terrible truth. For experts tell us that the world is now producing, and has at its disposal, enough food to feed the whole of humanity.

I believe that even if there were no other discrepancy to challenge our common sense of human responsibility than this – that millions of children starve to death when they could be saved with a fraction of the funds spent on the build-up of armaments – it ought to move us to anger. Nor should we allow ourselves to be fobbed off with nonsense couched in political leaders' jargon.

However, the number of those who recognize the existence and the glaring injustice of this discrepancy is growing, though such people may express what they feel in very different ways, because of their different cultures and political systems. Avoidable hunger *is* a glaring injustice, on a large scale. And systems, whether national or international, are to blame if they cannot overcome glaring injustice and avert great danger for mankind. There are many, particularly young people, who feel deep distress when confronted by persistent hunger among vast numbers of individuals over large areas of the world, when it could be relieved with a small part of the funds absorbed by ever-increasing military expenditure. (It makes no difference to this argument whether estimated expenditure on armaments is set slightly too high or actually lags behind the reality.)

A few years ago, an Asian friend of mine, now dead, put the question of priorities in his own way: why had President Kennedy appealed to his country's scientists not to be content simply to take up the challenge of the Soviet Sputnik (of which they had scientific understanding at the time)? Why had Kennedy set them the task of putting an American on the moon? And why had the scientists asked for ten years to do it and 20 billion dollars? My Nepalese friend, B. P. Koirala, who was even better acquainted with his country's prisons than with its seat of government, and who asked his questions quietly, having cancer of the larynx, but no less forcibly for that, wondered why fifty billion could not be mobilized to help conquer the worst of global poverty.

We are not concerned with details here, but with the basic principle, which is absolutely sound. Equally sound is the method of putting it into practice: initially by reallocating 10 or even just 5 per cent of global armaments expenditure, at the same time making it clear that this would be in the interests of the richer countries and the more prosperous sections of humanity themselves, and showing just how much that would be the case. But obviously many of those in power in the East and the West, the North and the South still (and for how much longer?) regard it as wrong to reduce arms expenditure by a modest percentage, and, instead, using the funds for productive purposes. Using them, indeed, to finance projects which would accord as much with the precepts of solidarity and love for one's neighbour, as with the well-understood self-interest of those states which would be most affected by this modest reallocation of resources – including, in the long term, the interests of their security.

It is now being said by eminent if not altogether conservative experts that the only way to overcome the international financial crisis will be to divert funds earmarked for defence budgets. Over the last few years I have said repeatedly (and I have not let the mockery of officialdom deter me) that the unrestrained squandering of funds on arms policies has contributed very largely to the current difficulties of the international economy. To put it even more bluntly: the arms race inhibits the development of the world economy.

Not only the economic consequences, however, but other connections in this context have long gone unrecognized. I remember a discussion in Berlin in the early summer of 1978, to which I was invited by the Aspen Institute. I spoke on the connections between arms and development, an unfamiliar train of thought to most of my otherwise knowledgeable audience, and I had no cause to complain of any inattention. Then, however, one participant of whom I thought particularly highly came out with his opinion that arms control was so difficult a subject, I would do better not to make it even more complicated by mixing it up with 'issues of development aid' . . . I have not been able to take that advice.

The tendency to keep East–West and North–South issues scrupulously apart – except in 'strategic' questions – has now slightly lessened. Reference to the way North–South relations have acquired a new dimension in the struggle for world peace is no longer contradicted with quite such a lack of understanding. And more people acknowledge that mass misery and extreme underdevelopment have become *the* great social challenge of our time. Such understanding alone does not, of course, get us very far. But in order to act judiciously we must realize some simple truths.

Where mass hunger reigns, we cannot speak of peace. If we want to get rid of war, we must ban mass misery too. Morally, it makes no difference whether human beings are killed in war or condemned to death by starvation. The international community – in the dual sense of concerned citizens and responsible governments – has no more important task, besides controlling the build-up of arms, than overcoming mass hunger and other sources of misery which could be avoided.

We must not let ourselves be blinded or paralysed by the gigantic, scarcely conceivable size of the figures involved. Nor is the moral challenge to our common humanity to be assessed by calculating whether the sum of human misery is even greater than the given estimates, or perhaps a little less, but solely by the possibility of feeding our hungry fellow men and women. We must come to realize that a sense of solidarity with those who are so much worse off is also the way to find partners in a world that needs cooperation; this is true not least of the economy.

Vast rounded-up numbers can easily make the fate of individuals involved congeal into statistics. Astronomical figures overtax our capacity to grasp them. I remember how during the Second World War under Nazi tyranny, a sense of the sheer extent of the toll being taken – the numbers of the fallen, murdered, imprisoned, exiled – was in great danger of being lost, or never even felt at all. Churchill once said that if a human being dies, it is a tragedy; if 100,000 die, it is statistics. We can identify more easily with a small number, particularly in a familiar environment. Victims on a scale of millions become an abstract idea, with no sense of closeness to it. One nought more or less conveys little to us.

But there is no help for it: we must familiarize ourselves with the reality behind those huge figures. We must try to make the meaning they obscure clear to ourselves (and others): 450 to 500 million people, at a cautious estimate, are undernourished or suffer chronic hunger. It is small comfort to know that the figure was even higher five years ago; in the report published early in 1980 by the Commission I chaired, the number of those suffering from malnutrition was put at 500 to 600 million. The impression of obscene horror is further reinforced by the fact that no institute – or governmental department, or international organization – is in a position to make calculations which are anywhere near exact and which agree. Often they disagree over the extent of the suffering, or they offer 'reassuring' information, such as the fact that the number of the starving seems to remain stable although world population continues to increase rapidly.

If we start from the notion of 'absolute poverty', of which more later, we get larger figures. However, we may assume that over the last few years, despite the new famine in Africa and the effects of the international debt crisis, not *everything* has deteriorated even further worldwide.

Recently, although the background remains very gloomy, there have also been encouraging signs. Great efforts have been made in, and with the help of, many of the developing countries, and they have not been entirely unsuccessful. It really is worth while contributing to projects of developmental aid and North–South cooperation and participating in them. I have been able to see for myself that it is not just a case of everything having become even worse.

There are impressive signs of changes for the better:

- India can now feed herself and is no longer plagued by regularly recurring famines. This does not alter the fact that great numbers of Indians are still destitute, suffering from lack of food and preventable diseases.
- In China, a billion people have enough to eat, where famines used to be the order of the day.
- In South-East Asia – in city states such as Singapore and Hong Kong, countries like South Korea, Taiwan and Malaysia – there has been an industrial explosion which retains its objective significance even where social reforms have left much to be desired. In some countries of this region, obvious progress has also been made in the provision of food supplies.
- Latin America, which is at an altogether more advanced stage of development than the other regions of the Third World, is going through a process of conspicuous if demanding renewal. One wonders if the new democracies will be able to cope with the burden of debt weighing on them, and how they will deal with their contrasting extremes: Brazil, for example, has risen to tenth place among the industrial powers, and exports food on a large scale, while millions of its own people live in the direst poverty.

Constantly we encounter serious inconsistencies in the Third World, and in the whole wide area of North–South relationships. As I write this, it is hard to tell how the two superpowers will make any real progress along the path of serious negotiations. I cannot see that those who wield political power are moving determinedly towards promising solutions to the crises of hunger, debt, employment and trade. We also have a crisis of the environment. Survival remains an open question.

2. Rapid Worldwide Change

A good twenty years ago I had to speak on the international situation, not for the first and not for the last time: I remarked that the world now changed more within a generation than it used to in the course of centuries, scarcely so bold an assertion as to lay me open to any charge of exaggeration.

Among the far-reaching changes of recent decades in my own country, and in many regions of Europe and America, are the new self-confidence of women and the perceptible steps being taken towards social equality. More questions are now asked about underdevelopment in other parts of the world – economic, social, cultural, juridical, political. Even discounting rhetoric, it is plain that greater recognition is given to the part played by women in the developmental process. That strikes me as being of historical significance.

Let us look at those other crucial changes that have confronted us since the Second World War:

- The number of autonomous states belonging to the United Nations has tripled: from the 51 original member states it has risen to 159 (the Sultanate of Brunei is at present the latest on the list).
- Former colonial dominance has been overcome, apart from a few lingering remnants, as witness the large number of nations which have become politically independent, and in so far are 'sovereign states'. A new epoch in the history of mankind is concerned with the struggle of these new states (many with a rich past of their own, others with their boundaries rather

24

arbitrarily drawn by foreign masters) for their economic decolonization – or simply their ability to survive.

- The population of the world has doubled to 4.8 billion.
- Gross world product as statistically recorded (that is, the sum of goods and services produced in the world's states or national economies) has quadrupled; so has energy consumption.
- There is still a gulf between rich and poor, and in some ways it is even wider, but the dividing line does not coincide with the division between developing and industrial countries: there is depressing poverty to be found in the North, and equally there is provocative superfluity in the South.
- Great achievements in science and technology must be set against a good deal on the debit side: natural resources are being plundered, and the process reveals the lack of restraint in an economy over-orientated towards a narrow concept of its own profitable interests – or towards bureaucratically planned targets which are remote from reality.
- The use of nuclear energy has become reality, but has not had the expected results: the problems of defusing anxiety about it have not been solved. Its military use could cause untold harm if theories of deterrence, or the nerves of those concerned, or computer reliability should fail.
- After an unmanned (Soviet) satellite began circling the earth in 1959, and a manned (American) module landed on the moon in 1969 – you will recall my Nepalese friend's question in connection with those events – a man-made device left the solar system for the first time in 1983. The militarization of space is now in progress, and has caused additional insecurity.
- While the East–West conflict and North–South problems mingle, the arms race between the superpowers has spread to large areas of the world, originally unaffected, where it has found company and been imitated.
- Despite all our progress in science and technology, in the dissemination and sharing of knowledge, the states of the world have not mastered their political, economic and indeed ecological difficulties, individually or as a body. Whether the point at issue is the arms race or world hunger, the environment or energy, unemployment or inadequate social welfare, we meet everywhere with irrational procedures.

My first thesis, nevertheless, is that in the medium and long term, North and South have more interests in common or running parallel – and so do East and West, particularly here in Europe – than most people have yet recognized. This should not be confused with having an eye to short-term economic advantage.

My other thesis is that a faster tempo of development in the South will also benefit people in the North. This proposition has been much criticized for being allegedly based on a 'Keynesian' concept, an objection which, however, has nothing to do with economic theory, but is part of an attempt to talk urgent problems out of existence and defend a form of international relations in which the weaker goes to the wall. Lord Keynes' theories aside, the regions of the world cannot afford an international economic policy of a self-centred and keenly competitive nature for very much longer. Global dangers are growing, and it is highly inadvisable to leave them out of our economic calculations.

In any case, the industrial countries clearly have an interest, one that needs no kind of interpretation in terms of economic theory, in strengthening their economic and in particular their agricultural involvement with other parts of the world. Any calculation, even one of only medium-term relevance, will lead to that conclusion.

Among circumstances that have changed is the fact that what was previously described as the 'world economy' has now, for the first time in history, actually become 'global', if not yet as unambiguously so as has technology. But while we can observe a process of internationalization in the economic area, many states are still excluded from decision-making. We also have the peculiarities of the system. Matters of international economic importance are still decided by those states which hold economic and financial power. Even in the European Community, we perpetuate the anachronism of making 'national' decisions on matters which can no longer be decided at national level.

How far can the uncertainties of the international economy since the early Seventies be attributed to the poor development of North–South relations? Can one deny that the oil price crisis had far-reaching effects, not least on the economic activities of those developing countries which are not oil producers? Is there any doubt that the rise in exports from the newly industrialized developing countries has created problems in many markets? And, can one seek the source of the worldwide economic failures of the last ten or fifteen years – with regard to monetary stability, growth, employment, international trade – anywhere but in the centres whence the great crisis of the Thirties itself proceeded?

As one who saw where it led last time, I ask: who can really tell whether the crisis of the Eighties will be overcome any better than the crisis of the Thirties? There are more than 30 million unemployed in Western industrial countries: that is no light matter. The figures in which absolute poverty is expressed can only horrify a normal mind. Reference to the depth of the structural change can at least convey something of the gravity of the problems we have to surmount. But one cannot see how the connections between issues of finance, trade, commodities and food are to be controlled.

The economic situation certainly appeared rather better in 1984–5 than a few years earlier; there was a remarkable upswing in the USA, and also in Canada and Japan, less so in Europe. There was no all-clear for the poorer countries; many of them experienced stagnation and retrogression. And there was widespread speculation as to when we might expect the next American recession. Meanwhile, the extent to which the United States was financing its budget deficits by 'blood transfusions' was something to be viewed with concern, as was the unfortunate effect of the high interest rates associated with them. (In the early summer of 1984, one of the big banks of the USA was barely saved from collapse.) World trade and economic activity, said one of the International Monetary Fund's forecasts, which are usually not so bad, would perceptibly lose impetus in 1985–6. For the rest, I can only suggest from my own experience that we should not let prophets bluff us over the international economy.

When my Commission published its Report six years ago, we thought it imperative for governments to apply themselves, urgently, to the issue of North–South cooperation and give it a more constructive form. Otherwise, we feared, the international situation would deteriorate even further. And we were right: the situation has indeed deteriorated. I am not suggesting that we should now resign ourselves to despair on that account. But why

A growing number of people will stand by these simple truths:

- That a precipitate increase in global expenditure on armaments is almost inevitably accompanied by economic setbacks and social damage – even if the great powers may sometimes manage to hang their own millstones around other necks.
- That the international monetary system has come adrift because it was not well enough adapted to fundamental change in the structure of the system of states.
- That even in the industrial countries, more employment could be created if we could at last manage to create the financial prerequisites for bringing together the unsupplied needs of the 'South' with our own surplus capacities.
- That it must impose intolerable burdens even on the industrial countries if the revenues of the developing countries from their commodity exports are reduced, as they often are, to a fraction of their proper value, while little consideration is given to anticipating the demand for commodities and energy in the years to come.
- That the debt problem – the position at the end of 1984 was that the developing countries were indebted to the amount of at least $850 billion – is due not only to the supposedly irresponsible governments of the debtor countries, but at least as much to their partners bearing responsibility in the creditor nations.

hide the fact that the dangers, taken as a whole, have grown even greater?

3. Comprehensive Answers to Global Problems

I cannot over-emphasize: if we neglect the tasks of the present and fail to invest in the future, we may arm ourselves to death without actually waging a major war, and bring our economies to the point of collapse. The North itself can survive only if the South is allowed independence and a decent life.

In 1984, a good deal was written on population questions; the second United Nations conference on population policy took place in Mexico City. In the field of North–South relations, only the Latin American debt mountain and the new famine disaster in Africa aroused anything like comparable interest at the time. Yet almost all that was said at that conference in Mexico had been known for years, and some of us had come to an agreement on it long before. We knew that:

• World population increases by over a million every five days.
• World population will rise from 4.8 billion in 1984 to 6.1 billion at the turn of the century: which means that in the Eighties and Nineties alone, i.e. within two decades, the human race will have increased by almost 2 billion. When I went to school in the year 1920, that was the number of people then living on the earth.
• Nine-tenths of the increase is in Third World countries, which have a very young age structure.

Thus, to a considerable extent, the future is programmed. However, it still remains to be seen whether world population can be stabilized at ten or twelve billion in the middle of the next century. I write this as one who has learned that this is another area in which excessive agitation is out of place. From all we now know, the earth has room for more people than was thought in my youth, and even later.

But world population cannot expand indefinitely, and faster than economic output. It is up to our human will and not Fate to decide whether the population explosion, as it is frequently called, actually ends in destruction or not.

Twenty years ago one aroused smiles, or outright laughter, by merely hinting at the consequences the ruthless plundering of the earth would have for future generations. Many people are now becoming aware of the dangers, and the measures we have failed to take. First the warnings of the Club of Rome, then the American *Global 2000* report, presented to President Carter in 1980, made it clear that protection of the environment is a genuinely global issue: there is *world*wide air pollution, there are serious *world*wide threats to our water and our forests; species of plants and animals are disappearing in great numbers and within a short period of time. Retribution is coming for the thoughtless and narrow perception of economic interests, and only a few people realize that there are limits to the exploitation of nature.

What it will mean if trees are no longer able to counteract the pollution of the air is slowly dawning. But can our imaginative faculties gauge the climatic consequences of the disappearance of the Amazonian forests? Many people on our earth are busily engaged in turning the dreadful vision of a global environmental catastrophe into reality.

In addition, an ever closer connection emerges not just between hunger and armaments, but between the environment and security. Here, even more than elsewhere, we see that the *status quo* must not be confused with stability.

Are we really going to put our faith in what is ideologically seen as the free play of supposedly free forces to save what may yet be saved? Or are we going to address ourselves to problems which can be resolved only by mutually coordinated action? It ought not to be hard to answer that question once we have even an inkling of, for instance, the effect of continued deforestation. I am not and never was in favour of playing off North–South and environmental issues against each other. When I received the Nobel Peace Prize, I spoke on both those aspects of our global domestic policy, and added, 'If the natural supplies of water, oxygen and living matter on our planet run out, then humanity, poisoned and starving, will no longer care about the peaceful order for which we strive today.'

Since then, argument has been piled upon argument in emphatic refutation of those arrogant folk who think they know everything, and do not; managers of the 'established disorder' who like to be acclaimed as practical politicians, but really thrive only because ordinary citizens do not see through (or want to see through) their complacent trickery. Human reaction certainly falls far short of what it should be to the consequences of the changes I have outlined. But a sense is spreading that we are dealing with problems that are more and more significant to the *whole* world. The worldwide interdependence of problems is a sign of the times in which we live.

And there is an increasing concentration of problems which

exist independently of a country's political and social systems and alignment within world politics. Whether research is done at institutes in Boston or Moscow, whether critical minds are debating and analysing problems in São Paulo or Bombay, Peking or Tokyo, Berlin or Paris, men and women everywhere are recognizing that not only they themselves, their country or their people are affected; the great questions of the future concern humanity as a whole.

I am not claiming that community of interests can derive from this except in the recognition of mutual dependency, and perhaps also in a growing understanding of the threats to the survival of mankind (which can only be joint survival). Among enlightened and open-minded people, there can be no doubt that we face the enormous task of ensuring humanity's survival *together*, and can master it only by international cooperation. Neither the rich North nor the poor South – nor the West without, and in opposition to, the East – will be able to control their problems alone and without mutually coordinated action.

We are thus concerned with more than 'aid for the poor' – important as empathy and a sense of joint responsibility for our fellow men are and will remain. We are concerned with a view of the tasks ahead of us in the international economic context. The production of goods and the provision of services are going to be increasingly based on the worldwide division of labour. The market – not automatically the same thing as space for un-restricted trade policies to have free play – for an increasing number of industries will be a worldwide market. International economy will not just be so called, it really will be international – for good or ill.

Potential danger building up in one region – whether in power politics, the economy, the ecology or perhaps in population policy – will no longer leave other regions unaffected in the long term. Ecological and economic interaction, in particular, extend far beyond specific areas. The threat of the consequences of the arms race has long been affecting more people than those im-mediately involved.

Global and interdependent problems call for comprehensive solutions. By this I do not mean that as many tasks as possible should not be tackled regionally; in many cases this is the only feasible way, particularly if it remains as difficult as ever to safeguard international interests through intergovernmental institutions. But the tackling of tasks on a regional basis will itself prove beneficial only if mutual consideration and the conciliation of interests are observed.

There is hardly a state in the world economically strong enough to do without the conciliation of interests. That also applies to blocs and federations of states. The really important problems are of a character that transcends systems. The political system of a country and the form its economy and society take will certainly influence its ability to solve problems. But many tasks and many dangers dependent on commodities, environmental threats, the results of technological change have to be dealt with wherever industrialization progresses. There will be a race between systems to see how problems can best be resolved. But there will be no more room for one region to pursue a path of its own without coming to an understanding with other parts of the world.

I am well aware that the thesis of *one* world, of the global nature of our problems and the interdependence of the world's various regions is sometimes dismissed as a myth – in the West, in the East, in the developing countries too. I have examined the arguments with the utmost readiness to exercise self-criticism, and I cannot find my thesis disproved. Indeed, many of the objections raised strike me as being marked, rather, by a disinclination to overcome cherished notions, egotism, or simply the defensive pragmatism of the politics of the day.

Over the last few years, we have frequently heard it said that the economic situation of the leading industrial countries must improve before more can be done for the developing countries and for North–South cooperation. I have always taken this for an excuse. For such an attitude fails to recognize the advantages that faster and better development of the Third World can mean for *all* concerned.

It would be presumptuous of me to examine those answers offered to my fellow men and women of widely differing cultures in response to the most profound of all questions. Or to whatever beliefs they hold concerning free will and what is allegedly unalterable. But without touching upon religious or ideological convictions too closely, I would say that not only should serious misgivings be voiced, a sharp protest must be raised if we – which generally means those who govern us – meet humanity's questions about survival with a positive unwillingness to take responsibility.

When the Federal Republic of Germany was still in its infancy, I said to my friends that we could not and did not wish to go without the friendship of the peoples of the former colonies. 'We do not want them as allies in the Cold War, but as friends whom we meet on terms of respect for their own ways, their own traditions, and their particular situations.'

At the time, 25 years ago, most of us did not yet realize that we were in a unique position. In the whole history of humanity, its survival has never before been in question. For in no previous generation have men and women been able to annihilate the species as a whole, whether as the result of a war waged with nuclear weapons; or as the inevitable consequence of continued exploitation of the environment and its natural resources; or the strangulation of national economies as an alternative to investing in the future.

4. *Whose Mutual Interest?*

Confronting and possibly overcoming the North–South conflict is *the* great social challenge of our time. It is worth while looking to see where – despite all the differences in our assumptions, standards, convictions and ideologies – areas of mutual or related interest between the industrial and the developing countries may be found.

I know that this attitude is regarded with considerable distrust in parts of the Third World: are factors that are really incompatible to be lumped together? Or is the idea to explain differences away instead of helping to overcome them? Is it perhaps a fresh attempt at exchanging direct for indirect dependence, promoting imperialism by other means?

To cite one extreme case of polemics: when I was in Latin America in the autumn of 1984, I encountered not only the hackneyed criticism of those who thought I should have expressed myself in friendlier terms where Washington was concerned; I was also harshly criticized by the 'Left'. A hostile Brazilian journalist thought that I had merely intended to 'throw sand in the eyes' of the people of the Third World with my speeches on disarmament and the debt crisis, and the same applied to the report of my Commission; that I was attempting 'to eliminate the class struggle on the international plane' with ideas of peaceful dialogue and cooperation; that I wanted to give a slightly more human face to capitalism, with the real intention of perpetuating it through the exploitation of the peoples of the Third World; and that I imagined 'the proletarian nations' as being 'on their knees, begging bowl in hand, meekly asking for a little improvement in the distribution of international revenues . . .'

It is hard not to return an angry answer, but to what end? Suppose we were all, each in his own sphere of action and influence, to make concrete efforts to identify and repel the enemies of just solutions? There are far too many, even among the rich upper classes of the developing countries, who parrot phrases about the 'class struggle on the international plane', instead of applying themselves to urgently needed reforms in their own lands.

The scepticism that I have in fact often encountered was related in no small degree – even when free of hostility – to the question of whether enlightened self-interest can be an element in the common interest, and to whether those who thought like myself really believed it was possible to do away with the fundamental differences between master and servant, exploiters and exploited. Did we seriously mean to patch matters up where a clean break was called for, to practise appeasement where a struggle was inevitable?

It is sometimes asked, rather sharply, in *whose* mutual interests adaptation or conciliation would actually be, and the suspicion is frequently voiced that people who think as I do may overrate the specific experience of their own countries. Yet was not a long and laborious learning process necessary before we ourselves came to realize that higher pay increased mass buying power and was a considerable spur to our domestic economies? Greater social justice is an incitement to economic development. Can conclusions of benefit to the world economy be drawn from that?

I do *not* mean that we want to make our own model a universal criterion, or assume that our own variety of capitalist development should be set up elsewhere. I reject such ideas of coercion just as I reject a paternalistic alternative.

Moreover, even a reformist must realize that gross economic and social inequality make political equality an illusion. The tradition of my own political thought forbids me to underestimate what can be done for large sections of society, in given conditions, by the adjustment of interests. Experience tells me not to avoid a tough conflict if it is forced upon one, but to look conscientiously at what can be done for the good of one's people, or the disadvantaged classes among them, by means of negotiation, persuasion, and efforts at adjustment.

My friends in the Third World must understand that we over here have to strive for a receptive attitude in those who do not, subjectively, see themselves as exploiters, and are not about to let dubious arguments persuade them that they have a very great deal on their consciences.

We certainly do have to face the fact that the peoples of the colonial and semi-colonial countries have been defrauded. However, many of those to whom I turn in our own part of the world are not bloodsuckers first and foremost, but understand the significance of social reforms. They want to know what international reforms will mean for them. A new North–South policy will win broad support only if it contains an element of healthy self-interest over and above the appeal to our common humanity.

I know the objection raised by many who speak for the South: they are tired of being imposed on and humiliated, and would like to get right out of 'the system'. But all probability suggests that getting out, detaching themselves from the system, will lead to disillusion and further collapse. Let us make use of every chance we get for practical cooperation – the possible spread of excessive harmony in the process is a negligible risk for a clear conscience to take.

My Commission's reports are based on the concept of mutual dependence. We were convinced that the era when one could simply say 'the rich must help the poor' was past. Today we realize that the developing countries are entitled to the just proceeds of their labour and their exports, and not merely on humanitarian grounds. Also that the industrial nations would be well advised to cooperate with them in a reasonable manner, for their own and the common good.

The number of responsible people who have adopted the idea of mutual dependence as their own, rather than simply paying it lip service, may have grown but is not enough to swing the balance. However, more people are now aware of our inter-dependence than was the case a few years ago. Their jobs, their supplies of foodstuffs and energy, even the stability of the banks in which they keep their usually modest accounts, all these depend upon the health of the world economy.

My colleagues and I said that the definition of 'mutual interests' was not an adequate basis for the necessary changes. With an eye to those who are particularly disadvantaged, we emphasize the obligation of promoting international justice. Only a new spirit of solidarity, founded on respect for our own and the common good, will help to smooth the way for the necessary practical solutions. Adjustment, and the sacrifice that adjustment entails, are inevitable if gross injustices are to be abolished – between as well as within states. In the long run no nation or group of nations will save itself by dominating others or by isolating itself.

The other simple realization is that starving people are not free. Nations need bread *and* freedom. This concise solution was proffered decades ago by my Peruvian friend Haya de la Torre and other leaders of social democracy in Latin America.

The unemployed, the 'new poor', or those who are otherwise disadvantaged cannot be expected to be receptive to the problems of the developing countries – unless they do realize that projects are under way, or soon to be under way, which are also in their own interests. In any case, appeals to the guilty conscience easily fall on deaf ears when directed at those who are not in positions of power, and have only a very limited share in decision-making about the future of their country.

And should the guilty conscience stir, it is easily quieted by luxury and extravagance, irresponsibility and corruption, which flourish on a large scale in the South as well as here in the North. Thus it is not surprising that new élites have established them-selves in the South beside or instead of the old ones. Today they frequently profit by their activities on behalf of foreign or multinational companies. There is certainly no less marked a propensity to despotism and self-enrichment in the governmental, party and military bureaucracies of many of the 'new' states than elsewhere.

After the terrible disarray which German history presented to the world not so long ago, we do well not to wag a reproving finger at our Third World partners. But there is no reason why legitimate doubts should not be expressed. A dialogue between North and South must be open on both sides. As to whether an indiscriminate increase in the developing countries' association with the great industrial nations is really in their best interests, that is another question. We have object lessons which teach us not to make light of the industrial countries' problems of adjustment. But politicians supporting certain kinds of order – the organizers of madness! – are bent on opposing proposals which they label as 'planned economy' and, as already mentioned, 'global Keynesianism'. My old friend Bruno Kreisky, for many years Chancellor of Austria, had a similar experience. At the very beginning of the Seventies, when the effects of a serious worldwide rise in unemployment were being felt, he suggested tying up European industrial plant which was lying idle with the African need for infrastructure. Back came the prompt objection that financing such plans would inevitably have inflationary consequences. Lack of imagination and a pathological aversion to planned projects won the day, and the chance was lost.

The rhetorically not uncommon cliché whereby we are all said to be in the same boat provokes a legitimate question as to who is steering it, and who is just there to row. I do not myself fear that the weight of interests involved will inevitably deprive demands for far-reaching reforms of their moral quality. I think there is still plenty of room for humanitarian commitment to helping one's fellow men and women. Moreover, gestures of disinterested charity are not the only things that count in this world. But our own interests will suffer if we fail to understand the interests of others.

To the surprise of many in the Federal Republic of Germany, it turned out, in a poll taken in the summer of 1984, that 57 per cent of voters felt personal concern over the poverty and hunger of the Third World. Perhaps word had spread, among some of those

canvassed, that the funds allocated to the much-disparaged purpose of development aid were not just being thrown out of the
window. The annual report of the World Bank Group said that
for every Deutschmark provided by Bonn, DM 1.81 flowed back
into German exporting firms. That comes to over DM 100 billion
from public funds in the last three decades – a considerable sum,
though in the opinion of a considerable minority an inadequate
expression of responsibility for our fellow men. And there is
another figure we should remember too: we spend rather more
per head per year on flowers than we spend on public development aid.

5. *Peace at Risk*

It is said that in the whole history of warfare, exceptionally
dangerous weapons have never gone off of their own accord. I
would not rely on that. History has never before known a period
in which there has been such comprehensive and thorough worldwide preparation for war.

The Cold War has hinged to a great extent on control of the
Third World. World power has never been so concentrated, yet
the great powers have never been so unable to establish world
order. Political thought has seldom been so far from the level of
scientific and technological development.

The remark, repeatedly heard, that nuclear means of mass
annihilation would never be used, but were merely serving the
cause of mutual deterrence, is not very reassuring, since it does
not take human and technical failure into account. And why
should one suppose that the ever-increasing extent of destructive
potential is a suitable way of reducing the idea of the use of those
means of destruction to absurdity?

It is worth taking another look at the dimensions. When the
Geneva negotiations failed in the autumn of 1983, experts estimated that around 40,000 nuclear weapons – some said 50,000 –
had built up in the arsenals of the two superpowers, with a
destructive power a million times that of the bomb dropped on
Hiroshima. Experts might argue as to whether it was now
possible to extinguish every human life six, seven or eight times

over. Europe was experiencing a long period of peace. But nothing could get around the simple realization that the development of modern weaponry had brought vast and hitherto unknown risks into being.

- The fact that modern engines of destruction could go into action independently, through technical error or human failure, cannot really be dismissed in deceptively reassuring terms much longer, and it cannot be repeated often enough.
- The increasing militarization of the developing countries is a cause of rising insecurity.
- In addition, we shall also have the consequences of the race which is now beginning for the militarization of outer space.
- Scientists are in no doubt that the northern hemisphere at least would be plunged into a 'nuclear winter' after an attack by nuclear weapons. Food supplies, the economic system, transport and health services would break down, not only in those areas directly hit, but in other parts of the earth as well. Many species of plants and animals would disappear. It is probable, but not certain, that mankind would be among the species entirely wiped out by a nuclear war.
- A study commissioned by the Pentagon has come to the conclusion that a nuclear conflict between East and West would cause a drop in temperature by as much as 25 degrees, and lasting months.
- Other studies have concluded that even a small-scale nuclear war would set off the 'winter effect', condemning a large part of the world to starve to death. Some forms of life would survive nuclear war: weeds, and worms living on the sea-bed.

I do not doubt that humanity – including political leaders in the East and West and South – would *like* to survive. That does not mean it *will* survive. Peace is not an original condition: we have to 'make' peace and safeguard it. It may be the aim of all systems of belief and basic philosophical attitudes, but it is contrary to all

39

historical experience and to our knowledge of human nature to suppose that such unanimity would prevent war.

In all the argument about the risks to peace it is easy to overlook the fact that the peace with which we are dealing is maintained in the midst of war. Since 1945, there have been over 120 armed conflicts in the Third World – seldom without foreign intervention, and claiming millions of victims, all as a result of 'conventional' warfare.

The realization that a nuclear war could mean the suicide of humanity, to many of us not an entirely new one, goes largely undisputed today. But our ability to make the earth uninhabitable is a new factor. In Africa, too, changes in weather and climate would make agricultural production impossible. In other developing countries not directly affected, the lives of most human beings would also be threatened.

Universal war would entail universal destruction. Its prevention should therefore be a universal duty. But what had Pierre Trudeau, Prime Minister of Canada for many years, to say when he had given up office? The leading politicians of the Western Alliance, he remarked, had almost never touched upon the subject of war and peace in their confidential talks at summit conferences in recent years. . . .

Repeated declarations of willingness to safeguard peace are no longer enough on their own. In view of the state of affairs in which the superpowers have involved themselves, the announcement of peaceful intentions is at best a friendly signal, and in fact falls far short of the requirements of our time. What we need is a well-considered policy in those states and systems which can mobilize sufficient strength and will – in theory and in practice, in the drafting of plans and putting them into effect – in order to reinforce world peace and make it indestructible.

As a step in the right direction, demands for a freeze on nuclear armaments have recently been made: 'A pause, firmly agreed and capable of being monitored, in the testing of new types of nuclear weapons and their launching systems, as well as a similar pause in the deployment of nuclear weapons systems' (Palme Commission, December 1984). Similarly, the Four Continents Initiative, meeting in Delhi in January 1985, in addition called for a freeze on the spread of weapons into outer space.

Slowly, the idea is gaining ground that we shall be able to safeguard peace, now in mortal danger, only *together with* the supposed enemy; that the alleged, and allegedly indispensable, balance of terror must be replaced by a concept of *common* security. To reach this point, and if possible to achieve a balance of good sense and reason, certainly calls for a process of rethinking, since the balance of terror runs counter to all that most people – and those who govern them – believe they know.

The question of credibility has been raised, particularly in Europe: can we rely on such safeguards if there were an emergency destroying what might be defended? Arising from this question, a transitional stage has been proposed wherein the potential dangers on both sides could be proportionately reduced, and thus lead to mutual security.

And would the idea of common security stand any chance beyond the opposing blocs themselves? Next door to Europe, in the Middle East – which as a danger area is comparable to the Balkans before 1914 – the idea may seem objectively cogent, but will still be hard to put into effect.

Political systems must ask themselves, and be asked, how a policy of security other than one of total deterrence can be drawn up. Serious dialogue calls for a *political* initiative. In the long run, security can be achieved only through political thought and action which considers the interests of both sides in security and in increasing it if possible. Every important step which unnecessarily alarms a potential opponent is a step backwards, creating new problems.

In the long run, security for *one* side cannot be achieved by armaments which reduce the security of the *other* side. Whether we look at developments over the last thirty or ten or five years, we see that in the area of major confrontations and the evolution of weaponry, no side will feel secure, high as it may pitch its own efforts, if the other side feels increasingly insecure.

Any dialogue must start from the realization that co-existence is forced upon the world, and it is more important to organize mutual security than to pursue undeniable ideological differences regardless. Existing differences should not prevent us from cooperating.

Risks to world peace were not reduced but increased in various ways (hard as they may be to assess) by the fact that the East–West conflict and North–South differences have become intertwined. When I spoke on co-existence at Harvard over a quarter of a century ago, I started even then from the premise that the East–West situation had been accompanied and influenced by the North–South situation for years; one day, I forecast, North–South issues could even be superimposed on East–West issues.

We have not yet reached that point. It has been shown repeatedly that the main danger to world peace still proceeds from the excessive rivalries of the superpowers. However, that indubitably increases the risk that the East–West conflict will continue intruding into the Third World, with unfortunate effects, and that many Third World countries will be drawn into the arms race between the great powers. Some are only too glad to let themselves be drawn in.

The militarization of the Third World is certainly not just the result of outside influence. Unresolved political and social problems play a considerable part in the setting up of military régimes. But such régimes are then generally incapable of mastering the social, political and economic tasks they face. The area in which they usually fail most conspicuously is that of agricultural production and the processing of agricultural products.

Their commitments in the Third World have not brought much joy to either of the world powers over the last few years. They have not achieved lasting success: either in Iran or Afghanistan, or in their tug-of-war for the Indian subcontinent; or in the strategic plays made for either the Middle East or North-East Africa; nor in the Gulf War, which started at the end of 1980 with American weapons on one side and Soviet weapons on the other; while Central America shows how badly imaginary dangers can lead them astray.

The militarization of the Third World is linked with – or derives its impetus from – extensive exports of weapons, also described as 'military development aid', from industrial nations headed by the superpowers.

That more and more weapons make the world not more but less secure has yet to make its impact, especially among the majority of those who bear responsibility for the Third World countries. Arsenals of weapons are still being stockpiled in many developing countries, mostly for reasons of prestige. We in Europe or elsewhere in the industrialized world should, however, beware of expressing our indignation too vehemently. For we have not set the Third World a very good example. Far from it: in a great many cases the colonial powers have left both the heritage of old and the germ of new conflicts behind them. Variants of the Cold War have been exported. And not only armaments firms but our governments too have played an extremely active part in the trade in engines of destruction.

6. *Indira's Legacy*

When I saw Indira Gandhi for the last time, in the early summer of 1984 – in the same garden at whose gate she died a few months later – she made a more urgent impression on me than ever before: when, she asked, would Europeans be ready and able to undertake joint action with major powers from the ranks of the non-aligned countries? What action? Bringing mutual pressure to bear on the superpowers! To what end? To find a common denominator for the subjects of the arms race and the international economy! How? By planning a summit conference, and preparing for it without delay.

I am not concerned here to pay tribute to the political achievements of Nehru's daughter, or to examine the criticisms levelled at her by her opponents in their time. I will concentrate on that remarkable woman's legacy to international politics:

• In March 1983, at the Delhi conference, Indira Gandhi, on behalf of India, was appointed to chair the non-aligned countries' movement. She defined it as 'the greatest peace movement in history'. Its programme, she said, was one of independence, freedom, and equality between nations. The closing 'political declaration on disarmament, survival and co-existence in the age of nuclear weapons' bore her stamp.

• In the spring of 1984, Indira Gandhi took up the Four Continents Initiative, which has been continued by her son and successor Rajiv. Together with Presidents Alfonsín of Argentina, de la Madrid of Mexico and Nyerere of Tanzania, as well

43

as Prime Ministers Palme of Sweden and Papandreou of Greece, India appealed to the superpowers to put an end to the arms race. Along with a large number of parliamentary representatives from many lands, I associated myself with this appeal. Julius Nyerere said, with the approval of us all: 'Peace is too important to be left to the White House and the Kremlin.'

- Indira Gandhi had concentrated more on North–South than East–West questions at the conference of non-aligned countries. She expressed the sense of disappointment that two decades had passed without any progress being made in the reorganization of international economic relations. (This choice of subject also had the advantage of helping to play down political differences within the non-aligned countries. The influence of a sometimes obtrusively one-sided prejudice against the USA was considerably reduced. One quarter of the participants inclined more or less towards the Soviet Union; half did not want to commit themselves.)

- The Prime Minister of India had appointed a group of experts from the non-aligned countries to prepare a report on urgent monetary and financial issues at the end of 1983; it was ready in July 1984, and was intended as the preliminary to a high-level conference in India in the autumn of 1985. Mrs Gandhi believed that 'if you leave a problem on the technical plane too long it can easily get lost in detail'. Thus, one must raise the subject to the plane of international politics, and only those chiefly responsible were in a position to do so (an assumption which admittedly said more for her notable self-confidence than her assessment of her colleagues).

- In our conversations of June 1984, in which the present Prime Minister Rajiv Gandhi took part, we discussed the connection between détente and cooperation. In Delhi, as on my preceding visit to Peking, the questions asked about the path Europe was taking and her ability to accept new forms of cooperation were sometimes of a hopeful, sometimes of an impatiently insistent nature. Our mutual friend Shridath Ramphal, the Commonwealth Secretary-General, had said, not long before, that a coalition of the medium-sized powers in East and West, North and South was needed: a coalition aiming for peace, more sensible regulation of the world economy, and preservation of

44

the natural environment. In concrete terms, it was a matter of how a dialogue between interested powers could be initiated at a high level and lead to a summit conference as soon as possible.

• All this coincided with the way other people were thinking, so that at every stage of my Latin American tour in the autumn of 1984, I was asked to support the idea of an international meeting at the highest level, to take place within the foreseeable future, on the subject of disarmament and development, and in particular on ways to overcome the debt crisis: a conference on the model of Cancun.*

In Delhi, we were agreed that if safeguarding world peace had become the prime target, then not only must something be done to counteract the arms race and heightened East–West tensions; it was even more important to abolish those dangers arising from poverty in large parts of the world. Famine in the poverty belts of Africa and Asia will not leave the better-fed parts of our planet unaffected for ever. Where millions go hungry, we cannot regard peace as genuinely secured. Overcoming hunger is the most elementary of human needs. The efforts of the international community must be concentrated upon this issue.

Safeguarding peace, protecting the environment, and organizing economic relations sensibly are the most important tasks that we and the next generation have to face. The struggle to overcome world famine is still the most urgent challenge to our common humanity.

I belong to a generation that has learned more than once in its lifetime how war brings hunger in its wake and can lead on to famine. Are we so sure that a future generation will be spared this experience in reverse? Is it really a mistake to suppose that hunger can lead to war? Or that the peoples of the northern half of the planet, having succumbed to despair, may simply blow the whole thing up some day? Or that as the population grows apace, misery may lead to chaos, unleash terror, and bring armed conflict in its wake?

I am told that people on the brink of starvation do not look for

* Cancun was the scene of the summit meeting held at the suggestion of the Brandt Commission in October 1981, on the Atlantic coast of Mexico.

45

a fight. But history can show us examples to the contrary. And as to the future, it is nowhere written that people cannot revolt in great numbers instead of dying in silence. I agreed with something I read in a major weekly journal: 'It is true that the hungry are seldom aggressive. But can we rely on the apathy of the poor once their own forests have been cut down, their own soil cropped to death, the foundations of their own lives undermined?'

In January 1984, at a joint meeting in Rome of the members of my Commission and the Commission on Disarmament and Security, under the chairmanship of Olof Palme, which had then published its report, we stated that in view of growing economic pressure and social crises, the political instability of Third World countries might well increase, involving other powers – with the eventual risk of a nuclear war, from whose consequences no country would be safe. Greater military competition, we said, was making the economic pressure worse. . . .

In June 1982, the report of the Palme Commission said that all states would suffer if expenditure on armaments were to undermine the economic welfare of those nations with a particularly heavy involvement in international trade. Everyone would suffer if the drain on national finances for arms purposes were to endanger foreign aid or development loans. Mutual security, said the Commission, could not be set apart from a course leading towards economic recovery and the concept of mutual prosperity.

Mass poverty *can* lead to war. Where hunger rules, peace has no firm footing. In the report of my Commission we said we did not believe that the world could live in peace, or that prosperity could continue indefinitely even in the North, if large areas of the South, with hundreds of millions of people, were excluded from all real prospect of progress and left alone on the brink of survival.

That war can lead to economic redistribution is not unfamiliar in contemporary thought. A French friend of mine, former Minister of Agriculture Michel Rocard, has said that if populations grow at a faster rate than the necessities of life, and if it is decided, in the name of liberalism, that there must be no state intervention, then there are parts of the world where the future of humanity will entail revolutions and military solutions.

Elsewhere, I have read that the destruction of the soil, the rivers and forests could become a major cause of political and military instability – which could lead to revolutions and perhaps to war. In any case, it does not take much imagination to envisage the growth of hatred among many of those who are forced to live in hunger and want through no fault of their own.

We need not listen to those callous bureaucrats employed in politics or economics who will not discuss simple truths, or who bury them in a mass of trivialities. Even supposing concern over armaments development and the waste of resources it entails were exaggerated – we are still left to wonder why it should not be possible to set aside some percentage of expenditure on arms, and why the nations of the world are incapable of so doing, in order to use the funds thus diverted for practical purposes that would promote peace, and abolish mass hunger and severe poverty.

We may assume that in 1986 over $1,000 billion will be spent, globally, on military purposes. Development aid as recorded by the international organizations adds up to less than 5 per cent of that vast sum. It is hard to see why at least 5 per cent, i.e. one-twentieth of world expenditure on armaments – in addition to present development aid – should not be used to overcome world hunger and on projects of economic cooperation. (Five years ago it was worked out that even 0.5 per cent could provide agricultural equipment to improve the agrarian production of most of the poor countries so much within a decade that they could feed themselves.)

At this point I ought to mention that there are no absolutely unanimous estimates of international expenditure on arms. But the trend is clear. The very reputable Stockholm International Peace Research Institute (SIPRI) estimates a figure lower than my assumed $1,000 billion. I am going by a study made by the US Arms Control and Disarmament Authority (ACDA), according to which a good $970 billion was spent on armaments purposes in 1984, NATO and the Warsaw Pact countries being responsible for three-quarters of that sum. Authoritative British circles have come to similar conclusions. (A slight reduction in the *increase* of the American defence budget for 1986, should such a reduction occur, would scarcely alter the overall picture.)

Meanwhile we have studies to soothe us – and where do we

not? If arms expenditure were frozen (in the West), we are told, we would not see any improvement in the international economy for another twenty years, and moreover there is no indication that the arms race is 'completely out of control'....

Years ago, I countered that attitude with some comparisons which are still relevant today:

- The military expenditure of half a day would be enough to finance the World Health Organization's programme to eradicate malaria.
- The money a modern tank costs could improve storage facilities for 100,000 tonnes of rice, so that annual wastage of 4,000 tonnes or more would be avoided – a day's ration for eight million people.
- The same sum would be enough to provide 1,000 classrooms for 30,000 schoolchildren.
- The price of a fighter plane would equip 40,000 village pharmacies.
- And my colleagues added this example: the price of a new nuclear submarine is equivalent to the education budgets of 23 developing countries with 160 million children of school age.

I am impressed to find how openly it is now being said, even by financial experts and leading bankers, that only an end to the arms race will extricate us from our common crisis. At the same time the connection between the arms race and the world economy, which strikes an instinctive chord in us, could do with more detailed scientific illumination. To the normal human mind, it is perfectly plain that social wealth is being devoured by armaments, while lacking elsewhere. Even scientific analysis will not reveal otherwise.

Meanwhile, time is running out. We are said to be approaching midnight, and I am afraid that is indeed the case. But I also think we should understand the full meaning of the French riddle about the nature of 'exponential growth'. In a pond of waterlilies, the riddle goes, there is a single leaf. Every day the number of leaves doubles – two leaves on the second day, four on the third day, eight on the fourth day, etc. 'If the pond is full on the thirtieth day,' the question runs, 'when is it half full?' Answer: 'On the twenty-ninth day.'

II

ALL THE PEOPLE AND THEIR DAILY BREAD

1. *An Unsatisfactory Balance Sheet*

North–South relations have not been making progress in the last few years, least of all in the poorest countries. To the contrary: warnings have been disregarded, even modest hopes have remained unfulfilled. Instead, we have seen the confirmation of many gloomy forecasts contained in the first report of my North–South Commission, published early in 1980. We were accused of pessimism at the time. If only that accusation had proved correct! But in fact it turns out that:

- The number of people suffering from malnutrition is still 500 million, and the number of those living in 'absolute poverty' around 800 million. These figures represent no deterioration, relatively speaking, only if we take into account the fact that world population is growing faster than the vast group of those who live a life of extreme destitution.
- At present, enough food is being produced worldwide. There is a greater supply of foodstuffs than for many years past, and international food reserves have grown – but famine disasters such as the African catastrophes still occur. Every minute, thirty children die for lack of food and clean water.
- The energy crisis seems to *us* to have slackened, but there is an increasingly acute shortage of firewood; this is the poor countries' real energy crisis.
- The threat to the forests and to water, the spread of deserts and exhausted soil, clearly show how great an ecological breakdown will face those who come after us.

- The export to the Third World of the East–West conflict, and the increasing militarization of the Third World, severely encumber the development process, as I have already shown, and mean the waste of a great deal of money that could be more productively employed, as well as the waste of talents and creative minds which might help to solve more meaningful problems. (It is estimated that out of every 1,000 scientists all over the world, 200 are occupied with research into arms technology.)
- We are facing a massive debt crisis, one of an order my Commission forecast at an early stage; I do not say so smugly.
- The further increase in trade barriers that we feared has come about – protectionism triumphant in defiance of all assurances to the contrary from official government sources.
- And more than one country is already shaken by social unrest. This is the consequence of the international crisis, and the reaction to traditional programmes for overcoming the *symptoms* of crisis.

It may be over-hasty to say that the real, acute crisis is actually upon us, for in the strict sense of the word, crisis means the state immediately preceding collapse or the beginning of recovery. I do not agree with those who believe that we are already over the critical phase, in that sense. I decidedly do not agree with them, for behind the obvious problems there looms the danger of the total extinction of life on earth.

When is the time to make the most strenuous possible of intellectual and political efforts, if not now? We are preparing to operate upon the very germ cells of Nature, we are playing Fate. So we are also, though in a very different way, responsible for our Fate. Either we live together in peace – at peace with our neighbours and with Nature – or we shall perish together.

Contrasts and contradictions mark the face of this world, and do so to an increasing degree. We have fundamentally changed the world. To a certain extent it has become smaller – particularly through new means of transport and communications technology, but also through our means of destruction. If we do not wish to decline entirely into becoming the agents of a destructive process, we must change our view of the world and our mental attitudes.

More cooperation, mutual security, mutual solutions to the problems of employment and the environment are all required, and indeed are imperative, but we still fall short even of those forms of cooperation which have already been achieved. Many of us resort to old remedies to cure new diseases. But only if we grasp the dangerous reality of our times can we hope to take any joint action to ensure that there will be a future.

2. Over Ten Billion People?

The catchphrase of 'population *explosion*' is no exaggeration. In a single generation, humanity has doubled its numbers. Every five days another million are born. In 1950 there were 2.5 billion people, in 1985 there are nearly 5 billion, by the turn of the century there will be over 6 billion. Those who live to be old enough will see the population of the world tripled within their time.

It would be an illusion to assume that the figure will stabilize at 6 to 8 billion. In the year 2050 there will be some 10 billion people or more – this, of course, is no more than a computation of probability. However, the progressive acceleration factor which has been a feature since the early nineteenth century is an established fact. In 120 years, one billion became two billion. Humanity reached its third billion within 32 years, and its fourth in another 15 years.

If we take the World Bank's development report of the summer of 1984 as a basis, the 6.1 billion people expected to be alive in the year 2000 would then be distributed between the continents as follows: Asia 3,600 million; America 898 million; Africa 828 million; Europe 520 million, the Soviet Union 312 million; Oceania 30 million.

Sceptics, however, observing current events, point out that the population of Africa need not necessarily grow, but could shrink to half its present size within less than a generation. And in the year 2050, again, the picture would look quite different from our assumptions of what it will be at the turn of the century.

Two other pieces of data have been recorded, indicating the course events are taking. Three-quarters of the world population live in today's developing countries, and this imbalance will increase. And on average, 44 per cent of the inhabitants of the developing countries are under 15 years old, as compared to 24 per cent in the industrial countries.

So far, the assumption that the sum of world population will reach equilibrium at 11 to 12 billion in the second half of the next century is pure wishful thinking. No real change of trend can be discerned. On the other hand, estimates of the number of people who can actually live on the earth range from 10 to 40 billion.

There is no doubt that all who are alive today could be fed, and millions more. So I would not call the situation hopeless, but it is certainly serious. And no one can contradict the World Bank when it says that without efficient family planning in the Third World countries, economic and social development will not take place. Robert McNamara, who looked into this matter himself during his time as President of the World Bank, and again spoke out clearly in 1984, goes further than that. He predicts that failure to practise efficient family planning will call authoritarian régimes into being, and those régimes will then take large-scale compulsory measures.

Such a viewpoint has given rise, and still does, to a sense of the urgency of making population policies involving birth control an important subject of international concern, and of advocating provision of the means to carry out this aspect of development policy. That does not mean exporting specific moral attitudes, but a serious approach to a political effort on whose success or failure much depends.

According to the predictions of the report already quoted, in the year 2050 India, with 1.5 billion people, will be the world's most populous nation. China, which has set itself to observe the rule of one-child families, will not be far behind, with an increase in population to 'only' 1.45 billion. What about the rest? There will be 470 million people living in Nigeria, 330 million in Indonesia, 360 million in Bangladesh, 300 million in Pakistan, 280 million in Brazil. I knew Burma and Ethiopia when they had 20 million inhabitants; in the middle of the next century one will have 100 million and the other 165 million. When I first visited

Tanzania (still Tanganyika at the time), the country had some 10 million inhabitants; by 2050 the figure will have grown to around 95 million. The calculations forecast that there will be 150 million people in Vietnam in the year 2050, 180 million in Mexico, 140 million in Iran, and 100 million each in Egypt, Algeria and Turkey.

Urban population is growing at an even faster rate than world population as a whole, especially in the Third World:
- There will be 21 Third World cities with over 10 million inhabitants in the year 2000, 15 of them in Asia: Mexico City will have 31 million, São Paulo 26 million, Shanghai 24 million, Peking 21 million, Rio 19 million, Bombay, Calcutta and Djakarta 17 million each, Seoul 14 million, Cairo and Madras 13 million, Buenos Aires 12 million.
- Other cities coming into the same category will be Tokyo/Yokohama with 24 million, New York with 22 million and Greater Los Angeles with 14 million.
- In twenty years' time, half of all Americans will be living in cities with over a million inhabitants, while the flow of people towards the big cities will continue all over the world.
- Conglomerations so huge that one can hardly grasp the extent of them are developing in the Third World. One wonders what will become of those squalid settlements known as *favelas* in Brazil, *barrios* in Mexico and *ranchos* in Venezuela, where redevelopment, if any, is making little progress.

Who would accuse those who hear the time bombs ticking away in cities, countries and regions of panic-mongering? The fact that a reduction in our own West German population is forecast for the next decade does not cheer me. Still, we might think ourselves lucky if that were our only worry. I know those who, all things considered, would be glad to change places with us. We need not fear the downfall of the West as yet. I am assuming that the Europeans – and within Europe, the Germans – still have something to offer the world.

The fear that 'they' in the South are to be kept down, while 'we' in the North only want to maintain our economic lead, has taken firm root in the minds of many Third World leaders. Many of them have thought, or still think, that a large population represents a power factor. There are also cultural, traditional and religious reasons for rejecting any kind of birth control. And finally, that simple fact expressed in South America by the saying that, 'The beds of poverty are fertile', still holds good. . . .

Only too often, however, population growth is regarded as the chief cause of hunger and destitution in the Third World. People prefer to suppress the connection between industrialism in the North and colonialism in the South. It is easy to forget that in the present state of the world economy, the poor are often too weak to defend themselves from exploitation.

The North and the West have frequently been accused of hypocrisy. It pays your families to have children, say the accusers, you get child allowances and tax relief, and then you want us to limit *our* families. As time has gone by, however, leading sections of the community in many of the poor countries have themselves come to realize that the benefits of an over-abundance of children can become a scourge instead, and that no amount of economic progress is of any use if it is literally more than consumed by excessive population growth.

There is a hint of the reversal of excessive population growth in some African countries. But the labour force of children who can help their parents still counts for a good deal, particularly in rural areas. And in the Third World, having children still represents provision for one's old age, something unobtainable from other sources. None the less, at the United Nations conference held in Mexico in the summer of 1984, which I have already mentioned, the representatives of the developing countries were in favour of expanding family planning programmes and stocking up on family planning material. Ten years earlier, at the first World Population Conference in Bucharest, opinion had not by any means been so decided.

This time, in Mexico, opposition came from the centre of the Catholic Church – and from the United States government. Washington had sent a delegation whose spokesman stated in all seriousness that everything would regulate itself if economic activity was left to go its own way. Economic liberalism as a substitute for contraception? In practical terms, all support for the termination of pregnancies should be withdrawn.

It was not surprising to find that the Vatican was of the same mind. Comments made publicly bore witness to the crisis of conscience obviously suffered by many millions of women and men whose Church is dear to their hearts. It was also reported reliably and uncontroversially that 'a growing number of priests view the conflict of aims between over-population and living conditions commensurate with human dignity with growing concern'. Very probably, contraception and abortion cannot be indefinitely equated in principle; the consequences extend too far beyond the field with which the morality of the Church is concerned.

The World Population Conference of the summer of 1984, however, made some meaningful recommendations; soothing reassurances had been granted in advance to the USA delegation, and – for the sake of peace – the Soviet delegation was conceded a passage relating to a policy of peace. And yet the President of Mexico, hosting the conference, had spoken out with refreshing bluntness against trivialization of the subject. The lowering of the birth rate, he said, was dependent on the resources available in the fields of nutrition, health, employment and education. My Commission had argued along the same lines.

Experience has long taught us that drawing up and equipping family planning programmes will be of limited efficacy if those programmes do not go hand in hand with the development of community life in villages or towns; higher social status for women; and better chances of survival for babies.

No nation has ever yet known its birth rate to fall without a previous drop in the mortality rate. Anything that helps to overcome poverty and promote better health makes a vital contribution to keeping the increase in population under control. The higher the proportion of those who can read and write and the greater the progress made towards equality for women, the more striking is the success of family planning programmes. It really does make a difference whether the women of the Nile Valley do or do not believe they will have no sons if they take the Pill, or if it is said elsewhere that the Pill is an invention of the enemies of Islam. The greater the share people have in the economic yield of their own labour, and the more intensively medical care is provided for the newborn, the more noticeably does the birth-rate sink; family planning is most unsatisfactory if it is divorced from a health service. And the sooner those concerned reach a certain level of education (and income), the readier they will be to use the family planning services.

Family planning has made considerable headway in such diverse countries as Colombia and Costa Rica, Korea and Sri Lanka. Even in a large country like Indonesia the number of couples who decide to practise birth control has risen from 3 to 50 per cent. The city states of Hong Kong and Singapore are frequently cited as being particularly successful, though the methods of reward or punishment employed there have met with much criticism. In India, where a sterilization programme was forcefully imposed in the mid-Sixties, the government met strong resistance. The concept of the one-child family decreed by the state in the People's Republic of China encounters understandable objections too; whatever harsh measures may be taken, the population there will still grow by several more hundred million.

It is easy, but not particularly helpful, for certain European resolutions to call for an end to the population explosion, while simultaneously maintaining that one should not encroach too far upon the rights of individuals to decide the size of their families. It is irresponsible to let things drift, in the name of a misunderstood notion of freedom, if population increases faster than the prospective means of subsistence. This is particularly true where countries trying to develop have their chances of development curtailed from outside.

3. All Could Be Fed

With our present opportunities for producing food, more people than are now living on the earth could be fed. However, the gap between the reproduction of human children and the production of the means to feed them is wider in some regions than others. So the question is, how can agriculture be made profitable? And how are the poor to be able to buy what they desperately need? And how are the export interests of large firms or of the state to be subordinated to basic domestic consumption? It makes no sense to export foodstuffs from countries where millions of people do not have enough to eat.

When global food production declined slightly a few years ago, the authorities responsible declared that the world food situation as a whole was not endangered. That makes the dreadful figures I am about to set out here no better. It is important to recognize the inconsistency of a state of affairs in which the international supply situation is comparatively better than it used to be, while at the same time whole regions are stricken by famine.

Let us recall those round numbers: over 500 million children and adults suffering from chronic malnutrition, over 800 million living in conditions of 'absolute poverty' – such was the estimate made by World Bank experts a few years ago. Their idea was to obtain points of reference for the large number of people who are barely able to survive, owing to a combination of undernourishment, disease, illiteracy, high birth-rates, under-employment, and tiny incomes. In 1979, according to the World Bank's estimates, there were about 800 million people in this category, as already mentioned, most of them in southern Asia and in sub-Saharan Africa. An estimate for 1985 would not look much better. There are varying forecasts of figures for the year 2000: in unfavourable circumstances, there would be a further rise from 800 to 1,000 million; in better circumstances, the figure might drop to about 600 million. A large part of humanity is thus affected by 'absolute poverty' in intellectual as well as physical development; many are condemned to perish miserably.

No, world hunger is not a hysterical flight of fancy. It cannot be argued away, nor can it be made to disappear by magic; at best it can be repelled, with much effort. The question is: practically and morally, how long can those immediately affected endure it, and how long can the rest of us endure it? I have already linked it with the waste of public funds on other purposes, and with issues of international security.

Let the experts debate the precise line to be drawn between chronic malnutrition and absolute poverty. The appalling pictures from East Africa made a deep impression on us laymen. Yet not a dozen years before, pictures no less shocking had appeared

57

in illustrated magazines and on our television screens, pictures from the Sahel zone in general and Ethiopia in particular; and from Bangladesh, and Cambodia, where there has been much misuse of international aid.

Many who saw those pictures from Ethiopia were overwhelmed by bitter memories – memories of 1945 and the skeletal figures emerging from concentration camps. I was reminded of a friend of mine, a Norwegian doctor interned in Sachsenhausen as a deportee, who had to bear the burden of deciding which patients in the infirmary were to get a chance of survival and which were not. I thought of him when I heard what was said by the nurses and emergency doctors who had to make similarly hard decisions at the gates of the Ethiopian camps; only a few children could be let in. One German nurse wrote: 'What I hate most is the moment when people have to be sorted out. I feel like a judge on life and death: one child gets a chance, another is condemned to die.'

In 1984, James Grant, director of UNICEF, stated that the numbers of children dying before their fifth birthday, from malnutrition and largely preventable illnesses, were:
- 15 million a year
- 41,000 a day
- 28 a minute

Mr Grant of UNICEF sees family planning as 'the best method of preventing the death of some 20,000 babies and small children a day'. None the less, there has been a distinct drop in child mortality in a number of developing countries during the last three decades. Looking at the world as a whole, it can be said, and this is very pleasing, that for rather more than a generation, there has been no rise in the number of children who do not have enough to eat and no clean water, and who at the same time are growing up without a minimum of educational and medical care. We may even speak of a declining trend. But the rapid increase in population, linked to environmental disasters and economic distress, could reverse that trend again at any time.

It is not just the situation in Africa that has come to a head. In India, despite a general improvement in food supplies, the health of a large part of the population is still threatened by inadequate nutrition. The same applies to other parts of Africa, and it still applies – or now applies again – to many people in Latin America.

Whether 12 or 15 million children are dying of starvation a year, whether 500 or 800 million people in the world go hungry, there is an individual fate behind every set of figures, however neatly rounded it may be: the fate of a human being with a right to life, a right not to be harmed, a right to a dignified existence.

Instead, a vast number are denied the simplest right a human being has, the right to live. This need not be so, and it would not be so if nations and their governments and the international federations could manage material wealth a little more sensibly, help one another rather more in the field of agriculture, and see their international responsibility to their fellow men writ a little larger.

The fate of every starving human being is a crime against the values, principles and aims by which many of us who do not go hungry claim to live, by which our governments claim to pursue their policies, and which are invoked at international conferences. Despair and rancour are growing in the minds of many who feel that all this need not be as it is. Even in those countries whose people are well fed, indignation is rising at the inadequate action being taken, the incompetence of civil servants and the indifference of humanity. The suffering is being discussed and accounted for. But action to relieve that suffering is either not taken at all, or is on too small a scale, or comes too late.

Unfortunately there are bureaucrats, including some in the diplomatic services, who will let any human feeling cool down until nothing remains of the initial impulse, however well meant, but a troublesome duty. I remember a conference of the Council of Europe. A minister from Northern Europe had been going to come and speak. He was unable to attend, and an ambassador was delegated to read out what had been conveyed to him as the minister's speech. It turned out that the speech was not even at an advanced draft stage, and contained nothing that had not been said before. The meeting was running out of time, but the ambassador, a man on the brink of retirement, insisted on delivering the speech, making matters no better by his soporific style of delivery. One wonders what such people can achieve when they do not just have to deliver speeches from their own ministries, but must negotiate difficult issues with actual Third World representatives, and when, this being the vital point, they are supposed to do something effective at home!

But are there still grounds for hope, all the same? The mere repetition of what may sound over-optimistic will not do. Everyone could be fed *if.* . . . And we must not dwell on superficial comparisons. Many of the developing countries start out from a less favourable situation than did those countries which went through their industrial revolution in the last century. None the less, I affirm my conviction that the task of feeding humanity can be solved, and can be solved primarily by agricultural reforms in the respective regions concerned.

Over and beyond that, biotechnology will open up opportunities of which we had no conception until quite recently. The next question is whether new methods of converting and storing solar energy can be put to work quickly enough, before the firewood disaster gets out of hand, and whether a breakdown of the water supply can be averted, and satisfactory use of sea-water made for economic purposes. I think both of these are possible.

In the autumn of 1974, with the famine disasters in the Sahel zone and Bangladesh still fresh in people's minds, World Food Day was announced at an international conference, and a rallying cry went out: within ten years, it was said, no child should go hungry. Some years ago, when I was to speak in Rome on the occasion of World Food Day, at the invitation of FAO (the United Nations Food and Agriculture Organization), I thought it would be appropriate, yet still rather bold, to extend that deadline just a little: 'By the end of this century, may humanity see the day when children need no longer go to bed hungry, when families need no longer wonder where tomorrow's food is coming from, and the future of humanity is no longer crippled by malnutrition.'

Will those who are young enough to prepare for a new century really see that day? Always supposing such a path is still open to humanity. . . .

4. *Hunger in Africa*

Two 'poverty belts' were described in the report of the Brandt Commission. One stretched across Africa from the Sahara to the northern banks of Lake Nyasa, the other from North and South Yemen and Afghanistan eastwards through South Asia and some of the East Asian countries. It can still be said that unless energetic and precisely defined measures are taken to improve agriculture, 'the Eighties and Nineties could bring even worse scenes of hunger than the Seventies. . . .'

That estimate has not proved false or exaggerated either. However, a correction should be made with regard to Africa: countries south of Lake Nyasa too, particularly Mozambique, are now suffering severely from food shortages. The same applies to a number of countries on the western side of the continent, such as Angola.

FAO's warning system forecast food shortages for 24 African countries, in essence as the result of drought. FAO has been criticized for not relating the warning clearly and urgently enough to Ethiopia. But criticisms are also made when the problems of a region seen as a whole are pushed into the background because of an acute crisis in one of its countries. We might, however, have expected those governments affected, and to that extent responsible, to be better informed about the vital problems of their countries, and more intensively concerned with them, than was the case in Addis Ababa and elsewhere.

Aid for Ethiopia took a long time to get under way. Its efficacy was impaired by the fact that the country, with an 'Eastern-bloc orientated' administration in power, was to a great extent cut off from international development aid, and that those very provinces worst affected by the famine, the northern provinces of Eritrea, Tigré and Wollo, have been arenas of guerrilla warfare for decades. Efforts to get hostilities suspended so that aid could reach all who needed it proved peculiarly difficult; resettlement moves met with criticism because ulterior political motives were suspected of being behind them.

On the other hand, despite all the polemic that went beforehand, this did not prevent the superpowers from acting together to help relieve famine on the spot. Soviet planes carried American

It was said of Ethiopia that:
- Even last time, i.e. in the 1973 disaster, drought and famine claimed 200,000 lives.
- In the first half of 1984, the talk was of 300,000 victims.
- By the end of 1984, it was estimated that of the 600,000 or more people suffering acutely from the famine, half would die.
- The full number of those affected by the famine, according to an estimate made by a UN representative, was said to be several million.

In Africa as a whole (south of the Sahara) we may say that:
- 150 to 450 million are suffering from inadequate nutrition.
- 30 to 35 million face the threat of famine.
- Famine is not just the result of natural disaster, but the consequence of political, economic and ecological mistakes.

wheat: a pleasing picture, like the smooth collaboration of the West German air force with East German units. Peter McPherson, head of the US development agency, specifically welcomed cooperation with the Soviet Union and other Eastern bloc states.

Undoubtedly there are three main causes of the disastrous situation:

1. Serious changes in ecological factors – deforestation, overgrazing, the spread of deserts.
2. Grave mistakes and errors made by the governments concerned, not least in imperial Ethiopia, and an almost incredible neglect of the agricultural sector.
3. A failure of international development policy, just where it ought to have brought about fundamental reforms to encourage agricultural production and supply.

The effect of the climatic change which led to severe drought, with the additional consequences of impoverishment of the soil and the destructive exploitation of forests, can hardly be overestimated.

At the turn of the year between 1984/85, it was calculated that 21 or as many as 27 African countries were stricken by drought. Besides Ethiopia and the Sudan, those particularly hard hit were Chad, Mali, Niger, Mauretania, Uganda and Mozambique, and not least affected were the refugee camps in the Sudan and Somalia. As I write this, it is to be feared that the disaster is not coming to an end but only just beginning.

The simple truth is: Africa south of the Sahara is a single great region where food production per head of the population has declined in the last two decades, and not just because of the catastrophic droughts. And one third of its entire population is undernourished.

What a vast change in the course of only a few decades! Around 1950, the developing countries as a whole, including the African developing countries, were still classed as self-supporting. Over the last few decades, they have needed more and more grain imports. How has this change come about?

The connection between food production and population growth is quite clear: the population of Africa is doubling within 25 years, and even faster in some countries. Nor must we overlook the fact that agrarian commodities have been unwisely exported, because it was in the interests of big business to export,

- Forty per cent of Ethiopia was forest at the turn of the century; today, it is only 2.5 per cent.
- The Sahara is extending, by about 150 kilometres to date (or 650,000 square kilometres of arable and grazing land in the last 50 years).
- Considerable parts of the Sahel zone have become semi-desert, with disastrous harvests, lost herds and abandoned villages.
- Extensive soil erosion has led to the clearing of land for cultivation by burning and complete deforestation; every year several more thousand hectares of forest become charcoal or firewood.
- We are seeing more and more emergencies, even in countries which normally have a high rainfall, such as Zaïre, or the countries on the west coast.

or exporting seemed advantageous to a country's balance of trade. But there were no funds available to pay for fertilizers and pesticides or agricultural implements; the dollar and oil prices had risen too high. Money for armaments, however, has usually been forthcoming.

One African head of state has observed, self-critically, that Africa's agriculture is sick. Agriculture has been seriously neglected in many of the countries that are now independent. That had to do with the notion of progress which was conveyed to them: industry was a good thing, agriculture not so good, and thus not so important either. And here governments must answer for what they themselves have done or left undone. I surely include in this criticism those who formed 1,000 tribes into 50 states, and provided the dubious models. But matters cannot stop at the allocation of blame. I myself found it helpful to hear how unsparingly an experienced African diplomat took various of his continent's governments to task for their false priorities, ineffectiveness, and failure to face problems. He said they ought to be ashamed of themselves; I replied that we should openly address ourselves to mistakes on both sides, and not gloss anything over.

Anyone who has any idea of the fertility of the land in Zambia and elsewhere – 'You could drive a walking stick into the ground and it would put out leaves,' was my own comment after a pleasant visit to Kenneth Kaunda – will find it hard to understand why six times as much grain has to be imported in the Eighties as in the early days of independence. Why did Zaïre, still an exporter of food in 1960, have to become dependent on food imports? Why must Liberia import rice it could grow for itself? (And in this respect the situation in the North African Maghreb area has not improved but deteriorated.)

The root of the evil usually lies in the fact that agriculture has become a poor relation, politically speaking. Food prices are held down to relieve the burden on the urban population. Governments cash in on agrarian exports. Farmers, on the other hand, get hardly any incentive to increase production. So the country becomes more and more dependent on imports, either bought or donated.

Emergency aid is necessary, but is no way to solve the problem. The unconventional Karlheinz Böhm, well-known actor and self-made development activist in Ethiopia, is right to remind us of the Chinese proverb which says, 'It is better to light a candle than complain of the dark'. I support all readiness to give humanitarian aid and every concrete project that will promote self-help – an example being friends in Bavaria who have 'adopted' two villages suffering from drought in Mali. But willingly as support may be offered, we should not forget that fundamental reforms are called for.

I am very much in favour of aid for Africa from the rest of the world, especially Europe. But we must be clear about three things:

- Except in genuine emergencies, it is irrational, because too expensive, to send highly subsidized foodstuffs to the developing countries instead of aiming for more effective results at less expense on the spot.
- Transport costs are often so high that they can hardly be justified – except, again, for emergency aid in disasters; funds should be invested in storage facilities on the spot.
- Something that is often entirely overlooked – by exporting our food, we are helping to introduce many of the developing countries to a form of nutrition that is not just expensive but wrong, and in addition to other things this is an injudicious import.

A good part of Europe's record grain harvest of 1984 went to increasing aid early in 1985. I can only welcome that, the more so as further aid in the way of encouraging self-help was planned. Large parts of Africa have become accustomed to eating wheat, which is not generally grown there. In West Africa, traditional foods such as millet have been displaced by rice, which also comes from abroad, and is either bought or donated. (Much money has been spent on rice fields by the Niger, but the people of the Sahel seem to have difficulty learning how to grow it.) To take another example: if we send milk from Europe to Africa, it finds its way into stomachs that are not used to it. And milk powder mixed with tainted water does harm, not good.

Another reason why food imports are not the long-term way to deal with the situation is that they offer no incentive to African

65

farmers, but, rather, discourage them. What is required is technical assistance, above all for the indigenous agriculture, and tools and committed experts, particularly to help cooperative institutions. Action must be taken against the disregard and neglect of the agricultural sector, and the fixing of agricultural producer prices which discourage production.

The 'green revolution' of the Sixties and Seventies, which achieved much in Pakistan, Sri Lanka, the Philippines and Indonesia as well as India, passed Africa by. But important results are expected from research at institutes in Nigeria (Ibadan), Kenya (Nairobi) and several other countries. The question remains: how seriously do we intend, over the years ahead, to encourage self-help in Africa and how much are we prepared to stand by the Africans if they are to bear the brunt of global political differences and of rearguard colonialist acts?

5. Reform!

Since the autumn of 1984 the World Bank has been trying to raise an additional $2 billion to relieve poverty in Africa. The programme had to be trimmed by half because of the recent US preference for avoiding multilateral arrangements, as they managed to do in this instance, thus setting the tone for others. (Though the United States gave, bilaterally, additional funds on its own account.)

One could not but feel doubtful of the policies of those governments in America and Europe which were now ready to help in the face of obvious famine, but had in the past either cut or discontinued their development aid – for instance, in Ethiopia. The US government rejected 50 credit proposals made on behalf of Africa by the World Bank and other institutions, among them six projects which were to have been to Ethiopia's advantage in 1984.

However, it was not and is not a matter of foreign financial aid alone; reform on the spot should be our chief concern. In many quarters there is still an aversion, ranging from incomprehension to hostility, to land reform and cooperatives. The subject thus tends to fare badly in resolutions which need unanimous support at government level. And favourable mention in a resolution does not necessarily mean that something will be done.

Internationally, agricultural production is coming to be valued more than it was only ten years ago. None the less, without fundamental changes there will be even worse shortages in even larger areas of the world over the next decade, particularly in Africa. Food aid can only alleviate, temporarily; it cannot solve the problem. It can be solved only by overcoming obsolete structures and ideologies, by actively including producers in their countries' policies, and by using the advances offered and promised us by science. And of course no progress can be made without capable administration.

There are now some countries in Asia and Latin America which show a relatively high growth rate in food production, and have become successful exporters, yet whose societies have large, poverty-stricken sections which are still inadequately provided for and undernourished. The food problem of such countries arises primarily from the fact that their people are too poor to buy what they need. It must be solved in the longer term by an improvement in income – which means providing remunerative jobs – for the members of these poor sections of society. That cannot be done without an economic policy which deliberately sets out to give revenues to those who need them.

Another group of countries is suffering chiefly (as seen in Africa) from the weakness of its agricultural production, poverty again being a factor, but the heart of their problem lies in the rapid decline in food production per head of the population. It is becoming prohibitively expensive to close this gap with imports. Environmental disasters and the destructive consequences of armed conflict add to these structural problems. But, first and foremost, in most of the countries with which we are concerned here, all progress made in food production is racing against population growth.

The already precarious situation became even more acute in the transition to the Eighties because of the devastating consequences of high oil prices in most Third World countries. More favourable prices or terms of payment, such as were granted to some of the poor countries by Latin American and Arab oil states, were not on the whole of any significance. The general situation was one in which, despite all economy measures, the oil bill consumed several times as large a share of export earnings as it had a few years earlier. Even in my Commission's report, we saw then 'no clear danger of a worldwide shortage of fertilizers', since only two or three per cent of oil production would be used for fertilizers. Nor was our observation wrong; it was just that prices rose sharply.

There was also another way in which the oil bill threatened food production. In many countries, people veered sharply to the use of wood as a fuel, with a consequent increase in wasteful exploitation and exhaustion of the land. Other alternatives, such as making petrol substitutes from sugar-cane, are highly controversial, since they do incalculable ecological damage, and decrease food production. What is needed is a programme to ensure world nutrition, based on the experience of recent years.

The *first* part of such a programme should be a purposeful increase in production. The main targets should be those countries with low incomes which show a deficit in their own production of foodstuffs. The increase could be achieved by price incentives and easier credit terms, and in many cases this could hardly be done without outside help. By increasing aid from abroad, an increase in agricultural investment at home could thus be encouraged. The least developed countries should be the chief focus of attention.

National and international *research* should concentrate, as much as they can, on the development of new, simple technologies suited to agriculture in tropical countries. They should be accompanied by programmes of joint study and organization. The developing countries themselves, with the support of their partner countries, would develop plans and programmes to deal with problems of marketing, transport and storage, and face the task, unfamiliar to their traditional agriculture, of supplying towns with food and opening up domestic markets.

Secondly, a supply of food from international sources must be secured. There should be a guarantee that at times of crisis, developing countries, particularly those agriculturally most at risk, could get supplies *in time*. However, the ultimate objective must be to strengthen those countries economically, to the point where they can supply themselves, in the world market if need be. Food aid for low-income countries should be stepped up appropriately; part of it (at least 20 per cent?) should be at the disposal of the United Nations' World Food Programme. Emergency reserves, as provided for by the International Wheat Agreement, should be stockpiled. Greater investment in storage capacity for the developing countries is needed too. Experts think that $1,000 million a year needs to be raised to create the necessary capacity on the spot *and* in the industrial countries.

Thirdly, we should look at international trade. For one thing, the producing countries should, at last, get adequate prices for their products. For another, tariff barriers should be lowered; one reason, but not the only one, is that it would then be easier for developing countries to increase their sales. In the course of the Seventies and the first half of the Eighties, trade in foodstuffs has made little contribution to economic growth in the developing countries.

Equal demands are made on the industrial and the developing countries. In the countries of the North, the attention of governments, of the public, and not least of influential economic circles, still needs to be directed to the urgent problems of the world food situation. Over and above emergency aid, an increased transfer of scientific and technical knowledge to the developing countries should be encouraged, particularly for the benefit of the great mass of the rural population. The countries of the South are confronted with the challenge to increase the value they set on their own agriculture. This would also mean letting the peasant population take a greater part in the decisions that affect them.

In 1984, the World Food Council came to the conclusion that over a 15-year period, $4 billion a year should be given for productive purposes and income support, in order to give 500 million people access to food by the end of the century. (My Commission set the figure at $4 billion a year over 20 years. It will be seen that the estimates are very close. Their ratio to arms spending is still horrific.)

The World Food Council was set up on the occasion of the World Food Conference at the end of 1974, when the famines immediately preceding it were fresh in people's minds. Two years later, the International Fund for Agricultural Development

(IFAD) was created, to boost agrarian production and food supplies with field projects, particularly in the poorest countries. The notable feature of this institution was the much increased participation and co-responsibility of the oil states. Western industrial countries, OPEC states and developing countries each had one third of the votes on its governing body, while finance ($1 billion in 1978–80) was originally divided between the industrial countries and the oil states. At the end of 1984 the activities of IFAD seemed to be under considerable threat, since the United States administration – in this as elsewhere – was anxious to take less part in international organizations (or multilateral agreements), placing more emphasis on bilateralism. Iran had stopped paying its contribution. Japan was also obstructing agreement, although this very fund had been seen as an excellent tool.

FAO, as the United Nations' special organization for food and agriculture, has not so far been affected. It has become the forum of worldwide discussion on agrarian policy; it also serves to coordinate concern about such questions as agrarian and nutritional planning, crop protection and the prevention of livestock epidemics. FAO has seen thousands of useful technical aid projects through. However, its headquarters in Rome has not escaped criticism. Even more than other international organizations, it has been accused of spending an increasing proportion of its budget on its own bureaucracy. Many of its critics, however, fail to make any comparisons with the growth of wages and salaries in their own national bureaucracies (or those of the European Community).

6. One Doctor for Tens of Thousands?

WHO, the United Nations' World Health Organization, which has its headquarters in Geneva, has stated its ambitious aim of making 'health for all' possible by the year 2000. WHO does not mean by this that it can eradicate all kinds of disease by then, but that it hopes to spread basic medical care and hygienic living conditions to all countries.

Dr Halfdan Mahler, the Danish Director-General of WHO, and his colleagues, strongly recommend concentration on basic care, with the provision of expensive equipment coming second. Most national health systems, they say regretfully in Geneva, cannot make good use of scientific and technical advances and achieve optimal effects in the face of their limited financial means.

However, we should cherish no illusions about the necessary expenditure. If the health strategy *agreed* upon in the context of WHO were put into practice, an additional $50 billion a year would be needed in the developing countries, i.e. rather more than the whole of present official development assistance. That seems beyond the limits of what we may now suppose feasible. Here again, however, it does no harm to remember the $1,000 billion a year which the human race thinks it can afford for military purposes.

Latest findings suggest that revolutionary results could be achieved in the battle against infant mortality, in return for a relatively modest investment. Experts cooperating with UNICEF, on whose authority I am relying here, give cogent reasons to show that a cheap and simple 'mix' of sugar, salt and water could save 20,000 children a day. (Seen in terms of a year's mortality figures, the lives saved would be equivalent to the entire number of children under five growing up in Great Britain, West Germany, France, Italy and Spain.)

The 'mix', also known as ORT (Oral Rehydration Therapy), is to counteract diarrhoea, which is a great threat to small children. Other elements in the coming 'revolution' are:

- an effective programme of immunization, for instance against measles, TB and tetanus;
- propaganda to encourage breast-feeding;
- simple measuring charts which would tell mothers if their children were failing to grow properly;
- the provision of food supplements where a proper diet is otherwise unobtainable.

For the rest, no effective war can be waged against hunger if conditions of hygiene are not taken into account. High child mortality, particularly in the developing countries, can be overcome only if we understand that we are dealing with a combination of different adverse factors.

In many places, lack of clean water is easily the highest health risk. Lack of drinking water, altogether, has become more and more of a problem; supplies are uncertain in half the world. The Nepalese friend I quoted in the early pages of this book said, of certain hospitals that he knew, that if there had been clean water available locally, 80 per cent of their patients would never have come into hospital at all.

Encouraging progress in the processing of water can certainly be recorded in more than one part of the Third World. And there has been considerable success in the fight against epidemics as well: smallpox was virtually eradicated in the Seventies – a triumph for the World Health Organization and the countries concerned; cholera and malaria were brought under control in the Sixties.

Since then, they have spread again, because of lack of funds. From a report made by German doctors bringing emergency aid to Ethiopia: 'We see every imaginable kind of disease. Malaria is rife. So is typhus, so is amoebic dysentery, so are a great many eye diseases of all kinds. . . .'

There is a very great deal to be done, if one looks at statistics like these:

- Only 10 per cent of children in the developing countries are immunized against the six major childhood illnesses.
- 600 million people live in areas infested by parasites; they risk disease carried by flatworms which live in the blood vessels of the abdominal cavity (bilharziasis – the disease is so called after a German physician, Bilharz).
- 300 million people suffer from parasitic worms.
- 100 million a year suffer from intestinal and respiratory diseases.
- Expectation of life has indeed risen, even in the Third World, but is still not much above 40 in a number of countries.
- In 1984, the USA had one doctor to 520 people, the Federal Republic of Germany had one to 450, but in Indonesia the ratio was one to 11,500, in Mali one to 32,000, and in Ethiopia one doctor to 58,000 people.

There is no automatic correspondence, however, between the average standard of living and health standards in different countries. Thus China and Sri Lanka may be extremely low-income countries, but they have an elementary health service for almost the whole of their populations. In Latin America, states as different as Costa Rica and Cuba lead the way in caring for the health of their citizens.

Politicians who are concerned with health and recognize their share of responsibility for the people of the Third World have begun to look at the problem of pharmaceutical drugs. This is all the more necessary as the avalanche of pills comes down on the developing countries too. Most of the products of the pharmaceutical industry used in those countries come from abroad. Quality and price are by no means always all they should be; one and the same drug often sells under different names and at different prices, according to the manufacturer's marketing power. Even worse: drugs which have been banned in industrial countries because of their dangers (for instance, because they are carcinogenic) are still being sold in the Third World.

Director-General Mahler of WHO has raised his voice in support of 'essential' medicaments: 'We have not yet been able to disentangle the complex relations between governments, national and international pharmaceutical industries, the medical profession and other professions in the public health services.' A statement which need not be taken as one of resignation.

7. Worldwide Assaults on the Environment

Concern for the health of those who live after us led me to the subject of environmental protection a quarter of a century ago. Members of the World Commission on Environment and Development established in 1984 were able to deliberate from a basis of extensive insights into their subject. They could assume that mutual dependency, to be observed at national, regional and international levels, exists between the economy, the environment, security and development. This Commission, which unlike mine or Olof Palme's arose from a resolution of the UN General

Assembly, works under the chairmanship of Gro Harlem Brundtland, leader of the Norwegian Labour Party.

Worldwide assaults on our natural environment went unnoticed for a long time. So too did the additional interdependency which now links the industrial and developing countries through their ecological problems. Only five years ago, when the report of my Commission was published, there were many people who preferred to ignore what we had to say, over and above matters of international economic and humanitarian concern, on the subjects of the arms race *and ecology*. We spoke out on the growing risk to 'international common property', a risk arising from:

• deforestation and impoverishment of the soil,
• exhaustion of pastureland,
• depletion of fish stocks,
• air and water pollution.

If it took so long, and was so difficult, to get clear facts and the risks they entail into the minds of people in the industrial countries, how can anyone be surprised to find the subject is considered even less relevant in large parts of the developing countries? A few years ago, in conversation with colleagues from developing countries, one had the impression that they thought ecology a Western luxury, and environmental protection a fanciful interest of culturally-minded tourists and big-game hunters. By now no one can fail to see that forests and water reserves are being depleted, while the deserts extend and nature is poisoned. Nor can anyone deny the consequences.

The poison gas disaster at the end of 1984 in the Indian city of Bhopal, which left 2,500 dead and over 100,000 injured, demonstrated the absurdity of the thesis that the protection of labour and the environment is only 'for rich countries, who can afford it'. On the contrary: attention was drawn to the fact that safety standards in the developing countries – as in that American pesticide factory in India – are set very considerably lower and applied far less stringently than in the countries where the technologies concerned originated. (In Bhopal, it was impossible, even months later, to predict the consequences for those babies whose mothers had been in contact with the poison gas.)

74

The poison gas case, the death of forests, the contamination of foodstuffs are all connected on a major scale. Is it true, one may ask, that mankind has loosed destructive powers whose final effect will be the suicide of our species? Is it true that something is going on not unlike the behaviour of lemmings? I would like not to believe the comparison apt, but it is not surprising that a sense of hopelessness is spreading.

There can now be no serious argument – as was possible only a few years ago – against the proposition that natural resources are not inexhaustible. But even today, many will not admit to themselves that if we continue to exploit certain natural resources, notably coal and oil, as they have been exploited hitherto, they will last for only another half-century.

Issues of the natural resources and the environment caused the United Nations to hold a special conference in Stockholm in 1972. It led to the setting up of UNEP (the United Nations Environment Programme), an environmental organization with its headquarters in Nairobi. Only recently, under the leadership of this organization, several governments have declared it their minimum aim to reduce the release of pollutants into the environment by 30 per cent by the year 1993. . . .

Together with UNCTAD, the United Nations Conference on Trade and Development with its Secretariat in Geneva, UNEP has particularly recommended the governments of those developing countries rich in resources to introduce an effective environmental policy. Environmental considerations should play a greater part in the processing of primary commodities. Appropriate programmes could be financed by taxing output or export.

Not *everything* has been negative and disappointing over the last ten years. Rivers and lakes have been cleared of severe pollution, and have come back to life. Reforestation has proved successful. It has been realized, if rather late in the day, that pollutant phenomena such as 'acid rain' could assume continental, even global proportions. And it had been widely hoped that the developing countries need not repeat all the same mistakes the industrial world had made.

In the course of the Seventies it became obvious that large parts of the Indian subcontinent, of sub-Saharan Africa, Central America and the Caribbean, and the South American Andes area are in great ecological danger. Destruction of the natural environment is the cause of periodic flooding in extensive regions of Asia.

If forests die, the entire vegetable kingdom is in mortal danger. Water and air and their degree of pollution depend on the forests to a great extent.

- Since 1960, FAO estimates that the world has lost half its forests.
- Every year forests all over the world shrink by a further several million hectares.
- The deforestation of large areas of tropical rain forest in Latin America (especially the Amazon basin), Africa and South-east Asia has far-reaching climatic consequences, going beyond the particular regions concerned; they are an encumbrance to agriculture.
- By the end of the century, the supply of usable wood will be considerably reduced; hundreds of millions of people will have lost their traditional fuel for cooking.
- Soil erosion, which has occurred on a large scale in, for instance, the Himalayas, is regarded as a direct consequence of deforestation and unsuitable hydraulic construction works.
- Some governments of developing countries themselves saw the problem earlier than most, and (as in East Africa) appealed to their people: 'Help your environment, and your environment will help you.'
- Years ago, in Tunisia and Kenya and later in India and China, I saw what efforts were being made to grow new forests; there are reports of similar efforts in Korea. (I shall come to Cuba and Israel later.)

In the field of *energy*, a start has been made on making a 'transition ... from high dependence on increasingly scarce non-renewable energy sources', as we put it in the first report of my Commission. Economic use of energy can be perceived in many quarters, and the deceleration of economic growth makes an involuntary contribution. The cartel of oil-exporting countries no longer strikes terror into us as it did a decade ago. The transition to inexhaustible energy sources has begun: solar energy in the widest sense, use of the biomass, the wind and the tides.

I remember, only a few years ago, the arrogant smiles of those government officials who could make nothing of reports about simple pumps powered by solar cells (for instance, to generate power for the lighting of a hospital at Bamako [Mali] and its operating theatre). Converting the rays of the sun, which in the tropics have until now rather been a draw on human strength, into a large source of cheap energy has become a major concern of our time.

The work necessary to make solar technology an economic proposition is in progress. I am told by experts that it will be only another few decades before solar power stations can be put into space to convert energy. (There is still controversy as to whether we can make the transition from the age of oil to the age of alternative energy sources successfully without increased reliance on nuclear energy; it may depend upon whether we can command *new* forms of energy.)

The USA did not accept our proposal for the creation of a global energy research centre under United Nations auspices and affiliated to the World Bank, to help in opening up new energy sources in the poorest countries. Intensive exploration into mineral resources in the Third World calls for such backing, since poor countries simply cannot raise the funds and should not be subject to unfair agreements. (There are huge reserves of hydro power in Africa which might be utilized.)

At the end of 1984 a private research institute in the United States warned that further waste of *water reserves* would lead in the next decade to a global crisis comparable to the oil crisis. At almost the same time, a Harvard University institute stated that *no* worldwide water shortage need be feared until well into the next century. But it entered a caveat: regionally, for instance in West Africa, a serious dearth of supplies must be expected. According to UN estimates, half of all the people of the Third World are today without fresh drinking water. Their number increases by 20 million annually.

The endangering of water reserves by over-use, excessive pumping of groundwater and its increasing degree of contamination has become a major political concern. In the summer of

1984, the Executive Director of UNEP,* Mostafa K. Tolba, said at a seminar in Japan that the growing scarcity of drinking water would aggravate international economic and political problems, impairing the security of many states.

We became really sensitive to the price of oil only when the oil states made it expensive. We still act as if water cost nothing, whereas in fact it can be as expensive as oil. In tomorrow's industrial society careful and thus sparing use of natural resources will have to be taken as much for granted as it is now (or should be) taken for granted that labour and capital will be employed as economically as possible in a business venture. One of the more cheering phenomena of a generally unpleasant international perspective is the fact that the superpowers have stated their intention of upholding the agreement which came into force in 1978, banning 'environmental changes for hostile purposes'. We should also welcome the fact that environmentalist objectives which would husband resources are beginning to take effect on economic cooperation, in sharp contrast to the state of affairs only a few years ago, and that demands are even sometimes made for them to be given equal status with the traditional areas of negotiation in foreign politics.

In 1972 the bad news emanating from the Club of Rome was widely considered much dramatized, more of a fanciful picture of the future than anything else. Not only do those in positions of political responsibility now know better; what is known is taken more seriously than a decade ago. Ordinary people are better informed, and expect political action to follow on the heels of knowledge. Majorities are beginning to realize that the protection of our living conditions is just as valuable as a modern economy which is technically up to date and which makes no more demands on people than is necessary. Humane labour, effective protection of the environment and an environmentally conscious management of the economy must complement each other and the safeguarding of peace.

* UNEP should not be confused with UNDP. The latter is the – technical – United Nations Development Programme, directed over a number of years by the energetic Bradford Morse, a former American Congressman who is now in charge of the World Bank's special programme for Africa.

III

THE POPE AND THE 'DIMENSION OF EVIL'

In the summer of 1978 I visited Rome as chairman of my Commission. Pope Paul VI, who obviously had little time left to him, set out his view that 'development is another word for peace', saying that in his opinion the social issue had assumed global proportions.

On my visits to Geneva, I met Philip Potter, then General Secretary of the World Council of Churches, which emphatically believed that peace is not simply the absence of war and that, 'Peace cannot be built on unjust foundations'.

In Germany I had a friendly reception from our two largest religious groups, the Catholic and the Protestant Churches, and other religious communions. The Pope, in moving terms, adjured us to continue our self-imposed task. The Commission, he said, represented 'hope for us and for the progress of the nations'.

At my meeting with Cardinal Arns in São Paulo, I sensed great understanding and encouragement. I must not enter into the theological side of the debate on liberation theology, but I was deeply impressed to find the clergy, particularly in Latin America, ranging themselves so unequivocally on the side of the poor and weak. The same applies to the earnest concern with which the bishops of North America present their joint pastoral message of an 'option for the poor', logically applying that message also to questions of international economic and trade relations. If such ideas are formulated within the Church of the richest country on earth, it may be an indication that the challenge of the South is to some extent beginning to be felt in Northern industrial states.

The commitment of the Church achieves much in the Third World; no criticism of outdated or unworldly attitudes – as in the area of family planning and birth control – can alter that. In West Germany, the churches have contributed in no small measure to arousing and deepening an understanding of the problems of developing countries. Their relief organizations and projects, like other non-government organizations, have helped to establish direct contact between the donors and recipients of development aid. They are aware that their efforts can be no substitute for what governments leave undone. No commitment on the part of the Church can compensate for exorbitant interest rates, or under-payment for raw materials, or state-imposed controls on imports from developing countries. But it is greatly to be hoped that the churches will not slacken their own efforts. Their work encourages the practical understanding of interconnections and circumstances which ought to be borne in mind when political and economic decisions are taken. And at that point too the churches should keep urging those in positions of political responsibility to do their part.

When I speak with prominent representatives of the Church, particularly the younger ones, and we explore the causes leading to violent conflict and war, our talk is not just of ideological confrontation and human rights, but is increasingly concerned with:

• high levels of armaments,
• injustices within the world economy, and
• the increasing hunger and need still suffered by so many.

Olof Palme and his Commission, and I and my own colleagues, were in Rome together at the beginning of 1984, at the invitation of our friend Bettino Craxi, the Italian Premier. Pope John Paul II received us. I told him we were not the kind of people who would ask how many divisions of soldiers the Pope had at his disposal: 'Hope is an important element in overcoming obstacles which might otherwise seem insuperable ... all who believe in the power of sincere convictions should reach out their hands to each other.' Our vision, I added, was of an international order in which the possession of nuclear weapons would not be the deciding factor in world politics, and security could be maintained at a much lower level, while material potential was used for the good of the peoples.

The Pope, for his part, reminded us that he had often referred to the links between those two great complex issues of North–South and East–West relations: 'The challenges and problems facing humanity everywhere now transcend national and regional boundaries. . . . If the social issue has today assumed global proportions, then the concrete programmes adopted by nations and regions must spring from a full awareness of that fact, and they must try from the first to assess the consequences such projects will have for the peoples and nations directly or indirectly affected.' Humanity, he said, will never let itself be reduced to a mere object or a one-dimensional factor.

In the autumn of 1984 the Pope described the great gulf between North and South as 'a universal dimension of injustice and evil'. A German cardinal was equally unequivocal when he added, a little later, that to arm ourselves for war was theft, 'since it takes the bread out of the mouths of the poor'.

I suggested earlier that peace may be seen as the objective or wish of all religions, forms of belief and basic philosophical attitudes. Should it not be possible, I ask once more, to deduce from this a *common* desire for peace, and draw from it the emotional and moral incentive to make fresh efforts? I added then that this was another point on which one should cherish no illusions: the creation of order out of contradictions seems to be humanity's eternal task. The momentum provided by the churches and religious communions *can* strengthen global solidarity and contribute to the solution of North–South problems.

IV

WHAT SHOULD BE CHANGED?

1. *Straight Talk*

What are the main tasks which face us in the area of North–South relations? There is still not enough clarity on this point.

First, we must understand that there is now a worldwide interconnection of effects. We speak of interdependency, or the globalization of interaction – the interaction of population growth, economic development, the use of commodities and energy, all bound up with rapid and accelerating technical developments. On the other hand, political capabilities and an understanding of international responsibility seem to be stagnating. There are clear signs of a retrogressive movement in many areas. In the struggle against unemployment, there is not a clear enough distinction between what can be done nationally and what must be attempted at a European or international level. As for environmental problems, international connections are coming to be recognized, if only gradually. But we are still slow to recognize that the question of our future-oriented realization of our own interests arises in our relation with the poorer sections of humanity.

Secondly, the ideological differences between powers and power blocs can no longer be resolved by violent conflict. That is ruled out once and for all by the very real danger, a danger of an entirely new kind, that we might mutually destroy each other – all of us, in the North and the South, the East and the West. Out of that comes the new realization that henceforth we can achieve security only together, *with* each other. What used to be a matter of goodwill is now an inescapable necessity.

82

Thirdly – and this surely is even harder – we must examine our own way of life, our ideas and what we believe to be our aims, and face the fact that poverty, ignorance and disease make large numbers of men and women the slaves of their circumstances. As long as those evils that could be overcome with more of an effort still spread, we must go on reminding ourselves that in the long run such a situation cannot last.

It can be seen without too much difficulty that these three main questions are very closely connected. This is particularly clear if once again we look squarely at the most important consequence of lack of undertanding of the interconnections – the senseless proliferation of weapons of destruction.

The ability of the generation now coming to the age of responsibility to solve the problems I have mentioned will decide how humanity copes with the transition to a new kind of global equilibrium. One may assume that urgently needed investments can be made only when a considerable part of our present resources is diverted to productive uses.

And considerable investments are indeed needed if a transition is to be made to a reasonably stable world with a population of ten or even fifteen billion in the next century. We know that the developing countries cannot raise the funds they need through domestic savings. But this problem *can* be solved. In principle, the resources required *can* be made available. Humanity *is* capable of solving the problem of finding those resources.

Quite another matter is whether we shall succeed in overcoming both the current lack of understanding of the interconnections, and the superfluity of special interests, in time. To succeed there must be much greater cooperation, both between specialists and generalists, particularly in development planning but in many other areas too. What we lack at the moment is an adequate link between expert knowledge and a contextual understanding. The present tendency is to undertake complex projects on the basis of simplistic assumptions, with the result that aims are only rarely achieved, while side effects which had not been envisaged further prejudice the outcome.

It is not easy to avoid such blind alleys. We should do well to forgo dogmatic trifling and speak clearly and to the point. This much seems obvious: it is only through greater global solidarity, through the pluralistic coexistence of differing principles, and through a greater ability to see the context, that we shall create a world in which many, and if possible all, will have their share of common welfare and justice. International cooperation in a spirit of courage and imagination can help to overcome the international crisis.

There is no sense in dogmatic disputes about free markets or central planning. Still less so when keen advocates of the free market economy sanction state intervention to benefit endangered branches of industry – dockyards here, steelworks there, this branch of industry today and perhaps that one tomorrow – while conversely the central planners in the East call for more personal initiative and introduce their own kind of market strategies. When Americans and Europeans alike have expensive market regulations for their own agricultural products, just as the industrial countries of the East do in some other fields, we ought not to reject corresponding demands made by the developing countries in the matter of commodities until we can say our own conduct is right and reasonable.

There is much argument as to whether the economy should be left to itself, or within what framework it should operate. The answer by no means decides *which* kind of economy and in particular what kind of price formation is preferable. Confusion reigns on these points. Whether a country inclines rather more to a market economy or to state control need not concern us. We have become used to seeing both coexist in our countries; why should they not coexist elsewhere too?

The sound of arrogant ideologists blowing their own trumpets is no less irritating than the self-satisfied air of those who regard themselves as realistic politicians, or the self-important gabbling of bureaucrats holding forth about concern for humanity. But the time bomb is ticking away, and despair is no help.

2. Not All in the South Are Poor

Political relations between the various parts of the world have changed fundamentally since the end of the Second World War. A

84

system built up over a period of more than 300 years collapsed within 25. First India, Indonesia and – in a different way – China, then the former English, French and Belgian colonies of Africa, and finally the former Portuguese colonies, all became politically independent; viceroys or governors or whatever they might be called went back to Europe. (The Germans were a special case, last out and first home again, having lost their colonies along with the First World War.)

Or is this view of matters wrong, at least when put that way? Is it too Eurocentric? Mention should at least be made of the Japanese, who ruled 450 million people in Asia around 1942, and were then thrown back on their native islands (losing some areas of those as well). And nothing can now be understood in isolation from the role of the two superpowers that emerged from the Second World War.

Of the 159 member states of the United Nations (in 1984) the numbers divided up into:

- 127 developing countries,
- 20 Western industrial countries,
- 12 countries with planned economies (of which China and Cuba are also classed as developing countries).

In some UN organizations, the following classification has been in use for some time:

- A: African and Asian developing countries,
- B: Western industrial countries,
- C: Latin American developing countries,
- D: Eastern planned-economy countries,
- China to a certain extent forms a group on its own.

A designation for the developing countries more generally used is the 'Group of 77', actually numbering 126 states at the end of 1984. This 'group' was formed in 1964, when UNCTAD (the United Nations Conference on Trade and Development) was first convened.

The oversimplified classification of countries into groups does not do justice to the complex reality. It is easy to distinguish

85

between former colonies and their former colonial rulers – but a distinction between North and South, if by that we mean to distinguish between rich and poor countries, can be drawn only if one adds some clarifications. In any case, the world is not so constituted that the North can be described outright as 'rich' and the South as 'poor'. Even apart from other differences, we all know that not everyone in the North is rich, nor everyone in the South poor.

'North', at the risk of simplification, stands for the 'old' industrial countries, not just for the West; 'South', at a similar risk of misleading simplification, stands for all the countries whose economic development has been retarded not exclusively, but largely, by colonialism.

The North–South split expressed in figures:
- Just under a third of the world's population lives in the North, with over four-fifths of the world's income at its disposal.
- Among the 'rich' countries, those with 'market economies' are far in advance of those with 'planned economies'.
- Of the poor countries, those with 'market economies' get a share of 12 per cent of world revenue, and the 'planned economy' countries of Asia (in particular China!) get 5 per cent. The gross national product per head of the population in most developing countries is between $150 and $1,500 a year.

Income per head and the share of the poor countries in world revenue are generally put even lower in statistics than they are in fact, since the barter economy and dealings in kind are hard to record statistically.

The make-up of the world by states offers a confused picture, and current concepts are not entirely suited to clarifying it:

- The 'North', as well as taking in North America, Japan, the European West and the Soviet Union with her European allies, is also understood to include two rich industrial countries south of the Equator, Australia and New Zealand.

- In Asia, Japan counts as part of the 'West', and so again do Australia and New Zealand in the Pacific.
- Japan, more heavily dependent than Europe on the developing countries, where she makes a very large part of her direct investments, rose to become the second strongest economic power in the world within a generation.
- Countries regarded as belonging to the 'East' are the German Democratic Republic, Czechoslovakia and other Central European countries, Cuba in the Caribbean, and sometimes Ethiopia in Africa.
- A country like Mexico may lie in the North, but counts as part of the 'South'.
- There are countries located in the South, particularly among the oil-exporting Arab states of the Gulf, which have a higher *per capita* income than prosperous industrial countries.
- Not all countries such as Nigeria, Indonesia and Mexico are rich because they export oil.
- In the 'South', as in the 'North', there are instances of extreme differences in prosperity; some countries sell a great quantity of foodstuffs while many of their own people do not have enough to eat.
- Ireland, Greece, Portugal and Spain belong to the European Community (and to OECD, the Organization for Economic Cooperation and Development, with its headquarters in Paris, which grew out of the Marshall Plan); however, they are nowhere near as prosperous as the USA, or the Federal Republic of Germany, or Sweden.
- Romania sets store by being included among the developing countries, and in that respect is comparable to non-aligned Yugoslavia. Does that decrease Romania's association with Comecon?
- Does the fact that Hong Kong, Singapore, Kuwait and Bahrain belong to the 'Group of 77' make them poor?
- The ASEAN group – the Association of South-East Asian Nations, including Thailand, Malaysia, Indonesia, Singapore, the Philippines, and latterly also Brunei – has a good chance of healthy development with considerable annual growth.
- Finally, it is surely confusing to lump together countries which have an old-established industrial base such as Argentina,

Brazil, Mexico, and Colombia and Venezuela, or aspiring countries such as South Korea, Taiwan and Malaysia, with the poverty-stricken regions of the Sahel zone, Bangladesh or Haiti.

And another thing to be remembered is that not everything which succeeds in Kenya will necessarily succeed in India. An Eastern European head of state did not hesitate to tell me one of his anxieties: it is one thing, he said, to build a factory in the Mongolian People's Republic, another to rely on its being efficiently run thereafter.

Not only in South-East Asia but in some Latin American countries too, industrial development has been erratic. The twenty countries which had the fastest growth in the Seventies were all Third World countries, and some of them stand on the brink of full industrialization. (Argentina, Brazil, Chile, Mexico and Uruguay are regarded as newly industrializing countries; so are Hong Kong, Singapore, South Korea and Taiwan.) The old industrial states have now lost their pre-eminence in a whole range of industries, not only in such areas as textiles and shoes, but in steel, ship-building, railroad construction, mechanical engineering, and the manufacturing of parts for the market in photographic equipment, electronics and computers.

The 'bloc of poor countries', if it ever existed, has been eroded by a number of very different circumstances and interests. On one hand, we find the rich among the oil-producing countries, into which money is still pouring at a considerable if no longer exuberant rate; on the other, countries like Tanzania, Cambodia, Bolivia and Bangladesh; in between them, newly industrializing countries with their debt mountains, to which I shall return when considering the case of Latin America.

The collective term 'Third World', which appears frequently in this book, has become customary to describe the developing countries. The expression was coined in Paris at the beginning of the Fifties, and applied to those countries which, exploited and despised like the Third Estate before the French Revolution, now wanted to 'make something of themselves'. No one was ever quite sure what the First and Second Worlds were supposed to be. The Old World and the New World, or the Western World and the

88

Eastern World? In Mao's time, the Chinese Communists tried drawing their own kind of distinction: the two superpowers or 'hegemonists' were the First World, the Western Europeans and some countries in a comparable situation the Second World, with the Second regarded on the one hand as a participant in the oppression of the Third World, while on the other it might be won over as an ally against the 'hegemonists'. . . .

So far as the governments making up the group of developing countries, or the 'Group of 77', are concerned, it is not essentially different from the uncommitted or Non-aligned Countries Movement, which has grown from 25 to 104. At its founding conference in Belgrade in 1961 – there was an Afro–Asian forerunner in Bandung in 1955 – the question of peace and the problems of development were described as of equal importance. Nehru, Nasser and Tito formed a kind of executive committee, and right up to the time of his death in 1980 Tito opposed all attempts to bind the uncommitted countries to one of the superpowers. The 'movement' has no permanent secretariat. Unlike the 'Group of 77', it has no group status within the United Nations.

I had a chance to see Tito's firm commitment to East–West and North–South issues for myself in the summer of 1979, when I visited him for the last time on the island of Brioni. Tito played a considerable part in making the non-aligned countries into a factor which cannot be disregarded and at times is influential, and in reminding the Northern part of the world of its duties towards the South, as well as in reminding the great powers of their duty to maintain peace.

(The Commonwealth, with 49 member states, plus Namibia, stands rather outside the rest of the scheme; a loose grouping, it is the legacy of the British Empire, and has launched many useful initiatives over the years.)

The 'action programme for a new international economic order' upon which a summit conference of the non-aligned countries decided in Algiers in 1973, was the subject of talks I had a few months later with President Boumedienne of Algeria, and with President Echeverria, then President of Mexico, after a Special Session of the United Nations had adopted a 'Charter of Economic Rights and Duties of States'. What they were advocating seemed to me very schematic, not free of contradictions, and also excessively sure of the value of resolutions. In fact, they had more right on their side than their uncomprehending opponents, though they did not take the far-reaching objective differences between developing countries into account, let alone the differences within most of those countries. But it was to be only a decade before an EEC Commissioner, the former French Foreign Minister Claude Cheysson, was to say that the creation of a new international economic system was an even more decisive factor for world peace than the resolution of conflicts between the superpowers. The one is certainly no less important than the other.

3. *Whose Development?*

At the end of 1982, three years after the first report of my Commission, we said in our second report that 'the Commission foresaw the world community in the 1980s facing much greater dangers than at any time since the Second World War'. The prospects had now, we said, become even darker, with:

- the international recession, which could deepen into depression;
- massive unemployment in the countries of the North, and the threat of economic collapse in parts of the Third World;
- acute risk to the international financial system, and growing disorder in world trade;
- the renewed arms race, as well as wars and civil strife in numerous Third World countries.

Another few years have passed since then. In the USA and some (but far from all) industrial countries, a certain economic recovery has begun. But this is still problematical, and there are hints of fresh setbacks. We cannot yet discount the possibility that the Eighties will become a decade of disasters.

The great contrast between the satisfaction of needs in North and South, and destitution in the Third World, have spread yet further. Thus it is only too easy to see why people wonder whether many of the developing countries could not do more themselves to get the problems under control. Indeed, one quite often hears it asked whether 'they' are doing anything at all, or just relying too much, and unjustifiably, on outside help.

This argument, if it is one, concurs with the misleading thesis of that Oxford international economist who said that foreign aid inhibits instead of accelerating development. But the assumption that public development aid has done more harm than good in Third World countries is downright wrong. The fact that some ambitious projects have turned out to be of little relevance is quite another matter. There is no doubt that the developing countries and their financial backers have had to learn from such mistakes and were often slow to do so. And no one is claiming that no more mistakes will ever be made. But why overlook the large number of defective projects in industrial countries? Why should the criteria be set so much higher for the developing countries?

The arch-conservative Lord Bauer, a Hungarian by birth, but who has worked at the London School of Economics for a number of years, goes further: development aid, he says, encourages a dependent mentality, begets corruption and shores up incompetent governments; it is 'the cause and not the solution' of the North–South conflict. Moreover, in his view, the population explosion does not impede but encourages economic growth. Nor does he see mineral resources as a necessary precondition of growth – it depends entirely on the correct economic policy and the values on which it is founded. Professor Bauer is among the harshest critics of the World Bank and other international institutions.

My old friend Gunnar Myrdal, the Swedish political economist and Nobel Prize winner – a man of wide interests, as expressed in his great work on the race problem in the United States and a major book on Asia – has been associated with criticism of this kind; unjustly, but there is no doubt that he did perform a considerable volte-face. His main targets are the enrichment of élites and the incompetence of bureaucracies and he deplores the fact that much aid was thus wasted. We should tell the Third World, says Professor Myrdal, that the new economic order has to begin in their own countries. In practical terms, this means the donation of aid in times of disaster, while normal economic relations should be the rule for the rest of the time. . . .

As anyone will understand, I cannot myself adopt this line, which betrays great disillusion. But let us not hide the fact that similar ideas are sometimes voiced in the South itself. B. P. Koirala, whom I have already mentioned, thought that foreign aid did not advance the cause of development, but merely created a new class whose prosperity had nothing to do with the condition of the people. 'The new class is not economically rooted in its country. It exists solely on a basis of the manipulation of foreign aid by means of corruption and illegal trade.'

In a report on Nigeria I found the following: 'Corruption in the economy, the administration and the military will persist as long as the immediate "survival interests" of poorly paid civil servants or the exaggerated material need for luxury goods are latent in the middle and upper classes of society.'

Abuse of power is an evil in *all* parts of the world. At my request experts gave me the names of the countries which would be at the very top of any ranking in this respect. Extravagance and corruption, abuse of power, militarization for the purpose of maintaining power, may be found in many parts of the world, not just countries of the South. We can speak of a good example being set by the industrial countries only to a limited degree. An open dialogue between North and South must mean that no subject is excluded: not the pressure exerted by strong governments, nor fraudulent dealings on the part of powerful business concerns, nor the abuse of power by so-called élites. And if we go by the United Nations Charter, the destitution of refugees, the mistreatment of minorities, and infringement of the simplest human rights cannot be excluded from a claim on the common interest.

At the same time, we shall have to live with the fact that the claim to sovereignty of representatives of some young states will be made particularly forcefully – all the more so when they can plead an old culture. We must realize that reproving forefingers raised too often and too easily lead to 'us in the North' having the record of our own sins held against us. And among them are those sins we have exported. The one-sided apportioning of blame is no help. It is important to recognize our own as well as the general responsibility, both in the present and the future, and to understand that small states, and states of medium size, and states of fairly large size too, must find a common denominator between their own interests and those of others if they mean to hold their own to any extent.

As for what development is really supposed to mean, and whose development we are talking about – there is more than one answer to that question. At least we shall not start out as confidently as they did a generation ago from the assumption that the 'underdeveloped' countries should be developed to conform with the material standards of ourselves (or the Americans) and that the whole world would be well advised to imitate the model of the highly industrialized countries.

These days, there is justifiable doubt in more than one quarter as to whether development can simply be equated with growth of every kind. It is hard to imagine development without growth. But not every kind of growth leads to development, let alone progress. The question is rather: *what* do we want to see grow, and *how*, in order to encourage *whose* development? Even in our own latitudes, there is an increasing number of people who wonder if it can really be humanity's highest aim to live in crowded accommodation, consuming unnecessarily large amounts of energy and eating fast food. The developing countries should go their own way. Their peoples must be allowed to decide for themselves what kind of progress they want, and what elements of *their* cultural inheritance they wish to perpetuate. It cannot be any business of ours to press new (or old) models upon them, act as their guardians or take them under our wing. Anyone who recommends a mere process of 'catching up' to our own level misunderstands the facts, or his own sphere of responsibility.

The real aim of a country's development should lie in its self-fulfilment and ability to participate in creative partnership. Our Commission assumed that development was in any case more than a transition from poverty to wealth, from a traditional agrarian economy to urbanized, industrial ways of life. The concept of development, to those who think as we do, contains not only the notion of material prosperity, but also the idea of something more in the way of human dignity, security, justice and equality. For the rest, we said, we were not trying to redefine the now questionable concept of development. Our concern was not with the niceties of theoretical notions, but with the fact that so many people are living in almost inconceivable poverty, and that so much needs to be done to help ward off the worst of that misery.

Attempts to penetrate the problem through theory – and there are several variants from the Marxist viewpoint alone – deserve some attention, and I would just like to mention two points: First, the current theory that imperialism is the exploitation of the 'periphery' by the 'centre' need not in principle be at variance with our present survival interests, which transcend all systems. Secondly, alongside the failure of 'liberal' strategies of the catching-up variety is the fact that a considerable trade is growing between developing countries, or some of them.

It is beginning to be widely felt that we must free ourselves from any idea of the desirability of spoon-feeding others. The point is not what others should do, but what we are ready to do together with them. The fact that development begins at home is one of the important realizations of the last few years. Ways of life and methods of production which are not destructive need encouragement. In the process, it will not always be technical quality which matters, but a new spirit of solidarity, and of respect for the space in which individuals have freedom to act and for the common good.

Among those in positions of responsibility in the South there are quite a number who speak frankly about the weaknesses of their associations; the moral corruption that always proceeds from absolute power; the flight from responsibility; the 'naïve belief in rhetoric and the volume of noise' (Ramphal).

The problems facing the South, which were described in detail in my Commission's two reports, can in all essential respects be brought nearer a solution only by the people of the South themselves. It was our colleagues from the developing countries who put forward this proposition, and set it down on paper. The countries of the South as a whole, however, have no machinery that is at all suitable for an era of negotiations. It is a drawback that the developing countries have not managed to set up a joint secretariat. And this is a task which could hardly have been solved *for* them, unless by a decision to make the necessary modifications to UNCTAD, with the agreement of all member countries.

In the autumn of 1984, shortly before I went to Cartagena in Colombia, representatives of the Group of 77 meeting there endorsed their intention of introducing a system of mutually preferential trading, in order to extend the exchange of goods between themselves; three years earlier, an action programme had been decided upon in Caracas. Bringing about more economic cooperation *between* the developing countries was another important subject discussed at the conferences of the non-aligned countries. A certain amount of progress can now be recorded, and we may hope for something to come of the South–South dimension in international trade.

The prosperous oil states have not yet managed to summon up any enthusiasm for a 'Bank of the South'. During Latin America's severe debt crisis, much was heard there of a coordinated approach to creditors, but nothing much of a practical nature came of it outside conferences. However, there is no doubt that cooperation in regional areas looks like becoming a more important factor. It is not something that can be kept on ice until all possible ills have been done away with in the individual countries concerned.

The familiar inconsistencies of human behaviour hold good of North–South relations, among them the fact that people think they must compensate and indeed over-compensate for losses. Material interests are frequently given an ideological camouflage. Much proselytizing is done, and massive influence is brought to bear, under the banner of self-determination. Particularly in cultural respects, anything but liberalism and non-intervention is practised – instead, influence is exerted according to whatever the proponent of non-interventionism wants. Development aid and economic cooperation are often enough pursued as a continuation of an old state of affairs by new means. Quite a number of former colonial civil servants meet again in the employment of the World Bank, or working as experts in their old countries, but now in the service of a new ministry for economic cooperation or similar agency.

To call incompetence, social arrogance and injustice in the Third World by their right names means not sweeping anything under the carpet, yet not making ourselves out to be any better than we are. Justice did not prevail in our own states from the very first, and it is still something achieved only with difficulty. 'They' in the South did not inflict economic crises and world wars on 'us' in the North.

4. *A New Bretton Woods?*

At the Bretton Woods conference towards the end of the Second World War, agreements were made which, under the leadership of the United States, were to prove their worth to the international monetary system (and to policies of financial cooperation) for an amazingly long time. Today, there is not a country which, on its own, has that concentrated economic power and discipline in monetary policy which would be necessary to help the world to a sound system. International trade and the interdependence of the international economy have increased far more than any participant in that conference at Bretton Woods may ever have imagined. Economic power has spread into a wider area today, and mutual international dependence has to a great extent become reality. Yet confidence in international cooperation has been shaken, and indeed is largely lost.

At Bretton Woods – which was nothing but a railroad station and the address of a fine, pleasantly situated New Hampshire hotel – the Americans and British between them laid the foundations of the financial and monetary system which turned out to be functional in its own way for nearly three decades.

The Bretton Woods negotiations themselves were described as difficult, although the number of participants was modest compared with the 146 member states which now belong to the World Bank. But even then, in that smaller circle, it was hard to convince many of those taking part of the benefits of international agreements. Even the Americans initially had considerable reservations, although the new system was much to their advantage. Harry Dexter White, leading the American delegation, warned his fellow countrymen and his own government that if success depended on taking bold action and taking it swiftly, they could not afford protracted negotiations, and where all-embracing economic, political and social questions were concerned, small national advantages should give way. In his own words: 'We must substitute, before it is too late, imagination for tradition; generosity for shrewdness; understanding for bargaining; toughness for caution; and wisdom for prejudice. We are rich – we should use more of our wealth in the interest of peace.'

The 'East' took part in the negotiations but did not join the institutions decided upon at the Bretton Woods conference; the Soviet Union was not happy about the idea of transferring part of its gold holdings. Numerically, the 'South' was poorly represented, although India and several important Latin American countries participated. Naturally the 'enemy states', headed by Germany and Japan, were not invited to attend. Better adjusted participation of all interested parties is thus one of the subjects which should figure prominently in any discussion of the reform of the international institutions which were then established.

The Bretton Woods system was visibly shaken by the oil crisis of 1973/74, but it had already ceased to function well at the beginning of the Seventies. The convertibility of the dollar into gold was abandoned in 1971, when the United States could not bring itself to cover the cost of the Vietnam War by laying a greater burden on its own national economy. It had been financing its deficits for too long by putting more and more dollars into circulation. The result was a change of attitude towards the dollar. Exchange rates adjustments were expected, and international capital movements began. The sudden reversal of the flow of international payments as the result of the oil price crisis finished the job.

Only very slowly, particularly in the USA, did people begin to understand that these changes had much farther-reaching consequences than what the long queues at petrol stations and the increased demand for smaller cars indicated. The people of the oil-exporting countries could not eat their billions, any more than they had previously been able to drink their oil. So to a great extent the money flowed back into the banks of the industrial countries, whether as direct investments or credits. 'Recycling', as it was called, was in fashion, and ostensibly it seemed to be a great success.

There was a similar picture after the second oil shock in 1979/80. The banks granted yet more credits, debts rose higher,

International institutions set up at Bretton Woods:
- The International Monetary Fund (IMF), to be the guardian of monetary order. It was to concern itself with stable exchange rates and liquidity to support free trade. Of recent years the debt crisis has altered and in some respects enhanced its role.
- The World Bank (officially IBRD, the International Bank for Reconstruction and Development). Its first task was opening up the way to reconstruction in Europe and Japan by means of loans. Later, its real work was to encourage the developing countries.
- Lord Keynes, the eminent British economist, wanted an International Trade Organization (ITO) set up at Bretton Woods as well, but the Havana Agreement, negotiated with this in mind, was not ratified by the United States Congress.
- The proposed ITO was also to have concerned itself with the stabilization of commodity prices. Had that suggestion been followed up, serious disagreements – and considerable damage to the developing countries – could have been avoided later.
- GATT, the General Agreement on Tariffs and Trade, was created as an indirect result of Bretton Woods. Its headquarters are in Geneva, and it now has 90 members. Originally intended only as a temporary arrangement, it turned into an important forum for multilateral talks on trade.

and no one felt too much concerned. But the flow of money was not quite so regular now. A huge so-called Eurodollar market (i.e. a market for dollars held outside the United States) had developed, the result of the circumstances in which some – the banks – were eager to invest their liquid funds, and others – not least the oil-importing developing countries – were equally eager to ask for new loans. The Eurodollar market grew from a few billion, originally intended only to balance payments at the margin and, as it were, keep the old system running, to a vast size, expanding to $1,000 billion or even $2,000 billion. For several years, and generally without any control by the central banks, money was moved from country to country, wherever there seemed to be the smallest danger of devaluation. Great fluctuations in exchange rates ensued, and entire economies veered off course. The end-product was high interest rates, for it had become increasingly necessary to halt inflation, and moreover the new sources of money were beginning to dry up.

Today one cannot overlook the fact that the world economy has been badly scarred. The scars stem from the fact that it was left to market forces to adapt the national economies to international shifts of economic power. In the process the oil-importing developing countries suffered the worst damage of all.

The chaos in international financial relations has contributed to the second deep structural crisis in the international economy in this century, involving:
- Massive unemployment, not just in the developing countries, but in many industrial states too.
- A dangerous increase in isolationism, much to the detriment of the newly industrializing developing countries.
- A fall in the price of commodities which is only partly absorbed.
- Disastrous debts, increased yet further by very high interest rates.

It is hardly surprising that critics observing the situation in the mid-Eighties think it even graver than the great crisis between the two World Wars. Once again we face questions that were to the fore at Bretton Woods. We in the West are not the only ones to feel the lack of a Harry Dexter White and a new Maynard Keynes, the other driving force behind the agreements at the Mount Washington Hotel. They were men with a gift for action as well as analysis, and it was they who worked out the details of the agreements and persuaded their governments to adopt them. They even took pains to ensure that the media could understand their message, and made detailed preparations for the negotiations, devising many clever manoeuvres. Incidentally, only seventeen days were spent on drawing up the terms for the creation of the IMF at Bretton Woods, while for the World Bank it took a whole five!

Today, it is said, things are very much more difficult, and in particular, the political will is lacking. And that is true. But it seems to me that the fundamental question is the same: do we work together or against each other? Despite all obstacles, shall we have cooperation, this time between East and West, North and South (and South and South), or shall we fight each country for itself, all against all, the outcome being uncertain?

The world *needs* a new Bretton Woods, if in a different place. On occasion I have suggested Berlin, politically on the border between East and West, as a suitable scene for such a meeting. For if reform of the international monetary and financial situation were pending, a serious attempt should be made to involve the Soviet Union on the one hand, and to enable the developing countries to participate on genuinely fair terms on the other. At the heart of major reform should be an effort to regulate relations between peoples and states in the name of equality.

The prerequisite would be to abandon that superstitious attitude which expects more of the market than it can deliver. For instance: a few years ago, the big banks protested against any criticism that they were cheerfully allowing developing countries more and more credit without troubling themselves much about their debtors' ability to pay. They presumably believed they were doing right and expected the world's thanks for dealing with a situation that baffled many governments. At first they made some money out of the requisite rescheduling of debts. Moreover, they thought any attempt to subject their operations to international control would only restrict their potential. An American expert remarked pithily, 'Exactly the way bankers argued in my grandfather's time, back in the United States, when national bank regulation was first introduced.'

In fact, too little rather than too much is being invested almost all over the world. But without some kind of regulating authority, the credit boom will get out of control, and the debt crisis can no longer be handled by any government acting alone. In a painful economic crisis, the United States saw the necessity of a controlling hand, and introduced bank regulation. Guidelines are necessary, and so are regulatory supporting actions if the possible collapse of a part is not to destroy the whole. The world economy finds itself in just that danger today. Those institutional safeguards we have at present are not enough to avert the danger.

Now a central authority to administer the world economy is as unlikely to come into being as a world government ruling all the world's different countries. But it is high time for very much closer cooperation and coordination in economic policy, particularly in the areas of currency and credit. The fact is that we are paying for our failure to act when we should have acted, at the time of the first oil shock. That is now over ten years ago. And there is still a good deal of resistance, and people still think along the old lines, advocating the remedies of the day before yesterday. We can see how hard it is to overcome such attitudes even in the narrower sphere of action of the European Community.

The reasons why the world economy finds itself in serious difficulties are of course of very many and very diverse kinds. Obviously none of the various economic theories or schools of thought has the magic formula which would help us to make steady and unproblematic economic progress. And it has become increasingly clear that no model can be put into effect anywhere in what might be called its pure form. So the first essential is for as many as possible of those who have to make the decisions not to let themselves be blinkered by dogma.

The much-vaunted international free trade is not so free at all. Neither world hunger, nor the destruction of the environment, nor the population explosion will stop of their own accord, nor will the arms race be checked by appealing to the free play of market forces. No: what is needed is purposeful concerted action to reach those goals. The same may be said of supplies of energy and commodities, or the control of internationally conditioned inflation and unemployment.

We should look soberly at the call for a new international economic order. I read an article in a French newspaper suggesting that it was time for us to realize that a new order was no longer merely something for the future. The multinational corporations, said the writer, have existed within a new system for quite some while; only politics lag behind the times and fail to provide the essential guidelines appropriate to the new situation. The multinationals succeeded through global planning and cooperation, and they also profited by the competition between governments, basing their activities wherever they found conditions most favourable. Moreover, said the writer, they have also been among the greatest beneficiaries of the monetary confusion of recent years. . . .

The present difficulties call for decisions taking more than the changes of the last few years into account. Governments should not pursue aims that are too contradictory, or adopt measures whose effects will be neutralized in the final analysis. The first essential is not just to talk about international economic inter-dependencies, but to take real account of them; the second is to act accordingly.

Until we have fundamental reform of the international monetary and financial system we must make sure that the Bretton Woods institutions have adequate resources at their disposal to carry out their tasks equitably. Secondly, the developing countries must be given the chance to contribute to their own welfare *and* to the prosperity of the world economy. And thirdly, the industrial countries must try to reach a national consensus, one that will outlast changes of administration, on the outlines of their economic activity, and to achieve coordination of their respective economic policies. Only then can they adjust with any prospect of success to international structural changes and adapt themselves to the modifications necessary. However, we cannot do without a new Bretton Woods.

5. *My Experiences on the 'North–South Commission'*

In the New Year of 1977, Robert McNamara, then President of the World Bank, sent a messenger to the South of France, where I was on holiday, to ask if he could rely on me to chair an independent commission which he thought was needed. I indicated that my present duties were fairly onerous, but I did not want to respond to this confidence in me with a blunt refusal. A month later McNamara, whom I had known since he was Kennedy's Defence Secretary, and whom I had met frequently, both while and after he was at the World Bank, made a speech in

Boston in which he mentioned his idea and my name. I did not make up my mind for some months, but then, at a press conference in New York in late September 1977, I announced my willingness to form, and act as chairman of, an 'Independent Commission on International Development Issues'.

A great many talks preceded this announcement. I was anxious to make it clear that the Commission did not want to complicate government negotiations in any way – a conference on issues of economic cooperation was meeting in Paris until the summer of 1977 – or interfere with the work of international committees. Rather, the group I was to appoint should see its task as making recommendations which would complement activities already in progress, and might help to improve the climate for North–South discussion. I also consulted Kurt Waldheim, then Secretary-General of the United Nations, who said he would be happy to receive the first copy of our report.

I let three considerations guide me in choosing the members of the Commission. First, Third World members should not be numerically in the minority, so that they could not be outvoted. (In fact, there was no voting.) Second, no impression of narrow party political constraint should be allowed to arise: hence we had Edward Heath alongside Olof Palme; along with Eduardo Frei, the Christian Democrat from Chile, a left-wing Algerian Socialist; the militant Commonwealth Secretary-General from Guyana as well as a banker who had been in a Republican administration in the USA; an experienced Indian governor and a Canadian trades union leader. From my exploratory talks, I did not think the time was yet ripe to try recruiting members from the Communist states. Thirdly, I was anxious for the members to be personally responsible for their share in the work, not following directives. We were assured of financial independence also of the World Bank. The government of the Netherlands was guaranteeing our expenses, and bearing half of them; the other half came from contributions made by a number of other countries and institutions.

One of the pleasant surprises of the Commission was that it did succeed in defusing current and future issues in the area of North–South relations of any ideological connotations, and in keeping them free of considerations of national prestige. I found it a fascinating and instructive experience to help in drawing up the report which was published at the beginning of 1980 under the title, *North–South: A Programme for Survival*. This report was translated into more than 20 languages, including Arabic, Chinese, Swahili and Indonesian. A second report, *Common Crisis*, appeared early in 1983.

One cannot say that the two reports failed to have any effect or exert any influence. Initially, they drew a number of comments, some more thoughtful than others, from governments, parliaments and organizations:

- 'We welcome the report of the Brandt Commission, and we shall look carefully at its recommendations,' it was said at the economic summit meeting of the leading Western industrial states in Venice, in June 1980. However, matters rested there.
- Parliaments of various countries and the parliament of the European Community debated the report. Working parties were set up, and several governments redefined their guidelines for development policy in the light of our recommendations, among them the governments of the Federal Republic of Germany, Great Britain and Switzerland. However, no notice was taken of our proposals for fundamental reform.
- International organizations accepted a number of our recommendations. The IMF and the World Bank adopted several of our suggestions – too few, and not quickly enough, but still it was something.
- As for any influence on interested groups and sectors of public opinion, it is hard to gauge. However, over and above serious comment, there were public gatherings with hundreds and even thousands of participants, for instance in Berlin, The Hague, and London. Ten thousand people came to Westminster to take part in a 'lobby on Brandt' and ask members of Parliament to support the report's demands.
- The media in the USA did not take much notice of us, not just because a great deal of attention was then being paid to the renewal of the Cold War. We had underestimated the need for well-organized publicity. However, the main reason might be sought in the change of administration, which also had a

detrimental influence on the effects of the *Global 2000* report in the United States.

Altogether, the immediate effects were restricted in extent. When a few years had passed, and the situation had deteriorated further, some of those ideas which had been dismissed as 'too pessimistic and too radical' were now taken up. Better late than never.

For the rest, I found it was very true that such work cannot be done without a capable secretariat – capable not just technically but in its specialist expertise. Of course it is also true that even the most capable of secretariats needs guidelines. It can perform its function only by reducing the friction between differing schools of thought and different temperaments to a minimum.

It is possible to mitigate but not eliminate the difficulties arising from the fact that a report of this kind must be produced by a number of different authors and editors from among the Commission members. I told some of my colleagues a remark I had just read in the work of an Eastern European dissident: to write a book is far easier for one man than for a collective. Given an authors' collective 40-strong, the writing can become a nightmare. Our own problems were not quite so bad as that.

I countered unreasonable expectations by saying that at worst, we would merely be adding one more book to the literature on development problems, and humanity had known worse things than another publication on a subject of increasing importance. In fact, at least 40 governments referred to our report at the Special General Assembly of the United Nations in 1980. But it was our bad luck to be putting forward our proposals at a time when there was a marked deterioration in the world political situation as a result of the Soviet invasion of Afghanistan and the confused state of affairs in Iran; relations between Washington and Moscow went on deteriorating. When I gave President Carter our report at the beginning of 1980, however, he did express a lively interest in taking some of the heat out of relations with the other superpower. His successor, elected at the end of that year, at the time conveyed no similar impression.

Our report influenced the international debate not so much by way of many separate proposals, as by emphasizing new features in discussions – others as well as ourselves were doing so at this time. We said that conditions for common *survival* were now the main concern, not development *aid* alone, important as that still was; not acts of benevolence, however laudable, but changes made to enable the developing countries to stand on their own feet. The process called for many erroneous ideas to be abandoned.

The Commission could not adopt, sight unseen, the all-inclusive, maximalist demands which many associate with the proposition of a new international economic order. We were unanimous in our view that the time bomb ticking away to the great danger of all could be defused only by making the successful breakthrough to fairly negotiated solutions. An 'all or nothing' approach was and is unrealistic. My colleagues and I settled for a combination of fundamental reforms and smaller steps to put right evils and aberrations. In all likelihood, the requisite changes could not be made in the twinkling of an eye. My reformist credo thus ran: we should keep the broad horizon in view, but not set immediate aims so high as to prohibit all chance of achieving them.

The first Brandt Report included an Emergency Programme for 1980–1985, feeling the world could not be offered long-term measures alone. We listed the equally important elements of the emergency programme as:

- financial aid;
- an international energy strategy;
- a global food programme;
- a start towards some major structural reforms in the international economic system.

An emergency programme of this nature was not meant to be a substitute for longer-term reforms, nor to be inconsistent with them. We said that immediate measures had to be taken if the world economy was not to suffer severely over the next few years. The idea of such a programme was widely discussed, and modified and supplemented, but not put into effect in any appropriate form. It did look as if there might be a chance when a North–

South summit such as we had proposed was envisaged for the autumn of 1981. Unfortunately, the idea did not get far.

6. The Cancun Summit

I had strongly advocated occasional summit meetings where serious talks could be held and possible compromises discovered by a limited number of people. Like others, I also realized that no state could make decisions for another at meetings of this nature, and the fundamental equality of all states must remain assured for actual decisions to be taken within the framework of the United Nations. None the less, I felt even more sceptical than many of my colleagues about mammoth conferences.

We therefore agreed that a restricted summit meeting between heads of government from North and South – 'if possible with the participation of the East and China' – might perhaps advance the process of international decision-making. We thought the number of participants should be kept small enough to make progress possible, and large enough to be representative and for what it said to carry weight. 'Such a summit cannot negotiate because it is not universal, nor will it be an appropriate forum to discuss details. But it can reach an understanding on what is necessary, and what is feasible, and how to harmonize the two.'

After laborious preliminary discussions, which I remember only too well, a first such meeting between the leading representatives of 22 states took place in Cancun on the Atlantic coast of Mexico in October 1981. The Austrian Chancellor had agreed to chair it jointly with the President of Mexico. Against all expectations and against advice, the new President of the USA, elected at the end of 1980, also decided to take part. After serious discussion of the invitation – as I was able to ascertain in Moscow in the summer of 1981 – the Russians did not attend. The Chinese were represented by their President, although he said very little. The participating states from the industrial countries were Austria, Canada, France, the Federal Republic of Germany, Japan, Sweden, the United Kingdom, the USA; those from the developing countries were Algeria, Bangladesh, Brazil, China, Guyana,

India, the Ivory Coast, Mexico, Nigeria, the Philippines, Saudi Arabia, Tanzania, Venezuela and Yugoslavia; the UN Secretary-General also attended.

Cancun was adversely affected by the fact that both Bruno Kreisky and Helmut Schmidt were prevented from coming by illness, and had to send representatives. The Canadian Premier, Pierre Trudeau, who was committed to North–South issues, took the place of the Austrian Chancellor as co-chairman; he was in no way responsible for the unsatisfactory outcome of the meeting.

Commonwealth Secretary-General Ramphal and I had submitted a proposal to the participants which was based on the four points of our emergency programme mentioned above. It laid most emphasis on the need for a global food and agriculture programme, and it did look as if in this area at least, Cancun would make some progress. (At this time, signatures were being collected in the USA for a resolution based on a thesis both brief and to the point: 'If we do not share the world's resources, there will be no justice; without justice there will be no peace; and without peace there will be no freedom anywhere in the world.')

We seemed to have moved closer together in Cancun – for instance, over the framework for the 'global' negotiations upon which the United Nations had decided in the autumn of 1979, though nothing much ever came of them. Important issues in the areas of commodities, energy, trade, development, currency and finance should be discussed, within their contexts. There was fundamental agreement on this point at the summit, even from the President of the USA, but subsequently, again, nothing happened. None the less, I and some others were inclined to consider Cancun a modest, partial success. At least one could learn from it.

I had comprehensive talks with three Presidents of the UN General Assembly – my countryman Rüdiger von Wechmar, the Iraqi ambassador Kittani, ambassador Muños Ledo of Mexico – and with the Secretary-General of the United Nations, on the difficulty of initiating global negotiations. In previous years, everything had seemed to founder on the fact that some spokesmen for the developing countries gave an impression of wanting to decide the future of institutions such as the IMF, and the policy to be followed by the industrial countries, by the force of their majority vote alone. Later, however, some very moderate and constructive proposals put forward by the non-aligned countries and the Group of 77 foundered on the delaying tactics of the US government and its hard-core allies.

In practical terms, the proposal was to depart from the idea of a vast 'global' round of negotiations and to tackle particularly urgent problems in an initial phase, concentrating on those areas where it was likely that consensus could be reached. In a second phase, attention could be turned to the really difficult problems, particularly those dealing with structural and institutional changes. From the angle of negotiating techniques, this combination of gradual progress and extensive discussion should be supplemented by an understanding on regional representation between the various governments, so that effective working parties could be set up. The influence of the moderate developing countries, led by India, melted away when their concessions – formally as well as in fact – were not honoured.

After the Cancun summit, President Reagan thanked me for the contribution of the North–South Commission. He emphasized the importance of development aid for many countries, insisting that private investment should play a greater part. The IMF and the World Bank, he said, were trying to put the resources available to even more efficient use. . . . None of this sounded hostile, but it did leave a basic question unanswered. In the poorest countries, the alternatives of private investment and public aid simply do not exist. As with the conflict of dogmas between free market and centrally planned economies, financial issues run the risk of arguing about non-existent alternatives. More private or more public investment? More multilateral or more bilateral lending? In fact both are needed. (The World Bank, which in any case is the largest borrower on private markets, is considered by experts more efficient than many of the internationally active commercial banks, as we are told in a US Congress study. That does not affect the necessity for reforms, for nothing is so good that it cannot be improved.)

The idea of resorting to summit meetings as an instrument – not just summit meetings of the great powers – has not perished. I have already mentioned the matters on Indira Gandhi's mind in the months before her assassination. It is not impossible that a selected group of heads of government may meet again to discuss certain precisely defined North–South issues (and their connection with East–West issues). The number of participants in such discussions should be kept to a genuine minimum. A certain amount of preparation is called for, but above all crucial questions must be discussed, and opinions on practical proposals exchanged. For the rest, it is an error refuted by experience for certain types of high-ranking civil servants to suppose that the future of the world depends on their rituals and compromise formulas, the leaders really being there only to read out prepared speeches, give their blessing to press releases on matters already negotiated, and observe the obligatory forms of protocol.

Security policy and North–South relations are matters too serious to be left to such officials alone, be they ever so competent. Or to put it less kindly: the leaders must not be let off the hook of doing their duty.

7. Proposals

No one can say that the recommendations of my Commission, particularly in the areas of development finance and monetary issues, are notable for radicalism. However, they have aroused a certain sense of discomfort. That was inevitable, in their very nature.

Reform of the international monetary system should, in our judgment, improve international liquidity and exchange rate stability, and also the reserve system and balance of payments adjustment, and should, moreover, ensure the participation of the *whole* international community of states in future cooperation: 'Mechanisms should be agreed for creating and distributing an international currency to be used for clearing and settling outstanding balances between central banks. Such a currency would replace the use of national currencies as international reserves.'

This international currency is envisaged as an improved Special Drawing Right.* We suggested creating new SDRs to the extent

* Special Drawing Rights, or SDRs, are the IMF's currency equivalent, and were introduced in 1969 as the first step towards an international reserve currency. Since 1981 the value of a Special Drawing Right has been calculated daily on the basis of a 'basket' of the five main currencies of the member states.

required by the need for increased (and as far as possible non-inflationary) world liquidity. The developing countries, we said, should have preferential treatment in the distribution of new liquidity, the process of adjustment should be accelerated, and should be seen in the larger context of furthering economic and social development in the long term.

The IMF should avoid 'inappropriate or excessive regulation of the economies' of the developing countries, and 'should not impose highly deflationary measures as standard adjustment policy'. Apart from various technical details, we wanted to further 'the demonetization of gold'; profits from the sale of gold should be used for the benefit of developing countries. We called on both the IMF and the World Bank to increase participation by the developing countries in their staffing, management and decision-making.

In our supplementary report, published early in 1983, we concentrated on these proposals. We repeated our call for the capital of the World Bank to be enlarged (to a modest extent, this was done), and for the 'gearing ratio' – the ratio of borrowing to capital – to be raised from 1:1 to 2:1.

In both reports, we referred to the 0.7 per cent target. In accordance with a decision of the UN General Assembly in October 1970, previously formulated at the first UNCTAD conference in Geneva in 1964, at least 0.7 per cent of the gross national product of the industrial countries should be made available for Official Development Assistance (ODA). We made other detailed recommendations. Here are a few comments on what actually happened:

- Instead of increasing Official Development Assistance to 0.7 per cent or even perhaps 1 per cent of GNP, several of the rich countries have moved yet further away from the 0.7 per cent target. At the beginning of the Eighties, the real value of development aid had sunk in both absolute and relative terms.
- At the 1983 UNCTAD conference in Belgrade, the USA, the Eastern bloc and New Zealand rejected the 0.7 per cent target in principle; the delegation of the Federal Republic of Germany was not empowered to agree to a fixed commitment.
- The Federal Republic of Germany did, however, approach the

0.5 per cent mark (0.49 per cent in 1985), while the North as a whole did not get above 0.36 per cent.

- In 1983 the net disbursements of the Western industrial countries amounted to 27.3 billion dollars (down by half a billion compared to the previous year), a good 12 billion dollars being accounted for by the World Bank group.
- Japan, whose performance in this respect had long been below average, has made efforts to increase its contribution over the last few years.
- The Netherlands and the Scandinavian countries, which voluntarily set themselves the 1 per cent target, have recently had difficulty in fitting it into their budgets.
- It must be borne in mind that only about 10 per cent gross investment of the developing countries are financed through Official Development Assistance. Thus they are financing the bulk of their investment with domestic savings.

The effectiveness of development aid has been considerably reduced or inhibited by:

- an increase in debts and in interest rates (the dollar exchange rate!),
- high oil prices,
- the market strategies of transnational corporations,
- armaments exports, including those forced upon countries.

At a conference in Paris in the autumn of 1980 a praiseworthy— and at first not entirely fruitless – attempt was made to stabilize assistance for the *poorest* countries, that is, those too poor to be able to incur any debts at all on the international capital market. It was agreed to double the aid for the 36 poorest countries until 1984; these countries included Ethiopia, Somalia, the Sudan, Tanzania, Afghanistan, Bangladesh, both the Yemens, Laos, Nepal and Haiti. At least 0.15 per cent of the GNP of the donor countries was intended to go to these poorest of the poor. In point of fact, the situation in these countries has deteriorated yet further.

The only countries to adhere to the agreed 0.15 per cent were Denmark, the Netherlands, Norway and Sweden. The Federal

Republic of Germany managed 0.12 per cent. The average was only 0.08 per cent. The failure in the replenishment of funds for the International Development Association (IDA, affiliated to the World Bank) placed a further burden on the poorest countries. And for another thing, checks must constantly be made to see whether the resources available are being effective.

When my colleagues and I spoke of the provision of additional funds, we were thinking of:

- first, an international system of progressive taxation, with the participation of the Eastern European states and the developing countries – excepting, however, the poorest;
- secondly, automatic generation of revenue (on a principle similar to that of indirect national taxation) by means of modest international charges which might be levied on, say, the manufacture or export of armaments, as well as on mankind's common property, in particular the resources of the sea-bed. International tourism and air traffic, as well as the utilization of space, were also mentioned as possible points of reference. (I will add here, as I have said before, that I do *not* think a country's share of world trade a suitable criterion.)

The creation of a new institution to provide finance, a 'World Development Fund', was also discussed. It would be supported by universal membership and act as a channel for such funds as were automatically raised worldwide. Despite doubts expressed not only by right-wing conservative and conservative left-wing governments, but in the upper echelons of the existing institutions, this idea should be given further consideration. The proposal worked out by our secretariat did not aim to replace existing institutions but to complement them, thus establishing credit policy on a broader basis. It has clearly been indicated that the credit flow into the developing countries from commercial banks and other private sources of finance should be increased at the same time.

We firmly believed that additional, multinational finance was needed for exploring and exploiting sources of energy and mineral resources in those developing countries not in a position to do it by themselves. The 'Energy Agency' we suggested for this purpose was in practical terms the only new organization whose immediate creation, with the support of the World Bank, we proposed. At first its chances looked quite good. Then the man at the head of one of the big oil companies turned to the American President (whose name did not happen to be Reagan at the time) and suggested to him that governments should keep out of a domain considered the property of the big corporations, on an international as well as a national level (even when they were inactive where, as in some of the smaller developing countries, there was little prospect of profits).

On the subject of *commodities*, my Commission recommended greater participation by the developing countries in their processing, marketing and distribution. We thought that measures to stabilize commodity prices should be undertaken as a matter of urgency. Work on an 'integrated' programme, financed by a Common Fund, had been in progress since 1973. We wanted such a fund to be enabled to encourage and finance effective International Commodity Agreements. National stockpiling should be encouraged too, so that commodities could be advantageously processed and marketed. Negotiations on individual commodity agreements should be brought, we said, to a rapid and successful conclusion. This was exactly what did not happen.

The work of the Fund should have begun on 1 January 1984. The Federal Republic of Germany agreed to it in the spring of 1985. But the necessary number of ratifications was not forthcoming, and the Eastern states were hesitant. It was feared, and not just in America, that commodity regulation – from coffee to cotton, from tin to copper – would pave the way for an international centrally planned economy. Should one forgo the doubtful chance of profiting from price fluctuations?

Anyone with an interest in calculability and guaranteed commodity supplies ought not at heart to be against remunerative and relatively stable commodity prices – if only because of the investment required to open up mineral resources. (When an outcry went up at the first steep rise in oil prices, at the end of 1973, most of the vociferous critics would not admit that the oil-producing countries had been defrauded over a number of years by prices which were objectively speaking too low; also, and inevitably, there was the widely and mistakenly held view that an inexhaustible supply existed.) One may, indeed one must, ask what happens to the people of a country whose government has to use a very large part of its export earnings for servicing its debts. What good is it to them if they have to pay for an imported tractor (or dollar) with an ever-increasing quantity of coffee or sugar? What is the effect on the people of Zambia if, with all her copper, she can only just manage to service her debts?

At the end of the Seventies there was a considerable drop in commodity prices. In Zambia we saw on the spot that the low prices for copper had not obtained since the Thirties. Compared with a few years earlier, the developing countries had to export twelve times as much coffee and twenty times as much sugar, and very many times as much sisal, to buy one and the same barrel of oil. At the beginning of 1984, even the Kissinger Commission, in its report on Central America, observed that the region was having to export twice as much as five years before in order to buy the same goods on the world market.

On the subject of *world trade*, we wanted to give the developing countries more opportunities, so that they could contribute to their own welfare *and* the welfare of the world economy. Among other things, our suggestions included:

- the concluding of commodity agreements, as already mentioned, which would contribute to the stabilization of prices and markets;
- improved access to the markets of the industrial countries, since only thus could the developing countries be able to buy goods for themselves or pay their debts;
- greater support for those developing countries making efforts to increase their production of food and energy.

We wanted effective national laws and international codes of conduct to prevent *transnational corporations* from indulging in restrictive business practices, and at the same time to have a positive influence on the transfer of technology. We thought these *multinationals*, in themselves, neither good nor bad, but we did query their conduct, their role and their accountability. Do they keep within the law? Do they invest a good part of their profits in the host countries? Do they have links only with an élite, or do they keep the interests of large sections of society in view? I shall be returning to this subject. The question is not whether a corporation does or does not have a transnational structure, but what is done with it.

For the rest, we firmly stated that permanent sovereignty over their natural resources is the right of all countries. However, it is necessary that nationalization be accompanied by appropriate and effective compensation, under internationally compatible principles. These principles, we said, should be embodied in national laws and increasing use should also be made of international mechanisms for settling disputes.

We also supported the view that greater efforts – international, regional and national – were needed to promote the *development of technology* in Third World countries. The transfer of technology should be supported 'at reasonable prices'. In saying this, we agreed that there is a cost factor, but said nothing about the function and cost of technologies that are 'appropriate' or 'conform to the situation', which are all the more important the less room there is for suspecting that conformity of such a kind is a way of perpetuating structural backwardness and traditional dependence. The fact that cost-effectiveness is also a problem when money is spent on foreign experts is so self-evident that it is sometimes overlooked.

8. *Diktat or Dialogue*

In the spring of 1984 I was to speak on the occasion of a rather curious anniversary. It was a hundred years since Imperial Germany made a brief foray into colonial history. The birthday of the German colonies is taken to be 24 April 1884. On that day, Bismarck telegraphed the German consul in Cape Town saying that the acquisitions of the businessman Lüderitz to the north of the Orange River should henceforth enjoy German protection. In the same year, Herr Nachtigal claimed Togo and Cameroon for the Reich, and a year later Carl Peters's acquisitions came under Imperial protection as German East Africa.

The end of 1884 saw the opening in Berlin of what is known as the Congo Conference, at which the interested powers agreed on the creation of a 'free trade zone' in Central Africa. This led among other things, and without the participation of any African representatives, to the founding of the Belgian Congo, under the sovereignty of the King of the Belgians. The interests of German liquor exporters were also concerned. The document drawn up at the close of the conference spoke of high aims; the intention was 'to create the most favourable of conditions for the development of trade and civilization in certain regions of Africa in a harmonious spirit of mutual understanding, and to obviate misunderstandings and disputes which might arise later from the occupation of further territories on the African coasts'. This document was 'mindful of finding the means to increase the moral and material welfare of the native tribes'.

All the interested powers had accepted the joint German and French invitation to Berlin. Besides the two hosts, the following were assembled in a pleasing spirit of concord: Belgium, Britain, Denmark, Italy, the Netherlands, Portugal, Russia, Sweden, the United States and the Ottoman Empire, now Turkey. What happened on that occasion in Berlin, a hundred years ago, was a case of unconcealed *Diktat* in the field later known as North–South relations. There was little criticism of the governments' actions. In the Reich, few people apart from Social Democrats thought colonial policy wrong or reprehensible. Things have changed since then, but it is not by any means certain that we can speak of *dialogue* rather than *Diktat* with a clear conscience today.

Dialogue is certainly not as yet the simple and clear alternative in North–South relations. In recent years some people have spoken – not unreasonably – of a dialogue between the deaf, or the delivery of parallel monologues. In addition, there is no strong lobby for development policy. However, even leaving aside moral objections, supposing they *can* be left aside, circumstances are not much longer in any way appropriate for *Diktat*.

Some feel concern at talk of partnership in development, reasonably enough envisaging unequal partners, and fearing that the phrase conceals the attempt to impose a *Diktat* by gentler but no less compelling means. And no doubt some of those involved will see it in that way too. Such attitudes must be firmly countered, for instance by greater participation of the Third World in the control of the international institutions. However, that cannot be done just by putting someone with the 'right' passport in a given place. (It is said that every one of the 'Chicago Boys' in Santiago is a Chilean.)

Nothing much will come, either, of drawing up as comprehensive as possible a catalogue of subjects for negotiation, making it clear that no issue is to be decided in isolation. The decisive factors are the attitude of those involved and the guidelines to which the negotiators must keep. Anyone who sees North–South relations only in terms of demands made by one side or the other basically misunderstands the question. And mutual interests cannot be defined or perceived in that way either. A *Diktat* is no kind of model for the future. As for dialogue – so far, only a few starts have been made, but that way hope lies.

Meanwhile we are facing a situation very considerably affected by new forces – forces which did not previously exist, and which draw their significance from new technical developments. What is often seen as government weakness is in many cases nothing but inability to control or deal with such new forces: multinational corporations, the international network of experts in the technology of the future, trades unions and other social groupings, churches, solidarity movements.

The importance and influence of such actors on the scene is increasing, and they are largely outside political control, particularly when their activities cross frontiers, while governments are hampered by the illusion of sovereignty. The part played by these new actors rests to a great extent on the frontier-crossing mobility of factors of production: goods, capital, technology and labour, despite all trends in the opposite direction, have an international market which is not decisively influenced by governments. That does not mean governments are not called upon at times of crisis, particularly when it is a question of unloading losses on the general public and transferring them to the taxpayer.

In the introduction to the first Brandt Report, I wrote that the shaping of our common future was too important to be left to governments and experts alone: 'Therefore, our appeal goes to youth, to women's and labour movements; to political, intellectual and religious leaders; to scientists and educators; to technicians and managers; to members of the rural and business communities. May they all try to understand and to conduct their affairs in the light of this new challenge.'

To put it even more clearly: pressure must be brought to bear on governments. If the moral reserves of many individuals are mobilized in favour of a development policy worthy of the name, that will be a help, and if besides complaints of the cumbersome nature of the decision-making process we also hear denunciation of the pettiness and frigidity not infrequently observed to accompany it, that will help too. (Development aid is not, of course, exactly at the top of the list of those issues that decide elections. Holland and the Scandinavian countries are good examples of the way a well-planned programme of public information can elicit a positive response. In the Federal Republic of Germany, we lag some way behind. In addition, a comparatively small circle of interested persons dispute the finer points among themselves, instead of getting together in the first place to canvass for more interest, commitment and resources.)

The way out of our present dilemma obviously does not lie in new international super-bureaucracies. Enough confusion reigns in those which already exist. But setting up a new institution to deal with an important and clearly defined area is a possibility. A thorough reform of existing institutions is more important, however. That applies not only to the United Nations and its specialized organizations. Internationally and nationally alike, bureaucracy proliferates. However, it is the governments of member states which bear responsibility for such a development in international institutions. With this in view, they should be called to a sense of their obligations by their national parliaments.

When the United Nations was created towards the end of the Second World War, it had roughly one third of its present number of member states. Since then, not only have many new nation-states come into being, there has also been a considerable fragmentation of the political map of the world. A large number of new states reflect the territorial boundaries of their colonial past; this is particularly clear in Africa. Which means that they often have to live with frontiers that are felt to be artificial. State sovereignty, which in many cases can be described as national sovereignty only with reservations, is supposed to be of primary importance. However, to respect frontiers once drawn is at the same time a prerequisite of regional cooperation.

Yet we live at a time when technical development, in what is in some ways a revolutionary manner, reduces the objective importance of state frontiers. A large part of international transactions takes place outside those controls which the authorities in individual states would like to or are able to exercise. That becomes especially clear when one realizes that the United Nations now has a long list of member states with less than one million inhabitants, some even with less than 100,000. On the one hand we have the United States and the Soviet Union, China and India; on the other we have Fiji and Papua New Guinea, the Maldives, St Kitts and Nevis. One can see at a glance how limited the areas must be in which equal voting rights are anything but a fiction.

Gunnar Myrdal, some years ago, pointed out the paradox of a situation wherein on the one hand states try to regulate their economic life, but on the other must take note of the fact that an increasing amount of production and trade is now removed from their control, and even their knowledge. There is no doubt that a growing economic and financial interdependence has developed internationally. Governments have not succeeded in bringing transnational companies under control through appropriate forms of cooperation, let alone in helping to coordinate the activities of trades unions. Even the international exchange of data for fiscal purposes has not proved particularly effective.

It is beginning to be said that the political autonomy of a state – independence is often a misleading notion anyway – should not be confused with its economic autonomy. Dependence, including dependence of an indirect nature, is made particularly obvious by the debt crisis. International organizations are ineffective because considerable elements of sovereignty of the great powers and influential states are hardly being delegated to the international plane.

However I do not look at global interdependency and jump to the conclusion that the creation of some kind of world government might be on the agenda. That will be kept waiting. And the matter is more complicated than it appears to many well-meaning people. Nor, if we are aiming at sensible objectives, can it be just a case of common action in the face of global challenges. It is equally important to define decentralized *regional* responsibilities, which probably is in the interests of the mini-states. It will be hard enough to overcome narrow-minded opposition to such ideas.

On the way towards a higher degree of common responsibility, questions concerning the point of big international conferences force themselves upon us:

- What can come of a meeting of several thousand people from a large number of countries, unless some provision is made to divide them up into working groups?
- Could not ministers stay at home and have copies of their speeches distributed, if their only reason for attending is to read those speeches, and then set off straight back home, perhaps after a few social events – leaving behind them civil servants without any authority to make decisions?
- Should not the UN General Assembly itself make efforts to set limits to the time allowed for the delivery of speeches? Is it not an illusion when the majority decides matters which the great powers, or groups of states, see as touching on their vital interests?

In many respects, technology is showing a tendency to run ahead of politics. It is as well to be aware of this, and compensate for it where possible.

9. Must Europe Wait on the Will of the Superpowers?

It would not be right to accuse others of failing to take their responsibilities seriously enough, and then fall considerably short of what we expect of others. We in Europe cannot hold our heads up if we shelter behind Russian obstinacy or American stubbornness, instead of asking ourselves about our own responsibility. If the superpowers will not accept advice from anyone, that does not mean others must accept all they are told. Nor need they go along with all that they are expected to do. They have to speak out where their convictions and understanding demand it. In the final resort, we too must pay for the mistakes of the great powers.

On fundamental issues I do not share the opinion of those who wield power in the Eastern bloc. We also have serious differences of opinion with regard to the treatment of North–South problems. I live in the West and belong to the West, and I know what strength we draw from the opportunities of a pluralistic system. It no longer bothers me to find reformist policies regarded as suspect. But one does notice the way people are dismissed as fools or worse for years on end, if they do not go along with every dangerous piece of nonsense, praising it as a manifestation of the utmost wisdom, as long as it comes from Washington.

I agree with Helmut Schmidt when he called upon the other industrial states to help the poorest countries even if the United States refuses to continue doing its part. That was with reference to the dispute in 1984 centering upon the International Development Association, affiliated to the World Bank, a dispute which led to a reduction in the opportunities for helping the poorest developing countries.

I say here, again: those who have power, particularly nuclear power, do not necessarily have morality or wisdom on their side. The great dangers to mankind proceed from the great powers, not the little ones.

In recent years, unfortunately, no more initiatives in the field of North–South politics have come from the USA, which in the Fifties was canvassing the Europeans for cooperation in development policy. There has been a lack of positive decisions, and the connection between arms and development has not been accepted; instead, we have seen a series of negative decisions and delaying tactics.

There is little point in vociferously drawing exaggerated conclusions from these regrettable facts, or in uttering condemnations. And in particular, it should never be forgotten that the USA disburses considerable funds for foreign aid earmarked for specific purposes. First and foremost, we should strive for more understanding in the USA itself of what many of their friends in Europe and the Third World expect of them. Consequently, the Americans should be invited to participate in renewed collaboration; they should not have the door slammed in their faces, nor be made the subject of hurtful criticism. That, however, cannot mean standing by, come what may; we should do as we think right in a given situation, even if we cannot do it (or cannot yet do it) in the larger context that was envisaged.

If I am critical in my attitude to United States policy, it is as 'one of the family'. Also as one who is sorry that official sources in Bonn do not say what ought to be said to official sources in Washington. Also as a European.

This concerns the European Community, and at the same time it concerns the stance taken by Europeans beyond the Community. For decades, particularly since the Second World War, there has been talk of de-Europeanizing the world. I think it may be said that that is followed, if slowly and as a contradictory process, by a Europeanization of Europe, including that part of it dominated by the Soviet Union. Over the last few years there has been more than one indication that European governments in East and West – with all their great differences, and with all the loyalties they feel to their respective alliances – have found a *common* interest in their wish not to bear too much of the brunt of extreme tension between the superpowers.

In any event, Europeans – or quite a number of them – will be less anxious than before to reject the idea of exercising a moderating influence in crisis areas, and will not want to leave those areas entirely to the superpowers. Our European contribution to ensuring peace must not lag so far behind opportunity as it has for a long while since the end of the Second World War. It is hard to see why it should, since Europe would be more likely and more intensively than any other region to become the actual arena of a nuclear catastrophe.

Europe might have a chance of pointing out new paths and taking them herself. It is to be feared that she will miss that chance, particularly with so many spanners being thrown into the works of the EEC. There is not much time left. Talk of the unification of Europe is nothing new, but little has come of it so far. And yet, over and above economic matters and a considerable share of world trade, the twelve states which today constitute the EEC have made some progress in coordinating their foreign policies. Something might yet come of that, if we do not delay too long.

Europe should have made her mark in development policy by her own efforts – working together, as appropriate, with Japan, or Canada, or Australia, or other countries. She might have been able to launch initiatives of her own, with practical projects. She should have dared to believe herself capable of a mediating role in getting serious negotiations going within the framework of the United Nations. Nor could anyone seriously have prevented Europe – I now mean in the sense of those various dimensions which go beyond EEC limits – from taking a clear lead in the fight against hunger.

Or we can start from more modest premises, and ask: why have the Western European governments not even managed to co-ordinate their activities in development policy better? Why are the already hard-pressed administrations of the developing countries, particularly the least developed, called upon to put up with such a vast quantity of parallel negotiations, visits and project surveys? Why must 20 ministers with responsibility for development cooperation visit the same countries, claiming the attention of their administrations, usually close on one another's heels? (And followed by civil servants from rival ministries and audit offices, and delegates of various committees, from almost all of those separate countries.) Political as well as technical coordination is needed! The European Parliament is in favour of it. The parliamentary assembly of the Council of Europe has endorsed the idea as well, and described the form it should take.

The EEC has had a good deal of experience, if nothing very exciting in the way of results, with the Lomé Conventions. These agreements concern previously dependent areas of Africa, the Caribbean and the Pacific: the ACP states, at present numbering over 60 members. A renewal of the Convention, to apply to the current five-year period, was signed in Lomé, the capital of Togo, at the end of 1984. The volume of finance provided – with a per capita drop – is in the order of DM 19 billion. In addition there are marginal concessions regulating access to the EEC market. Results have not come up to expectations, and not only the expectations of those who know that the EEC's agrarian market costs it DM 40 billion *annually*.

None the less, the Lomé Conventions, to which special regional agreements are attached, have features which could be useful as models in further North–South dialogue. Such is the case with the principle of aid for self-help, and with the Stabex mechanism, which involves compensatory payments for severe losses in export revenue to help mitigate the dependency from unbalanced export structures. It is also the case with environmental protection, which is at last, through regional projects and long-term programmes, taking on great importance. Despite all the criticism of governments which are behind the times, it should not be forgotten that the EEC has good dispositions for performance in development policies.

Much is still expected – or is again expected – of Europe. I sensed that in Latin America, just as I did in China and India, the Near East, Africa, and the other parts of the Third World. Sometimes one found it surprising that Europe, with all her inadequacies, still seems so attractive. Expectations are often pitched too high, and could hardly be fulfilled even if conditions were more favourable. But still, those expectations can be an incentive to regard goodwill as a positive challenge. Instead of complaining of lack of leadership from the great powers, we should have had the courage to go ahead ourselves – for instance, with a plan for long-term aid to Africa, with some kind of Marshall Plan for Latin America, with a perspective of productive global cooperation.

In an interdependent world, the principles of common justice and the general welfare cannot cease to hold good at our own frontiers. I believe we must do more in the way of cooperation, and indeed make more of an effort in many respects, without expecting miracles to occur overnight. But greater generosity will pay dividends.

V

THE INTERNATIONAL DEVELOPMENT
ASSOCIATION SCANDAL

In 1984 the World Bank tried to increase the funding of interest-free loans to those developing countries with particularly weak economies, or at least to make sure that it did not decrease. In the committees of the World Bank, the majority of governments agreed upon a middle way. However, the United States administration steadfastly refused to compromise. For the period 1985–87, consequently, there is less money available (when inflation has been taken into account) than for the three preceding years; not much more than half the previous sum, while the population of the countries eligible for this type of credit has practically doubled – for China is now among their number, and does not want to be treated any differently from India.

When this happened, the governments of Europe and Japan did not say they would stand by their word. Instead, they renounced any idea of an initiative of their own, and allowed an important area of development policy to suffer. I have called the argument over the International Development Association (IDA) a scandal, and I see no reason to withdraw that term.

The report of my Commission suggested that governments should make their contributions to IDA on at least a five-year instead of a three-year basis. We also said it was important that no political conditions were attached to the use of these funds. A large replenishment for the 1985–87 period would have contributed greatly to achieving the objective of increased aid for the poorest countries. In 1981, a conference was held in Paris, attended by the representatives of those countries whose economic development is declining and which receive less aid. It was agreed to double official development assistance to the countries by 1985. Both expectations and promises have remained largely unfulfilled.

At the beginning of January 1984, at the joint meeting of the Brandt and Palme Commissions, it was established that negotiations over IDA replenishment to date had lowered the amount actually available to below the sum many donor countries were ready to contribute. In view of the needs of the poorest countries, the amount of the agreed contributions was wholly inadequate: 'We support the proposal already put forward whereby IDA resources should be raised to at least $12 billion. We shall do everything we can to encourage the donor countries to change their attitude to one more worthy of the international community.'

What had happened? IDA funds for 1982–84 had been set at $9 billion. The World Bank, which is not prone to exaggeration, thought an increase to $16 billion was called for; the committees agreed on $12 billion. Thereupon, the USA said that they were not going to participate: they could undertake to contribute their 25 per cent share only of the previously agreed $9 billion, i.e. $750 million of the annual $3 billion. (The disputed $250 million per year would have amounted to less than 0.1 per cent of the US defence budget.)

The cutting down on replenishment means that in real terms there are now considerably less resources available than was the case in recent years, even though the need for them has grown: for another thing, the vast country of China is now a World Bank member and thus eligible to apply.

Together with Ted Heath and Sonny Ramphal, I turned to a number of heads of government. We received a predominantly friendly response – from Washington as well as the rest. We had appealed to President Reagan to change his administration's stance. He did not exclude the possibility of reviewing it in the next American fiscal year. However, there was no mention of any such review in the draft of the administration's next budget.

It cannot have been the money alone; another factor will have been the increasing efforts being made by the United States, in a spirit rather far removed from the principles of the immediate postwar period, to weaken rather than strengthen international organizations, replacing multilateral by bilateral agreements.

This generally means that the stronger party to the agreement is not really practising partnership, but is imposing conditions on the weaker party.

The European states that we asked to keep their word to the World Bank, making their contributions within the $12 billion context even after Washington's withdrawal, could not make up their minds to do so. Personal mediation in Bonn and Paris had no effect.

I do not gather the impression that anything very pointed was ever said to the Americans, as envisaged before the economic summit in London in the early summer of 1984. Chancellor Kohl had written to me in September 1984, saying that he too considered $9 billion 'too little' for IDA's seventh replenishment. But, he said, in view of the American attitude, it had not been feasible to fix a higher sum. In common with Japan, official opinion in Bonn was 'that a supplementary fund without the participation of the USA would have rather negative effects'. Only mutual understanding between all donor countries, he said, had led to the impressive contributions to early replenishments. In the interests of the developing countries, the same system of raising contributions should be retained for the future. The Federal Government had repeatedly made it clear that 'it could not make up deficits arising from the non-participation of a third party'. I was not convinced by these formal considerations, nor by the tactics involved, if tactics they be. Upholding the traditional way of distributing the load might once have made sense, as a means of persuading the US to participate, but today it is clearly to the disadvantage of the poorest countries (and allows hypocrites in Europe to save money).

At the annual meeting of the IMF and the World Bank in Washington, in September 1984, it was proposed to raise an additional $2 billion to relieve poverty in Africa. One may wonder why it was necessary to commission new 'studies' for this purpose first. A few months later, Tom Clausen, President of the World Bank, announced that it was hoped a special programme of at least $1 billion for the poorest African states could be decided on at the beginning of 1985. Meanwhile, the USA had again made it clear that they were not particularly interested in joint programmes; however, they said they would increase their own aid to Africa. In the meantime, the summit conference of OAU, the Organization of African Unity, could refer to the World Bank and their projected $2 billion a year. . . .

When President Clausen was canvassing for aid for Africa at the end of 1984, he put it to the rich countries, in front of the Press in Washington, that they might spend less on armaments and let the Third World countries have more resources instead.

However, it proved impossible to set up even the African programme as envisaged. Abdulatif Al Hamad, the Kuwaiti member of the Brandt Commission, raised a good half billion dollars for the World Bank, and the sum was made up to $1.1 billion by the inclusion of parallel national contributions. Washington's decision to set up its own programme caused Bonn to pull out too, announcing that it was making its own contribution of DM 100 million – provided by the reprogramming of funds already pledged. On the other hand, France, Italy and the Netherlands, among the EEC countries, did make direct contributions to the World Bank's Special Aid Fund.

It is worth setting the shameful result of the efforts made to raise money for the poorest countries against two striking comparisons: first, the German Federal Bank spent $1.5 billion within a week in order to stabilize the exchange rate of the Deutschmark; the net amount of currency reserves fell by that sum in the first week of March 1985. And secondly: every eight or nine hours, the world spends $1 billion – i.e. the entire sum provided for the Special Africa Programme – on armaments and for military purposes. That comes to almost three Africa Programmes a day, and it happens every day of the year. . . .

VI

DEBTS AND HYPOCRISY

1. *Debts upon Debts*

At the turn of the year between 1984 and 1985, the total indebtedness of the Third World was estimated to be in the region of $920 billion; some estimates made it as much as $1,000 billion. At least $360 billion of that amount – between a third and a half of it – fell to the share of Latin America.

Hence, Latin America's burden of debt became the focus of interest; it was its severest economic crisis this century, and has resulted in a distinct drop in the standard of living over the last ten years.

In September 1982, the tip of the iceberg showed in Mexico. An important country producing a considerable amount of oil, Mexico had become insolvent. The acute insolvency was pretty quietly eased, but turned out to be the start of a severe crisis which has not gone away. An eminent participant in the annual meeting of the IMF and the World Bank in Toronto in 1982 has spoken of the alarm he sensed 'when Mexico was seen to be insolvent and we didn't know if the whole situation might explode at any moment'. Those who handled the crisis did remarkable work: 800 foreign banks had to be induced to keep quiet. In addition to considerable interest payments they were compensated with fees of notable size in compensation.

The overnight Mexican collapse had been set off by changes in the oil market. Large finds were made in 1976–80, and on the assumption of high prices exports had been overestimated. In other parts other factors triggered the debt crisis. The international financial world felt not just alarm but almost as if the end of the world had come when, in the summer of 1983, Brazil refused to make its repayment due to the Bank for International Settlements in Basle: so said no less a person than the Swiss banker at the head of the BIS itself. There was another collapse to be averted in the spring of 1984, when Argentina had to be granted a bridging loan, a loan notable for the fact that – besides the USA – states participated, or were obliged to participate, which, like Mexico, were themselves deeply in debt.

These cases were not the only ones of their kind. Bolivia and Ecuador temporarily suspended the servicing of their debts. A call for a political solution came from the new democratic government in Buenos Aires. Other capitals echoed this demand, and in some quarters consideration was given to the idea of a debtors' cartel with the help of which at least a moratorium – that is, a deferment – might be enforced.

The real problems had arisen when short-term funds were used to finance long-term investments; the exceptional case turned out to be the rule. Unexpectedly high interest rates and export difficulties played their part. A greater and greater share of budgets and export revenues had to go to the servicing of debts.

Over the last few years, the world has seen an explosion of public debt. Everywhere – in small states and large ones, in industrial and developing countries, in the North and South, in the East and West – there was a similar rise in public debt, be it through internal financing in the industrialized countries or financing from outside in the developing countries, in some states in the East, and latterly in the USA. In the summer of 1984 the managing director of the IMF revealed that in the seven major Western industrial states, the ratio of national debt to gross national product had risen from 22 per cent in 1974 to 41 per cent in 1983. The debt crisis of the Third World thus coincided with high public indebtedness in the industrial countries. Some of those statesmen dispensing moralizing advice to the developing countries looked like drunkards preaching abstinence.

As compared with the situation ten years ago, the developing countries must now pay more in annual interest – over $100 billion – than the total amount of their debts then. (The African states alone are in debt to the tune of over $150 billion.) The annual debt service comes to three times the value of annual development aid from the West. Another and striking statistical comparison: the balance of payments deficits of the oil-importing developing countries have increased tenfold since the beginning of the Sixties.

Also in 1984 a considerable quantity of new debts was incurred, even if the proportion of short-term debts distinctly dropped. The fact that the Eastern bloc managed to decrease its international burden of debt brought about some changes. Between the spring of 1982 and the spring of 1984, the indebtedness of the Eastern bloc dropped by 14 per cent to $51 billion, and deposits made by those countries with international banks rose to $9 billion. Even Poland managed to decrease her debts during that period, though not in 1985. At the end of 1984 non-aligned Yugoslavia managed to obtain assurances from her creditors that debt service payments, some $20 billion, would be rescheduled.

Of total Latin American indebtedness, to the amount of $360 billion or more:

• Brazil accounts for $100 billion
• Mexico for almost $90 billion
• Argentina for $50 billion
• and Venezuela for $35 billion.

Three hundred and sixty billion dollars means $45 billion a year in bank interest. Rescheduling has resulted in additional fees and harsh conditions on the budgetary policy of the countries concerned and on the distribution of the burden of the crisis. As a rule, decisions have been made at the expense of the poorer sections of society, those with a low standard of living, and those who need public support or have no kind of access to any sources of relief – higher bread prices then just mean more hunger.

One may ask how such a mountain of debt, with all its consequences, could have come into being. The answer is only partially provided by miscalculations, as in the projected sales and price of oil, and by mismanagement on the part of the debtor countries, which could of course be noted as well. But when loans are taken up and applications made and granted for credit, there is a double responsibility: responsibility on the part of the lender as well as the borrower. In minimizing that responsibility, some speak of 'incorrect estimates of the scope for debt'. It is seldom admitted that the banks themselves indulged in an orgy of credit offers.

The Latin Americans are accused of having allowed a severe flight of capital to aggravate their problems. In 1984 flight capital amounted to over a third of their outstanding foreign debts. However, we should not forget that liquid capital is basically inclined to stray. Why should it show national responsibility for which there is little or no incentive in a given region, and when, moreover, the corresponding sense of responsibility is highly underdeveloped . . .?

Capital urgently needed in Europe is at present flowing out as well, and into the USA, complying with none but economic incentives: higher interest rates and greater security. The United States' high expenditure on armaments is known to be extensively financed by budget deficits – as at the time of the Vietnam War – which in turn send interest rates up, with the result that the developing countries, particularly the newly industrializing countries, who have gone into debt on a basis of variable interest, are unexpectedly encumbered to the tune of several billion dollars more.

At the meeting of the IMF in the autumn of 1984, even leading figures in the management of the World Bank rejected Washington's thesis that activity set off in the wake of the US budget deficit compensated for the major part of the burden of high interest, and the Third World must invest more resources and labour in exports. The reports of the IMF itself remark critically upon the fact that the mighty United States is solving its problems at other people's expense, importing capital which weaker countries need for their development.

In the USA itself, well-known economists are speaking out, expressing their concern at seeing their country well on the way to becoming the biggest debtor nation of all. Government experts expect a record budget deficit of $210 billion for 1985 (it was $175 billion in the financial year 1984). Another rise in interest rates is not impossible.

Experts dispute the question of whether the credit crisis has come about because of inadequate regulation of financial policy on the international markets, or whether the credit business has burst out of the framework which objectively should contain it. Why not assume a combination of both factors? In any case, there can be no doubt that in essence we are dealing with a decline in economic activity rather than the covering of credit as shown by the books. It is no contradiction that the excessive amount of debt worldwide must be reduced if the steep rise in interest rates is to be counteracted.

Future economic development had certainly been wrongly estimated in all countries, and in consequence, erroneous dispositions had been made. Just as certainly, there is a capital flight based on rules of conduct other than that of national responsibility. Those who are constantly demanding performance speculate on interest rates and through speculative capital movements. In any event, responsibility for the extent of the credit crisis should not be sought solely in the debtors.

2. A Blood Transfusion from the Sick to the Healthy

Over the last few years, debtor countries have become capital exporters – an absurd situation. An extensive net capital transfer from poorer countries to rich countries has set in, to a large extent to the private banks, improving their balance sheets. Debtors have had to borrow more money to service their debts with those same banks. Even in the USA, there has been talk of a 'perverse transfer of money away from the poor'. Another suggested metaphor was a 'blood transfusion from the sick to the healthy', and there are object lessons to show us the accuracy of that.

To take the case of Mexico: the second debt rescheduling, for a period of 14 years, will amount to *one and a half* times the original debt, i.e. $130 billion. At a meeting with government representatives in Mexico City, I asked if it was true that parts of the first rescheduling had cost 30 per cent in interest and fees. Yes, I was told, that might well be so.

We thus see circumstances such as the following arise:

- Latin America's foreign debts of $360 billion, with an interest rate in real terms of 'only' 10 per cent, mean that over $40 billion end up annually in New York, London and Frankfurt. In fact the Latin Americans recorded a negative net transfer of capital of $55 billion in 1984.
- When US interest on long-term loans rose by another 3 per cent in early 1984, the debts of Latin America instantly shot up by another $5 billion.
- The sum paid out by the countries of Latin America in 1983–84 in interest on their foreign debts corresponded to about 50 per cent of their export earnings.

The debtor countries have thus been obliged, and still are, to meet their interest payments with an excessive proportion of their export earnings. With the inclusion of redemption rates, the total came to over 100 per cent for some individual countries. The situation is becoming intolerable:

- In Brazil, the proportion of export earnings required to service interest on debts rose from 24 to over 40 per cent between 1978 and 1983.
- In Argentina, it rose from less than 10 per cent to 57 per cent of export earnings. (By now, if there had been no rescheduling, four years' export earnings would be needed for one year's servicing of Argentina's debts.)
- Mexico, an oil-producing country, will have to spend half its export earnings servicing its debts over the next few years – and that is after rescheduling.
- Peru would have had to employ 80 per cent of its export earnings in 1984 to meet its obligations. The country has temporarily relieved its burdens by refinancing and by leaving commitments unmet.
- Even in a small Central American state like Costa Rica, servicing its debts accounts for 50 per cent, and in Panama for 40 per cent, of export earnings.
- In the Dominican Republic, the debt service ratio amounted to a third of export earnings at the end of 1982, and it has since risen.

Rescheduling programmes generally are agreed only under pressure. Social consequences are disregarded. However, even in German banking and European economic circles, reference is sometimes made to the 'limits of political and social tolerance' which might be reached if financial rehabilitation measures agreed upon with IMF were to be put through. Even some politicians of a conservative tendency have pointed out that IMF would be inviting social and political unrest if it turned the screw too tight in the debtor countries and went so far as to endanger the feeding of their people.

These are not just theoretical considerations any more. Social unrest resulting from steep price rises in basic foodstuffs – as occurred in 1984 in the Dominican Republic, Mexico, Brazil, Argentina, Bolivia and Chile – may have been a portent of more serious protests to come. People have rebelled against the deterioration in elementary living conditions in other parts of the world too: in Tunisia, Morocco and Egypt on one hand, in the Philippines on the other.

It has become fashionable to make the International Monetary Fund an international scapegoat. I have serious reservations about it myself – they are set out in detail in our two reports – but I would not like to be a party to bringing criticism to bear in the wrong quarters. For neither the Monetary Fund nor the World Bank are institutions operating in a void. They do what the governments of their most important and vociferous member countries tell them to do, or what the member countries will allow to pass without contradicting. Those who complain of IMF or the World Bank should really direct their complaints to those governments who, in the last resort, have the say in decision-making.

In our two reports, my colleagues and I suggested ways in which these international institutions could be reformed. I have already mentioned the initial reactions of leading governments: either none at all or unfavourable. Only under the pressure of intensifying crisis does such an attitude slowly, very slowly, seem to be changing.

There is no doubt that in many respects IMF has played an impressive part. Its French managing director, with capable and sometimes too zealous colleagues from many countries, has performed Herculean labours, 'case by case', and not just during the Mexican crisis; commercial banks and international organizations, governments and central banks have all had to be brought together, transitional solutions have had to be found to avert worse developments. The people who work for the institution are authoritative experts, though they may have a rather conservative outlook and perhaps not enough insight into social needs. The waste of funds on military purposes is generally excluded from their discussions and statements, because many governments do not openly set out the relevant expenditure in their budgets, or are not ready to discuss the issue of national security with IMF. However, IMF itself, if often without public knowledge, has regularly endeavoured to obtain the relevant figures and information and not leave the subject unconsidered because of economic effects on the appropriate economic policy.

It is unrealistic to reject IMF conditionality in principle. However, it *must* be asked why conditions have not also been laid down for the industrial and other rich countries. The immediate answer is: conditions are part of an agreement made with IMF for balance of payments support, and only governments in difficulties will be concluding such stand-by agreements. But it is interesting and instructive to note that the tone of criticism of IMF was just the same, say, in Italy and Great Britain – at any rate at the time when those European countries were dependent on the help of the Monetary Fund and needed a stand-by agreement. Is such a thing quite out of the question in the case of the USA?

Those affected ask, rightly, why one cannot refrain from measures which mean economic contraction, fall most heavily on the poorer sections of society, and neglect long-term development. One might go further and ask: why not allow the developing countries too to practise whatever kind of mixed economy is suited to them instead of imposing ideological as well as material conditions? The answer is ready to hand. It is a question of whose word bears weight where. But that itself shows why the developing countries should have more of a say where decisions concerning them are made.

My criticism is thus mainly addressed not to IMF as such, but to the policy it pursues, which is decided by leading industrial states, in particular the USA. The USA stands in the way of IMF's ability to obtain more funds, under defensible conditions and less restrictions. The Fund lets the great powers off lightly, contenting itself with warily academic comments on high interest rates. Those who speak for Europe do not improve matters, since they either think their supposed national advantage more important, failing to recognize their international political responsibility, or because they have opted for a permanent fear of their great friend.

It would be wrong to suppose that these problems and dangers are not perceived in the United States as well. They often find public expression there, in Congress as well as the more serious sections of the press. When the Latin American debt crisis was looming, there was no lack of civil servants in the Treasury Department in Washington, if not at the very highest, politically occupied level, who issued warnings and made constructive suggestions. But they got as little of a hearing as those who tried to explain the character of the Central American revolutionary movements. Those who attempted to explain the Cuban revolution at the end of the Fifties had also found that their words fell on deaf ears, and the same thing had happened to those repudiated a decade earlier because they advocated a reasonable policy towards China.

Important as Latin America is, however, we should not overlook the fact that there are now Asian countries which are fundamentally no more solvent, to say nothing of most of the African countries. Referring to the latter, de Larosière, Managing Director of IMF, has said: 'This escalation of debt must not continue.'

Unfortunately, however, it seems that the rule applying to private debtors also applies, on a large scale, to states: if someone owes £1,000, that is his problem; if he owes £100,000, it is his bank's. Highly reputable financial journals have thus written, correctly, of the 'other' or 'forgotten' debt crisis, when referring to the smaller and poorer developing countries. These countries are neglected because their debts make up only a small part of the debt mountain, and because they generally have little to offer economically. Their people suffer no less from the consequences.

We may remember the wry joke about exploitation: if IMF comes along, things are bad; if it doesn't come along at all, or only late in the day, things are even worse.

In the long run, we shall not master this global crisis by

patching up holes here, there, and everywhere, but by making coordinated international efforts to begin reducing the size of the debt mountain, and taking the requisite reform of the international monetary and financial system seriously.

3. Latin America: Crisis versus Democracy

In the autumn of 1984, on a visit to a number of Latin American countries I was able to form an idea of the way the democratization process is going there, in the face of debt crises and severe economic difficulties. Both the pressing economic problems, and the clear drift away from military dictatorship and towards democracy, were more marked than I had realized from a distance.

I was well aware that several of those countries had made considerable economic progress in the Sixties and Seventies, though they were very far from having achieved social equality. But now constitutional issues topped the agenda:

- In Argentina, the new democratic order made its breakthrough with the election of President Raúl Alfonsín at the end of 1983. That election had repercussions on the whole continent, and symbolic significance too. However, we heard anxious questions: could the democracy expect support in good time, or would it come too late? That question has yet to be answered.
- In the vast country of Brazil too, the military dictators had shown their economic incompetence, thus preparing the way for the election of a civilian President, Tancredo Neves. He died before he could take office, but the interim coalition seemed to be up to its democratic task.
- I had met representatives of the Uruguayan democratic opposition when attending a conference in Rio. One of them, Julio M. Sanguinetti, was elected President shortly afterwards. The military judged it advisable to go back to their barracks.
- Peru was preparing for the democratic change by holding elections – for the first time in years. Although civil war was raging in parts of the country, the young Social Democrat

leader Alan García was able to take over as President, without further military intervention. He is pursuing a demanding programme of rural renewal and internal pacification.

- In Cartagena in Colombia, President Belisario Betancur – a conservative of an idiosyncratic nature, having been, as he himself says, 'baptized with reddish water' – told me how he was getting guerrilla fighters who had spent years in the forests to come to the negotiating table. When Betancur speaks of the 'objective agents' of subversion, he means malnutrition and unemployment, and the shortage of schools and hospitals.

- Chile is having particular difficulty in overcoming military dictatorship. One of the most moving experiences of my journey was the moment when the leaders of the Chilean opposition came to the airport during our stopover at Santiago; on the plane, a Chilean industrialist told me that he personally, like the trade unionists, was in favour of joint attempts at a new democracy.

Despite all these impressive experiences, however, the democratic process in Latin America is still at risk. Not just because of the pressing problems of foreign trade and finance, but on account of gross economic and social inequalities within those countries too. In Argentina, there was talk of inflation of the order of several hundred per cent (in March 1985, 800 per cent was the figure mentioned). Data from Brazil spoke of 200 per cent inflation, and the Peruvian figure was 125. In Bolivia, over 2,000 per cent was registered. The establishing of these approximate values is no doubt connected with the method of calculating them. President Alfonsín mentioned the total collapse of the German currency after the First World War, which I myself had witnessed as a child. Where was the present situation leading? And were we in the West going to help the new democracy or wait to lay wreaths on its grave? Another of the Presidents likened the situation to the painful experience of undergoing an operation without anaesthetic. And indeed, the outlook for the democrats of those countries is not particularly good, hampered as they are by the crippling debt service.

An extremely unjust distribution of income, inadequate food supplies, lack of social facilities, also of schools for the children of the poorer classes, are typical of the situation as a whole, with a generally low standard of living of a great majority of the population. It is obvious that there will be a struggle not just for the existence of political democracy, but for its economic basis and social orientation, for a new meaning to independence.

'More and more people have less and less to eat,' was the way a Brazilian bishop summed up the situation. While great quantities of food are destined for export, millions of Brazilians are malnourished. Wages in real terms have sunk below the 1970 level. The infant mortality rate has risen again, particularly in the north-east of that vast country. When Leonel Brizola, governor of the state of Rio de Janeiro, took office in 1982, 700,000 children had no schooling. Within two years, he told me, he was able to halve that number; one method he employed was the introduction of a school meals service.

Before the Second World War Argentina used to be compared with Canada, just as Uruguay was called the Switzerland of South America. Argentina is still considered a newly industrializing country, but like Uruguay can display alarming instances of the reverse of development. Today, and without any population explosion, those countries suffer not just from the consequences of dictatorship and the failings of the world economy, but to a considerable degree from self-inflicted and practically chaotic economic and financial conditions, high unemployment and exorbitant prices. The standard of living has sunk by 30 to 40 per cent since 1975.

In Mexico, wages in real terms dropped by 30 per cent in the two years after the debt débâcles of 1982; the proportion of unemployed and underemployed is estimated at almost 50 per cent.

In Peru, the President of the Central Bank observed: 'Our per capita income has dropped to its 1965 level.' Forty per cent of the population is described as undernourished. Export earnings from agrarian products have dropped even more sharply than those from mineral commodities.

In Colombia, the usual problems of the continent are intensified by the slow, and indeed in the short term imperceptible, progress being made in fighting the unwholesome influence of the drugs Mafia; that destructive factor looms even larger in Bolivia.

Even in Venezuela, distinguished by large revenues from oil and less population pressure, and on the whole better off than most countries of the South American continent, 20 per cent unemployment is presumed to exist, with a percentage twice that figure in the capital. None the less, my friend Carlos Andres Perez, former President of Venezuela, who accompanied me on an important part of my Latin American journey, remains as optimistic as ever about his continent's future.

He is not the only one to believe that the Latin Americans are incorrectly classified. They think of themselves as part of the Third World, but do not want to be entirely absorbed by it. The cultural heritage of Spain and Portugal, ancient Indian culture, modern American and European influences are all in a process of new amalgamation. Distrust of both superpowers is strong. So is the feeling of being neglected by Europe. There is no doubt that Europeans could do much good, and play a much larger part in Latin America than they do at present.

It would be a mistake, one to which many in the region are prone, to seek the causes of their troubles only outside themselves. In Latin America more than anywhere, the upper stratum of society bears a large share of responsibility for the existing misery suffered elsewhere. (As the Pope has said: 'The increasing wealth of a few stands beside the increasing misery of the masses.') If one is talking of exploitation, one cannot very well overlook the exploitation in the countries themselves. Crisis and democracy – it is a subject which cannot just be shifted on to the agenda of international conferences.

And incidentally, the member of a foreign delegation – or the visiting economist, or the prosperous tourist – will see little of what concerns and oppresses the ordinary people of the continent unless he or she takes a positive interest in it. Such visitors are accommodated in first-class hotels, welcomed into elegant offices and fine houses, and eat in good restaurants. Unless one is careful, one is in danger of altogether missing the reality of the country visited, particularly on a short stay in a Latin American country.

To be frank: anyone who arrives at the international airport in Rio or São Paulo, Mexico City or Buenos Aires, who is driven through office and business districts and spends a few days at a conference centre, must be careful that the long shadows cast by the country in which he is staying do not escape his notice. The same applies to Cairo and Delhi, Djakarta and Kuala Lumpur as to the capital cities of Latin America. If you see the considerable prosperity, sometimes the great luxury of the economic élite of society, and frequently of the political élite as well, you will find yourself wondering if you are really in a poor country after all.

In many cases, poor countries are those which, objectively speaking, are rich. The privileged, typically, are strikingly opulent; the lot of the poverty-stricken masses is unhappy, indeed desperate. Only the unobservant will fail to take in the whole of the truth around them.

4. *Alternatives?*

At the beginning of the Seventies the international monetary system was dismantled when it ought to have been renovated. The visible sign of financial instability came with the suspension of the convertibility at a fixed rate of the dollar into gold. The Eurodollar market was blown up to twice the official currency reserves, chiefly as a result of the oil crisis. The international financial system became subject to increasing privatization, while the developing countries had inadequate opportunities of obtaining finance. When loans were not repaid, banks were happy enough to be able to renew them and roll them over, to good advantage, since interest rates were rising.

However, the industrial states, led by the USA, had gone so far down the road of debt themselves that the consequences could not be long in coming. Even rather conservative Americans spoke openly of the defects of the international monetary system; many Europeans were no longer afraid to say that the United States did not live up to the responsibility imposed upon it by the role of the dollar. Some of the proposals we made five years ago were taken more seriously now. The governments of Europe found themselves required by the European parliamentary assemblies to aim to create an international reserve currency, taking the needs of the poorest countries into account. Basically, there are three main points at issue:

- First, can IMF be strengthened and reformed so that it assumes at least partially the role of a global central bank, and if so how? It would mean extending the role of Special Drawing Rights and altering the voting system in favour of the developing countries.
- Secondly, can the World Bank be put in a position to expand its annual volume of lending considerably, and ensure that the developing countries have more of a say? A word of caution: the Indian who graduated from Harvard or the Chilean who graduated from Chicago, whose family is not exactly poverty-stricken, and who has not overcome his own class-consciousness, is in no way a 'better' choice as colleague than an American or European, Japanese or Australian from a similar background. Nationality alone says little. (IDA, a subject on which I have already expressed my opinion, must also be seen as a part of the World Bank. So must IFC, the International Finance Corporation, which encourages private investment in developing countries by means of direct participation. The various regional development banks work in a similar way, and their activities deserve positive interest, though their role is not specifically elucidated here.)
- Thirdly, what should the nature of an international conference be to determine urgent issues of money, finance, and general economic matters?

Indira Gandhi had asked experts from the non-aligned countries to draw up the report which came out in the summer of 1984: it employed weighty if not particularly new arguments to set out the objections to an 'adjustment' providing neither employment nor significant growth. A conference with universal participation, planned for the autumn of 1985, was to take place in the context of 'directions in development policies', aiming for resolutions based on consensus; the preparations were to be made by a representative group from both industrial and developing countries, with the support of IMF, the World Bank and UNCTAD.

After Indira Gandhi's assassination, it turned out that more time was needed to realize these plans. But I am sure that her ideas will not be forgotten. Several factors indicate that we shall not master crises in the long term by dealing with them case by case. I would like to mention a few recent developments.

The resources of IMF *have* been stocked up considerably in recent years, but the governments whose word carries weight in the Fund do not want their *status quo* disturbed where Special Drawing Rights are concerned. Five years ago, we suggested a well-founded increase of $100 billion. American experts advocated just under half that amount, moderate European experts recommended an annual, quantitatively limited SDR allocation. They saw the solution as the combination of a smaller burden of interest with more – responsibly secured – new money.

The Western economic summits in London, 1984, and Bonn, 1985, were non-events so far as the debt crisis was concerned. The participants did rouse themselves to encourage the banks to make rescheduling agreements for periods of several years 'in suitable cases and in the presence of corresponding progress in adjustment'. At the same time, the governments declared themselves ready to negotiate rescheduling of official government loans. The progress made in 'adjustment' by the debtor countries was to be rewarded with more favourable conditions. Some governments did not agree with this excessively cautious approach. France wanted the creation of three additional tranches of $15 billion SDRs each.

The French representative at the United Nations said, in the autumn of 1984, that the world economic system must become less complex and should be marked by stability, and hence it needed restructuring. In the long term, steps must be taken to lay the foundations of genuine international currency reform; besides the dollar, the yen and the West European ECU (European Currency Unit) should be central factors in this future system. I regret that these French initiatives did not get support at least from the German Federal government.

Meanwhile experienced critics outside government circles have spoken out. Karl Schiller, for instance, reminded us of the old experience that as a general rule, a compromise settlement is preferable to the threat of insolvency. One of the big Swiss bankers said publicly and frankly that the banks must know they would not get back the money they had lent, and should be content with a moderate yield of interest. Other European bankers said that long-term rescheduling was better than short-term rescheduling whose conditions the countries concerned could not live up to. Finally, the head of the German Bundesbank asked for the phase of crisis management to be followed by a phase of longer-term consolidation, 'even if there were to be some uncomfortable consequences for the participating banks' profit and loss accounts'. In the USA, Henry Kissinger said that anyone relying on the present system of debt negotiations might just as well be playing Russian roulette. Declining to repay loans was no longer dismissed as immoral.

Meanwhile, the Latin American debtor countries had become impatient, and were speaking of financial colonialism and saying that South America must emancipate herself from foreign rule imposed by international financial circles. They wanted to negotiate only at a high political level. In practice, however, they had to climb down; the structural factors were altogether too powerful – or still too powerful. I can understand how the phrase 'imperialism through credit' arose.

At various meetings, in Quito, Cartagena, and Mar del Plata, eleven Latin American countries had agreed in principle on a common front to be presented to the creditor countries. Some of them talked grandly, speaking of landmarks along the road of concerted action against the industrial countries. But in practice, things looked different; talks on rescheduling continued as before between the individual debtor countries and their creditors, with either more or less attention being paid to their agreed debtors' principles.

Responsible people have said to me in conversation that here again it cannot be just a matter of distinguishing between multilateral rhetoric and bilateral pragmatism, closely as that would correspond to the facts. It is much more important, they say, to interpret the signs of the times correctly: the larger countries saw their agreements as a first step towards joint action by the Latin American family, which had met without the leadership of Washington for the first time, 150 years after independence. In that way, initiatives like those of Quito, Cartagena and Mar del Plata represented great progress.

There is a general intention of removing negotiations on rescheduling from the present technical level to a high political level, and conducting the discussion in the larger context of international economic relations, and paying particular attention to trade issues as well. The agreement made at the annual meeting of IMF and the World Bank in the autumn of 1984 to conduct such talks in the framework of the Development Committee – an important coordinating committee between the Fund and the Bank, if not at the highest level – was apparently not a large enough step.

When Tancredo Neves was elected President of Brazil, he ruled out the possibility of a moratorium on his country's debts. He wanted to start new negotiations on unreasonable conditions of repayment, while for the time being prohibiting the taking up of more loans from US banks. Only passing mention was made of a 'dangerous' cartel of debtor countries. (President Nyerere, who advised his African colleagues not to service their debts as a means of exerting pressure, was not representative in this respect.) Mexico's President de la Madrid declared himself in favour of a 'pragmatic dialogue', and emphasized the 'great variety of problems and positions' within the Third World. All governments were under pressure, but some less so than others. They all drew attention, he said, to their own particular circumstances, they almost all disclaimed the existence in the immediate future of any real alternative to the adjustments imposed on them and the resulting interim provisions. South America itself had only the beginnings of a regional mechanism with whose help effective preparations could be made for concerted action. If the process of coordination were accelerated during the current crisis, that, he said, could only be helpful to all concerned, including the creditor countries.

In October 1984, at a conference in Rio de Janeiro – Governor Brizola had invited the Socialist International – ideas for the management of the debt crisis emerged, which I put forward for discussion at the various stages of my subsequent Latin American journey, and for which I won the agreement of those concerned. They were as follows:

- a moratorium on debts; in addition, a waiving of the debts of the poorest countries;
- a lowering of interest rates, to be linked to the simultaneous

147

establishment of an upper ceiling; to the surprise of many, the Chairman of the Federal Reserve Bank of the United States himself also spoke of a 'cap on interest rates';

• the introduction of a 'social clause'. This would ensure that the programme of adjustment did not lower the standard of living of the poorest classes unreasonably; instead, the minimum acceptable living standard should be taken as a firm criterion;

• I would add here that an international conference on debts may well become unavoidable.

We shall have to wait and see when and how all these points are eventually taken up. I have already said that I think a second Bretton Woods is required. And one can only hope that those politicians chiefly responsible will apply themselves to the matter in time; for there are plenty of technical proposals, and in the long term experts are inclined to divide into two camps of equal strength: one camp puts forward all possible reasons for a given proposal, the other rejects it for reasons that sound equally plausible. But if one listens only to one camp or the other, one gets nowhere.

5. Unremitting Trade War

One of the many disappointments of 1984 was the failure of the UNIDO conference in Vienna. UNIDO (the United Nations Industrial Development Organization) was created in 1966 to promote industrial development of the Third World. In 1975, at a conference in Lima, it was still being estimated that the developing countries would command a quarter of global industrial production in the year 2000. In 1984 they had 12 per cent of it, and it was not thought likely that they would reach over 18 per cent by the turn of the century. The Vienna conference did not come up to expectations.

At that conference, the USA stated that in allocating development aid, they would give preference to countries with a free market economy. It is still not clear how that criterion is to be established, or to whose advantage such dogmatism is supposed to be. In several of the countries closely associated with the USA, and of which they approve – such as South Korea – a high degree of state control of the economy is practised. And when the United States and their principal European allies urge IMF to impose stringent conditions, they are not as a general rule aiming at free enterprise initiative but at practising greater government control in whatever country is concerned.

There is no doubt that the developing countries' access to the markets of the industrial countries is obstructed by the same groups that like to talk of free market economy and free world trade. At the annual GATT meeting at the end of 1984, it was pointed out from the chair that despite some increase in the volume of world trade, the climate of international trade relations had deteriorated; the growth of world trade, which could be attributed to the prevailing trend of economic activity in Japan and the USA, had been accompanied by a rise in protectionism. Those chiefly affected were the developing countries.

A clear trend away from multilateral free trade and towards the bilateral, controlled exchange of goods may be observed globally. There is talk of a 'fragmentation' of markets, creating insecurity in the economy and slowing down capital investments outside the USA.

The assurances given by many governments are highly disingenuous. Sixty per cent of world trade is transacted under 'non-free' conditions. Of the total industrial products consumed in the USA and the EEC, over 30 per cent are now affected by protectionist measures; a few years ago, it was about 20 per cent.

When a new round of international trade negotiations was envisaged in the spring of 1985, first in the OECD and then at the world economic summit in Bonn, there was no lack of warning voices to be heard from those who thought a link between trade and *monetary* issues was imperative. This connection is of particular interest to many developing countries.

In the first half of the Eighties, the developing countries were affected more than anyone by an increase in protectionist measures, particularly in textiles and clothing, steel, and agricultural products. UNCTAD registered no less than 21,000 cases in which 'non-tariff' barriers (i.e. barriers other than customs duties) had been employed – guerrilla warfare in trade policy, with permanent effects.

The tendency to short-sighted protectionism is spreading, while on the other hand the division of production – or chain production – plays an ever-increasing part in global economic cooperation, from footwear to car manufacture. The role of the multinational corporations is seen again here. To give a bizarre example: 95 per cent of all baseballs used in America come from Japan. First the hides of American cattle are sent to Brazil for tanning, then they go on to Japan to cover the baseballs.

With the restrictions and trade barriers of recent years, we have seen the shifting and interlocking of whole branches of industry between country and continent. Here are some examples (taken from John Naisbitt, *Megatrends*):
- Singapore comes in second place, just behind the USA, for orders for building offshore oil-rigs;
- Hong Kong and Taiwan are dropping out of the production of textiles and simple electrical goods in order to concentrate more intensively on computer technology;
- South Korea is challenging Japan's dominance in home electronics;
- The People's Republic of China, which concentrated on the export of commodities in the Seventies, is moving into the production and export of products of light industry, textiles, baskets, bicycles, radio and television sets.

Despite enormous shifts, it is not yet clear what opportunities will be offered to developing countries in the markets of industrial countries in the years ahead. The concept of an international society of unrestricted competition was shaken when competition itself was overcome in a number of branches of industry; multinational corporations and governments had made ample use of their opportunities. Exchange between the fundamentally unequal, in any case, entails its own grave problems, let alone the built-in handicaps in any race where a man with one leg is competing against a man with two.

As I have mentioned, the Allies' postwar planning envisaged an international Trade Organization (ITO). When nothing came of this, GATT, the General Agreement on Tariffs and Trade, became the most important liberator of world trade. Although GATT provides for the protection of a country's domestic economy exclusively by means of tariffs, and not without consultation, precisely the opposite has occurred in an increasing number of cases over the years, particularly in recent times. Trade restrictions are constantly supplementing or succeeding one another, and there are many cases of sudden action being taken, instead of serious efforts to reach understanding. Job losses in the industrial states as the result of imports from the South have in fact been less than was at first expected, while on the other hand the potentially growing significance of exports to Third World countries has been underestimated. Those who would reduce the export incomes of the newly industrializing countries should, however, be aware that they are simultaneously reducing the ability of those countries to buy capital goods.

With a view to comprehensive international trade organization my Commission recommended:

- creating *one* organization, which would incorporate both GATT and UNCTAD;
- protecting, for a certain period, endangered regions or branches of the economy, while paying serious attention to those structural adjustments necessary as a result of the international division of labour;
- regarding the protection of domestic markets in developing countries as entirely legitimate;
- giving strong support to increased South–South cooperation (and we have seen remarkable progress made in this area);
- recognizing the dangers which are the inevitable consequence of the further spread of narrow-minded protectionism.

In the American debate, too, those with international experience have suggested the kind of principles for necessary adjustments for which one should aim. If relatively free trade is to function, governments would have to overcome 'full laissez-faire'. This judgment has realism and honesty on its side, and so do those who now admit that they do after all recognize the advantage of an assured supply of raw materials at predictable prices.

However, some of the emotional attacks on European agrarian

policy are full of inconsistencies. I am one of the critics of the excesses of that policy, and have been for some time. I think they are also to be deplored and resisted from the angle of development policy. However, one cannot see the justification for American polemic against European subsidies if it is in fact only a matter of *who* is doing the subsidizing, and by *how much*. (In the USA, subsidies to farmers are more per head than in the EEC – a French friend of mine spoke of 'wallowing in the most consummate form of hypocrisy'.)

The agricultural policy of the European Community *does* need extensive revision. In the process, the interests of a constructive development policy must come into their own. By the way, it is only right that the EEC should not allow itself to discriminate in its industrial and research policy.

As for the multinational or transnational corporations, the negotiations in progress since 1977 over an international code of conduct have come to a halt; no agreement is in sight.

These were the recommendations formulated by my Commission:
- With regard to foreign investments, transfer of technology, repatriation of profits, royalties and dividends: reciprocal obligations on the part of host and home countries.
- With regard to activities of transnational corporations in matters such as ethical behaviour, disclosure of information, restrictive business practices and labour standards: legislation coordinated between home and host countries to regulate them.
- In matters of tax policy and the monitoring of transfer pricing: intergovernmental cooperation.
- With regard to fiscal and other incentives between developing countries in which transnational or multinational corporations are active: harmonization.

Over the last few years it has become even clearer what the transnational corporations represent. They control a third of world production, and transact 40 per cent of world trade between them. In certain sectors, particularly commodities, up to 90 per cent of the trade is in their hands. Over the last two decades, their activity has grown twice as fast as world production and world trade. Their profits in developing countries are on average twice as high as 'at home' in the industrial states. The multinationals are using their chances as best they can. Criticism should be levelled principally at the backwardness that marks the policies of many governments.

6. Natural Resources on the Sea-Bed

A disappointment in my own country was the refusal of its government in 1984 to sign the Law of the Sea Convention, which had come into existence two years earlier after very lengthy negotiations, and was perhaps the most important international treaty since the United Nations Charter.

When my Commission met in Ottawa at the end of 1982, and were putting the finishing touches to our second Report, we were visited by Elisabeth Mann-Borghese, Thomas Mann's daughter. She told us of the results of the work in which she, as an authority, had had a large share since 1958. Our Commission firmly believed that it was 'clearly in the interests of all nations to sign this Convention'. One hundred and nineteen states had agreed to the draft drawn up in Jamaica. The Convention was signed by 158 states and groups of states in 1984, though ratified by only a few. Among the overwhelming majority of the community of states that declared themselves in favour of this important treaty are almost all Third World countries, China, Japan, the Soviet Union and almost all European countries. The USA, which had once set the initiative in motion, was now simply opposed to it – influenced by the special interest of its private mining corporations in the future mining of the sea-bed – and secured the allegiance of the United Kingdom, the Federal Republic of Germany, and Israel.

I was very sorry to see the Bonn government, not for the first time, yielding so far to American intervention as to run the risk of isolating itself. An independent assessment of our interests in terms of foreign and economic policy would have led to a different view. German interests do not automatically coincide with those currently supported by the United States, particularly over the Law of the Sea, and not only because, unlike the USA, Germany is neither a world power nor the possessor of a large seaboard. Germany also lost its chance of making Hamburg the headquarters of the International Court of the Law of the Sea.

The Law of the Sea Convention is concerned with:
- regulating seafaring and fishing rights; and no one could expect that that might do away with the objective advantage of states with large seaboards;
- the demarcation of territorial and economic zones at sea (to which the same applies);
- measures against the contamination of the seas and the decimation of marine fauna;
- basic regulations for scientific and technical cooperation between North and South;
- regulations for deep-sea mining, although this will hardly be a very important factor before the year 2000.

The issue disputed most is the last point: under what conditions are so-called manganese nodules to be mined? Besides manganese, these contain cobalt, copper and nickel, and are found in large quantities on the sea-bed. The international treaty was to turn just these natural resources – a 'common inheritance of mankind' – to good account for all nations jointly, under the supervision of an international authority. The professional expertise of the few industrial states active in this area and in a position to build the expensive plant needed was to have been made available to the developing countries.

The objection raised was to the 'regulatory' powers of the envisaged authority, which it was supposed would offend the order principles of the free market economy. The fact was that certain large companies did not want to subscribe to a system of international law. Behind the principles of political order for which support is claimed, to impress the public, there lies a colonialist notion of the first law – also a kind of gold-digger's mentality, for which, however, there are no real grounds.

This is an area in which judicious international control is called for. And I would continue to plead for a good part of that common heritage of mankind to be freed for purposes of economic development.

The dispute over the Law of the Sea Convention is one proof among others of the dire straits in which multilateralism finds itself – and the present belief of many developing countries that they will do better if they concentrate on bilateral relations is certainly a contributing factor. Those who have long striven for the interests of such countries to be reconciled with those of the industrial countries are all the more discouraged.

7. A New Marshall Plan?

After the Second World War, the American Marshall Plan played a considerable part in helping Western Europe to get on its feet again; Stalin would not permit an extension of economic aid into his new sphere of influence. The United States made sacrifices, but they also got something in return. Over the last few years, it has repeatedly been asked whether the basic concepts of the plan named after Secretary of State (and former General) George Marshall could not be applied to the relation between industrial and developing countries.

Nor is the question unreasonable. A simple equation cannot, of course, be made. The existence in Europe of an industrial basis, preserved despite all the destruction, and of a large, experienced labour force, represented conditions there which are not present in large parts of the Third World.

My friends in the German Parliament took the idea as a starting point when they proposed a 'Third World Future Programme' in the middle of 1984. The introduction to their proposal says: 'The future of the Third World is not chiefly determined by outside aid. Rather, it is crucially dependent on the emergence of a more just economic and social order for the world as a whole.' The Future Programme was not, said the proposal, merely a humane requirement: 'It is not only based on the historical co-responsibility of the industrial nations; it is also in their own interests.'

After 1945, the Marshall Plan provided the impetus for the reconstruction of Europe and contributed to the recovery of the world economy. Today we need to make a similarly great effort to combat hunger and disease, the exploitation and destruction of the natural environment, the waste of energy and raw materials, ignorance and unemployment in the Third World: 'However, it cannot, as with the Marshall Plan, be a case of involving the developing countries in the political and economic system of the industrial states. What is required, rather, is global cooperation corresponding to the cultural and social identity and the political and economic independent responsibility of the developing countries.'

The basic principles of such a programme are simple: they consist of taking concrete action to bring about the necessary reduction in global expenditure on armaments and the use of the resources thus saved for the development of the Third World. But the aim of such a 'Third World Future Programme' goes beyond the call for funds to be diverted from military expenditure. It demands a new approach to international cooperation world-wide, for only thus would the anticipated resource transfer to the developing countries be possible at all. And an essential part of this approach is better cooperation between East and West. This is a return to the 'philosophy' behind our two reports: the peoples of the world have no choice but to secure their survival together. That can happen only if world peace is secured. And that requires the economic and social development of the Third World.

An emergency programme forms the nucleus of the project I am describing. Overcoming the international debt crisis will have a central part to play in the economic future of many countries not just in the Third World, but among the industrial nations too. A 'Third World' special programme cannot stop there. There are close connections here with the proposals of the Brandt Commission, since, as we said, 'the world cannot wait for the longer-term measures before embarking on an immediate action programme for the next five years to avert the most serious dangers, an interlocking programme which will require undertakings by all parties, and also bring benefits to all'.

Four large areas fell within the scope of the emergency programme as set out in our report in 1980:

First, a large-scale transfer of resources to developing countries, to be brought about by the provision of:

- aid for the poorest regions, which are worst affected by economic crises,
- aid for middle-income countries, by providing finance for their debts and deficits.

Second, an international energy strategy, to consist of:
- regular supplies of oil,
- predictable and gradual price rises,
- the development of sources of alternative and renewable energy.

Third, a global food programme, its aims being:
- increased production of food, with international assistance, especially in the Third World itself,
- regular food supplies, including increased emergency aid,
- a system for long-term international food security.

Fourth, the introduction of major reforms of the international economic system, to be achieved by:
- taking steps towards an effective international monetary and financial system in such a way that all could participate with equal rights,
- accelerating efforts to improve the developing countries' conditions of trade in commodities and manufactured products.

The 'Third World Future Programme' concentrates on the essential areas of:
- decreasing the burden of debt on the poorest countries,
- ensuring the satisfaction of basic needs, particularly through increased food production in the developing countries themselves,
- promoting trade and improved conditions of trade for those countries.

Responsibility for use of resources and control over such use could lie with a new international committee, North and South having equal representation on it. Implementing the programme should be entrusted to 'experienced international institutions within the United Nations'. However, there are good reasons to call for the formation of a separate 'World Development Fund', since the additional resources which would be transferred from military expenditure could not be lodged with proven institutions such as the World Bank or the Regional Development Banks, or be at the disposal of the general budget of the United Nations. As everyone knows, not all states belong to the Development Banks – or IMF – and at the United Nations the recipient countries, with their great majority, could make the decisions alone.

Such a proposal takes both the East and the West at their word. Both sides say that disarmament and development belong together, and resources from the first could be used for the other. This verbal unanimity at least offers a chance. And a global initiative in development policy can simultaneously open up a new dimension in global peace policies. Thus, such an initiative should first be prepared in the context of political cooperation between the EEC states, and then discussed with other European partners, as well as with the USA, Canada and Japan. The subject should be introduced into the East–West dialogue in such a way as to give an opportunity of a discussion as unpolemical as possible.

The connection between the necessary long-term change of basic conditions in the world economy, and short-term goals (the special programme) does certainly need further clarification. And overcoming the debt crisis and changing certain IMF practices are not enough. Above all, a joint international effort is called for, and a joint struggle against underdevelopment and negative development, including our own.

VII

NOT BY BREAD ALONE

In the debate on development policies, economic factors and considerations which do have great weight are often made to seem absolute. However, we must also keep the historical, cultural and intellectual inheritance of peoples and states and their political opportunities in view. Religious and traditional influences play a part, and so do the legacies of colonial power, and also those models, whether accepted or rejected, which have left their mark on more than one generation of leaders.

Our own experience in Germany of the disastrous consequences of destructive ultra-nationalism should not lead us to close our minds to the new nationalism, often deep-rooted, that we encounter in other parts of the world. Particularly in Africa, boundaries drawn by the colonial powers have divided tribes which share a common culture and language. Islam is gaining ground and making its militant mark on political events, but the fact that Islam is not necessarily militant, and has moderate and non-violent variants, is not widely known. Still less well known is the way in which the cultures of Latin America – the original culture, the culture of the immigrants and later cultural imports – rub against each other and interconnect, whereas over the last few years more attention has been paid to the cultural aspects of social and political change. No one now disputes that school and university education, research and technical training must be taken seriously and encouraged in Third World countries, particularly the least developed of them.

Literacy is of primary importance. UNESCO, the United Nations Educational, Scientific and Cultural Organization, has set itself the objective of eradicating illiteracy by the year 2000, but that is going to take rather longer than envisaged.

- In 1983/4, 29 per cent of the population of the world were unable to read and write.
- In 24 countries, over 70 per cent of adults could not read and write. And despite the great and persistent efforts that are being made, we must expect to see an increase in the *absolute* number of illiterates in the immediate future, owing to rapid population growth.
- In the developing countries, 300 million children between the ages of six and eleven do not go to school at all. And half of those who do go to school leave again before the end of their second year.
- We may expect the number of illiterates to be 900 million at the turn of the century.
- During my Latin American travels in 1984 I myself recorded figures: the illiterates of Brazil, some 30 million of them, were not allowed to take part in the elections; the proportion of illiterates in Peru was estimated to be 18 per cent, although they were not excluded from suffrage there; even in Argentina, there was estimated to be a similar percentage of 'functional' illiterates.
- Can we close our eyes to the depressing fact that, even in 'developed' countries, illiteracy is on the increase again?

Forward-looking North–South policies must give priority to the education of large sections of the population, or it will not be possible for those people to help themselves and further their own interests. However, we should not overestimate the value of formal education. (If that were all that mattered, the Germans would never have let Hitler come to power and wreak such havoc.)

Internationally – assuming that respective conditions are taken into account – we are concerned not just with aid in education and training, but with many additional and as yet unexplored opportunities for scientific, artistic and cultural exchange; not the kind of random exchange whereby skilled personnel are enticed away from developing countries without appropriate recompense. It is also a matter of getting to know the way other people live and think and taking part in something that, despite all public folly, may deserve to be called world culture.

In spite of some justifiable criticism, I think it is deeply to be regretted that UNESCO itself has fallen victim to narrow-mindedness. The USA, having given notice of its impending withdrawal from the organization a year in advance, did in fact withdraw at the beginning of 1985; the large US contribution of 50 million dollars a year is no longer at UNESCO's disposal. The United Kingdom* and some other countries reserved their right to follow the American example.

Washington's attitude is determined by the fact that the present American administration is withdrawing from international organizations where the rules are decided by majorities which cannot very easily be influenced; instead, it is using the more comfortable possibilities of bilateralism. I have already mentioned this in connection with the World Bank's proposals for Africa, the funding of IDA and IFAD, and the International Law of the Sea Convention. America's refusal to accept the jurisdiction of the International Court of Justice in the case of Nicaragua falls into the same category. It should be recalled that some years ago the United States withdrew from the International Labour Organization, which has its headquarters in Geneva, and came back when certain issues had been cleared up.

The decision to withdraw from UNESCO was taken against the advice of various important institutions and people of authority. It was coupled with an assurance that the USA would continue to promote certain UNESCO projects, and would moreover divert the funds saved to other relevant uses.

What, in fact, were the main arguments put forward in the UNESCO dispute?

• It was said that UNESCO had become unacceptably 'politicized', an accusation which makes no sense in those general terms, and whose drift becomes clear only when we know of the imputation that an 'Afro–Arab bloc' has gained excessive influence, with the cooperation of Director General A. M. M'Bow of Senegal – who is to be rated very high as a leading

---

* Since writing this, the UK has also withdrawn.

figure in the cultural field. (The treatment of Israel as if it were not part of the United Nations lent weight to this allegation.)

- Absurdly, the Director-General and his organization were also supposed to have committed themselves to a new international economic order, though surely anyone must know about the situation at the General Assembly in New York with regard to this matter.
- In my view, the objection that issues of disarmament and peace belong to the controversial field of 'politics', and are thus not within the scope of subjects to be dealt with by the United Nations' cultural organization, is particularly misguided. One might suggest, conversely, that far too little has been done so far to pursue those aspects of the peace issue which are 'not directly political'. If it is true that all wars have begun inside human minds, then human thought and philosophy could surely do a good deal to make lasting peace possible.
- Particular exception was taken to a so-called 'new international communications order', and here pertinent arguments were mixed up with dubious proposals. I would class as dubious those proposals which put the claims of governments before the interests of independent news coverage, while criticism of powerful agencies and media in the North which ignore or take inadequate account of the problems of the South is pertinent. (In my view, independently of criticism from the developing countries, one may object to the fact that the media in our latitudes pay far too little serious attention to Third World issues. News coverage of the United Nations, international organizations and North–South negotiations also leaves much to be desired.)
- There was also criticism of administrative shortcomings and the inflation of the bureaucratic apparatus, something which has become quite usual, not just in international organizations. Among those who raised objections of this nature were many who had thought the political accusations exaggerated, and would have considered it reasonable to concentrate on eliminating shortcomings in administration, routine and excessive expenditure.

The Council of Europe and its advisory assembly have now spoken out clearly in favour of taking seriously the cultural consequences of rapid social and economic change, and acknowledging the great significance to be attached to the cultural dimension in all areas of development cooperation. That includes the duty of protecting a country's artistic heritage and supporting cultural institutes in the developing countries.

Indignation has frequently been expressed in the Third World over the 'organized theft' of works of art, which has its roots in colonialism and thus in history. We are also concerned, however, with the frequent ignoring of the UNESCO convention of 1970, which dealt with measures to forbid and prevent the illicit import, export and acquisition of cultural items, in accordance with which museums and auction rooms should not accept goods illegally offered to them. Critics object to a trade which they rightly consider immoral, and which in fact contributes to annihilating the cultural heritage of the Third World.

Is it asking too much of us to object to such conduct as well? Let us not allow such ideological shadow-fighting as the dispute over UNESCO to obstruct our view!

VIII

SEEING IS BETTER THAN HEARING

1. *What Illusions?*

Ever since the early Sixties, the United Nations has repeatedly discussed a proposed fund to be financed from a modest percentage of military expenditure, and to be used for projects to benefit the poor countries. Regular and trivial objections to this proposal have been raised, just as they were raised to the idea of a levy on the arms trade or military spending, as sketched out in the Brandt Report. The present German Minister for Economic Cooperation, Warnke, has contributed an extremely questionable argument to the international debate. One should not, he says, create too close a link between disarmament and development. Connecting these two 'essential and independent aims' over-closely could distract our attention from the need to make progress in each of the two fields. I do not see that treating the two 'essential and independent aims' separately, as hitherto, has been very successful, nor do I see wherein the danger consists of linking them more closely at long last.

The danger lies, rather, in our persistent avoidance of making difficult but necessary decisions. When action is taken against famine and epidemic disease, extortion and its consequences, drug trafficking and criminal syndicates, 'independent' aims are served, but nobody would deny that links exist or dispute their mutual dependence. Certainly no sensible person would insist that measures should be taken to combat theft only if the receiving of stolen goods can be ended at the same time. But neither would anyone wish to separate opposition to one evil from opposition to the other, and claim to be thereby serving the common good.

The economic aspect of an extensive military build-up has not long been the subject of international discussion. But it is being asked, more critically than was previously the case, whether economic order is influenced for the better or destabilized. What will be the effects on the extent, tempo and nature of technical progress? What will be the consequences on infrastructure, education and research relevant to industry in the developing countries? Few would now dispute that armaments and development compete with one another in national budgets.

And many will now also agree that the enormous cost of the arms race does not merely restrict opportunities in development policy, but is a heavy burden on international economic relations. At the same time, we must realize that there is no guarantee that more funds will be available for development if a reduction in military expenditure should be brought about by international agreements. Should such a reduction be made, national needs would be competing with the claims of international aid and cooperation.

Pointing out the negative and harmful effects of the arms race is not enough. We shall have to get rid of the fear that the reconversion from military production to a civil economy will create insoluble problems. More economic cooperation does not necessarily, but *can*, mean more security.

The best historical example of the way in which the transition from war to peace can be made is found in the United States after 1945. The Swedish government has recently made an in-depth study which cogently shows that a change from military to civil production is technically possible and economically advantageous. One might think there were more than enough good arguments for it. But many people, including many of the decision-makers, are not convinced of the need for a basic change in policy until they see that such a change is possible.

Mutual economic dependence can offer hope for world peace. That was how I saw the trade policy components of our own *Ostpolitik*, and that is how I see the diverse forms of cooperation between the various parts of Europe. I am emphatically in agreement with those who regard more intensive interlocking of the world economy as an important factor in a peace policy. But we shall have to guard against the illusion of automatic effects.

There is no room for illusions, not least when they mislead us over deep-seated conflicts of interests and convictions. But do we not find the dangerous illusion-mongers where an outworn realism is cited as an argument for letting the breakneck arms race rush on, while world hunger is ignored? A new kind of realism is called for, one that takes our responsibility for our own heritage and a common future equally seriously.

One can no longer claim with a clear conscience that more armaments automatically mean more security. One can no longer dispute the fact that, on the contrary, humanity is in danger of arming itself to death. Thus, if an end is to be put to this madness in the mutual interest as properly understood, the resources freed must be at least partly made available for productive purposes in the Third World. That may still sound complicated, may seem (may still seem?) beyond our powers of imagination; and we have no familiar criteria.

Compared with the $1,000 billion which it was estimated would be spent on military purposes in 1985, the world makes a ridiculously small contribution to measures for securing peace in the strict sense of the word. If we put the United Nations budget and other international expenditure on peace-keeping measures together, the vast discrepancy is obvious. Globally, three to four hundred times as much is available for military expenditure as for the peaceful resolution of conflicts. It is important for this fact too to be made known to the world, since nothing much changes without the pressure of public opinion. Just 0.1 per cent of worldwide military expenditure would mean trebling the present resources the United Nations has at its disposal for peace-keeping activities.

When the Brandt and Palme Commissions met jointly in Rome in early 1984, we resolved: 'We urgently recommend govern-ments to divert a part of their military expenditure to efforts being made in the fields of development and the securing of peace.' Governments, we said, had been pursuing a policy of confronta-tion and brought the world to the brink of an economic and military catastrophe. 'The time is ripe for cooperation . . . all countries should have the opportunity and obligation to make a contribution to a new system of security . . . the United Nations remains the expression of our need for international order.' I

166

would add here that only fitful use has been made of the UN's opportunities of settling conflicts and encouraging the maintenance of peace.

The dream of making the Third World countries into areas free from intervention will find no counterpart in reality. But the idea of removing certain regions and countries from the quarrels of the great powers need not be unrealistic. Internationalizing the 'homemade' conflicts of a region simply involves too many dangers. It ought not to be difficult to make a choice between internationalization of this kind and the neutralizing of a potential source of conflict.

I know that European politics cannot be copied and exported. But among the experiences that most impressed me in the Sixties and early Seventies was the attempt that was made to replace a sterile and dangerous confrontation by limited, realistically significant cooperation, not allowing oneself the illusory belief that ideological opposites can be done away with, but resolving to relieve tensions in a way that might perhaps even help to change the character of the conflict, and could at least decrease its danger. I believe that if we should be spared a major catastrophe it will be possible and worthwhile to build on such experiences. With the help of acceptable intermediate results, practical cooperation and agreements capable of inspiring confidence could improve the political climate, make life easier for humanity, and help to safeguard peace.

It will surprise no one that this view influences my thinking on North–South issues, and I do not see anything wrong with that. I think highly of proceeding step-by-step. It strikes me as more promising than those grand designs which stay put on paper. However, such a strategy can succeed only if we recognize our mutual task and believe in our mutual ability to prevent nuclear war and secure the future of mankind. Any who cherish, even to the slightest degree, yesterday's dream of survival at the expense of others will find the way to fruitful cooperation closed.

One cannot rely on governments to do these things of themselves; most of them need something to set them going.

2. *Polemic Is Not Enough*

Over the last few years, about the most frequently raised objection I have heard is the following: let the East show how *it* is going to give aid first, because the 'aid' it gives, if any, will be only in the form of propaganda and arms. Widespread as this opinion may be in the West, it no longer conforms to the facts.

I write this as one who has long been critical of the foreign policies of the Soviet Union. If I had ever had any illusions, they would have been destroyed by Stalin's power politics and the decisive part they played in the division of Europe. I have observed the marked and frequent way in which Moscow's disarmament initiatives remained mere propaganda. How appallingly unnecessary it has been to make enemies of Czech and Polish reformers; or, within the Soviets' own domain, to treat human rights groups as criminals when they are doing nothing but asserting the principles of the Helsinki declaration of 1975; or to involve themselves in the Afghan venture with its thousands of victims, a venture that will end in neither lasting success nor voluntary approval.

And it is not so long ago that Moscow was clinging to the sterile thesis that the Soviet Union bore no responsibility for the consequences of colonialism, which were to be laid solely at the doors of the Western powers concerned. This was the accepted version, until one day the Third World leaders let it be known they were less interested in the interpretation of past history than in their future; they expected aid from the entire industrialized world, and not just from the Western part of the North. Moreover, it was no secret that countries such as Norway and Sweden made commitments without reference to their non-colonial past, explaining that many problems were not in any case to be ascribed to the colonial past alone.

And here as elsewhere it has turned out that polemic is not enough. If both or all sides had discussed the link between arms and development other than from the propaganda angle, the developing countries and the international community of nations would now be a little further forward. Eastern representatives made the subject a matter of public debate sooner than did others, particularly at the UN, but they did so with an eye firmly fixed on publicity requirements. I think that an effort should long ago have been made, in international forums, to get beyond the clichés which have become so usual there.

Moscow would have made a better showing had it given any prominence to the necessity for development on its home ground, particularly in the Southern and South-Eastern Soviet republics. It could also have been said that aid for allied countries figured larger than indicated in the statistics of the OECD or the World Bank. In 1980, the development committee of the OECD made an interesting emendation. Between one year and another, the estimated proportion of the Soviet gross national product devoted to development aid went up from 0.03 to 0.14 per cent. The explanation of this remarkable swing lies in the question of whether Cuba, Vietnam and North Korea are included or not. (The unfortunate habit of adding up military and economic aid, and thus confusing them, is not confined to the Soviet Union, but is embodied in the budgetary laws of the USA as well.)

That example shows that polemic is no substitute for checking figures. There has been some movement on the Eastern side; positions ranging from the dubious to the untenable have been examined. Scientists, quite rightly, have been somewhat ahead of the members of the political machine. Politicians active in the fields of economics and particularly of trade were ahead of those civil servants whose concern was the inheritance of the Communist International.

The tendency of world powers to meddle in the affairs of other countries has given rise to unprofitable polemic as well. What are the differences in the form this tendency takes? What is the specific relationship between power politics and ideology? We may doubt whether the race for the Third World and the absurdly excessive arms build-up can be moderated and controlled. But surely we must keep on trying if there is still, or again, to be any idea, for more than a brief moment, of reducing dangerous tensions?

It was no accident that the superpowers resumed their exchange of information about certain critical regions when they had agreed to new negotiations over the arms race and its possible limitation. One thinks first of the Middle East and Central America, but South-East Asia and southern Africa are in an equally critical state. And many people are unaware how dangerous the conflict over the Islas Malvinas (Falkland Islands) could have been if their 'nuclearization' had brought countermeasures in its wake, if only on the nature of plans, at first.

Reinforcement of the peace-keeping functions of the United Nations is essential for a policy of peace. These functions come within the scope of the Secretary General and in particular of the Security Council; the opportunities both offer for the settlement of differences should be extended and used more freely.

In the second half of the Seventies, the two superpowers tried to come to an agreement on the limitation of arms exports. Both sides thought at the time that this was more sensible than simply calling each other names. It does not look as if further progress will be easy. But the future belongs to those who are capable of applying themselves afresh to the problems of East–West and North–South relations, armaments and the economy.

A special conference of the United Nations is planned for the summer of 1986, on the subject of 'Disarmament and Development'. The French government has been particularly strong in its advocacy of this conference. A few years ago, a group of experts chaired by Inga Thorsson of Sweden did preliminary work for the UN Secretary-General. Important initiatives have also come from the Disarmament Committee of the Socialist International, chaired by Kalevi Sorsa, Prime Minister of Finland.

In April 1985, prominent representatives of East and West, North and South met at the headquarters of the United Nations. 'Survival in the nuclear age' was the subject of the symposium which I was asked to chair. We stated that:

There is a dynamic triangular relationship between disarmament, development and security. As long as the arms race continues, particularly where nuclear weapons are concerned, the world will not succeed in achieving either more stable and harmonious social and economic development within a more lasting international economic and political order, or global and national security. Competition in the field of armaments – quantitative and qualitative, conventional and nuclear – has had extremely harmful economic and social effects on the people of all nations, both rich and poor. If even a fraction of the valuable resources now being swallowed up by excessive military expenditure were diverted to social and economic development, particularly to combating the poverty of two-thirds of the world's population, it would make a very considerable improvement to life and security on our planet.

That New York statement continued:

This enormous and increasing amount of military expenditure is economically harmful, giving rise to inequity and distortion, and has contributed to the present deterioration of the international economic situation. Moreover, the spread of militaristic culture to the developing countries does further harm. The consequence of failure to control the arms race has been more confrontation and distrust, and the priority given to security issues has had unfortunate results not just for détente between East and West, but also for North–South cooperation.

We suggested that: 'Governments should plan and prepare for a process of the transfer of resources from military to civil uses. This would also, and not least, increase confidence in their serious wish for genuine disarmament.'

3. Changes in the East

Not surprisingly, I have been repeatedly asked since the formation of my Commission in 1977 why I invited no members from the Soviet Union, the Warsaw Pact states and the People's Republic of China to sit on it. The idea did arise, and I was certainly not hostile to it. However, I did not then think the time had come. Later, I was surprised to find that some people were absolutely set against having Russian representation on the Commission, and yet gave the opposite impression in public.

Our colleagues *did* manage to make contacts at the time, visiting Moscow and Peking on behalf of the Commission. I was able to form my own opinion in conversation with prominent people in the Eastern European states. In the summer of 1977,

Brezhnev said in a letter, 'that we approach the problem of relations between former colonial countries in a rather different way from the representatives of the Western states'. However, he said, they were ready to discuss contacts with the Commission.

Interest, mild at first and then greater, was shown in other quarters too. As one of the more open-minded of Eastern statesmen said: 'We cannot be indifferent to matters concerning future conditions of world trade, or the elements of a new international monetary system, or the international aspects of energy and food supplies.' That is as true as ever; some new problems have arisen since that statement was made, some have become more acute over the years. But while more contacts and talks would have been needed at least for discussion of certain practical and fundamental questions, and an agreement on them if possible, the gulf between the superpowers and the power blocs has grown even wider. Such a state of affairs need not persist. If détente were to figure more prominently on the international agenda again, North–South policies would benefit as well.

In Moscow, as elsewhere, I was able to discuss North–South issues as not just a human and political challenge, but a dangerous time-bomb. There was and there is a good reason to speak out *everywhere*, as distinctly as need be, on the disproportion between world armament and world development. It was therefore important that Soviet reaction to my Commission's second report was receptive on this point. The Soviet leadership wrote to me: 'Your report correctly indicates a direct connection between disarmament and the world's socio-economic progress.' The task ahead, said this letter, lay in actually putting an end to the arms race and employing the resources thus saved to solve the most pressing problems 'which a considerable part of humanity faces: hunger, disease and illiteracy'.

A leading Polish economist pointed out that there have been considerable changes in the policy of Comecon: until the end of the Sixties, the belief that the Soviet/Socialist economic model could be exported to the developing countries prevailed. Since then, he says, the basic premise has been that the right preconditions must be created in the countries concerned before 'a Socialist concept suited to varying conditions' could be introduced. It was also acknowledged that until the end of the Seventies, the former colonial powers were held to blame for the backwardness of the Third World; there was a widespread view that the Socialist states were not responsible for the misery in the poor and the poorest countries.

When I talked to Leonid Brezhnev in the Kremlin at the beginning of July 1981, he raised the subject of his own accord; he knew I would be mentioning it anyway, and was more forthcoming than before. He did not, he said, rule out the possibility of the Soviet Union's taking part in the planned summit meeting at Cancun: 'We do not say it will not be possible for us to participate in some way.' Some of the old arguments came up again: Moscow bore no real responsibility, and why did Western commentators rely on false statistics? We based our claims, he said, on figures which did not correspond to the facts. Why did we not count Soviet aid to Cuba and Vietnam, which were surely developing countries?

During my visit to Moscow in 1981, I went to the Institute of International Economics of the Academy of Sciences, of which the late Professor Inosemzev was principal at the time, and was impressed by the intellectual vigour more prevalent here than where politics alone were discussed. I spoke to a sizeable audience of professors and lecturers on 'issues which transcend political systems'. Despite our differing ritual in the way of presentation and expression, we soon found ourselves on the same wavelength. The scientists there knew what was in store for humanity, quite apart from political orders and social systems.

I had an opportunity to elaborate on this at the end of 1981, in Budapest, when representatives of institutes for development research from both sides of Europe invited me to a joint conference. The relationship between East and West, I said, still a tense one, and intolerably burdened by the arms race, and the extremely unsatisfactory relationship between North and South, were interconnected in a complicated and unhealthy manner. The industrial states of the North – in the East as in the West – were not, I continued, in a position to halt the squandering of the earth's natural resources and the laying waste of our planet in both North and South: 'Nor are they in a position to enable the developing countries to prosper, although that would promote their own economic wellbeing. This is a situation which will appear utterly absurd to future historians, should there be any; they will find it impossible to understand our present world's incapacity for action.'

Moreover, I said, the way in which interconnected problems were separated as if they had nothing to do with each other prevented this state of affairs from being rectified: 'That is the case with East–West and North–South relations and with interdependence between the two planes. It is the case with economic, ecological and militaristic issues. We must tackle these problems today in awareness of our mutual dependence, and in whatever area we are concerned, we must do so not in competition with each other, but jointly. Global and common or complementary solutions call for global negotiations.'

The great powers must thus include the dimension of North–South relations and of the global problems I have described in their policies, or they ensure their failure as we enter upon a new millennium. Creating concrete links, at long last, between the East–West issue and the North–South issue, bringing together détente and disarmament on the one hand and developmental and environmental policies on the other – for this there is no reasonable way without including the Comecon states in discussion of these questions. The Soviet Union is well known to have developed into a self-sufficient economic system, helped by the fact that it depends upon hardly any imported commodities. It has also long practised political exclusivity, so that no closer network of economic relations could be formed. Time has passed that attitude by. In future, if states allied to the Soviet Union want to reach their specific goals, they will have to depend more than hitherto on the exchange of goods with the rest of the world, and will be increasingly called upon to face problems of a global character, particularly in international environmental, energy and food programmes. The Soviet Union is in a rather unenviable situation, since its own agricultural performance has time and again fallen far short of the targets it has set itself.

Early in 1985, a study from the Friedrich-Ebert Foundation of economic cooperation in Third World countries said: 'The Soviet Union, which until quite recently rejected the idea of East–West cooperation in Third World countries on ideological grounds, is today regarded as the driving force and principal instigator of such kinds of cooperative action.' At the end of the Sixties, only Romania and non-aligned Yugoslavia showed not just readiness in principle but a lively interest in cooperating with Western partners in third countries. Of recent years, however, the Comecon states have succeeded, says this study, 'in securing considerable shares of the market in developing countries which used to be exclusively the province of Western industrial states'.

The East shows willingness, though one may not sense such receptivity to North–South issues everywhere as that of Janos Kadar, the Hungarian leader. Setting out from the appreciably different conditions of his own country, Todor Zhivkov assured me at the end of 1984 that he wanted to increase Bulgaria's small amount of trade with the Third World. And even Bulgaria has over 10,000 experts participating in projects in various countries anyway.

The German Democratic Republic is pursuing an active (also an ideologically active) policy in a number of Third World countries. In the economic area it has embarked upon joint projects with firms from the Federal Republic of Germany, in Libya and Ethiopia, for instance. What better could we wish for than more consistent joint action for the good of the developing countries on the part of the two German states, extending beyond isolated cases of cooperation?

Over the last few years, the People's Republic of Poland has been impeded in its economic as well as political activities abroad by its difficulties at home. But one success to Warsaw's name was the fact that in early 1985, there were no more apparent misgivings, even in the USA, about its application for membership of the International Monetary Fund. Romania and Hungary had been able to take that step some years earlier. Czechoslovakia, like the German Democratic Republic and Bulgaria, registered a distinct increase in business with the Third World.

The Comecon states are obviously trying to remove their ideological blinkers where the developing countries and international economic cooperation are concerned. Of course there is an understandable element of self-interest involved. Cooperation extends their own freedom of movement. Resolution of the principal differences between the Eastern and Western systems is not within the realm of possibility, but cooperation to the mutual advantage of both sides is, and so are measures to secure peace, and the definition of system-bridging interests. That seems to be the motto of the new Soviet General-Secretary. When I talked to Mikhail Gorbachev at the end of May 1985, I found increased interest, which I had not really expected, in two areas: North–South relations and Europe. An Eastern aphorism is thus confirmed: to see something once is better than to hear about it a hundred times.

4. *Peking and Delhi*

In the spring of 1984, I was asked by a newspaper what human achievement most impressed me. My answer was: 'The fact, if it is a fact, that China can feed a billion people.' After my visit to China in the early summer of 1984, which I had had to postpone several times, I would no longer have made that reservation 'if it is a fact'. Indeed, astonishing as it might sound, there was even talk of a certain grain *surplus* at the beginning of 1985.

Naturally one must not overestimate one's own impressions on a foreign tour. But I checked with well-informed foreign observers, and they confirmed the fact that since 1964, no Chinese had died of starvation. I consider this sober observation one of the great positive experiences of my time.

It is not for me to assess the economic reforms which the People's Republic of China – largely self-sufficient, and comparable to the Soviet Union only in that – has recently decided to push through. The combination of intensive agriculture, with clear incentives for farmers, and the production of consumer goods leaped to my eye and carried conviction. In Peking and Canton, and most of all in Shanghai, I saw busy urban life and considerable economic activity, and also real instances of European and Chinese industrial cooperation; there are good opportunities open to our own firms if they make the appropriate effort.

The industrial production of a city like Shanghai is, in absolute figures, four times that of Hong Kong and ten times that of Singapore. The thirst for knowledge and multiplicity of cultural activities exceed anything we in Europe can imagine of China.

Incidentally, when I was speaking on North–South issues at a Shanghai university, I was asked to use my own mother tongue; they needed no translation from the German! (The university was founded by Germans before the First World War, and continued its association with Germany – both West and East – after 1945.) The pressure of population is reflected in the severe lack of living space: 3.5 square metres per head in Shanghai. In the city itself, 6.7 million people live on a third of the surface area of Hamburg (with just over one million inhabitants).

During my talks in Peking I was able to take as a starting point the fact that China had already engaged in the difficult North–South dialogue. It had taken its place in IMF and the World Bank, without yet being conspicuous there for its contributions to the proceedings. It had also turned its attention to the Group of 77, and taken an interest in the efforts at South–South cooperation being made. I was aware that the People's Republic had varying experience of aid projects in some of the poorest countries, but I did not know that wind-powered pumps and the use of biogas to generate energy were now playing a considerable part in China itself.

The now legendary Deng Xiaoping was not lacking in self-confidence: international politics, he said, was not a card game in which China could be used as one of the cards. General-Secretary Hu Yaobang spoke of his people's wish to work with the people of Europe and the whole world for détente and an end to the arms race, adding that the emergence of the Third World into the international arena was an extremely important phenomenon of our time and also a powerful factor for the maintenance of world peace. 'China belongs to the Third World, and for better or worse is linked with Third World countries. China considers the preservation of the rights and interests of the countries of the Third World its international duty; it resolutely supports the Third World in its struggle for national independence and sovereignty, for the development of its countries' respective national economies, and for the creation of a new international economic order.'

Hu was in favour of support for the North–South dialogue, and declared his intention of taking an active part in South–South cooperation. The industrial countries, he said, should respect the independence and sovereignty of the countries of the Third

World, and pursue economic and trade policies advantageous to those countries. He thought that 'far-sighted leading figures in the developed countries' had seen that such a policy towards Third World countries would also benefit themselves in the long run. The Chinese party leader identified himself with my tenet that peace must come before ideology. He approved of my and my friends' ideas on the connection between disarmament and development.

I took with me to Delhi a critical remark to the effect that India might do well to restrain its 'sub-hegemonistic tendencies'. In answer to that, Indira Gandhi wondered ironically what plans the Chinese had for their own periphery. To counterbalance the ASEAN group mentioned earlier, India is in the process of preparing for a regional collaboration in South Asia, in which Bangladesh, Bhutan, the Maldives, Nepal, Pakistan and Sri Lanka are to participate. Agriculture, rural development, health and population issues are on the agenda for the envisaged exchange of opinions.

My visits to these two very large Asian countries gave rise to some comparative considerations, particularly with regard to population growth and food production.

The Chinese figures are well known. China's population of 542 million inhabitants at the time of the 1949 revolution had almost doubled to one billion by 1980. Since then there has been further growth. Officially, the population is to be kept below 1.2 billion and will stabilize after the year 2000. So far as total population is concerned, India will catch up with the Chinese. At the time of Independence in 1947, it had about 350 million inhabitants. In 1984, that figure had grown to 730 million, it will be a billion at the turn of the century, and is not expected to stabilize until the year 2060.

High priority has been given to birth control in both countries ever since the early Seventies, under state auspices. But there have been and still are great problems. Not all Chinese observe the norm of a single-child family, and many fail to observe it in spite of serious material disadvantages. And again and again one hears reports of parents wanting their only child to be a son. In one outlying province, there were recently found to be three times as many boys as girls among children under three . . . In India, Prime

Minister Nehru introduced a family planning programme at the end of the Fifties, with moderate success. Two decades later, under his daughter Indira Gandhi, an attempt to conduct a programme of compulsory mass sterilization failed.

The success of the Chinese in increasing food production to the point where hunger was overcome has won worldwide notice and respect. Comparatively speaking, less notice has been taken of the fact that India too can now supply its own needs. Grain production has quadrupled since 1967, and recently some rice has even been exported. Food production and population growth have almost reached equilibrium. A great achievement, in large part due to producers' cooperatives. However, almost half the entire population still lives below the poverty line. The lack of public health care is still alarming, although great efforts have been undertaken in this field too. Almost half the population still cannot read and write. It has been shown that farmers produce more not just when modern technology and modern means of marketing are available, but when enough serious attention is paid to the requirements of public education and health care.

India has made considerable progress along the road to becoming a great economic nation. It now has a large industrial sector, a highly developed technology, and a large number of skilled workers. A better balanced development of agriculture and industry could have beneficial consequences as a whole. One should learn from one's neighbours. North Korean agriculture is well spoken of. In some Asian countries which, like Taiwan, have intensively speeded up industrialization, agriculture does not seem to have kept pace.

5. Wasted Chances in Central America

On 25 October 1984, the Contadora document was to have been signed. That event did not take place; the United States thought it would not be in its own interests to sign, and won first Honduras and then other Central American governments over to its side.

Contadora is the name of an island where the conditions of a peace treaty for Central America were first discussed and then negotiated. The participants represented the Presidents of Colombia, Mexico, Panama and Venezuela. President Betancur of Colombia, whom I met at the time when the project failed, said it was as if the creation of the world had been interrupted on the fourth day, adding that every day that passed without major warfare meant success for Contadora. Who would have wished to dispute that? And who would not have been glad to hear that the heads of state concerned intended to continue their efforts, as all four of them told me?

In those October weeks Nicaragua was preparing for the elections to be held in early November, in which part of the opposition refused to take part; their American 'advisers' were against participation in the elections, just as they were against a ceasefire in the north of Nicaragua at the Honduran border; they flatly declined to exert a moderating influence on the Contras, the sworn enemies of the Sandinistas who have held power since the revolution. Instead, the unofficial war went on, in intensified form – involving intervention, sabotage, and economic strangulation. As a result, the Sandinistas became more dependent than would otherwise have been expected, and more than most of them liked, upon help from the Eastern bloc. There is no doubt the Soviet leadership would not miss any opportunity to needle its rival superpower.

It was nevertheless misleading to press the focal point of Central American crisis into the pattern of the East–West conflict. Even Henry Kissinger, despite his usually conservative position, held economic and social circumstances chiefly to blame for the crisis in that region. His Commission called for an aid programme, setting its immediate financial requirements at $1 billion.

The USA have always considered Central America and the Caribbean their back yard and the province of their big business. Their monopolistic claim to intervention in the area leaned heavily on indigenous oligarchies and 'friendly' governments, even when those governments might be brutally abusing power and opposing all the demands of democratic and social renewal. There have been other cases of the United States repeatedly allowing chances in the Third World to slip away, on narrow economic grounds and for reasons of ideological prejudice – the

East–West angle, lack of understanding for liberation movements.

As time went by, Central America increasingly became an arena for terror and persecution, a *danse macabre* of violence and counter-violence:

• Daniel Oduber, the former President of Costa Rica, estimates that there have been 150,000 to 200,000 victims of violence there since 1978.

• In Nicaragua, Somoza's reign of terror, the counter-violence it provoked, and the ensuing conflicts left some 60,000 dead. The estimate for 1978–79 alone is 35,000 dead, 100,000 wounded, and 40,000 children orphaned – and that with a population of less than three million. In 1984 the Contras were responsible for 5,000 victims.

• In El Salvador, between 20,000 and 40,000 civilians have so far fallen victim to oppression and civil strife.

• Guatemala has been the scene of particularly inhuman action against the Indians. Since the military seized power, 35,000 people have 'disappeared'. In the spring of 1985, colleagues of mine in the German Parliament, the Bundestag, who were touring the country ascertained that families are threatened if they search for disappeared relatives.

• Honduras, with its repeated violations of human rights, is not known to be governed according to the principles of a Quaker community either; recently there have been reports that leading military men are inclined towards taking an independent course.

• Here we should also remember the balance sheet of terror in the *South* American military dictatorships; 15,000 dead in Chile, 9,000 'disappeared' in Argentina, and many other deaths as well.

When Gabriel García Márquez received his Nobel Prize in Stockholm in 1982, he said: 'The country which could be formed of all who have been forcibly exiled and made to emigrate from Latin America would have a larger population than Norway.'

I would not want to pretend that I have been convinced by all the measures and views of Nicaragua's revolutionary government. But I have been able to assure myself of its determination to carry out reforms in the framework of a mixed economy system. And despite all untoward events, it has also achieved some notable successes, particularly in the struggle against illiteracy. The leadership was prepared to undertake a series of measures to work for the recovery of the country's economy. However, the opposition of Washington stood in the way of a loan from the Inter-American Development Bank.

The government in Managua was ready to sign the Contadora agreement, to pledge itself to non-intervention, and to guarantee that foreign military advisers should withdraw and no foreign bases be established. In Havana, Fidel Castro assured me that he too would accept corresponding obligations. In any case, conditions in Central America in his view are not such that the Cuban model could be exported there. No doubt analysis of Cuba's own interests lay behind that statement.

To return to October 1984: in La Palma, the parties to the Salvadorean civil war faced each other in talks for the first time. The Christian Democrat President, Napoleon Duarte, regarded with distrust by the extreme right, met representatives of the political and military opposition; since then there have been a few limited ceasefire periods. There is the suggestion of a chance for a peaceful solution. However, if Nicaragua were to suffer actual invasion, or were forced to its knees by some other means, there would be an intensification of guerrilla warfare in El Salvador, and it would flare up again in large parts of the region.

In that same autumn of 1984 the Foreign Ministers of the countries of the European Community, together with those of Spain and Portugal, met their counterparts of the Central American states and the Contadora group in San José, the capital of Costa Rica. The actual substance of the meeting was slight, but it had symbolic significance. It was not that anyone had forgotten what the map looks like, or would have wished to offend the USA. The idea was to demonstrate European interests, the wish for cooperation and at the same time the readiness to support those forces working for peace. I do not overrate the possibilities. But there is now a persistent demand in Central and South America for more cooperation with Europe. When the Commission of the

European Community announced a skeleton agreement for co-operation with Latin America at the end of 1984, the response was greater than actually justified by the content of the agreement.

What about Fidel Castro? He has shown how dubious a proceeding it is to try to master a national and social revolutionary movement by means of isolation and intervention. Castro has developed statesmanlike qualities, though Cuban military commitments may seem to suggest the opposite. His caution in Central American affairs is unmistakable; so is his wish for relations with the USA. Castro, who had tried to steer the non-aligned countries towards Moscow, now realizes how diverse the Third World is and in what a variety of ways it manifests itself.

He considers important what developing countries can do for each other, not least in the areas of health and education. Here we may sense a certain pride in the fact that Cuba and Costa Rica have achieved more than any other Latin American countries to provide schools and hospitals, 'leaving behind some industrial countries'; they even send doctors abroad, and there is thus no lack of reference to the fact that doctors sent from Western countries to the Third World cost very much more than Cuban doctors, for Cuba requires no direct payment in return.

Not everything one hears about Cuban agriculture is on the positive side. But if you fly over the island you cannot but be impressed by the progress being made in afforestation. Little has as yet been written about the role of deforestation in the Central American and Caribbean countries in causing their wretched living conditions. El Salvador is not the only place where the deforestation of a country has contributed to a crisis. More than any other part of the Caribbean, Haiti, a country known in literature as a 'land of woods and waters', now has more uprooted people than other parts of the Caribbean, people driven from the countryside by environmental causes, and Jamaica is a similar case.

6. *The Middle East*

The conflict between the superpowers has had particularly grave effects in the Middle East. The clash of their interests has mingled with the inter-Arab dispute and the antagonism between Arabs and Israelis. In recent years, two-thirds of worldwide arms supplies to the developing countries have gone to countries of the Near and Middle East.

- The United States indirectly became the protector of Saudi Arabia and the smaller, conservative oil states; up to 1978 the USA had close economic and military connections with the Shah of Iran; most important of all, it has guaranteed the existence of Israel, a country which is, of course, well able to assert itself too.
- The Soviet Union formed close links with Syria, and found Libya a solvent customer for armaments. Under President Nasser, it won influence in Egypt which then passed largely to the Americans under Sadat.
- The war between Iraq and Iran – both of them non-aligned countries – which has now dragged on for over half a decade is largely waged with imported weapons; before it began the Soviet Union had equipped one state and the USA the other.
- If it had been possible to impose an effective arms embargo on Iran and Iraq, that war would have been over long ago. Cynics add that weapons can be tested only on the battlefields of war. Saudi Arabia and the Gulf states spend 40 billion dollars a year on defence, by now rather because they fear Iran than out of any desire to attack Israel.
- Jordan is trying to obtain authority to negotiate for the Palestinians in its forthcoming negotiations with Israel. At the same time, it is anxious not to be entirely dependent on the West, but to have access to Soviet backing (and weapons).

The above summary indicates only a few of the threads that go to make up the Middle Eastern tangle. Who would venture to predict when it will be unravelled, or whether partial agreements between Israel and its immediate neighbours will last? Both superpowers have an obvious interest in limiting these conflicts and not leaving their respective allies and protégés to themselves. Hence there were confidential contacts over the Gulf War, and they agreed, early in 1985, not indeed to aim for an international conference on the Middle East, but to have an exchange of opinions without any commitments. Arms deliveries across frontiers are the order of the day in the Gulf War. A German firm – a large share held by Iran – delivered troop carriers to Iraq through its Brazilian subsidiary. Another firm on friendly terms with the first sent Iran tanks by way of its Argentinian partner. Italy has sent helicopters to one side and frigates to the other. Germany and other members of the European Community have exported electronic equipment to both sides at once. I will not go on with the list, but state my firm belief that the Federal Republic of Germany would be well advised to keep out of the international arms trade, particularly in the Middle East, even when others would then deliver the supplies.

When I was in Israel at the end of January, 1985, much of my time was occupied in talking to Arabs with responsibilities in that country itself, on the West Bank and in Gaza. My abiding impression was that small steps in the humanitarian, administrative and economic fields could serve as confidence-building measures on the way to a peaceful order. Israel had then begun withdrawing troops from the Lebanon. It urged the Egyptians to activate diplomatic relations. Jordan was informed what obvious subjects could be important in negotiations.

Prospects had once looked much worse. In this part of the world, as elsewhere, chances have been missed and wasted – by all concerned. But one chance has lain unused, never yet brought seriously into play. It revealed itself to me for the first time when, in the summer of 1978, with Kreisky in Vienna, I was present at a meeting between Anwar Sadat and Shimon Peres. Once matters of protocol and the politics of the day had been dealt with, both leaders turned to look at the future. A fascinating prospect opened – what could not be achieved if willingness to cooperate replaced military categories and destructive capacity! I could not but think of this memorable meeting when our Commission and other committees had to deal with the increasing militarization of the Third World.

The two participants in those talks at Vienna soon turned their attention to detailed discussion of ways whereby deserts might be made into fertile land, backward areas filled with productive activity, and to possible ways of promoting industry and the practical application of modern technological experience. It was an encouraging indication that solutions other than military ones can be found, even in the conflicts of the Middle East. Indeed, that in the last resort there can *only* be other solutions.

And deliberations such as those I have mentioned are not over. A promising attempt is being made to concentrate on the economic development of the entire region. We need not call on the Marshall Plan as a model in any narrow sense, and its scheme could not be transferred to that area. But I would like to plead for the superpowers, the Europeans, the Arab world and the Israelis to make an effort to clear the rubble away *together*, and to promote and stabilize the economic development of the region.

Nothing, of course, gets over the fact that the Palestinian question has come to occupy the centre of the Arab–Israeli conflict. That was how my friend Nahum Goldmann, for many years President of the World Jewish Congress, saw it himself. However, the important point should be to go on from stabilization of the dangerously volatile situation to genuine cooperation. And one must hope that it will then be possible to make progress in the struggle against the dangers of mutual destruction.

The Arab world, like Israel, has highly gifted people and great leaders. There can be no doubt that great progress is also being made there in the fields of science and technology, trade and industry. Model social institutions are coming into existence in many places; such is the case with oil-rich Kuwait. It is also true that relatively speaking, the oil states have done more than the industrial states for the developing countries. (Which does not, however, alter the fact that great poverty is to be found in the Arab world itself as far as the North African Maghreb region.)

I repeat: the question is whether, and when, use will be made in the Middle East of the chance which resides in sharing Israel's highly developed scientific and practical skills, not least in the field of agriculture. Israel is ahead of many other countries; its practical knowledge could be turned to good account not just for its neighbours but for the Third World in general. (It should be added that I speak not *only* of future prospects, for Israel is already successfully cooperating with several countries in Latin America and Africa.)

Anyone wishing to see what can be done with difficult soil should go and see what has been done on the spot. That may be said of more than one country. At the end of 1984, for instance, I saw for myself at the excellent Institute of Agrarian Science outside Sofia what has been done there to improve poor soil, to desalinate other types of soil, and to make soil destroyed by industry fertile again. This is a subject upon which work is being done in the Middle East, as it is in other parts of the Third World. The experience of Pakistan is regarded as so encouraging that it could be used in the Sahel zone.

Water is so important to this region that a member of the Egyptian government recently said he thought the next war could break out over it – the Nile, he meant, not politics. So far as irrigation is concerned, the Israelis, not the Kuwaitis, are ahead of many others:

- They have long been able to desalinate sea water, but this is a costly process, because of the high amount of energy consumed, and will have to wait some time longer.
- Besides making extremely good use of what water is present, the Israelis have been using brackish water in the cultivation of vegetable crops for a number of years.
- Over the last few years, they have succeeded in using sea water to irrigate several varieties of vegetable and grain crops. The process involves a drip system and plastic containers to filter out the salt and keep it from damaging the soil. Complicated, certainly, but think of the possibilities!

My Arab friends have not always understood why I would not associate myself with demands for normalization of the Middle East situation which neglected historical experience. However, I am the citizen of a country which will long have to bear the burden of its own history, and must never forget the responsibility laid upon it. What might appear normal could in the last resort be well-concealed brutality.

Facts are facts, and no one must be allowed to distort them. And there is no other way in which cooperation with the Arabs could really succeed; one cannot cheat by disregarding vital elements in the lives of nations.

7. *Development Aid for War*

International arms trade is a profitable business. Just how profitable one would not only gather from the Brandt report. Suppliers both old and new have between them distributed a scarcely imaginable potential for destruction all over the globe, and they even advertise the fact as well. Is it not, we asked, macabre to see so rapid and dynamic a transfer of ultra-modern technology from rich to poor countries in the area of deadly weaponry? As Alva Myrdal said: 'More and more states are buying more and more insecurity at a higher and higher price.'

The militarization of the Third World increases the incalculable risks for the superpowers as well. Their attempt to come to an agreement on the limitation of arms exports was broken off even before a new administration came to power in Washington. It is now more than uncertain whether the subject will arise again should the powers make any progress over the limitation of nuclear weapons.

In 1983 the Stockholm International Peace Research Institute (SIPRI) made the interesting and at first glance encouraging observation that world trade in conventional weapons was slightly on the decline. The reason was seen in the scarcity of money of the Third World. However, presumably an increase in the domestic production of arms has begun to play a part. And the situation as a whole was still far from inspiring optimism:

- In 1983, the monetary value of the arms *trade* was set at $135 billion, 70 per cent of that amount being the share of the two superpowers.
- The two superpowers were responsible for half of worldwide expenditure on *armaments*, and all industrial countries together for two-thirds. The share of the developing countries, including the oil states but not China, was some 20 per cent; twenty years ago it was all of 6 per cent!

• The two superpowers incontestably head the lists of big arms dealers, with a growing tendency for the USA to take the lead.

The American list of customers is twice as long as the Russian list: 39 major buyers as against 16, and in addition the USA are more generous in allocating production licences to Third World countries. Next on the list of arms suppliers come the West Europeans, first France, then the United Kingdom, the Federal Republic of Germany (with an increasing share) and Italy. The list continues with Czechoslovakia, Poland, North Korea, Brazil, Spain, South Korea, Israel and Switzerland. Recently China, South Africa, India and Egypt have featured on it too. In 1984 Brazil's dynamic arms industry made great strides in competition with the world's other arms exporters; its volume of exports reached some $3 billion. An arms deal to the value of $1 billion was concluded with Saudi Arabia at the end of 1984.

As regards arms *importers*, SIPRI and the American Arms Control Agency are agreed, though they are not quite unanimous over exact ranking, that the leading group consists of Syria, Libya, Saudi Arabia, Iran, Iraq, Egypt and Algeria. India and Indonesia also figure prominently. By now a quarter of the accumulated debts of the Third World are due to arms imports; the financial difficulties of the countries affected exercise a slightly moderating influence on arms buying. In some of the Latin American countries there is debate as to whether the new democracies must accept responsibility for everything the military dictators imported, making the burden of debt even heavier.

There is no doubt that the extent and nature of a country's military equipment has become a kind of status symbol in many parts of the Third World. In military dictatorships in particular, arms are a regular fetish. At the same time – and why hide it? – a country's military organization has sometimes had beneficial effects on literacy, road-building and other forms of modest modernization.

In Washington, Congress's research service calculated that the United States encourages bankrupt states to buy weapons which they often do not need, paying with money they do not have. Mark Hatfield, the Republican Senator from Oregon who is committed to a peace policy and who presented this study, called the present policy 'short-sighted'; he will have realized that that would be regarded as understatement. To give an illustration: in 1982–84, American aid for Africa rose by 40 per cent, but sales and donations of arms, by 150 per cent.

The rapid build-up of armaments industries in parts of the Third World has resulted in drastic changes on the international arms markets. Some countries are increasingly in competition in third country markets with the traditionally dominant arms industries, and are themselves now exporting to the industrial countries. As I have mentioned, Brazil is one of the biggest arms manufacturers in the world. There as elsewhere, they are trying to boost exports so as to lower unit costs and improve the balance of goods and services. Argentina feels positively dependent on the export of armaments. (Iran is not the only place where those tanks built with German assistance end up.)

About 40 developing countries now have their own industries manufacturing tanks, artillery and aeroplanes. The tendency is to move from production under licence to development on their own account. It is not so long since the developing countries had only a 5 per cent share in global expenditure on military research and development, while the share of the two superpowers was 80 per cent.

The Palme Report observed, much to the point: 'The major proportion of military budgets may be allocated to the payment of soldiers and civilian employees, and governments also obtain goods, services and buildings for defence purposes from the civil area. But since the beginning of the Eighties, expenditure on special military equipment and defence research has shown the biggest rise.' And further: 'More and more developing countries are importing technically sophisticated weapons systems, which must often be financed as normal purchases and not with military aid.'

The obsession with troops and weapons of many who bear responsibility in the Third World – laudable exceptions only confirm the rule – is unforgivable and cannot, objectively speaking, be excused. I say so at every opportunity, including in personal conversations. However, it is too easy to condemn the arms importers alone, and not address oneself at least as forcibly to those governments which supply or at least sanction the supply of arms.

What is more, it would be easy to prevent importing countries from spending development aid funds on armaments. One knows, after all, to whom money should be paid. It is quite another matter to know whether development aid is freeing a country's own resources for armaments purposes. However, the following forms part of an unvarnished picture of reality: food production decreased in the African countries south of the Sahara during the Seventies, and thus before the latest drought disaster, while in view of population growth it ought to have increased. Arms supplies to that region tended to rise; but funds were not available for fertilizers and pesticides.

Today no one speaks out openly in opposition when concern for security is associated with the economic objections to arms exports – war development aid! The militarization of the Third World increases the already considerable risks to world peace.

The proposal to set up a register of arms exports at the United Nations, which would also register plants destined for arms manufacture, deserves support, even if it does not attack the root cause of the problem. But one must not aim too high, and in view of the enormous increases of the past few years, registering and thus partially controlling arms production and export would represent some progress.

8. A Just War?

We know the saying that war is the continuation of politics by other means: once a viable calculation, as the question of which side represented historical progress was once viable. In the conditions of the imperialistic world system, *prevention* of war was at the heart of progressive foreign policy for large minorities. That did not alter the fact that in the face of Hitler's murderous régime, the embodiment of imperialism of a newly dangerous nature, the clear victory of one side over the other was necessarily desirable.

Among the most important outcomes of the Second World War besides the breaking of Fascism as a national power were the rise of the USA and the Soviet Union to the status of world powers, the ending of old-style colonialism – not exactly as some had expected; and – most important – the qualitative stride forward in arms development: the first manufacture and the first use of atomic bombs. After that, and not before, nothing was the same as it had been, unwilling as many still are to accept realization of that qualitative change, or readily as they have shaken it off again.

In principle since Hiroshima and Nagasaki, in fact since the early Sixties, the problem of war and peace has radically changed. I made these considerations the central point of a lecture I gave in Peking, where, under a previous leadership, there had been support for the thesis of the inevitability of another great war. By now, even in the Middle Kingdom, opinion had swung round to an understanding that prevention of war was in their own and the general interest.

But what about limited wars waged for national and social freedom? What about defence against hostile interference in a country's own affairs? What about protection from aggressors? Can one leave a small and threatened state unprotected? Should it be left to the East to provide material equipment for liberation movements in southern Africa? Does not the shortage of food and medicine create a kind of war situation of its own? At this juncture I cannot help pointing out that violent conflicts of a new and more comprehensive nature become more and more probable if we turn our backs on the hungry regions. And the battle against hunger can be won only on earth.

The struggle against the arms race, against the danger of a Third World War which would annihilate everything (or almost everything), together with the struggle against world hunger and underdevelopment, remains the top priority. However, the struggle for freedom and equality of nations is not a contradiction to that.

Democracy is not secured by the use of secret agents to carry out secret operations in defiance of international law. Freedom is not won with bombs, executions or other forms of terrorism. But who would condemn someone else for taking a social-militant path when the peaceful way is barred?

When global war is ruled out because it would mean the end,

the struggle of any movement, whatever it may be, has its limits where responsibility to humanity and humanitarian considerations begin. However, the dangers to mutual peace surely do not lie in the ardent striving for freedom of underprivileged peoples, nor even in the barely comprehensible irrationality of this or that region of the world, but in the tendency of third parties to meddle in the affairs of others or export the East–West conflict. A global peace policy and obligations capable of being monitored are called for to counteract that.

Nationalistic and hegemonistic reasons, and moral convictions too, may sometimes urge one to go to the aid of the oppressed, by the most drastic of means if need be. And yet experience and insight tell us to bring judicious restraint to bear on our humanitarian and idealistic impulses, putting them into practice with reason as well as passion. In this context it should be obvious that the responsibility of every state grows with the weight of its power.

In the autumn of 1973, I respectfully reminded the United Nations of Gandhi's policy of non-violent resistance. I think now, as I did then, that an additional comment is called for. There is such a thing as violence exercised through toleration, intimidation through inactivity, threats through passivity, manslaughter committed by a failure to act. That is a border at which we should not stop – 'for it can mean the border between survival and extinction'.

9. *Human Rights Are for All*

The right to life is the most basic of all human rights, and those who fail to keep men, women and children from starving to death transgress against it for a start. This is the first thing to be mentioned when we speak of human rights. What do freedom, justice and dignity mean to those who go hungry to bed today, not knowing if they will eat tomorrow? In other words: social and liberal human rights go together.

Human rights are trampled upon in many countries of the world. What, then, can we do to keep more and more people from

193

recurrent dreadful suffering? Ought terrorism to rule out development aid? Could the subject not be put more forcefully to the United Nations? And could not at least the Europeans agree on a common position?

These questions are understandable. But one may indeed doubt, and not just with reference to developing countries, whether one punishes rulers by striking at their victims. In any case, we should not adopt too righteous an attitude, forgetting what European history looks like, or the fact that German criminals brought torment, bloodshed and death down on humanity little more than a generation ago. Even today, it would be an inadmissible simplification to make human rights a stick with which to beat only those states whose governments are not democratic, or to permit any impression that a reference to 'human rights' really means 'American rights'.

The extent to which torture is practised in Third World countries cannot but horrify us. Amnesty International's 1984 report names many countries: 27 African, 16 Asian and 15 Latin-American states have made systematic use of cruel and degrading treatment to oppress political dissidents or to suppress, if not actually to annihilate, ethnic and religious minorities.

No constitution, no statute book, no code of criminal procedure describes torture as a reliable method of getting 'information', or allows it as a means of execution. And yet torture is to some extent methodically developed and to some extent systematically employed. There are indications from Latin America that torture is taught and disseminated there in supra-national establishments; we may doubt whether the experts who teach it are exclusively South American.

Let it be remembered, lest we overlook the mote in our own eye, that torture is by no means unknown in our latitudes. It was more widespread in Europe in the sixteenth and seventeenth centuries, when methods and degrees of torture were highly developed. Only in the wake of the Enlightenment was torture abolished – officially, at any rate – as a judicial measure and, with the advent of progressive constitutional and liberal thought, discredited as an affront to human dignity. Today the prohibition of any kind of 'torture or cruel, inhuman or degrading treatment

The global balance-sheet of death is depressing:

- Over half a million and probably more than a million of the Khmer people of Kampuchea have died.
- And what about the massacres perpetrated by Emperor Bokassa, not really such a comical figure? Or Idi Amin's 'Lumpen-militariat'? 300,000 or more died, many of them after being tortured, out of a population of 12 million, and even five years later there was no end to the violence.
- How are we to understand the excesses committed in the name of the Prophet? Or the terror in the Middle East? Or the sufferings exacted from the Afghans?
- According to reports from Amnesty International, over a million people have been murdered by order of governments, or with governmental collusion, over the last ten years. The horrors that occur are often the systematic work of a state-controlled machine, the victims are men and women from all classes of society. Children are tortured in Central America. Children have been forced to watch their mothers tortured in the Middle East.
- The bloody conflicts in Sri Lanka, most conspicuous among them being the terror inflicted on the Tamil minority, have aroused indignation, and not only in India.
- The plight of the Kurds, denied a peaceful existence and a secure future by several of the states to which they are indigenous, can only inspire helpless despair.
- In 1984 Amnesty International, looking back over the previous year, stated that political prisoners had been killed, or tortured, or subjected to degrading treatment, in at least 117 of the over 150 sovereign states of the world. That was stated also with reference to China, Indonesia and Pakistan. Amnesty particularly criticized the Soviet Union for consigning dissidents to psychiatric hospitals.

or punishment' (the wording used in Article 6 of the Universal Declaration of Human Rights of 10 December 1948) is part of our understanding of human rights.

A retreat into autocratic or dictatorial forms of government has generally brought torture in its wake. In my speech accepting the

Nobel Prize I said: 'We have learned into what barbarism human-ity can relapse. No religion, no ideology, no brilliant display of culture can exclude beyond all doubt the possibility that hatred may erupt from the depths of the human spirit and drag nations down into the depths.'

Torture was also a phenomenon accompanying colonialism; the final phase of French rule in Algeria attained a sad notoriety. It may thus be that the use of torture in the Third World is also a colonial legacy, just as political acts of violence in general are a prime article of export. Today an African professor need fear no contradiction when he says that, in his own part of the world, the technology of destruction is far in advance of productive tech-niques.

The deliberations of the 1975 convention which ended in unanimous condemnation of torture and other cruel, inhuman or degrading treatment or punishment seem to be making headway, but with what practical significance? The expedient of interna-tional ostracism is to the fore, and should really apply to interna-tional aid in the context of torture too. In future the prohibition of torture ought also to apply to exceptional situations such as those involving martial law or the threat of war. And an order from a superior should not be accepted as justification. For the rest, one should beware of the illusion that corrupt civilians are any better or more harmless than corrupt members of the armed forces. The mere existence of a written constitution is no guarantee of constitutionality. And the application of Western European criteria to the whole world is misleading anyway. So far as Africa is concerned, tribal realities currently carry more weight than the prospect of a multi-party system.

And what do the criteria of human rights signify in view of vast refugee movements? In the summer of 1984, the United Nations High Commissioner for Refugees, my former Danish colleague Paul Hartling, spoke of four million refugees in Africa alone. In fact, there are more refugees today than ever before in human history; for some years, two to three thousand people have joined their ranks daily.

• In this century, 250 million people have so far fled from their homes.

- According to Hartling's information, the number of new refugees has remained constant at 10 million over the last five years.
- Pakistan alone estimated the number of predominantly Afghan refugees there at about 2.5 million; there are probably more than 1.5 million in Iran.

It is as true today as it ever was that the international community of states in general, and democracies in particular, must take the victims of intolerance and brutality under their wing. Countries next door to any regime that causes an exodus of refugees have a great burden to bear. It should be shared, in a spirit of solidarity, by the better off. The Federal Republic of Germany cannot avoid realizing this basic insight. The fact that we cannot be a haven for all the tormented and outcast of the world, certainly not for all who would just like to be better off, is another matter – but that is not the real point at issue.

We must also face the challenge presented by the victims of South African apartheid. If even conservative circles in the United States say that 'peaceful change' is in their own interests, then more Europeans than before must try to work towards that change. Black South Africans not only have to bear the humiliating burden of apartheid; many of them are condemned to live below the poverty line in the 'homelands'.

The European Community has tried, without much success, to add a clause on human rights to the new Lomé Convention. It will continue to be sensible not to make development aid dependent on clauses demanding 'good conduct'. To determine what constitutes good conduct in a given case is a difficult undertaking anyway. In addition, there is by no means always a clear connection between human needs and the conduct of governments. It is a most debatable point whether aid for the poor helps to stabilize dictatorial régimes. In any case, there is no evidence that the denial of aid in itself helps to shorten the life of such dictatorial régimes. The contrary seems to be the case.

Human solidarity cannot be limited by the bounds of diverse political systems. It carries conviction only if it takes universal effect. We must neither be blind in the left eye nor reel with shock when the Left represents democratic values. And those things denied to the majority of humanity contribute to the conflicts which impede the relations between states and threaten peace.

Not our own generation alone, but those of our children and our grandchildren are still prone to an unfortunate colonializing romanticism, which seen in the sober light of day is nothing but a far from romantic history of extermination. Yes, we have always entertained an idea of the noble savage, and the impressive dignity of children of nature. None the less, those children of nature were regarded as simple souls, and as a general rule might was right. How long ago was the perfidy of the conquistadores, the endless chain of broken promises and treaties, that turned free peoples into an endangered and isolated minority, and not in South America alone?

But more and more people are coming to realize that the pressure of problems which originally hung together, and are now once again interconnected in their effects, can be countered neither by the misty twilight of myths and legends nor by the alarming simplification of the past. Today, the appeal to reason and humanitarianism points the way to our own future.

So let us break through all callous attitudes to those who are endangered or actually threatened with extinction. We must keep our minds alert to all the misery that still, and unceasingly, arises from blind striving for power and the unscrupulous representation of particular interests.

And experience shows that development policies can further the process of democratization. There are many who should ensure that they are better informed, so that they will not be taken in by empty phrases; many must be active themselves, and make sure that what is done in their names or at their instigation has real meaning – in their own communities, churches, parties, in their schools and their unions and associations. And we ought to begin with ourselves.

INSTEAD OF AN AFTERWORD:
PEACE AND DEVELOPMENT

On 25 April 1985, I received the Third World Prize at the United Nations headquarters in New York. I made a speech of thanks which expressed the ideas and the content of this book, and my doubts of whether any real improvement is taking place. This was its text:

Let me begin with a confession. It crossed my mind that it might have made more sense not to deliver a lecture on this occasion today. That way one would have demonstrated that with all our speeches so far we have made little impact in averting those dangers that threaten the very existence of mankind.

But no one need fear, or hope, that I will not make a speech; otherwise I would not be here today.

In any case I would have wanted to express my deep-felt gratitude towards those who have bestowed this great honour upon me. In doing so I think of all those with whom I have had the pleasure of cooperating in recent years. Without an exchange of views and ideas, and without the encouragement of others, I would not have dared to step into that field strewn with pitfalls – that area that links peace and development.

Now it could rightly be said that there is really no need for another analysis of the state of the world; of its growing problems; of its immense dangers; of our persisting inability to change things for the better. Conclusions have been drawn from the many analyses made – in terms of methods, substance and policies, even in terms of institutions. There is a wealth of proposals and formulas, in almost all areas. They range from economics to armaments; from currency and finance to hunger;

from drought and deforestation to the rapid growth of world population. There is a wide choice for everyone willing to choose. The supermarket of world problems and their solutions offers a complete inventory. There is hardly any gap on the shelves.

However, demand is not very strong. And this is so despite the fact that the vast majority of those who bear political responsibility for their people and nations are full of good will, and intend to solve the problems and let our world reach a state of security and well-being: a state which in accordance with the abilities of its members, could overcome oppressive misery and develop its immense resources.

I do not want to play anything down nor to paper it over. Of course there are those unable to do anything even if they wanted to. And there are those who take it upon themselves to do what they should not: the authors and victims of ideological presumptions, including the nice but ineffective preachers of a world without violence. Let us be quite clear: when I speak of peace I am thinking of all those who suffer from war or who are oppressed by it. But what concerns me today is worldwide rearmament and the obvious dangers of war, and their objective stark contrast to meaningful development, national and international.

To put it more forcibly: There is no point in worrying about cooperation and mutual interests, if we fail to avoid a nuclear holocaust; or if we fail to master the consequences of famine on continental scales.

People of my age have more than once known the experience of war leading to hunger. Can one deny today that hunger and mass misery can create the conditions from which new wars arise?

Indeed, alarming contradictions are a sign of our times. Our objective ability to solve most problems has grown almost as much as our capacity to destroy everything. Science and technology have made mankind capable of both, to a previously unimagined degree. Scientific and technical discoveries grow at seemingly unlimited speed. We are becoming aware of new dangers and new problems. But it seems as if mankind is helpless in the face of the irrepressible flood of new discoveries – yet unable to master the opportunities they offer.

Here one cannot but remember the genius of Albert Einstein who – like other great minds – had the gift of reducing highly complex processes to a simple formula. I am referring to his statement that the atomic bomb has changed everything except the mind and thinking of people. Indeed, he who looks for reasons why what should and could be done doesn't happen will find that *Homo sapiens* has developed the technical, and in a narrower sense the economic, capabilities of his brain much faster than his political and community-building abilities. Or one might say that the formation of character and of moral values has not kept pace with the rapid progress of technology. Those are the qualities needed to live with oneself and to deal with oneself, and with others, with one's neighbours – on both a personal as much as a national plane. The economy aims for output and profit, today no less than 2,000 years ago. Weapons are geared towards easier handling, greater distance and precision just as for the past 2,000 years. And the conflicts between people and nations: the criteria by which we measure them – sovereignty, prestige, power, dominance, hatred towards the enemy – unfortunately all this has changed little in 2,000 years.

There is one exception: it is slowly dawning that we cannot go on behaving as we used to some hundred or even fifty years ago if we all want to survive.

The fear that human history may end could give grounds for hope. But fear, as a general rule, is not a reliable prop. Where then are we to find the strength to change our way of thinking, and what shall our criteria be?

Historically, there have been three basic attitudes in the relations between peoples and states: conflict, co-existence, cooperation. Nobody can argue that is no longer the case today. In conflicts between villages, tribes and nations many lives have been lost. But mankind could afford it. Even today, as long as these conflicts are local or regional, as long as they are sufficiently limited, we continue that way. A global conflict, however, would mean the end for all of us: a nuclear winter would descend even on those who now live in perpetual summer.

If survival is the top priority – and I can think of nothing else on which we could more easily agree among religions, ideologies and scientific viewpoints – then the preservation of world peace is our most important objective, dominating all others. Only if we avoid the self-destructive catastrophe of mankind will we be able to continue quarrelling about our different ideas, about the best way to achieve happiness for all. An end to global conflict without compromise is the precondition for coexistence and cooperation. Or put another way: without it a continuation of history appears impossible.

In global terms this means that worldwide there is no alternative to common security. The report of the Independent Commission on Disarmament and Security Issues under the chairmanship of Olof Palme, the Swedish Prime Minister, elaborated on necessary details three years ago.

The world can afford the coexistence of peoples and nations with their different views, the multiplicity of their ideas – real or imagined – on paths to welfare or happiness. Peoples and states may even turn their backs on each other as long as they do not dispute each other's right to exist. This holds worldwide; but it would also apply regionally, as the world might still be able to countenance regionally limited conflicts – terrible as they may be. The Gulf War, by the way, is a frightening example of how a military conflict of this kind can start with arms supplied by both superpowers which then find it difficult to control or stop what is happening.

Some of those wielding a great deal of power may admit it or not: by and large our actual interdependencies are increasing and the objective need for cooperation is growing. The debt crisis is a threat not only to the nations of Latin America; extremely high interest rates in the United States create problems for many other countries, not the least for the weakest among them. Drought and large-scale starvation in Africa do not stop at national borders. The energy crisis – which is far from over and which is not just an oil crisis; the threat of a drinking water crisis; the various ecological threats which had been largely neglected for a long time – all these problems extend across borders between political systems. I am sure the World Commission on Environment and Development chaired by Mrs Gro Harlem Brundtland will provide the international community with important additional suggestions in this area. My own country, the Federal Republic of Germany, suffers from acid rain and dying forests no less than its neighbours, the German Democratic Republic, Czechoslovakia or Switzerland.

In sum, many of our problems are of a global nature, they transcend systems, and their number is growing. Reason calls for the adoption of global rules far beyond the traditional ones, and it calls for mechanisms which guarantee the observation of such rules. It seems of little importance whether or not this is called a matter of mutual interest.

Egoism and narrow-mindedness have so far prevented any rapid progress in areas where the East–West conflict and North–South issues interact – in fact developments have advanced at a snail's pace at best. And it shows a considerable degree of stubbornness if people still refuse to admit that immensely rising worldwide military expenditure is not only politically damaging but does a lot of harm economically.

Those $1,000 billion which the world spends on military purposes this year really amount to a death sentence for millions of human beings. The resources which they would need for living are actually spent on armaments.

But there is another obstacle to understanding the need to see ourselves more as partners in common security, in military and in economic terms; there is not only stubbornness but also the lust for power. Nobody can deny that the desire for power in individuals as in nations is a strong motivation which, when it comes to most mistakes and catastrophes in the development of mankind, we cannot explain away. One could even see our history as a development in which force – in its unrestricted expression, also known as the law of the jungle – had to give way step by step to the rule of law, although there were many setbacks. Limits and rules of behaviour were adopted which everyone has to observe. Each treaty voluntarily agreed is another step in this direction.

Celebrating their fortieth anniversary this year, the United Nations stand as a symbol of a step forward – and of the inevitable difficulties associated with it. The mechanism of the Security Council and the veto may be taken as evidence of the cool realism of its founders who knew that it would have been too much to expect a world organization to overcome real power by schematic majority rule. One might also say: joint decisions, agreed rules and comprehensive arrangements within the United Nations as well as elsewhere demand the cooperation of the powerful, especially of the superpowers.

Here we have witnessed a development since 1945 which in the context with which I am concerned nobody has expressed better than President Raúl Alfonsín of Argentina. As you know he belongs to the group of six heads of state and government from five continents who got together last year to voice their own and many other people's concern and their alarmed impatience with regard to arms control. In January at their meeting in New Delhi the President of Argentina stressed the legitimate interests of big powers and superpowers, in particular regarding their security from each other and thus their ability to defend themselves. But, he made it clear, it is an undeniable fact that their military forces and their weapons' arsenals have grown far beyond their defensive requirements. They have acquired the capability – only the two superpowers have it and nobody else – to eradicate all life from this planet. Thus their power has objectively become a threat to all people. The decision to use those weapons is exclusively theirs. This implies that some individuals, their advisors, small élites – few people in any case – hold the power to destroy the basic right of all people; their right to live.

In all civilizations and cultures, in all religions of all societies and continents, the right to live was considered something special. Therefore, it is unacceptable to the 5 billion people or to the 160 states, it is terrifying, that they should depend in their right to live on a small group of people in one or two capitals; that they should have to trust in the wisdom and restraint of those few not to abuse their power and not to make that one irreversible mistake. The preservation of world peace is too fundamental a human right, and a right of nations, to be left to the leadership of superpowers alone.

From that right to live all those of us with less power derive our right to put pressure on the two superpowers to limit their power and to agree on common rules of conduct in the interest of maintaining world peace. This would not reduce their power. And I entertain no thoughts of neglecting political differences. But a global code for preserving world peace must be effective especially for those very powers who hold the means to destroy it.

When the President of the United States and the leader of the Soviet Union meet in the near future – here in New York or elsewhere – the world does not necessarily expect them to become friends, or to wipe away their differences by magic. They are not expected to announce cooperation in matters where there can be no consensus. We do expect them, however, to end the threat of an all-destructive world conflict. Obviously this will only be possible if they do not question each other's right to exist. And only if they manage to agree that they themselves will only be able to achieve security together – and thus banish the danger of extinction which threatens all of us.

This would mean at least an interruption of the arms race while negotiations continue. And it means negotiations on critical areas as much as on destabilizing military projects. It also means confronting the links between the arms race and development, between hunger and weapons, and making this issue part of the agenda.

To me the aim of such an urgently needed summit meeting of the superpowers should be nothing short of an agreement which rules out a Third World War. This would mean more than most of what is being said now as we look back to May and August of 1945. It would mean nothing less than the opening of a new chapter in the history of mankind.

Peoples and states must demand such an agreement, otherwise security is not to be found – either in East–West problems which will continue to exist, or in North–South problems which become ever more pressing. On the basis of such an agreement many issues would be easier to control, and the export of East–West controversies into the Third World could probably be reduced. A halt to further excessive arms build-ups would become plausible. And the ever-increasing accumulation of destructive machinery would come to be seen as even more perverse – an arsenal which kills people without ever being used because it eats up the money without which people are condemned to death through starvation.

When the United Nations hold their Special Conference on disarmament and development in 1986 – once more drawing on the commendable work of the group of experts chaired by Inga Thorsson – much will depend on curbing the tendency to trot out tedious propaganda slogans on the one hand and to discuss abstract anaemic theories on the other. Nor must participants be held back by the self-declared realists who accompany their inaction with nicely chosen rhetoric about disarmament and development being objectives too important each in its own right to be linked together. Even if only modest amounts would be affected in the beginning, the redirection of resources should be made a reality and as soon as possible. And this should include a discussion of the rather dubious and damaging aspects of much of what constitutes the international arms market.

However, it is only on the basis of an agreement which rules out a Third World War that we will be able to choose easily or indeed at all between the proposals for resolving the North–South conflict. This will become immediately obvious when we think of the forthcoming Geneva talks. How can one ever decide on what steps to take without first having made the new perspectives clear?

Now, as for North–South issues, it will come as no surprise to you if I reiterate the proposals – which ranged from emergency measures to structural reforms – presented by the Independent Commission which I chaired. Most of our findings remain valid today. It would have been better if we could actually claim that some problems had been resolved positively. Unfortunately this is predominantly not the case, and many issues today present themselves in yet more serious terms.

Many of those points surfaced again when representatives of non-aligned countries put their suggestions for a realistically comprehensive dialogue down on paper. And also when Indira Gandhi, who will live on in our memory, envisaged another North–South summit for the second half of 1985. But instead, we now witness considerable skills being applied in the areas of currency and finance to patch up holes, but the necessary reforms being avoided. The same goes for international trade and other areas well known to all of us.

As yet we see no sign of action which might set in motion what has ground to a standstill in such a frustrating way: I mean the intended 'global' discussion, under the auspices of the United Nations, about those issues important to a restructuring of worldwide economic relations. The responsibility for the complete failure has to be lain at several doors. But one thing is clear: if certain important countries had been willing to move, a general deadlock would not have come to pass.

I stress the paramount responsibility of the superpowers. At the same time I want to warn the big countries – and all others concerned – not to allow the destruction of multilaterialism and its institutions, imperfect as they may be. Europe should, and must, realize that it has to play a role in counteracting negative developments. There is no reason why Europe should always wait for others to take the lead. And much less should it jump on band-wagons which may be big but are moving in the wrong direction – or ending up nowhere.

When I speak of multilateralism, I want to emphasize that there is still more scope for it in a peace-keeping role than many people believe. The decisions which the superpowers must inevitably make would harmonize well with better use of the peace-keeping potential of the United Nations. And a fresh, serious look should be taken at the conciliatory powers of both the Security Council and the Secretary-General.

At the same time it is of primary importance that the rest of us who have power neither over the bomb nor the veto are no longer allowed to lose sight of the links between crises of security, world economy and environment. I would like to use the award bestowed upon me as a contribution towards an independent clearing house for 'Peace and Development' which would bring together realistic ideas from all over the world, and thus establish a constructive link between East–West and North–South issues.

I am now coming close again to making proposals whose practical value I questioned at the beginning of my lecture. Presumably it has become clear where, in my view, the key to a solution of our most pressing problems lies. Disputes will lead nowhere as long as they are about isolated issues, such as debts or commodities, food or birth-rates, or soil erosion, deforestation and other appalling environmental damage. Or on whether attribution of blame and responsibilities should be on a national or international level. On budgets too, and absurdities of budgets which allocate funds for armaments that are lacking for education or health care. The key to a solution not of all but of many problems is in the hands of the superpowers. The question is whether they can succeed in limiting their fruitless conflict and their power to destroy the world, at least to the extent of agreeing on a code which would make a Third World War impossible.

That cannot mean that the rest of us should hide behind the responsibility of the nuclear giants. We must shoulder our own responsibilities. And this includes applying all possible pressure and telling the powerful of this world what they owe mankind.

I put it this way: since there can be no survival without the prevention of a Third World War, since development means peace, we must at last begin to organize ourselves to cooperate and give peaceful development a chance. That chance is in trust for all of us and alone gives us hope that future generations will actually live after us.

About the Author

Willy Brandt, born in 1913, fled Germany in 1933 and lived in exile in Norway and Sweden during the Second World War. Having joined Germany's Social Democratic Party (SPD) in 1931, he entered politics after his return home in 1945. He was Governing Mayor of West Berlin from 1957 to 1966, in which year he became Vice Chancellor and Foreign Minister in the CDU/SPD Coalition. From 1969 to 1974 he was German Chancellor in the SPD/FDP Government.

He has been President of the Socialist International since 1976 and, from 1979 to 1983, a member of the European Parliament. In 1971 Willy Brandt won the Nobel Prize for Peace.

He is the author of many books and essays and the Independent Commission on International Development Issues, which he chaired, produced two reports —*North–South: A Programme for Survival* (1980) and *Common Crisis: North–South: Cooperation for World Recovery* (1983). Willy Brandt has been Chairman of the SPD since 1964.